Bright New World

The eighth Otto Fischer novel

Jim McDermott

Copyright Jim McDermott 2020
All rights reserved

Abbreviations and acronyms used in the text

CDU – Christlich Demokratische Union Deutschlands: Christian Democratic Union party of Germany

DDR – Deutsche Demokratische Republik: German Democratic Republic, or East Germany

DPA – Deutsche Presse-Agentur: German news agency, founded in 1949

EPD – Evangelischer Pressedienst: German Protestant news agency

HIAG – Hilfsgemeinschaft auf Gegenseitigkeit der Angehörigen der ehemaligen Waffen SS: lobby group comprising and working for the rehabilitation of former Waffen SS personnel (though Allgemeine SS personnel were also accepted).

KDP - Kommunistische Partei Deutschland: German Communist Party

KGB - Komitet Gosudarstvennoy Bezopasnosti: state security agency of the Soviet Union, formed in 1954 by the amalgamation of former domestic (**MVD**) and foreign (**MGB**) security agencies

KNA – Katholische Nachrichten-Agentur: German Catholic news agency

MGB - Ministerstvo Gosudarstvennoy Bezopasnosti SSSR: Ministry for State Security, counter-intelligence successor organization (from March 1946) to the former **NKGB**, and part-forerunner of **KGB**

MVD – Ministerstvo Vnutrennikh Del SSSR: Ministry of Internal Security, domestic intelligence successor organization (from March 1946) to **NKVD**, and part-forerunner of **KGB**

SED – Sozialistische Einheitspartei Deutschlands: German Socialist Unity Party, a Soviet-imposed merger (in April 1946) of the **KDP** and **SDP** in the Soviet Zone of Germany. From 1952 its sister organization in the west ran (very unsuccessfully) in Federal elections

SPD - Sozialdemokratische Partei Deutschlands: German Social Democratic Party

WASt – Wehrmachtsauskunftstelle: German Government agency maintaining records of servicemen killed or missing it action; now Deutsche Dienststelle

Prologue: December 1955

For weeks now, the building had been under suspended sentence of death. It overlooked Holsteiner Ufer and the Spree, a solid, mid-nineteenth-century apartment house, one of the few on Hansaviertel's northern flank that had not been atomized by Allied bombing in the final months of the war. That was part of the problem – it had stood almost alone for a decade now, orphaned, damaged, serving no purpose other than as a cautionary tale, an unbottled specimen from a time when Germans couldn't have conceived the rubble yard their capital would become.

The district wore its wounds starkly still. Other parts of central Berlin had been cleared and rebuilt in recent years, but Hansaviertel, tucked between the Tiergarten and the river, had always been a repository, rather than a producer, of wealth - a suburban oasis for the genteel sort, fleeing westwards from the overcrowded old city. Gentility, however pretty it had once been, was no priority for a nation dragging itself from ruin.

Now, though, a great clearance had begun, and from the old ruins would rise the spirit of capitalism made concrete and steel, giving the finger to its socialist counterpart, Stalinallee, directly to the East. On a blank sheet, dozens of renowned architects were designing au ultra- modern suburb with new schools, churches and an American-style shopping mall, and all the World would come to Berlin to see how the new Germany advanced, leading the march into Tomorrow.

The building was in the way of this. As fine as it was (and repairable, had anyone the will to see it done), it was out of its time. One of the consultancies competing to redesign the district had suggested that the collision of (a very little) old and new would give the rebuilt Hansaviertel a sense of continuity that the RAF and USAAF had done their best to sever; but Berlin's Senate had disagreed, insisting that anything that was staid or likely to awaken memories had to go. And so, finally, the demolition men arrived to sweep away what bombs had almost missed.

It needed to be done carefully. Old wounds made it difficult to judge how the building would collapse if they tried to undermine or explode it (and rubble falling on to Holsteiner Ufer was likely to embarrass passing motorists). The only safe option was to take it down course by course, as if it were a factory chimney close by houses.

The men started three weeks before Christmas and then paused for the holiday. They returned the day after St Stephen's Day with just the ground floor still to remove. The surveyors had reported that the building had no cellars, so the job was expected to have three of four more days' life in it at most. The foreman at least was relieved about this. His wife was pregnant, threatening to pup at any time, and for some reason had insisted that he be close at hand when she did.

On a cold, wet Thursday mid-morning, he was overseeing four of his men as they removed the monumental lintel above the building's main entrance when he noticed an old fellow sitting on the now-derailed garden wall. This wouldn't have made an impression, usually (any demolition work attracted the attention of old folk with memories of better times), but the rain was coming down hard and the gentleman didn't seem to mind. He was as settled as a scholar in a warm library, and as intent as he could be upon a business that wasn't his own.

After half an hour during which the hairs on the back of his neck stood resolutely upright, the foreman stopped pretending to do his job and went across to the wall. The old man's eyes remained fixed upon the stump of the structure until the view was blocked by a body. He looked up, surprised by the interruption. The foreman tossed his head back towards his team.

'We're making coffee soon, Father. Come and have some.'

The old man smiled and lifted himself from the wall. He was too well-dressed to be homeless, but the rain hadn't done his clothes any favours. If he had a wife still she'd raise five shades of Hell when she saw the state of him.

The workers had set up their kettle at the back of the main hall, where a fragment of ceiling offered some shelter still. The foreman lit the tiny gas stove beneath it and waved the old man to an upturned box. As he sat down his eyes were moving nervously, scanning every surviving surface as if willing a story to pour from it.

'Do you know the place?'

The visitor jumped slightly at the noise, and nodded. 'I was the *portier* here, until the end.'

No German needed to ask which *end* that was. The foreman glanced around. Though ruinous, enough of the building's expensive facings remained to hint at days of glory. When it went up during the *Grunderzeit*, the city had been expanding rapidly, bursting out of its old Customs Walls, propelled by confidence, new money and a desperate need to put on a face both to outshine the Austrians and match the damned British.

'It's a nice old pile. A pity we're pulling it down.'

'It's best that it goes.'

'Why?'

The old man shook his head and said nothing. He looked down, noticed his clothes for the first time and tried vainly to brush the excess moisture away. The frown disappeared when the rest of the gang piled into the hallway. They glanced at their visitor disinterestedly, and he moved slightly to make space as they crowded around the kettle. One of them pushed his arse onto the upturned box next to him and nodded.

'Who're you?'

'Gregor. Gregor Schultz.'

'He minded the building. In the old days.'

Old days needed no more explanation than *end*. One or two eyebrows went up in polite acknowledgment, but the revelation stirred no further questions. The foreman, having started something, tried to keep it going.

'What was it, back then? It's hard to tell with the fittings gone.'

Gregor gestured towards the emptied stairwell. 'A few wealthy families kept home here since before the First War. In the twenties, some of the city's bigger companies bought up space and had hospitality suites for visiting clients.'

'And after that?'

'It was requisitioned by the Government, like many of the buildings around here.'

'They put up a roof-aerial, did they?'

Much of the foreign diplomatic community had been resident just across Tiergarten (and were returning gradually to their sovereign territory as old, bombed-out embassies were being rebuilt). A five-storey structure across the green space would have been ideally situated to intercept confidential radio-traffic, but Gregor shook his head.

'It wasn't that.'

'What then?'

'They gave it to the police.'

Everyone took care not to notice his slight hesitation before the noun. It was history and therefore none of their business - just one detail in a vast tapestry of shit, now sluiced away. They drank their tea, swapped opinions about the St Stephen's Day football matches, lit cigarettes, farted and generally behaved like workmen with a small mission, now almost completed. Their foreman cradled his coffee, thinking about his wife and the thousand small things yet to be arranged for their imminent first child.

When he had drained his mug the old man stood up and nodded his thanks. He turned to go, but a thought held him. He cleared his throat. 'What's going to be built here?'

One of the workers snorted. 'Something too expensive for ordinary folk. And fucking ugly, no doubt.'

The foreman knew a little about this, and didn't want to waste his expertise. 'It'll be a high apartment block, with balconies at every level. A famous Dutch architect designed it.'

The snorter had another go. 'He won't *live* in it, for sure.'

'Anyway, *we* just demolish things. Once this floor's cleared we're off to bring down what's left of the old Menzel *realschule*.'

The old man frowned. 'You're leaving the cellars where they are?

'The surveyor told us there aren't any. You'd think there would be, a building like this.'

'He's wrong - there *are* cellars, two small ones. They were blocked off, but not filled in. There ...'

He pointed to the outline of a door in one corner of the hall's rear wall. The work was professionally done and the surface painted to match the rest, but no-one had thought to remove the frame. What remained looked as if art thieves had cut out a painting and fled.

The surveyor was a lazy cock, obviously. The foreman got up, went over to the wall and knocked with a fist. It was plaster on brick, as they would have discovered at some point in the coming hours.

'Get hammers.'

In less than five minutes his men had made a space large enough to climb through. Later, of course, they all wished that they hadn't. The foreman told them to say nothing and went to telephone the site supervisor. He refused to state his business until he had the great man himself on the other end of the line, and then a sort of hell broke over things. He too was told to say nothing, and later that afternoon it was he and his men alone, directed by the supervisor and some smartly dressed fellow, who cut down the bodies and wrapped them. It took no great effort (the flesh long since having fallen from the bones), but he suspected that the memory would never leave him. After all, it wasn't every day that a man got to lay hands on a general and not suffer for it.

Part One

1

It only occurred to him much later, how little *moment* had marked the moment. A captain came into the yard, blew a whistle, delivered the news in bad German, took no questions (not that anyone was as stupid as to ask one) and waved them back to work. Briefly, they had all disobeyed by default, looking around blankly, catching each other's eye, and then carried on with their tasks at half-stunned speed. He didn't recall that anyone had smiled, much less given three hurrahs.

The Red Cross came two days later and recorded the customary lies in their notebooks. Everyone was in good health and spirits, the diet was fine, the work not too onerous and no, of course there were no complaints. Curiously, the last was as close to the truth as any lie could be. If this wasn't all just a sadistic joke, anything that was wrong or might otherwise cause concern would soon pass, and therefore was not worth mentioning.

After the well-meaning gentlemen went away a meal was served at tables set up on the assembly ground. Some of the weaker ones began to fear that they were hallucinating, not least when they found that their otherwise standard-issue broth contained meat (unidentifiable but definitely not a species of rodent). A little later, at dusk, they were deloused in the wash-block and told to surrender worn out or damaged clothing, which was replaced by items so lacking in obvious signs of hard usage that their previous owners must either have been on clerical-detail or shot in the head before the end of their very first shift.

A train arrived the next morning, and the surreality continued. The locomotive was dragging passenger cars rather than cattle-wagons, and though their fittings were at best peasant-class, no man took his seat without a sense that he had somehow wandered on to the Orient-Express. A guard was placed in each carriage but rifles remained on shoulders, pointing downwards, their owners taking every chance to doze between cursory inspections by a young lieutenant whose own heart and head were clearly elsewhere.

These disruptions had confused him as much as any of his comrades, and it was only on their fourth day on the train that he began to hope. They had been moving westwards, and there just wasn't four days of Soviet west from where they had begun their journey. He knew that the others could see it too – their attention had sharpened, taking in more of the world than tired, broken minds usually did (though none of them had yet found the nerve to speak of it). When locomotives were being changed, one of them heard a conversation outside on the opposite track, and hope became something else (they didn't entirely believe him when he swore that he understood the difference between Russian and Polish). After that, it took only a further three hours before the sound changed beneath the carriage wheels and they all looked out onto the broad, beautiful sweep of a river and the growing German skyline beyond.

When the train stopped they fell out on to the platform and allowed themselves to be herded by men who spoke their own language. They gave their names and units, last places of residence and names of (hopefully) surviving relatives in the same passive, respectful manner that had kept them alive all these years, content to be told how, when and in what order things were to be done. After this, he and several others were taken to one side. He knew what was coming before the policeman opened his mouth to address them.

Their home towns and villages were no longer part of Germany, they were informed (as if this was news to any of them), being in provinces annexed as part-payment for the crimes of the illegal, fascistic former regime. If any of them knew or suspected that some members of their families survived still, the German Democratic Republic was willing to provide further transportation, even to those regions currently comprising the Bundesrepublik. Men forced to fight for the fascists, they were told, shouldn't be regarded as culpable for the crimes thereof, nor kept against their will where they didn't want to be.

He wasn't fooled by this compassionate offer. *We're volksdeutsche now, refugees without ties or a future, and they'd much sooner the capitalists bore the expense.* When asked to express a preference with their feet he was one of those who stepped forward immediately. They were separated from the rest and, half an hour later, fed coffee and plain pastries at a station cafe (it so overloaded their blighted palates that several of them puked their thanks, drawing complaints from the official photographer who had been charged with recording this fraternal act of charity). Then, they were loaded on to another train with those of their comrades whose homes lay in the West. When it pulled out of the station he looked back to get a final impression of what he had been told was Frankfurt-on-the-Oder. He had never before been here, and he doubted that his affection for the place would ever fade.

He'd been fortunate to keep down his strange breakfast, because the final leg of their journey consumed the better part of that day. He was no stranger to the city they came to in the early evening; before the war he had sailed here often from his home town, and recognized the twin towers of the almost-rebuilt Marienkirche several minutes before the train pulled into the main station.

When they had disembarked and given their names, units and other personal details once more they were told that they were now free men, though this wasn't quite true. Outside, they were kept together while some fool of a politician regaled them through a microphone, explaining to them that they were heroes while a heart-torn mob of elderly women pressed around, holding up small posters, each carrying a photograph and the plaintive exhortation: *Who has seen my son?* A very few received the miraculous answer of the object itself, pushing out of the crowd to be embraced by a mother who'd feared him long-dead; the rest scanned faces desperately, hoping to find what had been taken from them more than a decade earlier. He didn't see anyone he recognized. As far as he knew his sister lived still, though where and how he couldn't say.

The fool finished his speech with the revelation that they were the last of the last - that they comprised some of the final twenty-six thousand German soldiers to be released from Soviet camps (curiously, this did not make any of them feel luckier in their skins), and that they should thank Chancellor Adenauer for his unsparing efforts to bring them home. Then, they were dismissed graciously by a hand, allowing the rest of what remained of their lives to proceed.

 He noticed a line of tables bearing an Inner Mission banner, and wandered across to them. He received some Deutsche Marks (he examined them curiously) and an address where he could get a bed for a few nights and advice on work vacancies in the area. It was the last that made him think for the first time about what came next. He had been trained as a carpenter, but the Ivans hadn't thought to utilize those particular skills and he was certainly much out of practice. Other than that, he had a great deal of experience in the heaving-rocks end of the (re)construction business, a knack of not letting things climb too heavily upon him (a faculty that had almost certainly kept him alive as more morose men succumbed to years of half-hearted mistreatment) and a way with an anecdote that made light of the very great and varied deal of ordure he had been obliged to taste over the past fourteen years. He wasn't sure how employable any of that would make him in the modern Germany.

He didn't even know if there *was* a modern Germany. Were there jobs to be had, or was it like '32, when men wandered the streets with bootlaces in their hands, trying to earn or beg enough to keep their kids fed for another day? The nation had been through a defeat far more impressive than that of 1918, and revolution had followed the earlier debacle. What could he look forward to this time?

His fears were soon dispelled. As he walked through Lübeck's streets, trying to find the address he had been given, he couldn't help but notice how new fat sat easily upon folk. There was a preoccupied busyness to commuters, a hive-shiver of industry, that made him feel like a Greek priest, useful for nothing but getting in the way of things moving from *here* to *there*. Strangely, his invisibility was a comfort, shielding him from too much that was too strange. It made him feel a little better about a day that should have been more of a celebration than it was.

An old lady opened her door to him. She was pinched-faced but led him inside with a hand resting gently on his forearm, and made tea while she spoke of her son, lost in Tunisia in 1942. She offered her given name, Else, and told him he was welcome to stay as long as he wished, though she would need a little help to meet the cost of his rations. There was always work to be had at the docks – he could make decent money loading and unloading cargoes, if he didn't mind heavy lifting and foul language. He told her he'd go there first thing in the morning, and meant it.

He asked if there were any decent bars nearby, where he could end his long fast with a beer – only the one, he reassured her, to celebrate the day. She gave him directions and the use of her son's jacket, a poor thing that he took with as much reverence as if it had been a saint's finger. It was like putting on a new skin - that of a man who had never needed to wait to be told to eat, or piss, or breathe.

The bar was an old place that had survived the RAF, and its plain, late nineteenth-century wooden interior was as welcoming as any could be. He kept his promise but made the beer last almost an hour, accepted a cigarette from a rough-looking fellow and an interrogation from half the clientele. He told them about the miracle, his death and resurrection as a prisoner, his years of wondering whether he was the most fortunate or cursed of men, and let them judge the matter.

This was a weighty thing, so they took their time with it. Had he been lucky as a boy? How many of his comrades had survived with him, and for how long? What unit had captured him, and were they Europeans, Cossacks or Mongols? How cruelly had he been used during the years in which so many others had died? What was his astrological sign?

He answered everything as truthfully as he could, because he was genuinely interested in their opinion. One of them seemed to be taking it more seriously than the others, and pressed him closely. He gave the man his unit (why not – he had given it to just about everyone else in Europe over the past few days) and the location of its last, desperate battle: the overwhelming numbers thrusting into their badly-sited line, the air and artillery onslaught (so much more deadly than any exhausted enemy would have been capable of mounting) and the attempted breakout in the evening, straight into a ring of steel placed precisely to sweep them up or cut them down. As far as he could say, only he and eighteen of his comrades had survived the day, and by the end of the month just three of them were above ground still.

Where did this happen?

He told the man, and the serious frown deepened.

I've heard of it, but I don't know when, or why.

One of his friends laughed. *It wasn't Goebbels who mentioned it, that's for sure.*

No, it was much more recently. It's not a big place is it? A famous battle?

He reassured the man that it was a rural hole in a land full of similar, memorable for nothing, the 'battle' no more than a frantic, lost brawl. If it marked anything at all, it was one of the many points at which the so-called German redeployment from Moscow was shown to be what it was – a hasty back-step.

Then why ...? The serious man (an old fellow in rough working clothes) stared at the pitted floor and scratched his cheek ... *does the name of that place bite me?*

There's a bordello there, and it's where you picked up the thing that bites you.

Shut up, Klaus. May I ask your name, sir?

He gave it, and the frown moved a little, rearranging the forehead. Then the head came up, the eyes cleared, and the serious old gentleman nodded.

That's it. You died.

He smiled and said that he often felt as if he had, and no doubt he had been marked down as a corpse; but the explosion that should have torn him apart lifted him instead and carried him about twenty metres through the air, to a patch of soft moss that caught him as gently as if his mother's arms had been outstretched. He was dragged into captivity without a single scratch on his body. It was why he had since wondered if he were very luckiest of men or the very …

The older man shook his head. *No, I mean you died last year, in Berlin. I read about you in the newspaper. It said that you were on your way to meet an old comrade from your unit when you were gunned down in the street. I shouldn't have recalled it, but yours is a very unusual name. I wondered at the time if you were French.*

2

Having circled it interminably, Otto Fischer arrived at a decision about twelve hours before a long-feared encounter made it redundant.

For months he had pored over a number of possibilities (most of which, upon closer reflection, turned out to be nothing of the sort), hoping that a neat, clean solution might present itself conveniently. He kept telling himself that he was living under threat, but it was a vague one and couldn't be measured accurately; so, like most idiots, he allowed the pleasant inertia of his untroubled routine to push away the moment at which mild anxiety should have become panic. Winter had come and gone without any great trials, business was modest but steady, nothing tragic of note had occurred in Germany since Thomas Mann's death the previous August, and only yesterday, rumours had started to circulate that in Moscow, Khrushchev had actually denounced Stalin and his works. A man could let all of that blunt the edges of his nerves.

Still, half his mind had continued to search for something to ease or remove the threat. Two weeks earlier, a casual conversation had reignited – or at least made less preposterous – one of his more frivolous ideas. The other party had been Josef Pfentzler, proprietor of *Pfentzler's Modes*, a couturier's that catered for the generously-proportioned lady, plying its trade four doors from *Fischer's Timepieces and Gramophones*. Pfentzler had been dining alone at a modest Italian restaurant just over the border in Steglitz when Fischer arrived for his weekly self-indulgence. The old man noticed his fellow entrepreneur, and, though they were passing acquaintances at most, invited him to his table with a wave of a hand.

Pfentzler was in a fine mood, which was unusual. The word around Lichterfelde was that his wife's death some years earlier had excised his more amiable qualities, leaving a hardening crust of dyspepsia that had gradually driven much of his clientele elsewhere. This was unfortunate (and unwise), because few areas of south-western Berlin accommodated so many ladies of large appetite and deep purse as did the district of Lichterfelde. On this particular evening, however, travails of the marketplace were clearly far from mind and heart.

Fischer discovered the reason for his table companion's genial mood as he examined the menu. An offer – a very generous offer – had been made for *Pfentzler's Modes* by a Frankfurt clothes chain looking to gain a head-start in Berlin's old-fashioned, largely owner-occupied retail world, and what should have been Herr Pfentzler's working hours were now devoted to researching residential properties on the shores of the Bodensee. He urged Fischer to test the waters himself, arguing – very persuasively - that a well-provided retirement was no less than a scarred veteran deserved.

In the following days, Fischer thought more about giving it all up than he had ever done previously. His shop wasn't going to be involved in any bidding frenzy, but it was well-situated and quite up-to-the minute, decor-wise. He had built some reasonable goodwill over the past five years and was the district's only official retailer for the Decca, RCA and Deutsche Grammophon record labels. With more expenditure on advertising he might have gone further, but that would have required expansion, and he wanted to manage other people as much as he'd ever coveted a position on a firing squad. Someone with more commercial bounce could make a great deal of the business.

Of course, he would have to give notice to his assistant, Renate, but kicking her out of the door would be almost an act of mercy. Since her mother had gone on the run with an ex-lover and Fischer's cash the poor girl had taken up the flagellant's scourge and demanded that her pay be cut by a hundred DM each month. She was much thinner now, and it was only by having their lunch delivered each day from a local café that he could be sure she took in at least some fuel while doing the work of a pair of field-oxen. For a good Protestant she was being willfully Catholic about it, and urgently needed a way out of her present employment that wouldn't further torture her conscience. Redundancy, with adequate severance pay (her agreement to which might require actual torture), would ease the burden on both their consciences.

The principal attraction of retirement was little to do with money, though. With even a modest price for the business he could take himself far from KGB's headquarters at Karlshorst, where his name was pinned to a file marked Pending Sacrificial Lamb - a hanging gift from his 'friend', former Major Zarubin, for having got the man back to the Soviet Union in less than several pieces. A new billet in Spain or Portugal (where communists were not so much unwelcome as blood-sported) would both remove that burden and ease a war-wounded shoulder that increasingly objected to cold, damp winters. He'd heard that life out there could be lived well for very little, and it wasn't so far from home that the mind would play the exile tricks that wither a man. The more he thought about it, the harder it was to dismiss the prospect.

And then, just when a promise of Iberian languor had settled on his lap and started to nibble his ear, someone at Karlshorst scratched 'Pending' off the file's cover. It was a Tuesday morning, nondescriptly grey, and twenty minutes after opening time *Fischer's Time-pieces and Gramophones* had yet to see a customer. The proprietor was stripping down a Victrola in his repair-room and idly imagined the noble city of Guimarães (having thumbed through *Baedeker's Spain and Portugal* the previous evening), while Renate busied herself hunting down specks of dust that somehow had survived an earlier offensive. Truly epic bad news deserves a thunder-clap or comet, but Fischer's had to make do with the doorbell, and came in the form of a well-dressed, middle-aged man. He paused just inside the door, glanced around the premises as if a stranger to this sort of enterprise, and, when confronted by an attractive but rather thin young woman, asked to speak to Herr Fischer.

His accent placed him as a native of what used to be East Prussia, though this was lost upon Renate (who had never visited the province in the days when it was part of Germany). She went to fetch her boss while the prospective customer examined a selection of repaired but unclaimed wristwatches, now for sale. When Fischer came into the shop, he removed his own item and asked if it might be mended within the following three days. It wasn't an unreasonable request; the piece had a slightly modified Swiss movement, quite familiar to any experienced repairer, and it wasn't as though the stock-room was presently over-pressed with urgent work. Still, Fischer's gut rolled over. The faceplate bore no maker's name, but the back was inscribed in Cyrillic script which identified the piece as having been manufactured at the Petrodvorats Watch Factory. The common trend in *movements* of wristwatches over the past decade had been very much from Germany to the Soviet Union; those that came the other way usually travelled beneath the sleeve of a Red Army uniform.

Fischer wrote out the ticket and asked for an address. His new customer gave it easily, without hesitation, and the only thing wrong with it was that the street lay three kilometres east of the Line. Even the proud proprietor didn't believe that *Fischer's Time-pieces and Gramophones*' reputation was such that it might drag a man across Berlin, not when so many perfectly adequate enterprises serviced the ground between. On the evidence before him, a promissory note he hadn't ever intended to put his name to was now being presented.

At the other counter, Renate seemed oblivious to the slight change in air pressure that warns of coming deluges. She looked up as the gentleman opened the front door once more and managed a smile and farewell - she had been practising the former, a facial expression she rarely employed - while her employer stared down at the wristwatch (which was working perfectly well) and wondered if this was how things were done these days.

He felt curiously short-changed. Even a wink or a tap on the side of the nose would have hinted at business too delicate to be mentioned in company, but this had been about as portentous as – well, what it looked like. If a man was about to become a traitor, an outcast, he wanted a drum roll at least, not a brown envelope through the post-flap.

Guimarães was beckoning frantically, but he very much doubted that KGB would sit back and allow him time to put his business on the market, sell it and pack a trunk. Presumably, the detail of the matter would be stated in three days, when … he glanced down at the ticket

… Herr Globnow returned for his wristwatch. He had precisely that period during which to think of a cast-iron excuse for giving Renate a day's leave. She was as faithful to him as any dog, but he didn't want to test his charms against her love of country.

He examined his own conscience only briefly. There had long been a space where a sense of identity, of loyalty to a particular form of social order, should have nested. The protagonists in this new struggle, straddling Germany's corpse, took care to paint their respective philosophies in stark shades of black and white, and neither of them had convinced him. On a purely practical level, he preferred what was familiar to a rolling, five-year stagger from one failed economic plan to another (with the occasional purge to keep spirits low); but that didn't amount to faith, either in democracy or capitalism. He'd had more than enough of being told that *this* was utterly evil, and *that* was divinely-ordained - that the fight was one for civilization itself, when really, what it was would have been familiar to a Hittite, or a Roman, or the ear of Herr Jenkins. He couldn't go so far as to *believe* in anything, and he resented those who expected him to try.

But if the prospect of committing treason didn't weigh too heavily, its consequences definitely did. Being caught by Gehlen's people whilst on KGB's payroll would be slightly less disastrous than the reverse, but that was to say very little - and even a bullet to the back of the head might begin to seem the merciful option after several years on latrine-cleaning duties. He hardly entertained the prospect that he might not be caught. His only prior experience of the spy's life had offered no evidence that he had any aptitude for it.

He must have been wearing his fears on his face, because Renate came across from her counter and squeezed his arm gently. She assumed, of course, that he was thinking still of the monies he had lost to her mother. All penitents bear deeper scars than they deserve, but she took her sufferings to a virtuous excess. Actually, he had been quite delighted when Frau Knipper fled to Bruges (her only letter to her daughter had been posted from there) rather than remain in Berlin, plotting his downfall into darkest matrimony. He wanted to tell Renate as much, but it was the sort of truth that would hurt more than the lash she applied to her back.

He couldn't take his eyes from the wristwatch. What the hell could they want him for? He was acquainted with no government officials, military masterminds or any members of the Allied Commissions, so what remained? Was he to subvert the time-piece-repairing economy in West Berlin? Sow relativist doubts among the prosperous citizens of Lichterfelde? Whatever it was, his half-ruined face would allow him to pass as unnoticed as fish-paste in a diving-bell. They might as well scour the circuses and find someone with a red nose and big feet to do the business.

'Marcel Dalio.'

Renate said it almost in his ear, and his feet tried to leave the floor.

'What?'

'That man. He looks a little like Marcel Dalio.'

The name was vaguely familiar, but Fischer was in no mood to search for it. 'Who's that?'

'A French actor. He plays sophisticated characters. My … Mother likes him.'

A small bell pealed. 'Isn't he Jewish?'

'I think so, yes.'

She was right, their recent visitor *did* resemble Dalio - a man whose ethnic origins were as plain as any caricature. How had a Prussian Jew survived the Reich, unless…?

In 1919 the *Freikorps* had ended German Communism's brief stab at running the nation, and many of the survivors had fled to the Soviet Union, their only viable sanctuary. Others had followed a decade later, when National Socialists began to crowd the Reichstag. Fischer had always assumed – without thinking too much about it, either way – that the long-term exiles who returned with the Red Army in '45 had scrambled to take the best political jobs in what would become the DDR, but why should that necessarily be the case? An army needs men of all ranks to function; perhaps Herr Globnow was one of their foot-soldiers - an infiltrator, a subverter, perfectly at home in West Berlin yet utterly apart from it.

And what would Otto Fischer be? During his brief time with the Gehlen Org, the world had been much more conveniently chaotic. The Game had just moved into a new phase, and its players were unfamiliar still with the ground upon which they fought. Back then there had been blind spots, through which he and his friends passed out of plain sight, creating lies that had stood for want of evidence otherwise. It was different now. Both Germanies had cleared the rubble, the players were well-practiced and the ground – once crowded by a shuffling mob among whom a man could lose himself easily – was laid out neatly, its grids comprising rules, recourses and sanctions. Anyone trampling through that was going to be visible, sooner or later.

He wasted the afternoon brooding, sent Renate home at six o'clock, and after closing up shop went upstairs to his apartment and opened a bottle of wine. Wine was for weekends, but this was a special day, one in which a wise man could make a start on drinking himself pleasantly to death. As it happened, neither alcohol nor the Weiner Konzerthausquartett's best efforts lifted the weight even slightly. He thought wistfully of Josef Pfentzler, planning his easy descent to the grave having managed, apparently, to avoid most if not all of life's ordure-smeared complications. What did a man have to do, to earn a bland, eventless span in this world?

He played out the self-pity for a while, and it helped a little more than wine and music; but he slept badly that night, poked by half-waking dreams of rainy street corners, turned-up collars and races through dark woods, lost to under-fed attack-dogs. At dawn he rose, had a quick shower and went for a groggy walk through Lichterfelde's almost deserted streets. A familiar-yet-resented shift had begun; what a day earlier had registered in his subconscious as normality now wore a sheen of once-removal, as if he had been lifted and set down on the other side of slightly dirty glass. A few shift workers walked by him, preoccupied, heads down, and his maudlin mind told him he was already passing, unseen, from their ordinary world. The illusion cracked slightly when he tripped at a kerb on Weddigenweg, stumbled forward cursing and raised a smile from a passing street-vendor, pulling his bockwurst cart to its plot. He tried to return it, but the result felt ugly even on his face.

His mind had found no sort of peace by the time he returned to his shop a little after seven-thirty. It was just as well, because Herr Globnow was standing in the doorway, waiting, pretending to find the side-window display more interesting than it possibly could be. He was two days early, which in any other circumstance might have seemed overly-impatient, or hopeful, or ill-mannered; but neither man mistook the visit to be upon a point of wristwatches, working or otherwise.

He found a cheap hotel in Moabit, near the Navigation Canal. The old man sitting at its brown, dingy reception asked to see his papers but changed his mind when he was offered three nights' payment in advance, cash. The room for which he provided a key was also brown, and dingy, and smelled faintly of urine, and Jesus kept a careful eye on things from the wall opposite its only window.

The name he'd given – Walter Senn – belonged to someone else, but he was certain that no offence would be taken. It had been floating in the wind, unclaimed, for eight years now, since the day its owner had stepped backwards to admire his bricklaying skills and dropped several storeys to a Stalingrad street. A good fellow, Walter, with a bad habit of letting his attention wander.

By the time he reached Berlin he had spent almost all he'd managed to save. Weeks of working as many double shifts as possible had given him an illusion of relative wealth, but he hadn't even begun to gauge how expensive modern Germany could be. Had he continued to stay at Frau Weltmann's house in Lübeck he might have managed very comfortably - she hadn't named a price for bed and board, but when he offered what he thought was fair her eyes had lit up, and after that he'd eaten as well as he could remember. Her home comforts had both attracted and frightened him, though. To have stayed would have been easy, and convenient, and as if to surrender like an insect in deep honey, enjoying every moment of its drowning.

So, that morning, while she was still sleeping, he'd left fifty marks on the hall table, his thanks to her for not allowing hard times to blunt her soul. After that, the train-fare to Berlin and the advance payment for the hotel room had made his wallet much less likely to ruin the cut of his jacket. He was skating close to where ice becomes water, and as yet he had no real idea of why.

He had to *know*, naturally. After that, he couldn't say what he was going to do. A man who'd survived the worst sort of encasement didn't come out of it with any plans worth the name. He was used to obeying, to expecting things to proceed without playing any part in how they did so. Initiative was just a word - he knew what it was supposed to mean but couldn't recall anything of the manoeuvre.

His obvious first step was towards a library, but it was now early evening, so he put his almost-empty rucksack in the room's only wardrobe and went downstairs to ask the *portier* where he might find a meal that didn't break the bank. The directions were straightforward, and in a few minutes he was in Birkenstrasse, a busy, well-lit thoroughfare, excusing himself to a succession of people who seemed to think that he was occupying their *lebensraum*. At the corner of Perlebergerstrasse he found the restaurant and spent the next few minutes staring at a hand-written card in its window, trying to understand German words that attempted to describe Albanian cuisine. When he went inside he ordered a beer and pointed to something on the menu. It tasted like lamb, another memory that had almost escaped him.

Afterwards he walked through the streets for an hour, taking in the feel of the place. He had never been here before, not even during the Peace, and he decided that he liked it. It didn't smell too clean, wasn't nearly quiet and seemed to wear very little lace on its knickers - Moabit, at least, was what he'd always imagined all of Berlin to be. He stopped at a narrow little bar and had another beer, and as he finished it he realised he had no idea how to get back to his hotel. When he asked directions, two large, half-drunk fellows with tattoos on their knuckles insisted on walking him there, for the price of his joining in every nonsensical chorus of *Dort droben auf dem berg* and having his back pounded horribly by way of farewell.

The bed in his room was as bad as it looked, but he slept well (his spine being far more familiar with rough terrain than angels' caresses) and as soon as the *portier* arrived to prepare his guests' breakfasts the next morning he asked about the nearest major library. This drew a blank stare, so he explained what it was that he needed to research.

The old fellow shrugged. 'You'll have better luck at the *Morgenpost* archive. I expect they have all the papers there.'

At precisely nine o-clock he was outside Ku-damm 21, waiting for the doors to open. He had no idea whether they welcomed casual enquiries from the public (nor, he suspected, had the *portier*), but it wasn't as though his question couldn't be answered by dragging out a report or two. He'd wondered whether he might bribe someone to be amenable, and then remembered that bribery had certain protocols, not the least of which was funds to do the business. All he had was his endearing personality, an asset that had failed to move even his mother to more than what the paperwork demanded.

Once more, his thin expectations were confounded. The very lovely young lady to whom he was directed gave him a preliminary sneer when he admitted that he had made no appointment; but when he mentioned the matter and the (approximate) month in which it had been reported she looked puzzled, as though she were being teased.

'Is that all?'

He assured her that it was.

'Wait, please.'

Despite his best efforts he couldn't help watching her rump, calves and ankles closely as she retreated down the corridor (they being items to which he had long been a distant - though no less loving -

stranger). She returned within ten minutes, and it was all he could do to keep his eyes on her face as she approached.

She had brought three newspapers, only one of which was the *Morgenpost*.

'I remember this', she said. 'It was an *assassination*, apparently.'

He took the newspapers to a reading desk and sat down. The *Morgenpost* had run the story briefly on page three, while the *Berliner Zeitung* had given it more prominence, devoting half a column on the front page to the details offered by the Police. The third paper – a rag he'd never heard of, the *Süd-west Berliner Zeitung* – had treated the incident as though it ranked with the invasion of Poland, splashing all kinds of supposition (with very little facts) across its first two pages.

The old gentleman in the bar in Lübeck had been right – he'd died that day. His name, former unit and place of birth were all stated accurately, and his body had been identified by a friend of the family who'd come forward.

What should he think about it? His first reaction was to laugh, but that didn't seem respectful. Though he had no place in the world to lose, he was who he was, and having always been so felt quite comfortable with it. If some other fellow had wanted his name, the least he might have done was to take care to keep it off a headstone. He wasn't worried about the obvious implication – that it was almost certainly some sort of criminal business that had required a man to take someone else's identity. It wasn't as if its real owner could be tainted with any illegality - a hard bunk bed in a forest in the Ukraine, and half a regiment of second-rate Red Army conscripts to guard it, was almost the perfect alibi. But it was an immoveable fact that a borrowed name, attached to a murdered man, had acquired a new, permanent home.

Some people might think him blessed, to be extracted from all past associations and sins. He was a blank sheet, unstained, ready to re-make a mark in the world. He could be anyone at all (anyone who wasn't actually someone already, that is), go anywhere, do the best he could to make a new life, but...

But nagged more than it should. He had lost everything already, even his home city, in the fourteen years he had spent out of the world. If he was obliged to give up his identity also, what would keep him from blowing away in the wind?

He told himself not to be stupid, that he had begun this journey already without the assistance of the man who had died badly on ... he glanced down at the story once more ... Schloss-Strasse, Steglitz. Each time he'd been asked for his personal details in the past few days he had given Walter Senn's name and a street in Danzig that hadn't quite been his own. Why had he done that? In the camps there might have been good reason for it, but now? He was guilty of nothing, so was it natural caution or an intent to some purpose he couldn't yet quite see? In the event, he had swiftly become grateful for the lie. On the platform of Lübeck station they had each been given a piece of paper and told that they must call the telephone number upon it as soon as they had a permanent address, in order that they might be interviewed *officially*.

About what? Whether they had become Soviets in all but name during their long captivity? Whether they might be of some use in future, as if they hadn't given enough already? It smacked of a State Security agency (he couldn't know which, of course), wishing to squeeze out what little remained of a man, and he wasn't going willingly into that slaughterhouse. Given that to all practical, possibly sensible ends, he had made himself Walter Senn, it seemed hardly reasonable that he should be so reluctant to part with his real name.

He could see too little to think it through clearly, but at least his next task was obvious. He had to find this *friend of the family*. He re-read the *Morgenpost* piece and memorized the name at the Police Praesidium to whom all information should be addressed. The killing had happened almost ten months ago, so he doubted that they would be interested still in any revelations. That was fine; he was going to be asking, not offering. He just needed to find a way to do it that didn't raise further, difficult questions.

4

'You're not serious?'

Herr Globnow smiled. 'Really, it isn't a joke.'

'But ...' being a matter about which he was profoundly disinterested, Fischer had to search his memory for the date; '… it won't happen until the end of '58.'

'That's why I'm here now. You'll need plenty of time to get yourself known around Lichterfelde and Steglitz.'

'Known? For what?'

'For being the right man, of course.'

'But I'm *not* the right man. I have no idea what it is I'm supposed to care about, nor what I'd do if I did.'

'I can prepare you for all of that. The point is, you're a fairly familiar face in this part of the borough already, so when you announce it the word will spread quickly.'

Fischer wondered if *familiar* was the right adjective to describe his face. Repulsive, possibly, or demonic, and certainly singular. Christ, what if he was expected to kiss babies?

'I assume I'd be standing for the KDP or SED?'

Globnow laughed. 'Don't. The Old Communists have been under a hanging death sentence for years – they'll never fight another election in West Berlin. And the SED? When they ran in '54 they got two-point-seven percent of the vote and precisely no seats. We want you to influence decisions in the *Abgeordnetenhaus*, not press your nose forlornly to its windows. You're going to be a Social Democrat.'

'But ... we have an SDP Representative already. In our district, I mean.'

'He has a past, and it'll be coming out.'

'What sort of past?'

'I don't know. We haven't decided yet.'

'You can't just ...' Fischer paused. Of course they could, in a hundred ways. It might be sex, or criminality – anything to point a finger away from someone who was genuinely on KGB's payroll.

Evidence was whatever they decided to make it, and would cost nothing to fling. Even if any doubt remained, no-one would take a chance on a man with damp stains on his coat.

Poor bastard.

Globnow was still smiling. 'The CDU would be the most suitable home for a small businessman, naturally; but that would put you among a lot of competition. The SDP don't attract many heartfelt capitalists, so you'd be a bit of a catch for them – proof that they appeal across the usual boundaries. In any case, they're by far the biggest group in the House, so you'll be more effective on their side.'

'But what would I preach? To convince people?'

'What you'd expect - worthy, left'ish stuff, nothing to make the horses bolt. Once you're in with the Party we'll make sure that you're putting out the right message. You don't need to make it up.'

So the Fischer trajectory was to continue, gloriously upwards. From reluctant *kripo*, unlucky parachutist and very minor tradesman to dispenser of fantasies - a professional dissembler whose success depended upon enough decent people putting aside the sort of common sense that makes a man jump into water when his arse catches fire. Either God, Khrushchev or some anonymous handler at

Karlshorst had an excellent sense of humour, and for a moment he suspected that the latter might be Zarubin - it was precisely the sort of thing he *would* conceive, had he been stationed in Berlin still. His career would have needed to falter badly to bring him back to the city, though, and the Soviets had neater ways of showing their dissatisfaction with a man's work.

He wondered how bad it was going to be. He had feared that he was going to be a link, a passer-on, a sleight-of-hander between those who put themselves into the confidences of important people and the ones who waited, hands outstretched, for the information – a middleman, whose loss would hardly be noticed, much less mourned. *This* was a longer game, a career in playing at something he wasn't, for a purpose he probably wouldn't ever be told. And when it all fell to shit – as it must – his best hope would be a midnight flit across the line, with a grossly underfunded retirement in exile to look forward to. Guimarães, Moscow – he hardly needed a coin to flip that choice, nor a seer to tell him that it wasn't really a choice at all.

Globnow was watching him, content to let the bad news work its way through the system. He seemed a genial sort, for someone whose job it was to steal lives. Perhaps he had an innate bonhomie that protected him from its worst passages, or a native sadism that relished them - either way, he seemed not at all ruffled by the turmoil he had unleashed. When Fischer (retracing his thoughts in the hope of finding a misplaced trap-door) rubbed his head distractedly he held out a hand, palm upward.

'Don't be anxious – we won't be on your back all the time. You might go on for months, doing good work for this part of Berlin. It's only when minds, dirt or attention need to be shifted that you'll be required to step up, and none of it will come back to bite you. We don't risk our people for nothing.'

Fischer's spirits might almost have rallied, but *for nothing* sent them back into their dive. What constituted *something*? A major East-West confrontation, the atomic bombers in the air? His handler having a bad day at the races? This was going to be like living with a disease that had been diagnosed variously as nothing to worry about or don't make any plans.

What did they have, to prevent him from merely refusing to cooperate? His (unwitting) part in the death of an unfortunate young man? Surely that wasn't going to be resurrected, not when it would drag a former KGB-StB operation into the light. What else? Over the years he'd done a great deal to irritate any number of powerful people, but nothing that would find its way onto a charge sheet. His intimate life was above reproach (one of the few things for which he could sincerely thank his ruined face), and if anything in his safe was traceable, it was only to the church mice that had passed around the hat to raise it. What, other than …?

Stupid, Otto. He was looking at it from the wrong direction. What they had was *him*. As Zarubin had said, he was reliable, respectable and very, very available. As for the stick, it was much the same as the one that was about to bloody one of Steglitz-Lichterfelde's current SDP Borough Representatives, which was to say whatever shape, size and type of wood that they wanted it to be. Evidence – of anything - was the easiest commodity to manufacture.

Globnow stood up. 'I'll be in touch again soon, with paperwork to join the SDP and a few testimonials to your wonderful character. May I have my watch, please?'

Fischer retrieved it from a drawer and held it out. Despite everything else that crowded in, he was mildly curious. 'It's a good piece. Where did you get it?'

'It was a birthday present, from my wife.'

'Ah. Is she in Ber …?'

'Your people shot her, outside Kharkov, in August '43. She was a second lieutenant with the 1st Ukrainian Front.'

'I'm … sorry.'

The other man smiled thinly. 'No reason why you should be. She was a Uighur, so most of the fine men I worked with in Moscow looked upon her in much the same way as the bastards who killed her. Germans have no monopoly on thinking themselves superior.'

'Yet you've stayed loyal to them.'

'You make choices. As time passes, they cease to be so.'

Globnow left without another word, and Fischer went upstairs to try to force down some breakfast. His head and gut were suspended between two states – the detached, oblivious condition that allowed him to plod through every normal day's routine and the needing-to-be-elsewhere, upright-collapse that precedes every dawn offensive. This was going to be unbearable. He was to be placed in parlous danger – but not quite yet. He would put one face to the world and hide another, be respectable and perfidious, serve and betray his fellow Berliners, and all the while wonder when and how it would end. It was a threat of some form of hell, with a ticket to queue beforehand.

He was still upstairs when Renate arrived. She called to him twice before he answered, and it took a great effort of will to join her in the shop. He asked if she'd slept well and taken some breakfast, and scolded her mildly when she lied about both, and set out his tools as he would on any other workday, and half an hour later couldn't have recalled any of it if he'd tried. He had three repairs and a gramophone-service waiting – a perfect day's quota (not too much to fret about; not too little to make time drag) that he almost certainly wasn't going to meet. He was thinking about the months he'd squandered, waiting like a too-tall conscript in a forward trench for the bad news to arrive. He might have settled himself in northern Portugal by now, coming to terms with the local wine, trying to develop a taste for reconstituted dried cod and reading three-day-old copies of the *Frankfurter Allgemeine* whenever nostalgia pressed (if it ever did), and when Herr Globnow turned up at Curtius-Strasse he would have glanced up at the wrong name on the shop sign and scratched out one of the entries on his own quota. A perfect non-consummation, all shrapnel avoided.

Fleeing was no longer an option, though, and attempting to preempt Karlshorst by handing himself over to Pullach would be merely to jump the queue for Hell a little. What remained was to wait, to savour his helplessness in the meanwhile, and then - surreally – to attempt to put some enthusiasm into being a local politician. Putting it another way, the weather had turned for the worse once more, and Otto Fischer was on parade in his underpants.

5

The reception area at Friesenstrasse Police Praesidium did no justice to the fine old red-brick building in which it squatted. It was cramped, under-provided with over-distressed seating and smelled of too much humanity. He almost decided to reverse course and send in a written application instead, but he recognized the urge for what it was and steeled himself.

'May I speak with *UnterKommissar* Holzmann please? It's about the Schloss-Strasse killing, in May last year.'

Both of the large *wachtsmeister*'s elbows were settled comfortably on his counter, and this request did not incline him to shift them even slightly. He sniffed.

'He's a *kriminalkommissar*, now. Do you have an appointment?'

'No. I've only recently seen the request for witnesses to come forward. So I did.'

'That was ...' the *wachtsmeister* squinted at some point on the wall opposite; '... nine months ago. You've only just seen it?'

'I've been away from Berlin.'

'Oh. Wait over there.'

He sat on a bench and rehearsed what he was going to say. His accent would help, of course, and he wasn't going to make the mistake of over-complicating his story. It was entirely feasible – even to be expected – and unless this Holzmann fellow was a proper bastard he could hardly refuse to help. It wasn't as if he'd be required to do more than open a file.

It was ten minutes before one of the elbows shifted sufficiently to allow a hand to pick up the telephone receiver, but the *wachtsmeister* tossed his head a moment after it went back into the cradle.

'Second floor. He'll meet you at the top of the stairs.'

Kriminalkommissar Holzmann was a young man, as cleanly presented as to make his visitor feel shabby. He had the sort of serious frown on his face that hadn't quite got over the promotion, but he held out a hand.

'You have information on the killing of Rudy Bandelin?'

'I don't. I didn't want to mislead you, but it's important.'

The frown deepened. 'Important, how? Did you know Bandelin?'

'A long time ago, yes. We grew up in the same *heimat*. I haven't seen him since the war.'

'I keep hearing that. The fellow must have been living in a badgers' sett. What is it you want?'

'The newspapers say that his body was identified by a friend of the family. May I ask who that was, please?'

'What is it to you?'

'It's that it might be … I've been away for a long time, a prisoner of war.'

'Until *now*? Oh ...'

The pfennig dropped, and Holzmann's face softened slightly. 'That's a hard sentence.'

'It was. I had family in Danzig, but of course it's Poland now. I haven't been able to trace anyone. Can I ask … was the person who identified Rudy a woman named Else Senn?'

He had no idea who Else Senn was - if she was anyone at all – but that hardly mattered. Holzmann put a hand on his shoulder.

'I can't recall. Come on, we'll see.'

He was led to a small, two-man office. The single desk was occupied on one side by a burly fellow with a moustache who glanced up briefly when the door opened and then went back to his one-fingered typing.

'What's your name?'

'Walter Senn, Sir. Else's my Aunt. She was very close to the Bandelins, lived two doors away from the family. It's why I thought she might have been ...'

He trailed off, hopefully, and saw the pity in Holzmann's eyes. It was a distant chance at best, but exactly what a desperate man might chase. The *kriminalkommissar* opened a filing drawer, flicked through its contents and lifted a file from it.

'It was ... no, I'm sorry. The name I have is Anna Felder.' Holzmann looked up. 'Yes, she was about your age, perhaps a little younger. Good-looking, with dark hair.'

Anna was the name of his sister's lifelong best friend. Around the time he'd marched off to war she had been keeping company with a

Danziger low-type named Georg Felder. It couldn't be a coincidence.

The shock must have been plain on his face, and it was neither rehearsed nor pretended.

'She knew my sister. You don't have an address for her?'

Holzmann looked doubtfully at his partner, who shook his head slightly. It was probably against any number of rules to hand out information – particularly about a female – to someone claiming to be something without any evidence to prove it. He searched his memory frantically.

'She … has a harsh voice, as if she smokes heavily. She doesn't, though. It's always been that way, like for Dietrich. And as you say, she's pretty. She and Margret were always popular with the boys. If you wish, I could speak to her here, if she can be brought?'

It took no effort for him to sound plaintive. If they said no, what could he do - stick up posters in the street, asking Anna Felder to come forward to … where, and to whom? He recalled the old ladies at Lübeck station, and the pathetic signs they held up – *Who has seen my son?* The answer was many people or no-one, and nothing – absent a flash of blind luck - could be done to determine which.

The Moustache sniffed and shrugged, and Holzmann, after pondering both for a few moments, re-opened his file.

'The address we were given last year was in Wedding - Utrechterstrasse 148, apartment 12. Obviously, we haven't checked since.'

'Thank you. Did you ever find further evidence about what happened? To Rudy, I mean?'

The two policemen looked at each other once more. Slowly, Holzmann shook his head. 'It was assumed to be a revenge killing, given the method. Your friend seems to have been involved with bad people. It happens a lot, with ex-soldiers who can't go home.'

He nodded and tried to look sad. 'He was always a bit wild, was Rudy. Not too fond of an honest day's work - not of what it paid, anyway.'

The policemen nodded, only half-listening, and he got the strong impression that Rudolph Bandelin's death had long since been assigned to a space between concern and oblivion. A few minutes earlier he might have resented that, but having taken with the one hand they had offered him a chance of seeing his sister once more, and if family didn't keep a man in the world, what could?

Holzmann had been kind and he was grateful for it, but one thing a man learns when he relies utterly for his life on the whims of others is never to waste a hint of humanity when it presents itself. He cleared his throat.

'May I ask something else, sir?'

The look on the policeman's face told him that he'd pushed a little too far, so he spoke again, quickly, before a refusal nailed up the boards.

'It's just a name. If you have it, that is.'

'Otto, you old Bastard! What's your news?'

'Hello, Freddie ...' Fischer caught a movement at the edge of his vision and nodded at Renate's economical, one-handed explanation that she was popping out to speak to her fiancé, three doors down; '... nothing much, really. How's life on the mighty Moselle?'

'Sickeningly pleasant, thank you ...' a child's laugh pealed close to the receiver; '... get off, you little thug! Your namesake here pissed on my lap yesterday - have you been giving him orders?'

Fischer had urged Holleman's son not to name his first-born Otto, and begged to be excused duty as his godfather, and been ignored on both matters. What a godfather *did* eluded him, so he sent a birthday card each year and put money into a bank account for when the lad needed it, and otherwise recalled his existence only when precious moments like this occurred.

'Pat his head for me. How's Kristen, and why aren't you working?'

'Ravishing, and piles.'

'Ouch! When did this happen?'

'The fruits have been ripening for a couple of years now. I can bear it most days, but I tore something straining on the latrine this morning, and ...'

'... and you've just saved me the price of lunch. I take it you're standing for the rest of the day?'

'Lying coquettishly on my belly, actually. Listen, Otto ...'

Freddie Holleman never picked up a 'phone to offer or hear the latest gossip, so Fischer had been bracing himself since the conversation began.

'... why don't you come for a holiday? To Trier?'

'A holiday?' The word was vaguely familiar but hard to place, like *Alleghenies*.

'You haven't had any time off since your ten months in the burns ward – and Sachsenhausen, obviously. It was Kristen's idea, and a cracking one. We can hire a boat and bugger around on the river like two proper old farts. Or go hiking!'

'With your tin leg?'

'Alright, not hiking. What about motoring? Old churches, drunken lunches, cheap hotels, and if the mood takes us we can invade Luxembourg on the odd afternoon. What do you think?'

Fischer thought it a marvellous, inspired idea, and he searched quickly for a plausible reason to say no. In his present distracted mood he would ruin any holiday, but if he said so Holleman would want to know the reason, and then Christ alone knew where the damage would end. Claiming he was too busy with broken time-pieces wouldn't do it, nor pleas of poverty (Holleman would empty his wallet in a moment, and then Kristen would have to kill them both). No, when an enthusiastic avalanche poured towards a man, a handy side-step was the only sound strategy.

'It's a fine thought, Freddie, but not in February, surely? What about September, the golden month? That would give me time to arrange things here, so I could take two or three weeks without fretting about the shop every day.' *And I'll have plenty of time to think of a proper excuse.*

'Hm. I got the impression that Kristen wants a holiday from *me*, but you're right, it would be better in early autumn. I can tap into next year's leave allowance then.'

'And your arse might have stopped singing in the meantime.'

'I can only pray. September it is.'

Fischer thought about the irony of it for most of the rest of the morning. First Pfentlzer, and now Freddie Holleman – a pair of remarkably ugly sirens, singing to him of happier places while Herr Globnow stood behind them, large rock in hand, ready to lob it into any craft that wandered too close to shore. Facing all that, a man might feel that he was being toyed with.

Renate returned to the shop after a startlingly long absence and apologized abjectly, though he stopped listening about three minutes into the explanation. It was something to do with wedding arrangements, a topic upon which he felt himself to be horribly over-informed already. Both she and her fiancé were orphaned (Jonas Kleiber actually so, she by reason of her mother's absconding), so details usually kept within the decent confines of a matriarch's parlour were being aired wantonly. Kleiber had the instincts of a rock when it came to the proprieties, but Renate wanted it all done by the book and was demonstrating a tighter grasp of fine detail than OKW had ever managed with *Barbarossa*. Fischer genuinely wished the young couple all possible happiness, but his pulse failed to race even slightly when each day's planning crises erupted singly or as a herd.

At some point during his latest failure to pay attention it occurred to him that he was allowing his own calvary to distract him, so he thought about ways to make amends. In the back of the shop he had an old Hermle, a fine piece that had stopped working some years earlier and was uneconomical to repair (he doubted anyone would pay the price he'd expect for it). Restored, it would make an excellent wedding present, and he decided to make a start the following day, other business allowing. In the meantime, he sympathized vaguely about the local church choir (two tenors short) and the city-wide run on white roses that was making them impossibly expensive, and then suggested to Renate that she take off the afternoon to track down a cheap-but-wonderful caterer.

All this selflessness raised his mood, and he did a lot of useful work before closing time. The weather outside was fine for February, and usually it would have tempted him to his favourite bar; but he feared that Jonas Kleiber would have the same idea, and then the evening would be spoiled by more grumblings about wedding arrangements (though this case more directed to *why* than *how*). Instead, he ate a supper of blutwurst and cabbage and then read the newspaper, a pleasant enough occupation until he came to the story of the hour - the re-appearance in Moscow of the fled British traitors Burgess and Maclean. Curiously, he hadn't thought to put himself in their forlorn company until that moment, but when he did so his supper almost returned. He had a sudden, icily clear vision of himself, confronting a bank of flash bulbs, delivering an earnest political manifesto from a text carefully prepared by others while trying not to seem as if his life had come effectively to its close. What would it be like to spend his final years in that bleak other-world? Were there any decent bars in Moscow? Any Italian restaurants? And if there were – he doubted it greatly – would he be allowed out in the evenings?

Bugger Jonas. He threw the newspaper at the kitchen bin, put on his jacket and found his wallet. It was almost eight o'clock, and Kleiber couldn't hold his drink nearly as well as the average twelve-year-old. With luck, any rants about wedding preparations would be incoherent or even mumbled by now, and lost beneath other observations from the bar's over-opinionated clientele.

He must have stretched his legs, because he was at the bar in less than fifteen minutes. As he entered he half-registered the noise level, which was considerably higher than usual. What snatched more at his attention was the sight of Jonas Kleiber *sans* trousers, leaning on the bar with a clutch of his friends around him. Instantly, the former *kripo* threw himself upon the clues – the similar display of naked legs by several other young men, the prevalence of beer bottles on every surface (the landlord, Kaspar, usually swept them up before the foam disappeared from their necks), the song presently being assaulted (a foul parody of *Lili Marlene*), the cake, the hint of vomit – and felt a strong surge of relief. It appeared that he had not been invited to Kleiber's bachelor farewell.

'Otto!' Kleiber tried momentarily to release his grip on the bar, but thought better of it. 'My old street-fighting comrade!'

Fischer made a gap through the bodies and shook the young man's free hand. 'My sincere condolences. Why so soon, though? You're aren't getting married until March.'

'I'm not. But I have instructions.' Kleiber giggled. 'I get a lot of those. She said I was to do what boys do in plenty of time to recover. I would have done it next week, but I'm ...'

'What?'

'I ... forget. Never mind. You must hate me, Otto!'

'Why would you think that?'

'I didn't tell you about tonight! Renate said she didn't want you to see me drunk!' Slowly, Kleiber stood straight. 'I'm not though, just relaxed and cheerful.'

'And trouser-less.'

'And that, yes. I lost a wager.'

'Which was?'

'That I could take them off without spilling a drop. No-one else has managed it, either.'

Beaming, he held up his bottle to his friends, who roared and did the same. Fischer took a step back and nodded at Kaspar, who reached for a *Spezial*. Kleiber, frowning at the gap that had opened between them, moved to fill it. He put an arm around the older man's neck and squeezed.

'I'm marrying Renate.'

Gratefully, Fischer imbibed the heavy scent of beer and at least two meals. 'Yes, you are. She's a wonderful girl.'

'She's very ...'

'Very what?'

'Extremely, even. I'm lucky, aren't I?'

'Yes, you are. And forget about not inviting me. It's a young man's thing – you don't want an old sod spoiling the atmosphere.'

Kleiber giggled again, but then frowned and squeezed a little more tightly. 'Listen, Otto.'

'I'm listening, Jonas.'

'Hm? Oh! There's someone looking for you.'

'For me? Why?'

'I have no idea. Herr Grabner took a call this morning, about you. Well, the man who called asked about you.'

'Why would he call the *Süd-west Berliner Zeitung* about *me*?'

There was short pause while Kleiber stared at a small area of regurgitation on the floor. 'That's a *fucking* good question. I have no idea, but don't worry, it's fine. Herr Grabner said, *Don't talk to me about Otto Fischer! Because I don't know him!* And then he put the 'phone down.'

'Did he really say that?'

'I paraphrase, obviously. But your secrets are safe.'

'What secrets?'

Kleiber beamed. 'That's the spirit!'

As a new song began (an equally obscene re-working of *The White Cliffs of Dover*) Fischer retreated with his *Spezial* to a quieter section of the bar to ponder the mystery. Why would anyone think a local newspaper had information on him? Why wouldn't an enquirer come straight to the horse's mouth? His name was above the shop, the business was listed in the Berlin Directory – hell, he placed occasional advertisements in the *Berliner Kurier* and *Spandauer Volksblatt* which went out of their way to direct the potential customer to Curtius-Strasse 21. Someone wanting to find Otto Henry Fischer hardly needed to pull down the brim of his hat or climb over back fences. On the other hand, it hardly seemed to be something he should worry about. A man wishing harm wouldn't announce himself beforehand to the Press, surely?

Sometime during the third verse the bridegroom-to-be toppled like a tree, and as drunken confusion reigned Fischer paid for his *Spezial* and departed quietly. He had started to strip the situation to its individual parts, which killed any chance of the evening sliding away comfortably. What had Grabner *really* said to the anonymous gentleman - and what, precisely, had been asked? Kleiber sat directly opposite his editor for much of each workday, but recently he'd been distracted – not least by Renate, who was invading the *Zeitung*'s premises each time a clock chimed to demand his input (which was then promptly ignored) on the latest urgent decision. Could what he recalled – even when sober - be trusted?

During his years as a guest of NKVD, Fischer had taught himself that what couldn't be altered shouldn't be fretted about, but the lesson had stayed with him only as far as Sachsenhausen's front gate. Out in the world, an illusion of freedom told a man that some matters couldn't or shouldn't be left hanging, and this one was dangling in his face. Before he was halfway home, he knew that had to interrupt Ferdinand Grabner's evening.

It was an easy decision, but making his escape afterwards would be a problem What Kleiber was doing to his entrails this particular evening, Grabner did *every* evening. The man drank heroically, his means of mourning a fled young wife; but unlike most professional alcoholics he preferred company. Fischer was a widower, and Grabner considered himself to be such in all but name – they shared a brotherhood of loss that a glass of whisky would cement like tempera to an altar panel. Neither aviation fuel nor bullets had managed to damage the Fischer liver, but an hour in Grabner's company might do the trick very well.

The editor of the *Süd-west Berliner Zeitung* lived on Lipaerstrasse, a suitably staid address for a long-term pillar of the local community. It was almost nine-thirty by now and getting colder, and Fischer forced himself up the garden path to the front door of number 87 as his shoulder started to complain. He knocked twice before hearing movement inside, and then Grabner was stood in the open doorway, his shirt collar open and sleeves neatly rolled up.

'Ah, Herr Fischer.' He said it with little more surprise than a receptionist would a name on her appointments list, and stood back. 'You'll be wanting to hear about the 'phone call.'

The odour of alcohol was barely noticeable, and the man seemed firm on his feet. Fischer allowed himself to be led into the sitting room, where Richard Strauss was providing the entertainment (if *Elektra* could be mistaken for that).

'Would you like a glass of wine?'

The question was so unexpected (Grabner's preference was for wine-glass measures, but of spirits) that Fischer accepted graciously. His host lifted a bottle from a small table and offered the label, as if what it said mattered to the process of finding oblivion.

'A Haut Medoc only, but quite bearable.'

Fischer made a pleased noise and held his glass while it was (steadily) filled. It was damned good – excellent, even - and a fine way to end oneself, if it had to be done slowly.

'The fellow didn't give his name.'

'Jonas said that. What did he ask?'

Grabner shrugged. 'He said that he'd read an old piece in the *Zeitung* – our initial report on the Schloss-Strasse killing, the one before Jonas went mad with his *what ifs* and *what aren't we being tolds*, and asked if he might have your address. It put me on my toes, because we didn't name you, just referred to *an old comrade* of the deceased man. I asked why he wanted to know. He told me that he'd been a friend of Rudolph Bandelin back in Danzig before the war, and was making enquiries on behalf of the man's mother.'

Rudy Bandelin. One of the reasons Fischer had resurrected the man from a hundred thousand other corpses was that his relatives would never know of his apparent survival. And now an old woman had suffered her beloved son's death twice over. *Shit*.

'Did you ask how he got my name?'

'No. I just said that it wasn't the *Zeitung*'s policy to give personal details to casual callers. He was very good about it – thanked me for my time and such, and then hung up. I doubt he'll have any trouble finding you. He only has to open a telephone directory.'

But why didn't he do that in the first place? Fischer sipped his wine and tried to think.

Grabner scratched his head. 'I've wondered why he didn't do that in the first place.'

'I expect I'll find out soon enough.'

It took some effort to refuse the second glass, but five minutes later Fischer was out in the street, shivering as he half-walked, half-trotted under light rain, wondering now if an evening out of doors had been the sharpest idea. By the time he turned into Curtius-Strasse his shoulder was throbbing keenly, hinting at a night of sudden, painful awakenings. As he approached the door of his shop he fumbled for his keys, juggled them badly in one hand and dropped them in from of his stoop. Indulging himself in a single *fuck* he bent to retrieve them, but loss the race to a set of bony knuckles, sweeping them up from beneath his outstretched hand.

When he straightened the keys were being held out to him, and he was torn momentarily between thanks for the gesture and an apology for the *fuck*. As it happened he needed neither, because the kindly samaritan had already caught a glimpse of his face.

'My God! Is that what it did?'

7

Fischer made coffee slowly, taking his time because his next words eluded him entirely. An apology was so inadequate as to be insulting, but what else did he have?

The other man stood uncomfortably in the middle of the sitting room, dripping water, shifting occasionally from the rug to the polished floorboards and back again as if unsure where the least damage could be done. He was - had been – a well-built specimen, but the frame was hollowed out and the clothes draped oddly from it, like a wrong-sized tarpaulin tacked to tent poles.

He took the coffee and nodded awkwardly, still fascinated by what he was seeing but trying not to be obvious. It gave Fischer an opening he hadn't expected. He waved a hand over his face to introduce it.

'To answer your question, yes. Did you see, when it happened?'

'I wasn't paying attention. Obviously, something heavy hit us. One of my crews was nearly wiped out by what got yours, but the rest of us kept firing, trying to swat locusts. I remember hearing someone screaming. It was you, probably, because they didn't drag anyone else out of it.'

Fischer nodded slowly. It – the single most unforgettable *it* of his life – had happened almost exactly fourteen years ago, yet this was his very first eye-witness account. As a historical event, he could look at it quite dispassionately, and was grateful for the other's man's memory. He hadn't been much inclined to take notes himself, at the time.

Bandelin was looking at his neck, and the damage there. 'How far does it go?'

'The right shoulder, and quite a bit of my back, though that's never been much trouble.'

'Does it hurt still?'

'Only the shoulder, in bad weather.' Fischer put down his mug and took a deep breath. 'Look, I did it because ...'

'You needed an identity for someone. It's alright.' The big man shrugged, like it was a trifle, hardly to be mentioned. 'You thought of me – that was clever, given what happened that day.'

Fischer had been carried from the field, a death-in-waiting. In the hours that followed, the rest of the regiment had been cut to pieces, and the survivors were swept up in the woods that evening as they tried to break out, to be carried off into Siberian oblivion. Almost eleven hundred men, wiped from the slate by bad military intelligence and the piss-sour luck not to be somewhere else. If a name was needed to attach to someone who could use it still, what better place to pluck it from?

'I truly believed you were dead.'

The genuine, kosher Rudy Bandelin shrugged. 'I should have been, but it seems that you stole all of my bad luck that day.'

'I wouldn't call fourteen years in Soviet camps a happy fate.'

'It got better, over time.'

'You mean you got used to it?'

'That too, but the first year was the worst for all sorts of reasons. We didn't get nearly enough food, or penicillin, or pain-killers; but like they used say, if they didn't have it for their own people they weren't going to lose sleep about us. After '42, the state of emergency relaxed a little, they fed us more and fewer men just dropped dead in their tracks. Still, the war years were a real test. It was only after the surrender that things really improved.'

'How?'

'We were put to work – proper work, not the punishment battalion stuff they kept us busy with in the POW camps. It was fair enough – they made us rebuild what we'd knocked down. I was at Stalingrad, then Kharkov, and in the last few years a labour camp near Smolensk. Towards the end we had as much to eat as the dissident Soviet politicos there.' He pulled a face. 'I used to gripe as loudly as the next man, but I doubt that we treated *our* prisoners as well.'

'Not those from the Eastern Front, that's for sure.'

'We saw a few of those, too, the lucky ones - I mean, lucky like really, really unlucky. The poor bastards managed to survive the Reich, came home and immediately got arrested and punished for not having died heroically. You'd have to wonder which god you'd offended, to earn that weight of crap.'

Bandelin paused, took a sip of his coffee and glanced around the room as if weighing the owner's taste in décor. Fischer, still disoriented from the shock of seeing the living, breathing article, couldn't make sense of how this was going. He would have expected recriminations - a demand, at least, to know how he'd dared do what he'd done; but the man seemed about as concerned for his stolen identity as the corpse he'd been mistaken for. It had to be a pretence.

'Forgive me, Rudy, but why don't you care about this?'

'What, you using me? Why should I? In a way, I've been saying goodbye to Rudy Bandelin for years now.'

'Why would you do that?'

'In the camps, men were desperate not to be forgotten. Most of us had lost our *soldbuchs* in the fighting, but the Red Cross were allowed in occasionally. They took details and left with earnest messages for family and friends.' Bandelin shook his head. 'That wasn't me, though. My parents are dead, and I never married. I have a sister, but for as long as I expected to die a prisoner I didn't want her hopes raised. It was better she thought me dead, or as good as. After what happened that day at Okhvat, I assumed that WASt had informed her the chances weren't good.'

Fischer was so relieved to hear that there wasn't after all a broken-hearted Frau Bandelin that he almost forgot the obvious next question. 'Who *were* you then?'

'For quite a while, no-one at all. The Ivans worked by headcount, not roll-calls. If any of the guards asked I told them *Hans Schmidt* and knew that they'd forget even that. Then a comrade died in an accident, and with what I knew of his life it was a comfortable fit. I've been Walter Senn since then, if anyone cared to know.'

'You don't worry about his family?'

'Like me, he was raised in Danzig, but at the Johannis-Gasse orphanage. He has no history that can hurt anyone.'

For a few moments Fischer said nothing. He was immensely relieved that the man found no reason to hold a grudge for what had been done, but a host of other questions pressed that he might or might not have a right to ask. He decided to keep to the ones that involved himself.

'You were the one who called the *Zeitung* about me, obviously. Why didn't you come straight here?'

'I wanted to give some warning that I was about to drop on you. If the shock had been too great, you might just have said no.'

'No? To what?'

'To helping me.'

'How?' Fischer thought of his safe, emptied by Renate's mother. He could – and would, gladly - offer some money, but it wouldn't go far.

'You could do for me what you did for the other fellow, the one who got my name and a bullet. Now that I'm back in the world I'll need to prove to all sorts of people that I'm Walter Senn, but if I do it the legal way they might ask questions I can't answer. I don't have money, though.'

As far as Fischer knew, the forger Norbert Roth was plying his illicit trade still just a few hundred metres from Curtius-Strasse. Bandelin had an identity ready and primed, so the only difficulty would be the expense. It was more than *Fischer's Time-pieces and Gramophones* could bear easily at the moment, but the moral debt he owed was immense.

'It'll take a few days. Have you somewhere to stay?'

Bandelin removed two head-and-shoulders photographs of himself from a pocket and placed them on the table. 'Not yet. Is there a Mission in the district?'

'There used to be. I'll clear a space in the box room downstairs. We'll make up a bed.'

'Thank you.'

'Is there anything else you need?'

Bandelin scratched his chin. 'I don't think so. I'm going to try to find my sister, Margret.' He smiled. 'My corpse was identified by a good friend of hers, so she may have got out of Danzig too.'

Fischer frowned. 'The dead man was half your size and a dozen shades darker. Why would this friend say that it was you?'

'It's a very good question. I'll be sure to ask it when I see her. The police gave me an address.'

'Was it them who gave you *my* name?'

'Yeah. For a while I couldn't place it, but then the screams came back to me. You hadn't been with the Regiment for long when it happened?'

'Three months.'

'To be honest, I couldn't recall your face until I saw it again.' He waved a hand. 'I mean, the part of it that looks how it did before. I suppose that, in different ways, we've paid our accounts in full.'

'That would take an evening's philosophizing, at least.'

Bandelin snorted. 'Then let's not bother.'

'Would you like to eat? I have blutwurst.'

For a half-skeleton, Bandelin gave a good account of himself, and the next two days' meat allowance disappeared swiftly from a plate upon which the cabbage remained largely untouched. He refused wine, drank a beer, and then, as if a switch had been thrown, slumped slightly over the table and began to snore gently. Fischer tidied the table around him as carefully as if he was defusing a primer and then went to bed.

He drifted for a while before sleep came. He had just assumed another burden, yet he had been absolved of a minor crime and a greater wrong, and the price of it was negligible – at most, five hundred marks (less, if he could negotiate Roth down). His conscience was tender, much more so than the skin that housed it, and prone to bruising – a strange affliction in someone who had volunteered to be soldier. However strange and unlikely the balm, anything that eased guilt was welcome.

8

When he rose at dawn, Bandelin – Senn - was gone, the front-door key posted through the letter-flap. He ate breakfast and tidied the apartment, and went downstairs when he heard Renate arrive. She was subdued, preoccupied, and he made a point of not raising dust by asking why.

He had decided already not to tell her the truth about Rudy Bandelin. She knew something of the story, having met the poor young man who died in that borrowed skin; but as the original item was about to disappear forever, *Walter Senn* would do if introductions needed to be made. As for her fiancé (who knew *all* of the story), the less he was told the better. Fischer had a great affection for Jonas Kleiber, but his mouth and that of a starving wolf were equally capable of remaining closed.

In his repair room he opened up and tried to diagnose an ailing Phonokoffer, but the pending task distracted him. Renate was mumbling to herself and almost certainly didn't listen to why he would be gone for about an hour (a lie, it didn't deserve an audience), and he was out on Curtius-Strasse a minute later, struggling into his jacket, trying to recall the address. His feet retained a vague memory of it and pointed him in the right direction, and as he walked his mind's-eye caught a glimpse of magnolia trees, a deep front garden, the house too small for the plot it sat upon. By the time he reached Finkensteinallee he knew precisely where he was going.

With only their early buds the magnolias looked forlorn, and the house, less prettily framed, plainer than he recalled. He knocked on the door and stepped back.

Norbert Roth had aged considerably in the nine months since Fischer's only other visit. The hollow chest had sunk further than the *Scharnhorst*, and the scrawny neck, uncovered by his shirt's lack of a collar, resembled something in a butcher's window that had failed to sell on Christmas Eve. The scowl was the same, though, and just as welcoming.

'What?'

'Hello, Herr Roth. Perhaps you remember me? I ...'

'I'm not senile.'

'No, of course you aren't. You'll recall I asked you to do a job for me?'

Briefly, the frown became a squint. 'Rudolph Bandelin, born Danzig, present identity papers issued by Hanover administrative district.'

Genuinely impressed, Fischer nodded, and for the first time his keen eye noticed that the lower half of Roth's body was encased in violently purple baggy trousers, set off nicely by a pair of golden, upturned-toed slippers. The other man's eyes followed his downwards.

'I'm the robber knight, in our *fastnachtspiele*.'

'Our?'

'The Lichterfelde Minstrels. We're doing a children's show at the Titania Palast next month.'

The prospect of Norbert Roth – a living template of misanthropy - performing for impressionable minds was almost too startling to contemplate, and Fischer had to remind himself that an infinite world must hold infinite possibilities.

'Ah, tremendous! I was hoping that you might do another piece of work for me?'

The other man sniffed. 'Not for a criminal?'

'Not at all – in fact, the reverse. A man who's only just been released from a Soviet Prisoner of War camp.'

'Then why does he need a new identity?'

Because I stole his. Look, may I come in and explain ...'

Roth stood back, and Fischer paused as he recollected the deadly threat that lurked in the darkness ahead of him.

'Your cat ...?'

Roth's face soured (if that were possible). 'Himmler died last November, two days before his twentieth birthday.'

'Oh, I'm sorry, well ...'

Fischer paused, sneezed explosively, and through tear-filled eyes barely made out a tiny ball of white fur settling between the gold slippers.

'This is Heydrich. Come 'round the back – we'll speak in the summer-house.'

Dabbing his eyes, Fischer followed the gaudy apparition through the side-garden to a windowed shed. Inside was just room enough for two men standing. Roth lit a small kerosene burner and closed the door.

'What do you want?'

'The same … excuse me ...' Fischer sneezed once more and wiped his nose with a sleeve; '... as before. This man is also from Danzig, also needs Federal grey papers, and Hanover District would do fine, if you have any stamped ones still.'

'Photographs?'

'Will these do?'

Roth examined the two that Bandelin had supplied. 'Yes, they're good.'

'Height and eye-colour are on the back. There's one thing ...'

'What's that?'

'I can't afford five hundred marks – not at the moment.'

The photographs began their return journey. 'I don't offer credit.'

Fischer searched his memory. It was hardly as capacious or well-ordered as Sherlock Holmes' *mind-attic*, but it could manage other areas of a house quite well, and he recalled that Norbert's sitting-room had missed something.

'Herr Roth, have you ever thought that a man needs music?'

'I have a radio.'

'I mean real music, the kind a man chooses to colour his life. I can provide a gramophone ...'

Roth's head began to shake, and Fischer pressed on quickly. '... and help you build a collection, free of charge.'

'How free?'

'Three recordings each week, for ... a year. I'll advise on which are the best available, naturally.'

Roth squinted at his guest for several seconds, weighing how much more than five hundred marks the offer was worth.

'I don't like Schumann.'

'You don't need to, believe me. I stock other German repertory, and French, too. I have some Italian opera, and even English ...'

'Meadow music?'

'Well then, no English either.'

Slowly, Roth nodded. 'Alright. But *four* each week for the first three months, then three.'

Whatever profits Fischer derived from his recorded music sales would be skinned by the arrangement. He held out his hand, and Roth took it.

'Five days.'

'Thank you.'

He was almost half-way home when snow began to fall, and as always it cheered him. By the time he reached Curtius-Strasse it was as if the clock had been rewound two months and the pavements spruced with a thin dusting of as-yet virgin whiteness. Outside his shop, Josef Pfentzler was shivering in his shirt sleeves, straining to pull down the awning, and Fischer, unseasonably well-disposed, took a grip on the pole and strained with him.

'Herr Fischer, thank you! Come in for a moment.'

Pfentzler's Modes was an older-styled emporium. More modern ladies' outfitters in the district affected the Manhattan style of minimalist display, where the eye was lucky to find half a dozen items for sale; but Pfentzler had an ironmonger's feel for fashion and kept every possible eventuality stocked somewhere on or in his many shelves and drawers. Fischer had often thought it a pity that such expertly-run places might pass, but passing they were. He didn't doubt that the Frankfurt purchasers already had plans to strip out every fixture and replace it with the latest in plastic bareness.

The proprietor seemed as cheerful as during their recent lunch. The stoop was gone, and though the face couldn't be improved without drastic restructuring it wore its smile creases comfortably. He brushed snowflakes vigorously from his sleeves in the middle of the floor, well clear of the many crowded surfaces.

'Have you thought any more about my suggestion?'

'Retirement? I have, though I don't think it's for me quite yet.'

'Really?' Pfentzler looked concerned. 'A man shouldn't die in harness, like a horse. My own father went like that, always telling *Mutti* one more year, one more year, and then there weren't any left for him. Such a great pity.'

Fischer had his weary days, but he hadn't yet pictured himself dropping in the street like an abused nag. He supposed it was natural for a recent convert to speak with a certain evangelical fervour.

'I don't intend to go on and on. Perhaps until I reach sixty – that's less than two years now.'

'Hm.' Pfentzler nodded, but he seemed unconvinced, or preoccupied. 'Well, think of what you could be doing with your time. Ha – time! You of all people should keep an eye on it!'

With that feeble joke, Fischer excused himself and made careful snow-prints back to his own shop. Jonas Kleiber was there, looking morose, taking precise, detailed instructions from his *inamorata*. He half-turned and nodded at her boss, offering a glimpse of eyes that looked as if they had been poked vigorously with a stick. The only other presence was an elderly gentleman, flicking his way through A – M in the Chamber Music section, so Fischer went over to ask if he might help. That required another ten minutes of his *time*, as the Juilliard Quartet's Bartok cycle wasn't in stock (nor ever likely to be, given Lichterfelde's strong resistance to musical modernity) and his stab-in-the-dark opinion was sought on the Vegh alternative. Mindful of his looming losses from this sliver of his trade, Fischer made a herculean effort to persuade the gentleman to dip his toe in the shallower end of Debussy, and failed.

Kleiber followed the disappointed customer out of the shop, pausing only to turn to Fischer and pull a face.

'She's got a favour to ask.'

Though he'd been waiting for this for several weeks now, Fischer hadn't thought of any decent way to refuse. Renate's face was flushed, and he decided to spare her the further pain of putting the question.

'I'd be honoured, Renate. There's a condition, though, and it's a strict one.'

'What is it, Herr Director?'

'That you never, ever call me *Herr Director* again. It's Otto, as if we were friends, or family. You can't go down the aisle linking arms with a stranger, can you?'

'No … Otto.'

The first time, it sounded startlingly intimate. For a moment Fischer could have wished that he were thirty years younger and a whole continent prettier, but his Old Fool soon passed and he turned his mind, finally, to that day's work. This admirable state lasted for about twenty seconds, as long as it took for him to get to his bench and lift the first repair ticket. Renate had followed him into the repair-room with a piece of paper.

'This came in the post. You've been accepted.'

'Have I? For what?'

'Your membership, of the Social Democratic Party.' She tilted her head and frowned slightly, a gesture hardly less endearing than the way she'd caressed his given name. 'I didn't think you were the political sort.'

He asked directions at the Seestrasse bus halt. They were clear and accurate, and within ten minutes he was where he wanted to be, at the junction of Turinerstrasse and Utrechterstrasse. At the same moment he saw the latter's street sign he saw her also, standing directly across the road from him, and the stark coincidence made him stop dead, stupidly, in the middle of the street. Had she been looking his way she must have noticed him immediately, but her head was turned southward, down the length of Utrechterstrasse. She raised a hand and waved; he followed her gaze and saw another woman of about the same age approaching, also waving. For a moment he felt a raw burst of hope, but the hair colour, the build and deportment were all wrong. It wasn't Margret.

He didn't dare introduce himself now, so put his back against a wall, lifted the newspaper he'd found on the bus seat and waited. The two women double-kissed and then, linking arms, set off towards the main junction with Müllerstrasse. He followed about fifty metres behind, keeping an eye on passing buses, not wanting to be surprised.

They waited at a halt on Müllerstrasse for five minutes, giving him plenty of time to slot himself four commuters behind them in the queue. The bus they took was posted for Siemensstadt, and when he saw it he crossed his fingers – a wasted gesture. Twenty minutes later they pulled up at last stop on the route, almost opposite the old Siemens Headquarters building on Nonnendammallee, and the only person other than himself who didn't immediately pile off the bus and march through the front gate was its driver. There was no way that she could be followed, cornered and spoken to in that maze, not without a town's-worth of eyes witnessing it.

He paid the driver his return fare to Wedding and sat once more. She worked a day-shift, so he would be obliged to kick cans down the street for a few hours and then try to pick her up once more on Utrechterstrasse, hoping earnestly all the while that she wasn't planning an evening out with friends.

The cans proved elusive, so instead he explored Wedding in some depth, ate a sparse lunch at a worker's cooperative near Leopoldplatz and then walked the park there until his legs ached. A little before five o'clock he resumed his station against the same wall that he had used that morning. A decade-and-a-half-long career as a prisoner of war had excised his boredom gland, so the active mind wandered widely while the eyes missed nothing.

It was dark now, but the street-lighting was perfectly adequate. Utrechterstrasse linked two thoroughfares, and plenty of folk passed by in the hour he stood there. He wasn't bothered by that; she was distinctive, the more so for being a rare artefact from a gone life. He was more likely to mistake his own reflection for someone else.

It was cold now, but Berlin cold couldn't compete with its east-of-the-Urals cousin (and he'd borne that in the tattered remains of his tunic). Even so, he was beginning to think of stamping some feeling into his feet when she stepped off a bus about two hundred metres down Utrechterstrasse. She was alone, head down, walking quickly as soon as her hand released the door-handle. He couldn't have wished for more.

He came up behind her, silently, and coughed gently. Even so, she almost leapt into the air, and he spoke quickly to reassure her.

'Anna, it's Rudy Bandelin.'

Her eyes and mouth opened widely, but she recognized him instantly and didn't recoil. '*Rudy?* But you … died.'

He smiled. 'It's not so bad. They let us out to haunt every Thursday.'

She shook her head, ignoring his weak wit. 'What happened to you?'

He gave her the concise version – which, given the tedium of his Soviet exile, was all his story required. She listened at first, but it was obvious that something else was crowding her attention, and she hardly let him finish.

'Listen – last year, I ...'

'I heard about it. Why did you tell them that it was me?'

'Not ...' She glanced around, hoping to see no-one. 'I live close by.'

The apartment building was an old three-storey block, slightly shabby but solid. As he entered her apartment he checked the hook behind the front door to reassure himself that she lived alone and followed her into the sitting room.

She turned, keeping distance between them, and he tried to find conversation small enough to ease her mind.

'So, you married that scoundrel Georg Felder?'

'Yes. He died in the Breslau siege.'

'I'm sorry.'

'I'm not. He was too good with his fists.'

He nodded. It certainly sounded like the Felder he remembered. Why did nice girls fall so easily for hopeless pricks?

'But you managed to get out. Of Danzig, I mean?'

'Yes, during *Hannibal*. Rudy, I ... '

'What?'

'I was frightened when I read your name in the newspaper. It sounded so much like what gangsters do that I almost didn't come forward. I had to know, though.'

'I don't see how you thought the corpse was me.'

'I didn't. I was relieved about that, truly.'

'So why did you tell them it was?'

'Because the dead man had papers saying he was you. I didn't know if you were involved with that. What if the killers were looking for someone called Rudy Bandelin, not a face? It seemed better just to confirm what the police thought already. I'm sorry if ...'

'It's alright.' He took half a step forward. 'I had nothing to do with any of it. I was in Russia until a week ago. And I've been using another name for years now, so it's not important. Anna ...'

'What?'

She looked nervous still, and, needing to know more yet dreading the question, he felt every bit of it.

'Do you know if Margret got out Danzig?'

She opened her mouth but nothing emerged, and when he saw the tears in her eyes he knew the answer.

'She ... died there, in 1945. I'm sorry, Rudy.'

He had hardly known his sister, even when they lived in the same city. They had different friends, followed different routines, had too many years between them to feel close. But after a long and bitter exile, with the rest of his posterity expunged, she was important by default – the last sliver of everything. He felt something in his throat, expanding.

'How?'

'She ...' Anna waved a hand helplessly; '... was killed by a soldier, after ...'

It was hardly necessary for her to go on. When the first wave of Soviets troops hit any German city, they claimed the wristwatches and gramophones. The second wave took the women - hundreds of thousands of rapes and murders, the reckoning for what the *Wehrmacht* had visited upon what they had been told were beasts. It was impossible to call it unjust, unthinkable to excuse a single innocent death.

The Soviets had taken years of his life from him, a man who had never knowingly hurt anyone who wasn't trying to do the same to him. He hadn't wanted to fight on their soil - hadn't chosen to be in uniform, even. And his sister was guilty of nothing other than being a Danziger, but for that they had stolen her life. At that moment he wanted very much to kill someone – anyone - in a Red Army uniform, and several if it could be managed, and he knew that the thing was impossible. He had no redress, no possibility of finding comfort, no choice but to bear the pain.

Anna stepped forward and put her hand on his shoulder. It had no weight to it, yet it warmed slightly. He looked up and tortured himself a little more.

'Was he a European, or one of their Asians?'

'I don't ...' She paused, puzzled, and then her eyes widened. 'It wasn't the Soviets. A German did it, a man who asked for her help. A pig who called himself Feyerabend.'

'Called himself?'

'It's the name he gave to the Red Cross when he arrived at Danzig from Pillau, during the evacuation. He said he was *volkssturm* – he was wearing the insignia – but he had no papers. Your sister had volunteered to help at the Port, and as he was wounded she tended him at the first-aid station. I was there too. It was like hell – two ships had managed to get across during the night, but the Soviets had strafed them badly. When they were unloaded we had hundreds of people stacked on the quayside, the dead with the living. I lost sight of Margret at some point during the morning, and when I saw our matron she told me that Feyerabend had said he had family in the city, and had asked Margret to help him find them.

'I didn't think too much about it, but matron looked worried. I asked what it was, and she told me that one of the Red Cross people, a fellow named Braun, had challenged this man. She hadn't heard what was said, but the poor fellow got punched for his trouble. Later, Braun told her that he had known Feyerabend personally – the *real* Feyerabend: that he had been the *volkssturm* commander at Palmnicken, near Konigsberg, when the SS arrived and marched thousands of Jewish women through the town to the beach. They ordered the *volkssturm* to turn out and come with them, and when they got to the waterside they said that the women had to be shot. Feyerabend refused, and when they said he had no choice he told them that he did, then took out his pistol and shot himself in the mouth. The women were killed – all of them, there on the beach, like dogs. One of Feyerabend's men got out of Pillau two days later and told Braun what had happened.'

Anna paused to remove her coat. 'When I heard the story I wanted to find Margret immediately, but I couldn't leave the quayside until mid-afternoon. I went straight to her apartment, but when I knocked she didn't answer. I didn't know what to do, so I went home. The next morning my father came back with me, and when we couldn't get in he took the lock off her door. She was ...'

The tears welled again. 'I think it must have happened the day before. He was gone of course. We told the police, but it was breath wasted. The rumour was that Danzig was now to be evacuated, so who cared about a girl's death? I swear, Rudy, if I could have helped her ...'

'I know. How did she die?'

'He broke her neck. Her underwear was ...'

'Don't.'

If the murderer knew that the real Feyerabend was both *volkssturm* and dead, then he had been there, on the beach at Palmnicken.

'This man – you saw him. How old was he?'

'I don't know. Not forty. I thought he had a sweet face, until ...'

So, not *volkssturm* – their ranks were filled with teenagers and the elderly, not men who could serve in a real unit. Which meant that he had to be SS. And if his vital task at the end of days was to murder Jewish women, he probably wasn't fighting SS but one of the scum who had given all Germans a filthy name.

'These Jews – did Braun say where they came from?'

'No. But Stutthof had many subsidiaries camps. I assume they'd been cleared out of them as the Red Army advanced.'

When he'd gone off to war, Stutthof had been a small civilian detention facility still, an *arbeitslager*, where whores and other undesirables had served their mandatory sixteen-week sentences. It was hard to imagine the sprawling corner of Perdition that it had become.

He shook his head, trying to get the image of Margret, violated and then murdered, out of it. For a few moments he had entertained a pretty thought of catching this man and putting him where he belonged, but common sense told him that the pig was gone, years gone, safely dead or anonymous. And even if he could be caught, what could be said or done? To someone who had worked in one of the death camps, a solitary murder would hardly have registered as a crime. What others might consider foulness was to him a sort of normality, indistinguishable from the casual hurts he inflicted during every working day. A man who didn't fear for his soul could hardly be brought to understand his sins, much less repent them.

'Christ.' He hadn't ever felt so helpless, not even during the years when a guard's bad mood might have put a bullet in his head. He couldn't lay flowers on her grave (if she had one); didn't have the nerve to ask God the Stranger to forgive her small earthly sins; would never be able to put her to rest in his heart. He swallowed painfully.

Anna hugged him, told him again how sorry she was that she hadn't done anything to prevent it, and that was all that could be said. He was learning, a decade later than his compatriots, how it felt to lose the German way, the entirely just punishment deflected cruelly onto innocents.

When he began to feel a little more ridiculous than bereft he released her, rubbed his face hard and gladly accepted the coffee she offered. While he waited he noticed her apartment for the first time. It was under-furnished to the point of bareness, but she had attempted to brighten it with a few mementoes – old photographs from Danzig, a red scarf draped artfully over the back of a threadbare sofa, a worn but intricate piece of embroidery that sat on a small, scarred table and a porcelain dog, sitting on its haunches in a blocked fireplace – that declared the place to be as much a home as any refugee could make. Not much to show for ten years or more of exile, but he had already guessed that her job wasn't up to financing the good life.

He took the cup from her, and, like an idiot, asked the wrong question.

'You didn't re-marry?'

She shrugged. '*Volksdeutsche* aren't considered prize catches, even in Berlin. Plenty of men want to get into my pants, but when they hear the background story they don't come back.'

The casual crudity shocked him as it might from his own sister's mouth, until it came to him that he, a near-stranger, had seamlessly inherited some degree of the intimacy that she and Margret had once shared. They were from the same street, had known – and now mourned - the same people, wished themselves back into the same, lost life. Who else could she say such things to?

'You work at the Seimen-Schuckert factory?'

'In the offices there. I manage the typists.'

He recalled that she and Margret had taken a secretarial course together before the war. It had been a proclamation of sorts - that they had no intention of coming out of school and straight into marriage. Back then, it had been a brave decision – and unpopular, with German Industry, the Unions *and* the Führer conspiring to keep women on their backs or at the sink. He wondered if either of them would have found the courage to do it alone.

She was having trouble saying something, so he managed a smile, raised his eyebrows and let silence tease it out.

'Do you have somewhere to stay? I'd give you a bed, but there's only mine, and ...'

The very last thing her reputation needed was another notch on the post. 'An old comrade's putting me up. In Lichterfelde.'

'What will you do?'

'I don't know. Find a job, look for somewhere to live - there must be plenty of vacancies in Berlin.'

'Don't ...'

'What?'

'I mean, why Berlin? The west has far more opportunities, and better paid. There's less *history* over there. People are getting on, not looking back.'

'Then why don't *you* go? It's not like you have ties here.'

She shook her head. 'I've been in the city too long. I've made some friends, and I know Wedding now – it feels almost like home.'

He wasn't convinced. Why would he leave, when the only two people he knew still breathing lived here? Did she *want* him gone? He'd made no advances, hinted at nothing she might need to repel, not attempted to borrow a pfennig from her – was the threat of his vague proximity so unsettling that she could be so blunt about it? The earlier hint of closeness jarred now. He had misread either that or this, and hardly knew what to say.

'What's wrong, Anna?'

'Nothing. Why?'

The lie was written plainly across her face, yet still he couldn't read it. She was worried, and unless an insanely jealous husband was about to walk through the door, Rudy Bandelin couldn't be the cause of it, not on some ten minutes' re-acquaintance. When he spoke again he put an edge to it.

'If it's *any* of my business, tell me.'

Again, whatever she wanted to say hit a blockage between mind and mouth. The silence lasted longer this time, and only the risk of killing a friendship in its cradle made him hold his temper. He said nothing, and willed it out of her.

'You … can't stay. In Berlin, I mean.'

'Why not?'

'The man who killed Margret, I saw him two months ago, here in the city. You can't touch him, though. He's beyond anyone's reach.'

On the whole, Fischer approved of the venue. If it was necessary that he live the spy's half-life from this moment, it should at least have the correct backdrop, and a park bench surrounded on three sides by dense bushes couldn't have been bettered as a cliché.

Herr Globnow was there when he arrived, dressed for the office but sitting comfortably, reading the *Frankfurter Allgemeine* with apparently deep interest. When the shadow crossed his face he looked up, smiled and waved a hand.

'I've never been here before. It's very pleasant.'

Fischer disagreed, but didn't say so. He and Lichterfelde's Botanical Gardens shared too much bad history, and it was none of the business of his new and unwanted employer. They were close to the southern perimeter, less than a hundred metres from a squat, ugly tower, the terminus of an old air-raid tunnel that ran under Unter den Eichen, connecting the Gardens with a modest five-storey red-brick building, former home to *SS Wirtschafts-Verwaltungshauptamt*, the main economic and administrative office of a pariah organization against which Fischer and his friends had conducted a small, extremely circumspect war during the final winter of a much larger one. The tale wasn't one to pass onto a favourite grandson, much less a man who specialized in using histories against his hapless victims.

It was warm for late February, a swerve in the weather to encourage Berliners towards a bout of pneumonia. Fischer owned one jacket and one coat, each too warm for summer and not quite warm enough for winter, but today he had guessed right and left the coat at home. He cut a poor figure sitting beside Globnow, who appeared to be able to draw upon KGB funds to the extent of presenting himself as a man of means. He noticed the up-and-down that his new recruit had imagined he'd deployed with subtlety.

'I'm an engineer – that is, I was. Now, I manage men who do the real work.'

'Management? How very bourgeois.'

Fischer had meant to pierce the man's genial mood, but it only raised another smile. 'It is, but every revolution re-proves the necessity of hierarchies. You can't have people doing whatever takes their fancy, otherwise it's the Wild West.'

'I suppose not. Why am I here?'

'Your SDP membership has been accepted.'

'I know. I got the letter.'

'It isn't as if they'd turn you down. All the main parties are trying to recruit new members at the moment, but we live in an unenthusiastic age, politically.'

'I wonder why.'

Globnow snorted. 'Everyone needs to get over Fascism. Who rules still matters.'

'The quiet life seems to be the rage at the moment, if you see what I mean.'

For the first time in their acquaintance, Globnow looked irritated. 'It's a pause, not *quiet*. It can't last, not with the Americans seeing everything as a struggle between good and evil.'

'And you *kozis* don't?'

'For us it's a question of systems, not morality. Whenever we seem overtly judgmental it's to move opinion, not because we believe any of it. Anyway, you asked why you're here.'

'I did.'

'What do you know about the SDP in West Berlin?'

Fischer blew out his cheeks. 'As much as anyone who isn't remotely interested. Ernst Reuter and Willy Brandt are on one side, Franz Neumann on the other; both sides are saying nasty things about their competition. I assume that you think Neumann's in the right?'

'He's more a traditional socialist. Obviously, Brandt is an American puppet.'

'So, you want me to be a Neumann supporter?'

Globnow shook his head. 'He tried and failed to stop Brandt becoming President of the *Abgeordnetenhaus* last year, so you'd be pissing into a headwind. Obviously we'd like Brandt's upward trajectory to be as turbulent as possible, and if you dig up any photographs of him with his cock in a young boy we'll give you a good price for them. Failing that, we want everyone to see that he's basically CDU in the wrong suit – a slightly pink capitalist.'

'How would I do that? Assuming, of course, that I'll ever be in a position to do *anything*?'

'You will be. You'll sponsor or support policies that play to the SDP's traditional left-wing constituency – for the workers, not the bosses. Brandt, of course, will resist, and with luck he'll use his weight as President to stamp on them. Each time he does, he paints himself as what he is.'

'What's the point of it, then?'

'The *point* is to draw the battle lines more clearly, so people can see what the Americans are doing before it's too late.'

'What *are* they doing?'

Globnow rubbed his head. 'Is *everyone* in the West blind? They're turning the Federal Republic and West Berlin into their anti-Left proxies. First, they get the KDP banned. The SED will be allowed to participate for a little while longer, but only to give the illusion that pluralism still exists. Eventually, all that remains will be two principal parties that you won't be able to drag a cigarette paper between – like the Republicans and Democrats. It's conquest by ballot box.'

Fischer couldn't see any of it - and even if it were true, a choice of two bland, largely inoffensive ways to be governed was probably just what the German people needed for a decade or two; but then, his ideological commitment to the job probably wasn't required. He sighed.

'When is this going to happen?'

Until two days ago, I would have said that we'd start giving you a public face sometime towards the end of this year. Something's happened, though. Your SDP Representative has been caught with his pants down – literally, I mean.'

'So you went with sex.'

'We didn't *go* with anything. It's one of those happy moments when the enemy puts a gun in his own mouth - or, in this case, his pants. The gentleman has ardent feelings for his constituency agent, but not so much so that he'd leave his wife for her. The disappointed lady is making loud, inconvenient noises about it.'

'Is adultery a capital political crime these days?'

'It is when you soil your own doorstep. The local Party has the choice of disciplining him or ejecting the young woman for allowing him to fuck her. The latter wouldn't look good, even if it's the pragmatic choice.'

'So, he'll go. What makes you think I'll slip conveniently into the space that creates?'

'You won't, it's too soon; but the new fellow – *any* new fellow – will be vulnerable to, ah, revelations regarding his past. He won't yet have the Party machine fully behind him, nor the tenure to make removal harder. In the meantime, we can make a great deal of your heroic past and blameless present, get you onto a few committees and then, when the new scandal breaks, push you forward as the necessary clean break from a run of sordid episodes.'

'Heroic?'

'Your wounds shout it out. And, of course, your Knight's Cross.'

'You know about that?' Eleven years earlier, Fischer's medals had disappeared into the furnace of a burning railway station during the American Eighth Air Force's attempt to make glue out of the once-pretty port of Swinemünde.

'You lost the bauble, not the record of it having been awarded. What better man to represent the new Germany than one so nobly unstained by the crimes of the old?'

Globnow sounded sincere, which made it seem almost more than nonsense. The Knight's Cross had been 'earned' for somehow avoiding death at the hands of New Zealander machine-gunners, an honour that might as easily have been conferred on Rolf Hoeschler, Fischer's good friend and the man who'd squeezed next to him in the shallow depression at Maleme Airfield that had become a toilet at some point during the afternoon of 20 May, 1941. Why he had won that toss of the coin he couldn't say, and it had puzzled him ever since. If it was now to launch him on a political career the world was beyond mad.

He stared at a passing pair of ducks without really seeing them. How did one feign strong political beliefs for more than a minute or so? How could he persuade others of his value if he didn't see it himself? Freddie Holleman would know – he had been a KDP politico for several years, and could cheerfully lie through his teeth without losing a moment's sleep over it. In fact, he gave the impression of seeing politics as one of the performing arts, success in which was measured by degrees of deception. Fischer doubted that he had a similar talent.

And *committees*. Evenings squandered in the company of fellow-travelling scoundrels, all professing their devotion to whatever cause pushed them further up the ladder, when he could be doing something life-enhancing instead, like drinking wine and listening to Adolf Busch, or paring his toe-nails (his own, not Busch's). Not even KGB had the right to steal his evenings.

Globnow stood suddenly, frightening the ducks into a half-airborne, half-bouncing manoeuvre that carried them to a safe distance. He turned to Fischer.

'There's a town-hall meeting in Steglitz next week, to discuss what's to be done about the Camp Andrew rapes. You should attend, and say something to get noticed.'

The Camp Andrews rapes. Several local women had been violated in the past few months, the perpetrator in each case a man in a US Army uniform. Rumour had solidified into near-certainty that he was a member of the garrison stationed at the old *Leibstandarte SS Adolf Hitler* kaserne, and that the authorities there were purposely dragging out their investigation until the outrage died down, after which the ladies could be compensated and the offender shipped quietly home. Whatever the local SPD Branch 'discussed', they weren't likely to influence events any more than they might the weather.

'What sort of something?'

'The sort that makes people feel better. Like how outrageous it is, that ten years and more after the war Germans are still being subjected to this. That more must be done - put, of course, as a question – why isn't more being done?'

'What good will that do?'

Globnow sighed. 'Speaking the mob's mind is never breath wasted. In time, you'll get the knack of knowing what it is they should be thinking before they think it, and afterwards they'll firmly believe that they've thought it all their lives. It's what made the Führer a master of the art.'

'It sounds like you admire him.'

'For creating national imperatives from his personal derangements? Who wouldn't? Josef Stalin was a great fan.'

Fischer was so heartily depressed by the conversation that he didn't notice Globnow leaving. He sat for almost half-an-hour, putting himself several ways into a politician's shoes and admiring none of the results. He tried, briefly, to see himself in heroic pose, a latter-day Lenin exhorting the workers with raised fist; but a counter-image of a wild-eyed lunatic, rousing his fellow villagers to burn a mildly eccentric old lady and her cat, washed away the other entirely. Strangers would consider him an unprincipled opportunist; his friends would wonder how they could ever have regarded themselves as such. What he would think of himself could hardly be guessed at.

'They should tidy the bushes more often. It looks like a wilderness.'

An old lady had filled the space on the bench vacated by Globnow. A disapproving frown sat so comfortably on her face that he suspected they were no strangers to each other. She folded her arms under her bosom, deploying it like twin turrets towards the many objects of her complaint. He gave the latter a brief, inexpert examination and could see nothing of the wilderness about them. They certainly weren't topiary'd into submission, but nor would one expect lions or fugitives to emerge from their very slightly unkempt ranks.

'Oh, they're not so bad. The Gardens' management can't afford enough staff to keep them as they did in the old days.'

He considered this a masterful response, seasoning gentle half-agreement with a hint of nostalgia, but all it raised was a disbelieving sniff.

'No-one *cares* anymore. Lichterfelde was such a pretty, well-ordered place when I was a girl. Now, it's no better than Steglitz.'

Give that revolution, several bouts of semi-starvation and the Red Army had marched through since her youth he considered that the district had borne things fairly well, but saying so would only prolong the torment. He stood, wished her a good day and pointed himself at the South Gate. His momentary relief at escaping further punishment was just that, and before he was out onto Unter den Eichen it occurred to him that this was his job from now on – to be a repository for the gripes, grudges and crushed hopes of the

Borough's voters, his bread-and-butter compensation for the turd goulash of a spy's existence.

By the time the traffic parted sufficiently to allow him to cross the road, Fischer's First Conundrum had come to him: if almost all the World's ills could be laid at the door of politicians, who of sane mind would wish to be one?

11

He walked for hours through dark streets, imagining his sister's death. It was a historical event, one of the innumerable tragedies visited upon German women in the final days, yet to him it was as raw and new as a bleeding wound. He thought of his heedlessness, of how little he had noticed her being in the world at all when he might have been a brother instead. What would have been different, if he'd tried?

He recognized self-torture for what it was, and still it hurt. At one point, crossing a park so poorly lit that it might have been the Grunewald, his legs stopped working under their weight of grief and he stood senseless for minutes, not knowing what he was doing or even what could be done. The city was as still now as cities could be, its noises blurred into something almost subliminal, and the sudden shriek of a copulating owl in trees nearby would have startled someone less detached from his senses. His ears registered the sound, but the information was lost on its way to the brain.

In all the years he'd had no choices to make, any wrong step had been punished, missed or overlooked, and that was the end of it. Being without alternatives was a wonderful thing, absolving a man of almost any crime (other than stealing a comrade's rations). Freedom had come as an inundation, scouring his fallow conscience, raising old husks that he had drained and dropped unthinkingly when all the time in the world had seemed to stretch out in front of him. He had made himself an empty life, and now he would have to live in it.

Walk. His legs moved unwillingly, carrying him back into the sodium-lit streets, a place called Charlottenburg (he'd heard the name, of course, but when or why he couldn't say), and read the name of the place in which he'd almost given up: *Schustehruspark.* After that, he moved south, across a wide, arrow-straight east-west thoroughfare along which not a single vehicle moved, and into more new territory. He marked his way by district signs - Halensee, then Wilmersdorf and Schmargendorf - and at some point it came to him that he was wholly lost. Had it not been for the asphalt beneath his feet and the structures all around he might have imagined that he had walked clear out of Berlin by now and was well on his way to Ludwigsfelde, or even Luckenwalde (though of course he would have needed to cross a Red Army or *VolksPolizei* checkpoint on the way). He began to imagine fresher air, country smells, the temptation of escape for its own sake.

And then he found himself *in* countryside, or at least a fair illusion of it. Only the neat, winding paths told him that this was an affectation, a pretence to keep minds from feeling the squeeze of urban sprawl. It was too dark still to see where he was going, but to his left a faint glow in the sky hinted at dawn, a natural compass to keep his head pointing south.

He emerged onto a road he had crossed only a day earlier, and immediately his route from Wedding was thrown into perspective. His feet had guessed well, making only a few missteps to get here. Within ten minutes he was on Curtius-Strasse, standing in front of the shop, and the matter of a bed pressed itself. He was much too early, of course, and being grateful for the offer had no intention of abusing it. He drew his coat tightly about him, sat on the stoop and tried to get comfortable.

A policeman nudged him as he was drifting away. He explained the situation and gave a name, and to his surprise both were accepted as fact. He was directed to a street-sweepers' hut three streets away, where a man with a couple of marks and the right attitude could probably get a hot drink and a chance to warm his arse in front of the stove while he drank it. The suggestion was an excellent one; he found the hut easily, told his story once more and had his money refused. The coffee was decent, a bacon roll sublime, the stove a God-send and the conversation only slightly hampered by his fourteen years' distant exile from German league football. In half-an-hour he made two friends, Ernst and Bobby (both Prussians like himself) who gave him the latest word (plenty) on vacancies in their venerable profession, and an address nearby where he might find a cheap room with half-decent rations (the only disadvantage to it being a landlady who insisted that her clientele be – or become - abstainers).

Had the previous evening's revelations not chained his spirits to the floor they might have been raise hugely by this encounter. It was the first time since returning to his country that he sensed a small possibility of finding a place for himself. He had no great ambitions for a late career - streets needed cleaning as much as ships needed building, or bridges raised, or cysts removed. What he *did* didn't matter as much as being able to qualify for a small portion of what was considered to be normality, or close to it. With a roof and regular food, Rudy Bandelin (or rather, Walter Senn) would be content in and with his much-belated lot.

Except for the other thing. Normality was a hope suspended – deferred until what was abnormal could be settled. The thing stood foursquare in front of him, blocking the forward view, and there was no way around, only through. He was almost relieved that he had no say in the matter. The old, pre-war Rudy could always put off not prevaricating, but the new one had no distractions, no other claims upon his attention. Even the warmth in his stomach and the glow of recent bonhomie couldn't douse the persistent, insistent need to purge what infected his head.

As he arrived back at the shop a good-looking young woman was unlocking the door and letting herself in. When he took the closing door from her grasp she opened her mouth to shoo him away, but Fischer was there already, telling her not to worry, that this was a friend, an old comrade from the war. He smiled, nodded and gave her his name, *Walter*. Her mouth twitched in a hint of acknowledgement, but she didn't seem the type who tried or wanted to make new friends. That was fine. He had no intention of pushing himself into anyone's company.

Fischer tossed his head, and he followed him into a back room where broken clocks and gramophones awaited resurrection. He didn't know the man well enough to judge with certainty, but he seemed preoccupied by something. He gestured vaguely towards a corner.

'I thought you'd be needing a bed last night, so I put you over there.'

'Thank you. I had some business that kept me late.'

The mattress lay in a narrow space between two shelving units, but it was neatly made up. To a man who was familiar with the finest hospitality a Soviet work camp could offer – and who had slept for about four minutes in the past twenty-four hours – it was no less enticing than the matrimonial suite at the Adlon.

He could hardly throw himself on it, though, much as the prospect appealed. In any case, what he had to say couldn't wait for sleep.

Fischer, distracted, might be better worked upon than Fischer clear-headed – what he was going to hear made little sense, after all.

'I told you yesterday there was nothing else that I needed.'

Fischer nodded. 'You did. But you can't anticipate everything. What is it?'

It could be put several ways. The man deserved a full explanation, with time to consider the ups and potential downs; but in this case there were no ups, so time would give him room to find the many sensible reasons to say no, of course not. The thing might be half-put, with a moral imperative left hanging to tease out the correct (but probably stupid) answer. It might be framed as a question – *what would you do, Otto, if you were in my worn boots*? There were many possible things he might say to that, but only one that wouldn't be craven. None of that would be fair, though, because *it* wasn't something that should be asked of a man at all. So, he thought, perhaps it shouldn't be put as a request, but as what two soldiers would understand as a necessity when faced by an enemy.

He made sure that he was looking Fischer in the eye when he said it, because he didn't want there to be any doubt about whether he was serious.

'I'm going to kill a man. It'll probably be suicide too, and I need your help.'

12

With great care, Jonas Kleiber gave the special advertisers' section of the *Zeitung* a final, careful examination to ensure no mistakes had been made, and handed the proof back to the Georg the compositor. The thing had been his idea, pushed with considerable effort against the inertia of his editor's instincts (which had strengthened considerably in the months since he'd allowed Kleiber his head on the Schloss-Strasse slaying story, with disastrous results).

Lichterfelde – A Shoppers' Paradise! The statement probably wasn't entirely accurate, but nor was it capable of being contradicted in legal proceedings. It headed a full-page feature, each local business advertisement boxed nicely to distinguish it from the others, at a thirty-percent premium over the usual cost. Kleiber had arranged with a counterpart at the *Steglitz-Zehlendorf Kurier* for that august organ to carry the page also, free of charge (in return for a reciprocal gesture later in the year). With that agreement, he'd been able to sell the project to the district's notoriously tight-fisted tradesmen (including Otto Fischer – who, usually, could be persuaded to pay for advertising as easily as a priest could a Black Mass). Even Herr Grabner was impressed by the result, and its promise of a revenue bump.

It wasn't an exercise that Kleiber ever intended to repeat. Negotiating with tradesmen wasn't something to stir a journalist's Hemingway gland, but he felt he owed the proprietor a gesture after the previous year's debacle – one, furthermore, that might convince the old man that his beloved child was in safe hands, if or when he decided to step down. In the five years since joining the *Zeitung* as a cub reporter, Kleiber had very gradually come to think of what he did as more than water-treading, and with his shareholding in the business he was beginning to feel almost Hearstian about it. Renate didn't think of it as quite a real job, but *quite* was slightly encouraging, given the strength of her opinions on so very many other matters. A business was a business, after all, and if he could make a success of it once Herr Grabner went on permanent gardening detail she would have to respect him – or the achievement, at least.

He was thinking of her still, and how she would react to *Lichterfelde – A Shoppers' Paradise!*, when Otto Fischer's head appeared slowly at the top of the stairs to the newsroom. With satisfaction, he noted the surprised look on his friend's face.

'You've had them repaired!'

'Rebuilt, actually. We wearied of your old-lady-moaning about them.'

For several years now, the *Zeitung*'s staircase had been a less secure option for the visitor than abseiling, blindfolded, through the newsroom's glass ceiling. Everyone commented about it, of course, but none more persistently than Fischer, who had a hero's aversion to entirely gratuitous risks. In fact, the incentive finally to meet basic safety standards in the workplace had been Grabner's recent weight-gain and the concomitant prospect of his retiring to hospital rather than the garden.

Fischer cleared the top of the stairs, turned to give them a brief appraisal, and nodded. 'Good job.'

'Expensive, too. How may we assist *Fischer's Time-pieces and Gramophones*? It's too late to pull the advertisement.'

'I've written that off as a lost cause already. What can you tell me about the *Interbau*?'

'Plenty. What do you want to know?'

'All that I don't know at present, which is everything.'

Kleiber squinted through the glass above him. 'Twenty … five hectares, thirteen hundred housing units, to be built by a galaxy of renowned architects, our magnificent, futuristic contribution to the 1957 *International Bauhaus* Exposition.'

'That's the puff-piece. I want to know *about* it.'

'It's going well, apparently. No industrial disputes; no arguments between the architects – not since Otto Bartning banged their heads together at the end of last year; no slippage in the timetable; and it can't go over budget because there isn't one – it's going to cost the fucking Earth. In all, a non-story, which is why we aren't covering it until we have to.'

'Still, a project so prestigious must be being watched carefully by the politicians?'

'Naturally. Nothing must be allowed to go wrong, or the new Germany will look to the world like a conglomerate of cocks.'

'So, who's overseeing it? A committee in the *Abgeordnetenhaus*?'

'You're joking, naturally? Trust it to that rats' nest of chancers? No, Mayor Suhr and the Senate are giving it their personal attention. They appointed a steering sub-committee and incorporated a private company to buy up all the land that isn't the City's already. Nothing will be allowed to wander from the master-plan.'

'Um.'

Kleiber frowned. 'From memory, you aren't a building-site enthusiast. Presumably, you have some cunning scheme to get your repaired clocks and gramophones to the attention of the World's Press next year?'

'That would be nice, but no. How is your advertising project coming along?'

'It's Come – look.'

Kleiber passed his mock-up page to Fischer, who examined his own advertisement with rather more care than the rest. He noticed one other, though.

'Christ! You managed to put your hand into Josef Pfentzler's pocket?'

'I did. *Pfentzler's Modes* is officially a part of the Lichterfelde's Shoppers' Paradise promotion.'

'He's a strange one, isn't he? He's been pushing me to retire, for God-knows-what reason.'

To Fischer's surprise, Kleiber laughed loudly. 'I'm right, then!'

'About what?'

'He's been doing the same with Grabner – I mean, *really* pestering him about the sweet life he could have as a man of leisure. So, my theory is that Herr Pfentzler's Frankfurt buyers want the entire block, and their offer to him is … what's the word?'

'Contingent? Conditional?'

'Yeah, both – on him getting everyone else here to sell up, too.'

It made sense. There were five small businesses in the one block, whose amalgamation into a single space would probably make worthwhile what Fischer had been struggling to understand about the apparent interest in Pfentzler's small, over-stuffed premises. If the Frankfurt people came at it themselves they would run up against at least one – and probably more – hold-outs who didn't like the idea of their shops disappearing into a faceless retail maw. One of their own, however, whispering visions of well-cushioned retirement, might well do the job.

Fischer himself would have shrugged off the temptation, usually, but nothing was *usual* right now. With an eager buyer poised, he might be able to extract himself before Globnow and his KGB employers could apply the standard, violent deterrence. Even if they heard of the offer, he could tell them that he was moving to premises nearby – hell, he could even put a small rental deposit down to confirm the fact, and then do a moonlight flit to Portugal with the rest of the proceeds for *Fischer's Time-pieces and Gramophones*. What could they do about it, after the event?

That was the problem, though – the *event*. He was putting himself in Pfentzler's shoes, hoping that everyone else on the block would agree to sell. Grabner was a fair bet, probably (unless Jonas Kleiber could somehow raise the capital to buy him out and keep the *Zeitung* going); but Frauen Opitz (shoes) and Riehm (hair and nails) were recent arrivals, and probably loath to kiss goodbye to what paint had yet to dry upon.

'Otto?'

Kleiber was regarding him curiously. He pushed away thoughts of escape, reminding himself that any 'plan' that relied on one of Kleiber's hunches being correct was a leap into unrelieved darkness.

'Sorry. The *Interbau* ...'

'Why *are* you interested? They're rebuilding Hansaviertel – so what? It's only happening there because it's close to the Line, and the capitalists can get one up on the *kozis* for Stalinallee – in fact, the whole thing will stare right down Stalinallee, which will get right up Walter Ulbricht's arse. Is it the architecture? I can get hold of some of the competition plans if you've got an erection about what's being erected.'

'It isn't the architecture. I want to know who's liaising between the Senate and the site.'

'Oh. Well, I don't know. I can find out, though.'

'How?'

The city's annual report. Any part of the project that gets cash from Berlin rather than Bonn goes into it, and they're obliged to provide the information if anyone asks. The Third Estate asks often, as you'll imagine.'

'Someone will be named?'

Kleiber shrugged. 'The Steering Committee's expenses will be in there, obviously, and the consultancy that's handling the day-to-day administrative business. The property-holding company also, I expect.'

'Could you get the report for me, Jonas?'

'I could, if you tell me why.'

'If you knew you wouldn't want to, believe me.'

'Oh. Alright. It'll take a day or two.'

'Good. Don't rush it. How are the wedding plans coming?'

The bridegroom-to-be groaned. 'Why we couldn't have eloped I don't know. A little ceremony in Bad Gastein, with a bartender conscripted to be my ring man - it would have been perfect, and we could have spent all the money we'd save on ourselves.'

Fischer smiled. 'You'll find that a wedding's like the *Interbau* - expense doesn't matter.'

'I'm finding it already. We'll be eating pilchards until 1965, at least.'

Fischer left Kleiber in a markedly lower mood than when he'd arrived at the *Zeitung* offices and returned to his shop. His guest was fast asleep on the floor in the stockroom, and Renate had a tense cast to her shoulders that told him what she thought of it. She was uncomfortable with strangers, and more so with those who put down roots on her territory. Fischer had calmed her slightly with the news that Herr Senn was looking for lodgings, but until he was gone and she could disinfect the stockroom floor the atmosphere was going to be charged. If she'd known what the situation really was the roof would probably need replacing, too.

Repairing an early-model Dansette quietly was a difficult job, but Fischer let the challenge distract him from the several piles of excrement that had stationed themselves on his near-horizon. When lunch arrived from the cafe he woke the squatter and told him what he'd discovered while they ate and Renate kept shop.

Senn nodded to everything but said nothing, and Fischer began to feel as if he were pushing himself forward on a narrow ledge.

'Are you *sure* we're looking in the right place? You said your sister's friend saw him only the one time.'

Senn wiped his half-full mouth with a forearm. 'The one time was a four-hour visit. Siemens are going to do a lot of the electrical and telephony work for the Hansaviertel site, and this was a big, preliminary meeting. She saw him during coffee breaks, huddling with the architects and civil engineers. He's definitely close to them.'

'And it *is* him? Definitely?'

'You think I didn't squeeze her hard about that? He walked right towards her when the group arrived at the office, and she almost fainted. He didn't recognize her, just offered her the sort of vague smile you give a dog when it's a breed you're not fond of. He looks older, obviously; but not nearly enough to make her doubt who he was.'

'Did she get his name?'

'No. She asked afterwards, but no-one could recall that he'd given it - at least, not to anyone who wasn't a director.'

'He looked important, though?'

'His suit did, the shoes too. Anna said he had that air about him, of someone who told rather than got told. And the other thing removed any doubt.'

'Other?'

'He made a 'phone call from Siemens. The story went around the office afterwards about who was on the other end.'

'Who?'

'Three people. An exchange telephonist, then a secretary, and then Federal President Heuss.'

Part Two

1

'The meeting will come to order.'

Berend Kahl had a carrying voice, that broadcast to just this side of pomposity. It made him an effective chairman at times when a single voice needed to be heard, but in conversation gave him more an air of dogmatism than authority. He was not entirely unaware of this, but as a minor politician – merely the SPD Branch Secretary for Steglitz Borough – he was far more aware that deference, reticence or outright invisibility did little to push a man into the limelight.

The meeting was not well-attended. Being in ruling coalition with the CDU (their alliance controlled 108 of 127 seats in the *Abgeordnetenhaus*), the edge of felt injustice that usually propelled SPD members into having their say was largely blunted. In any case, a little money was being spent at the moment on policing, housing, education and public health (the four minefields around which all local politicians took care to dance lightly), so on this particular cold evening the lure of warm hearths was exerting a greater pull than it might otherwise. The church hall had seating for about two hundreds, which for this audience was a four-fold excess.

Still, Kahl was pleased to notice at least one new face - or rather, half a face. The poor fellow carried his war all too plainly, and the result wouldn't have eased nerves in a dark alley. The wounds probably extended much further than the visible damage, because the man didn't seem at all comfortable in his chair. Kahl thought for a moment of offering him the cushion that relieved his own ordeal during these meetings, and then about how the gesture would be received by the audience, and then it occurred to him that sometimes a man could be *too* political. He coughed.

'Minutes of the last meeting were distributed a week ago. Are there any comments or proposed alterations?'

Most of the thin throng in front of him didn't bother to shake their heads. A solitary hand went up.

'Yes, Karl?'

'You spelled my surname wrong.'

'Any objections to reissuing the minutes with Karl's name spelled correctly? No? So ordered.'

Matters arising from the previous meeting were dispatched quickly. A report was then read out on the presentation of the district branch's congratulations to Representative President Brandt on the success of his visit to Sweden the previous year, followed by the Treasurer's statement of finances, including subscription arrears (Kahl gave the audience his standard pursed-lips-and-glare at this point), and a brief statement from the local Police Praesidium on the alleged molestation of local women by GIs was entered officially into the record (at which point, Half-Face opened his mouth as if to say something, but changed his mind). That being done, any other business was opened to the flagging membership.

To Kahl's surprise, the mutilated fellow promptly raised his hand (or, rather, claw).

'The Chair recognizes …?'

'Otto Fischer. I'm a recent member.'

'And very welcome, Comrade.' Inwardly, Kahl winced. The new ones usually came with bespoke grievances - petty gripes about this or that for which they craved a captive audience. *This* was probably going to be about littering in the Botanical Gardens, or a black American soldier eyeing his daughter, or the price of cheese even.

'How can the Committee serve?'

'Why isn't out new Representative here to introduce himself?'

Kahl glanced sideways at his fellow committee members. It was a good question, one that several of them had asked before the meeting commenced. The answer, of course, was that the man didn't think it a good use of his time, but it would hardly be *politic* to admit it – or that, had he attended, it would have been his first visit to the Borough, ever.

'He, ah, he had urgent business at the Rathaus this evening. He sends his apologies.'

Half of Herr Fischer's face registered mild surprise. 'Surely his most urgent business is to reassure the people of the Borough that someone they haven't had the opportunity to elect has their interests at heart?'

A low burble of agreement from the floor made Kahl wish suddenly that the question had been about the price of cheese, or Negroes. Fischer glanced around, acknowledging the support, and carried on before the Secretary could think of a polite way to close him down.

'Forgive me for saying, but the whole situation hasn't been well-received in Lichterfelde. As a *Fallschirmjäger* veteran I'm familiar with parachutes, and it seems pretty clear to me that this gentleman has used one with the Party's blessing. If we couldn't elect a new Representative – and I understand the circumstances – surely a local candidate should have been given priority?'

For almost three weeks now, Kahl had been dreading the question. It could hardly be answered honestly (the gentlemen to either side of him having heard something very similar from his own mouth); fortunately, however, hypocrisy was only considered a vice in political life if discovered. He frowned and shook his head.

'All proper procedures were observed. There was no other candidate with such experience available.'

Another hand went up, and Kahl's heart sank a little further. Alaric Gutzeit was a pedant, and therefore incapable of being fobbed off with a snatched-out-of-the-air answer.

'The Chair recognizes Al Gutzeit.'

'How many names were considered by the Candidates' Committee, Berend?'

Kahl was certain that the man knew the answer to this already, but had caught (and was enjoying) the scent of blood.

'Only the one. No-one else came forward during the application period.'

'Which was three days.'

'It … yes, three days. Due to the unfortunate circumstances regarding Comrade Hamm's resignation we felt we had to move quickly to restore confidence.'

'In what?'

'In … the process.'

'It doesn't strike me as *much* of a process, if you made a choice from a list of one ...''

The new fellow's hand went up once more, and Kahn was almost relieved. 'Yes, Comrade?'

'I'm sorry to ask what might be an obvious question, but what qualities make Herr …. I mean, Comrade … 'Fischer glanced around, and his closest neighbour whispered the name; '… Baumann particularly suited to his new post?'

With as much conviction as he could put into it, Kahl tried to look enthusiastic. 'He's been Branch Treasurer for the Charlottenburg Party, for eight years.'

Fischer nodded. 'Ah. Charlottenburg. Thank you.'

He sat back, apparently satisfied, but Kahl wasn't fooled for a moment. With great subtlety, he had left it hanging, as clearly as if it had been painted in pink: *Jobs for the Comrades*. One of the pitfalls – or, more accurately, serrated man-traps – of politics in the outlying Berlin Boroughs was the lunatic parochialism of the local memberships. It was probably a hangover from the relatively recent past, when their little towns had enjoyed clear green space between the high street and metropolis. They were Steglitzers, or Lichterfelders (never both), and could no more think of themselves as Berlin SPD than as members of a universal socialist brotherhood. The Committee had managed to rush through Baumann's nomination while the local membership were still reeling from revelations about their former Representative's cock-athletics, but had braced itself since for the backlash. And now the other attendees were leaning across to Half-Face, nodding, agreeing with him, and Gutzeit had his hand outstretched, introducing himself to the Branch's newest awkward bastard.

As a veteran of hundreds of political meetings, Kahl knew how to use a distraction. He tapped the table once with his gavel before the audience could fully work out why it was becoming outraged.

'Any other business?'

Hastily, Half-Face raised his claw once more. Not trusting himself to speak, Kahl waved towards the cause of his growing indigestion.

'Could you tell me who in the local Party deals with housing issues, please?'

'Issues? What *issues*?'

The one good eyebrow rose innocently. 'Oh, anything, really.'

'Walter Gropius is being difficult.'

'Really, Heinz. Had you wished to astound us you might more usefully have said that day has followed night.'

All but one of the men around the table laughed, the exception being the youngest of them (who found the comment funny but couldn't yet see his career-path clearly enough to take risks). He smiled politely, and no-one noticed.

The wit - a sleek, handsome man of middling years - beckoned the wine-waiter with a finger. He had been asked at short notice to host this lunch by his boss, a man who needed to be coshed from behind to relax in company. However, it being one of his primary tasks to ease open doors and smooth brows, he had long since taken the precise measure of every one of his fellow diners (other than the polite, unimportant young man), and made it his business to be their first telephone call whenever their roads ran anything but straight and true. They knew that at such times they were being manipulated, of course, but such was the man's charm and ever-open purse that no-one found cause to resent it, much less object.

He put down his glass of wine and leaned forward slightly. 'So, what's ruffling his hair?'

'The brown concrete on his apartment buildings – it isn't *brown* enough.'

'Oh, God. Try to persuade him that the facings and balconies aren't *white* enough – they'll be much easier to change.'

Even the young man laughed this time. Their host frowned briefly, picked up his fountain pen and made a note in the pad that lay to his right side - an affectation, to demonstrate that he was taking the matter seriously. In fact, he had an excellent memory, and would make it his business to see the concrete browned further before the sun set that day, if he had to shit in the mixers himself.

'What Walter wants, Walter gets.'

'Thank you, Florian. He'll be pleased.'

During the fifth and sixth courses they discussed their respective timetables, the landscaping plans and the extremely optimistic completion schedule, all of it interspersed with minor gripes about their architects, project managers, workmen and contrary winds from the Senate House. It was the wives' and mistresses' turn over coffee and liqueurs, and, as usual, their host Florian led on the latter (it being common knowledge that he objected to ploughing just a single field at a time). Being worldly men they laughed at his anecdotes, nodded knowingly and quietly promised themselves that the plough would never be allowed anywhere near their own fields.

When the reckoning arrived the fountain pen signed it (Florian was never so crude as to reach for his wallet), and then they all pushed back their chairs, thanked him for a wonderful lunch and went back to their offices without knowing what it had all been about – and indeed, the business they'd discussed could have been dealt with easily by telephone or memorandum at no cost whatsoever. It had been a long lunch as always, taking a hefty (though extremely enjoyable) slice of their day, and had they been quizzed about it by their staff it would have been difficult to justify as time well spent. And yet it was, and no-one did, and as always they each felt a little reassured about how things were going in those parts of the project that they didn't get to see, usually. There wasn't yet a commonly understood term for what Florian did, but they all had a similar sense of what it was – a lubrication of invisible wheels, by an expert mechanic.

Florian himself enjoyed such occasions hugely. He was on his own ground, playing at serious business, keeping difficult men happy enough not to add to the many problems that a vast, complex undertaking could attract as honey did a bear's snout. Nothing in his employment contract had made clear precisely what was expected of him – that had been explained by his only superior, the man responsible for all of what they were doing. 'See holes ahead of time and guide me around them' he had said; 'all that matters is that this is done right, and without any grief.'

That man – Rolf Schwedler, Senator for Building and Housing and one of the city's two Deputy Mayors – was no coward. His decision to demolish entirely two of West Berlin's most beloved ruins, Anhtalter and Görlitzer Bahnhofs, had made him one of the city's least beloved politicians. The *Interbau*, though, was something that couldn't be allowed to fail, or even be seen to have been fumbled. It was the Federal Republic's answer to Ulbricht's mad rush to rebuild east of the Line, the show-piece of modern western German ingenuity that sought to bring fled industry back to Berlin - and, not least, give the city a final chance to make its case as the Republic's capital against the almost done-deal that was concentrating power in Bonn. The slightest shiver in the progress of construction would kill at least one and probably every ambition that had made it the greatest urban project since Albert Speer's preposterous *Germania*.

Florian was perfectly aware of this, and that Schwedler's failure would be his own. One didn't walk lightly away from the ruins of a dream, not one that was shared by everyone up to and including the Federal Chancellor – and certainly not when the Americans themselves had invested money and their can-do reputation to see the project succeed. The prospect of bad endings worried him less than it should, perhaps, but he had never been much of a brooder. All would be well, or not. All things were well, or not. It was always best to stand with the Stoics, he'd found

As usual, a pleasant lunch had given him the taste for something else. He had several options, though the readiest (and most tempting) was the wife of one of his colleagues at Rathaus Schöneberg, a pretty, depraved young lady who was always willing to receive a casual caller and accommodate whatever fancy moved him (as long as it caused her a little pain and a little more humiliation). Her home was near a u-bahn station in northern Wilmersdorf, and therefore as accessible as the woman herself. He made a quick telephone call, enjoyed the filthy detail she put into her whispered promises, and almost decided to defer his only other task of that day.

It wasn't in his nature, though, to leave things untidy. He picked up the receiver once more. As usual, the dial tone sounded four times before he heard a voice.

'Linde.'

'It's Florian. Have you met with him?'

'Yes.'

'And?'

'He's in a bad condition - almost certainly an alcoholic, and he hinted at some ailment that's going to kill him sooner rather than later.'

'The conversation?'

'It took a while. I got him mostly drunk and then told him that I'd served in an einsatzgruppe, but he was as paranoid as hell. I think he thought I might be Jewish, until I offered to pull out my cock and wave it at him. It was the only time he managed to raise a smile.'

'Can he identify Manfred?'

'He didn't recognize the description I gave him. He said he recalled the incident and was proud of the part he played; but he'd been brought into the unit only two days earlier and it was dissolved less than a month after that, so he doubted that he'd know that man if he saw him.'

Florian had an excellent memory. It had sounded off when he'd heard the name, four weeks earlier, though it had been quite a while since he'd been obliged to hunt down information on those involved in the incident. Linde was a good judge of men, and he sounded quite relaxed about what he'd heard. It was very likely that Manfred was safe, at least from this fellow's memory. Still...

All would be well, or not. Sometimes, though, it wasn't sensible to be merely philosophical. A man who mixed with very well-known people (as Manfred did) could find himself photographed, and Florian could do nothing about that. The risks that *could* be removed were better not left untouched.

'I don't trust *sooner rather than later*.'

'When, then?'

'Immediately. Your choice, but an accident, naturally.'

'We don't need a honeymoon, darling.'

As he spoke, Kleiber recognized *the look* - one he suspected would become a close companion during their life together. Had it been merely a sulk he might have learned to ignore it, eventually, but it was more than that. It conveyed displeasure, sorrow and a hint of reproof, all wrapped in a cast that told him he was in an initial negotiation, not a surrender ceremony. The fact that she had come armed with brochures meant that some thought had gone into it already, and she didn't like to waste thinking time.

'We needn't spend a lot of money. A week in the Rhineland, or on the Danube – we could take a tent and a stove.'

'We'd need a car, too.'

'Herr Grabner said he's pay to hire one for us, didn't he?'

He had, and Kleiber had thanked him almost heartily for the offer. With what they were spending on the wedding he doubted that his bank account could meet a day-trip to the Tiergarten, much less a week on terrain where local folk were adept at emptying visitors' pockets. As for camping, if he wanted to test his powers of endurance he might more conveniently punch a policeman in the mouth and take the six-week tariff. At least he'd be fed, and the bed would be off the floor, and there would be just as many opportunities for sex (if not quite the sort he wanted).

'Um.'

It wasn't his best argument, but he needed time to think. A honeymoon was a holiday, and he didn't take holidays, not by choice. Marriage was a commitment to compromise, he knew that, and on all the little matters regarding which he had no opinion he was ready to give way gracefully - he just hadn't expected any lines in the sand to be drawn so quickly, or adeptly. It made him appreciate that he had skills to learn, particularly one that let him gauge precisely how much she wanted a thing, so he would know how far and how hard he could push back against it without declaring war. Unfortunately, skills only came with time and familiarity, and by then he'd probably have lost the will to resist.

He was saved from further prevarication by a grunt from the stock room. Renate's antenna, extremely sensitive to a particular frequency at the moment, swivelled instantly away from honeymoons. It was Otto's old comrade, Herr Senn the not-quite-lodger, rising from his camp-bed. Kleiber had met the man just once, and had yet to form an opinion. Without further data he felt himself to be somewhere between Otto and Renate, the one quite happy to have the man squat here, the other wanting him somewhere far away, and yesterday if possible. Their only conversation so far had lasted some thirty seconds, during which Kleiber had taken an impression of a little wit, sprinkled over a carapace formed in equal parts by shit and grief, and he hadn't felt encouraged to go after the details. No doubt Otto would offer more information, if he saw fit.

Scratching his head, Senn came into the shop. Renate regarded him coldly.

'Would you like some coffee, Herr Senn?'

'Yes please, *schnucki*.'

Kleiber winced. Renate stiffened but kept down whatever she would have preferred to launch at him. Terms of endearment didn't work on her any more than ribbons did on boars. A few months earlier she had dealt firmly with a difficult customer, and afterwards her amused employer, overhearing the conversation from his repair-room, had called her *barchen* - little bear. The look it earned hadn't inclined him to repeat the error.

Senn didn't seem to notice her glare – but then, he didn't seem to notice much about Renate, so perhaps *schnucki* was what Danzigers said to women generally, in the same way that Kleiber's Lancastrian camp-guards had thrown *love* at anything in a skirt. The man was preoccupied by something, the mouth half-twitching in secret conversation, and he only came out of it when Fischer walked through the front door, bringing the fine smell of fresh bread with him.

He tossed his head, and without a word Senn followed him upstairs to the apartment. This left Kleiber alone with honeymoons once more, so he took a lungful of air to fuel his excuse for leaving suddenly. Before he could deliver it, however, Renate had put a finger to her lips and positioned herself at the foot of the stairs.

'What is it?'

Furiously, she waved him quiet and tilted her head. Something was being said upstairs, but it was much too hushed to be overheard. Kleiber took this as clear evidence that it wasn't meant to be, but his fiancée interpreted it rather as a challenge.

She came over to her *beau* and whispered. 'Jonas, think of a reason to go up there.'

'Why?'

'They're planning something.'

'Are they? Is it our business?'

'I don't know!'

'Well, *you* go up.'

'I can't. I'm watching the shop.'

'No, you're not.'

The look she gave him made it clear that further such observations, however accurate, wouldn't be tolerated. He sighed.

'Alright.'

The ascent comprised only eleven stairs, but Kleiber didn't need to think too hard on the way. He was a journalist, to whom superficially plausible reasons for bothering people came as easily as sleep did a cat. In any case it hardly mattered, because Otto hadn't closed the door to his kitchen. Both men heard him approach and their conversation had died before he reached the landing. He walked into two questioning stares, and gave them his innocent face.

'Otto, that stuff you wanted about the *Interbau*?'

'What is it, Jonas?'

'I don't have it yet. The guy at the Senate office who deals with the Press is in Bonn this week, and no-one else can shift in a seat without him saying so.'

Fischer pulled a mildly disappointed face. 'That's alright. Whenever you can manage it.'

Kleiber nodded, turned, and went downstairs to report his failure to Renate. She wouldn't be pleased, but that, too, hardly mattered. He was intrigued now despite himself, having noticed Senn's reaction to the word. It hadn't been so much as a twitch as a start – as obvious as a wink (the more so for being suppressed swiftly). So, Otto was delving into something not for his own amusement or curiosity but that of his friend - and it wasn't a casual thing, not when it could draw a reaction like that.

He told Renate that he'd heard nothing (but omitted to mention the rest) and got the rolled eyes treatment. She said nothing more, however. Her mother's reputation as a minder of other folks' business had been famed enough for the daughter not to want similar, however close to home her concerns. She told him that he'd better get back to work, which was her usual way of letting him know that he had fallen somewhat short. He went, gladly for once, and wondered how far he could or should press his nose into a business that might bite it. He trusted Otto's judgement without reservation, but it was a fact that the man attracted falling masonry like a cellar – not least, because he had a habit of placing himself directly beneath it.

That last thought made him pause mid-stride on Curtius-Strasse. Was something going wrong up in Hansaviertel? Why would Otto and his friend Senn be interested in the *Interbau*, otherwise? Hell, a thing that large and costly, with so many exalted reputations tied to it - it would be the story of the year, not only in Berlin but the whole of Germany, West *and* East.

He breathed carefully, trying to calm himself. He'd made the mistake of launching into something the previous year, and the consequences for his friend – and his own job – had been almost disastrous. A good journalist didn't write the story and then scramble around for the evidence to support it; he went after it carefully, painstakingly, not letting the objects of his attention see him coming; he gathered his facts, shuffled them into order and only revealed his hand an hour before publication, when asking his hapless adversaries for any comments they might wish to have included in the breaking story. Above all, he was *discreet*.

A mental image of this new Jonas Kleiber pleased him hugely, though enough remained of the old to indulge a vision of the awards ceremony, the guest-of-honour's quiet modesty as some of the Industry's shining lights took their turn to praise him to the balconies and then, as the champagne poured, quietly beg him to accept a senior position at their newspaper. If – *if* – he could do this properly, Renate might have as many honeymoons as she wished, and in proper beds too, and a new car in which to transport her to them.

Two hours later, as the *Zeitung*'s entire, two-man editorial team prepared to get out its special advertising edition, Ferdinand Grabner had to ask Kleiber to please stop whistling before it parted him from the very last of his nerves.

4

Fischer waited, listening for the lowest stair to make its habitual complaint, before continuing.

'I met the SPD's Housing Secretary for Steglitz Borough, but he's small fry, and happy to be so. He's hasn't even visited the *Interbau* site, much less met any of the people who work on it.'

Senn was examining a small area of the kitchen table's surface, and didn't speak.

'What he *did* say was that he's sick and tired of his job. He only gets expenses, and the post seems to entail being the butt of complaints from folk who've been on the housing list for months or even years. I sympathized with him and asked if a recent member might be considered for such an important role within the local party. For a moment I thought he was going to grab my head and kiss it; but he recovered himself, pretended to think about it and then suggested he put my name forward.'

Senn looked up. 'Why would you want the job?'

'To get where I can find an excuse to meet people – people who might know our fellow.'

'I asked you to help, not be an accomplice. If you can get me a pistol and three or four rounds ...'

Impatiently, Fischer spoke over him. 'Don't start that again. There are plenty of ways to lay your sister to rest without dying yourself. And what use would a gun be if you had no idea who to point it at?'

'I can go up there ask around. There'll be plenty of workmen on site who'll recognize the description.'

'And of course they'd chat to you, rather than call security about the wild-eyed fellow with the bulge in his pocket who's looking for one of their bosses.'

'What the hell else can we *do,* then?'

'Plenty. This is an important man, and his sort have friends you can't cross. But if you were to light a fuse and stand back ...'

'Fuse?'

'He murdered your sister. To you, that's a crime; to anyone else, it's history. But he also helped to kill several thousand Jewish women on a Baltic beach, and that's ongoing business. If you shot him he might not even feel it before he's gone. I promise you he'll feel months in a prison cell, imagining the gallows on the horizon.'

'It won't feel like justice, not to me.'

'What will? From whatever moment you put a bullet in him, *feelings* will last as long as a hangover. After that, there'll be nothing.'

'So, we just denounce him?'

'That won't work, without evidence. We'll need proof of who he was, and *where* he was on the day those women died.'

'How the hell do we do that?'

'I don't know, yet.'

Senn shook his head. 'It's too thin. We could spend years looking and still not come up with anything damaging. This isn't something that due process is going to solve. He's one of thousands who'll never pay for what he did if *I* don't make him pay.'

Fischer said nothing. He was right, of course - without a lot of help and access to the files of the Jewish Nazi-hunters in Linz, how could they hope to embarrass an acquaintance of the Federal President? Perhaps a very personal and messy revenge was not only the realistic option but also the cleanest – a quick execution that had as much process to it as the whim that had ended all those lives on a pretty beach. If no one would know why he had been killed, was that so bad? The dead couldn't rise, the bereaved couldn't forget, no blood-price could begin to meet the immense wrong done to a generation of Jews. None of them were the business of Walter Senn, whatever he thought of it. No one man's shoulders were broad enough to carry *that* responsibility.

And yet. Senn probably had enough anger to carry him joyfully through the act, but Fischer would be the cold accomplice, a matter-of-fact abettor, and he didn't think his conscience could wear that coat. Perhaps it had tried to salve itself with visions of witnesses, and courts, and judicial executions, rather than face the bald reality that some crimes could only ever find off-the-books restitution. This was old, cold business, but not to the man who needed – and was owed – his help. He couldn't refuse it, but he hardly knew how far he might have to go.

It was a mess, and for once Otto Fischer was striding willingly into it, eyes wide open and bootlaces flapping. At least his KGB handler Globnow would be pleased that he'd stirred himself, met the local SPD apparatchiks and put a foot on the Party rung; though no doubt he'd wonder why his hapless new agent was pointing himself towards housing matters, rather than trying to embarrass Willy Brandt and the Americans …

Globnow.

'What?'

Senn was looking at him curiously.

'Nothing, just a thought. Look, whatever's to be done, we need to know who and where this man is, and the best way to do that is unnoticed. I'll find a reason to go up Hansaviertel and ask questions on site. When we know more, the possibilities will be more obvious.'

The other man pulled his face but nodded slowly, and Fischer, grateful that his effort to stretch out the business hadn't been recognized as such, relaxed a little. That *thought* had stirred his head, and he couldn't say why. He dismissed it, and tried to keep his mind on the real problem, which was time. He had no doubt that Rudy – *Walter* – would waste none of it, once he had the information he needed, and if Fischer didn't supply the firearm he'd either find it somewhere else or settle for a length of lead pipe. *If* there was another possibility, it would require that some way be found to slow the momentum other than an appeal to common sense, and Fischer had at most a very few days to find it. If he failed, he would be an accomplice in a righteous killing that would look very much like murder.

Gregor Schultz was picking potatoes when his heart all but gave up the struggle. A few minutes earlier his wife Brenda, standing at their kitchen window, had cast her eye over their garden crops and tried to decide whether to make fried potatoes with cabbage, cabbage and potato soup or potato cabbage bake. She still hadn't made up her mind when the moment came for Gregor to take up his trowel and bring in the harvest, but as there was a cabbage sitting on the kitchen table already it required no great perception on his part to know what else was required.

Ironically, he was worrying about his knees when the attack commenced. They didn't like gardening, and had told him so many times over recent years (particularly during cold or wet weather, and Berlin enjoyed plenty such). He feared placing himself in the genuflection position one too many times and then having to call Brenda for help. If it was muddy (and his plot could often do a fair impression of the Ypres Salient) she would be obliged to go next door and conscript old Erno Stiller to help her, and then God alone knew how much worse it would get. So, in permanent residence behind the kitchen door was an old crutch, an implement upon which he'd limped home from the First War and kept for sentimental reasons, but which now made the garden genuflection slightly less of a reckless gamble.

The crutch was resting at an angle, its crosspiece on the low wall Gregor had built to separate flowers from vegetables, when he toppled sideways and broke it. If this caused any pain he didn't feel it, because his left shoulder and chest crowded out any competing claims on his attention. How long he lay there, how his wife – with or without Erno Stiller - got him out of the garden, and how he came to be in an acute-care ward in the Krankenhaus Moabit he couldn't say, nor really cared. His first clear thoughts came four days later, though he retained vague impressions from the intervening period, mostly framing Brenda's worried face, staring down at him.

A young doctor told him that he was very lucky - that they had needed to resuscitate him six times before his heart stabilized sufficiently for them to dare to send their new closed-chest defibrillator elsewhere, and that he was going to need considerable care before he had another go at his potatoes (or anything else, for that matter). Though not normally the sort of man who enjoyed taking instructions from others, Gregor had nothing to say to the last. He was frightened, more so than at any time since that day …

He had never spoken of it, not even to his wife. Eleven years of silence, broken only by default on the one occasion - a secret he didn't want nor had been asked to keep, a weight upon his soul that God would probably forgive but he couldn't. He wondered now if he was paying the price for leaving it unsaid, when so many others had either opened their mouths or reassured themselves that such things had never happened. He wanted to ask Brenda what he should do, but having said nothing to her about it in all these years didn't know how to broach the matter; he considered speaking of it to the Krankenhaus's resident pastor, but he feared that the sin would be recognized in him. He wanted, above all, to forget that he had been present that day, when a work routine had become something terribly *else*.

He couldn't, though. He was lying in a hospital bed, perhaps at the uttermost point of his life, and enough of the old religion sat upon him still for him to know that a debt hadn't been discharged. So he fretted, and felt his newly-outspoken heart complain about it, and almost, nearly, half-started to tell Brenda every time she came to visit. Yet still the thing weighed him down.

On his tenth day in the Krankenhaus he came to a decision. In the bed next to him was Lothar, another bad-heart case, a man in his 70s who nevertheless retained a keen eye for the ladies. They hadn't yet acknowledged each other's presence beyond the occasional nod, but Gregor had observed and admired the other man's easy way with nurses and his advances (of varying indecency) to them. Most of the young ladies laughed him off, but today one of them - a serious, quite beautiful woman – took objection and rebuked him furiously, appealing to his Christianity, his sense of decorum and the granddaughters he must have, whose own respectability he besmirched with such talk.

Lothar took all of this silently, without obvious contrition or offence, and when she turned to go he pulled a naughty-boy face and winked at Gregor, who laughed for the first time since before his illness. It wasn't much of an introduction, and surely it said nothing about Lothar's better nature, but Gregor had a sudden, strong sense that a shameless sinner was just the sort of person to whom a sin could be confessed.

Two further hours passed before he spoke of it, and only then because Lothar had introduced himself in the meantime, indicated which three of the nurses felt the greatest sexual attraction for him and promised Gregor the use of one if he couldn't please them all simultaneously. It wasn't the sort of offer that could be spoken over immediately, so Gregor thanked him and waited a few minutes until they had both suffered their bed-baths (during which Lothar signally failed to show any symptoms of virility), and then threw it out without preamble.

Lothar listened silently to the whole tale, frowning during the relevant passage and then considered the matter for some minutes. This played on Gregor's nerves, but he didn't say anything more for fear of prompting a half-thought-out answer. Eventually, Lothar shook his head.

'You couldn't have done anything about it then, and you can't now. There's no fault on your part.'

It was what Gregor had told himself a thousand times, and while he felt a little better for the confirmation, he wasn't satisfied.

'I should have said *something*.'

'When? At the time it would have got you killed. A little later, whoever you told would have said *don't bother me, I've got more important things to think about*. Now, people will just shrug and ask what point it is you're making. It's one of those things - a very *bad* thing, but all done and forgotten,'

Gregor was almost certain that this was precisely what Brenda would have told him, had he confided in her. She was a practical woman, who had never done or witnessed anything for which she needed to search her soul, and who wouldn't therefore understand how he felt. He sighed, and contemplated the shape of his feet as he moved them beneath the blanket.

Lothar sniffed. 'Do you feel better for telling me about it?'

'I … suppose I do. A little.'

'Well, then. Tell everyone.'

'Everyone?'

'Get it off your chest. Climb on to a roof and shout it out. Or bother people in the street. The more you tell it, the less it'll sit on your shoulders.' Lothar shrugged. 'It won't make any difference to anyone or anything, but so what? It'll be out, squeezed like a boil.'

Gregor thought about all of this for the rest of the afternoon, until Brenda came to visit. Of course he wouldn't climb on to a roof (he hated heights), or importune strangers as they passed by in the street, but considering the thing rhetorically it was likely that a secret shared widely would lose much of its weight (and it certainly wouldn't be a secret any more). Some people might consider him a coward for having been silent all these years, while others might understand how difficult it had been to say anything, ever; either way, he would be able to put it away, at least as far as any unpleasant memory could be.

It needed to be done correctly, though. He had an obligation to the memory of men whose names he never knew, whose crimes – if they *were* crimes – he could only guess at. And a few minutes before Brenda arrived he had a glimpse of how it might be done. The thing had been a secret in so many other ways than that which tortured his conscience. It had been intended never to be discovered by those who planned and executed it, yet they had carried it out almost casually, as if they were tying the last of very many loose, inconvenient ends. It had been brutal yet abrupt, terrible yet inconsequential. He wanted it to make it more than *inconsequential*, to flush it out as something more than a detail.

His wife seemed relieved that he was more cheerful, and he ate one of the apples she brought to prove that his appetite was returning (it wasn't). The doctor had told her that if her husband's heart continued to behave he might be allowed to go home in a week's time, so she was full of things to be arranged – his bed to be brought downstairs (poor Erno!), a new tablecloth for when the district nurse visited and a dozen other little adjustments to their home that he let slip from mind as soon as she mentioned them. He was just happy that she was happier, that it was becoming less likely she was going to be alone. The world was better than it had been, but it wasn't yet nearly a safe place for widows.

He didn't tell her what he'd told Lothar, of course. At the moment, she'd panic if he tried to go to the toilet unaided, so a hint that he was planning to stride out into no-man's-land would put her straight into the women's ward next door. It would require a very gradual escalation, the sort that warns of an approaching avalanche by firstly shifting the crockery. Gregor hadn't much experience of subtlety, and less of heroism, so he would have to learn as he advanced (much as soldiers did on their first offensive). It scared him to think of it, but that was alright – he had a great deal of experience of *scared*.

6

Florian frowned at his telephone. He was preparing the regular progress report for the Senate, and was irritated because his secretary had standing instructions that until the said piece of corner-rounding, exaggeration and wilful optimism was signed off each fortnight he was not available to callers. He was tempted to ignore it, but as his concentration had been broken he picked up the receiver, ready to be brusque.

'Florian, you old dog! Lunch today?'

He relaxed slightly. He really had no time for a lunch break, but as he'd intended to speak to the other party this was serendipitous.

'If you don't mind just the one course, and two drinks at most. I'm due at Rathaus Schöneberg this afternoon.'

'Lovely! I'll meet you at the canteen, then. Noon?'

The canteen was their code for a Hungarian restaurant in one of the surviving pre-war buildings on east side of Claudius-Strasse. It was small, dark, quite shabby and outrageously expensive, and for all those reasons not frequented by anyone else working on the *Interbau* Project. Being seen together would not have raised any suspicions (their arcs of responsibility crossing at several points), but for different reasons both men regarded attention as something to be avoided. In any case, his dining guest (Florian always pocketed the bill) had spent time in Hungary before the war, and was as besotted by the country's cuisine as the other man might have been by its younger, slimmer womenfolk, had he ever had the opportunity to browse.

The report was finished by ten-thirty, and he passed it to his secretary to type and duplicate. He then spent twenty minutes on a 'phone call to Bonn, to Victor-Emanuel Preusker, Federal Minister for Buildings and Urban Development. Preusker was perfectly aware that his political career had come to be as tied to the *Interbau* as the price of coal was to the weather forecast, and fretted horribly over problems about which he hadn't been informed and which hadn't arisen anyway. Florian didn't mind soothing his nerves; in fact, he had gone out of his way to make himself Preusker's first call in a crisis, rather than Senator Schwedler, his logical recourse (who in any and all cases would have referred the Minister directly to Florian anyway). When, two months earlier, a rumour percolated back to Bonn that land-rights issues were holding up a decision on the route of the pedestrian tunnel between Hansaplatz and Zoo Station, it was Florian who had personally assured Preusker that heads had been banged together and all matters resolved satisfactorily. They hadn't, of course, because no *matters* existed; but Florian had taken pains to ensure that no-one in the Ministry knew it when first he had planted the said rumour.

Today's call was not about crises, however (though as an aside Florian managed to infer – without giving details – that something minor but troublesome had been nipped in the bud). Preusker's niece, an architectural student, very much wanted autographs from Otto Bartning, Walter Gropius and any other member of the original Bauhaus project now working on the *Interbau*, and could it be arranged? Florian felt obliged to tut, mmm, sigh, and make a wholly unfair aspersion regarding Gropius' temper in order to wrack up the favour to something more that the trifling thing it was, and was rewarded with yet another hint that he would one day be recognized for all his good works.

The Minister satisfied, Florian signed a few dictated letters, asked his secretary to arrange for a taxi to pick him up at two o'clock and stepped out of the office without telling her where he was going (he rarely did, given the tendency of so many colleagues to regard their little inconveniences as epic disasters). In eight minutes he was in Claudius-Strasse, at the door of *Carpathia*, and before he could place his hand on the door it had been opened by the proprietor, László, who gave him a comical little bow and waved him in.

His guest, already halfway through the first of his permitted two glasses of wine, stood as he approached the table.

'Hello, Manfred.'

'Hello Florian.'

The names fell easily from each man's mouth, though neither had been their respective parents' choice. Manfred, who wore his years every bit as well as Florian, gestured easily to a waiter and indicated his own glass. The wine was the same type and vintage as always, one of the establishment's more expensive offerings (from a list upon which nothing was cheap or even reasonable), and Florian's was poured with appropriate reverence. He lifted the glass, sniffed, place it on the table and turned to the waiter.

'What's the special today, Tomi?'

'*Vadas*, Herr Geist.'

'With real venison, presumably?'

Outraged, the waiter drew himself up by several centimetres. '*Carpathia* serves only the genuine recipe.'

Florian knew this perfectly well, but was in a mood to tease. 'Wonderful. For two, then.'

As Tomi retreated, the smile fell. 'What is it, Manfred?'

'The business we discussed, last time?'

'It's dealt with.'

'He won't talk?'

'He *can't* talk, unless he gatecrashes a séance.'

'Ah.' Manfred relaxed visibly. 'I don't recall him being there, but ...'

'He didn't recall *you* being there, but ...'

This raised only a half-smile. Florian could sense that his lunch was about to be spoiled by the all-too-familiar whine about *necessities*, and *doing one's duty*, and how little people understood *what it was like*, so hurriedly he tried to move the conversation elsewhere.

'Is Bartning managing to herd the architects?'

The other man shrugged. 'Well, you know, geniuses don't make for easy pets. Most days he has to sooth at least one tender brow. He sits them on his knee and tells them they're his favourite child, and they go away happy for the moment.'

Manfred played with his wine, saying nothing more, until their *vadas* arrived. As secretary of the Exhibition Committee he was very well placed to report on any breaking problems before they metastasized into something troublesome, which is why Florian took care to shield the man from the consequences of his wartime record. He did the same for several others involved in the *Interbau* project, and for no other reason than that he wanted no further obstacles to its success than financial tremors, difficult architects or God Almighty could provide. Unlike many of his compatriots who had served in uniform and since prospered, he had no ideological commitment to keeping faith with the old days and ways. He didn't secretly donate, act as a conduit, provide accommodation or otherwise wave on hunted men with his handkerchief; nor did he feel any particular regret when a new 'martyr' created himself by imagining it was safe to emerge into the light once more. The past, however heroic or stained, was just that, and very likely to remain so; it held no opportunities, only obligations, and it was up to each man to accept or ignore the latter. If Florian chose to help someone on a matter of their uncomfortable history, it was only to help seed his own future.

Manfred was easily the most troublesome recipient of his attention, though he didn't mean to be. He was charming, good company and a very effective mover of difficult loads in committee, and Florian couldn't imagine having a more effective ally in the task of pointing a hundred conflicting priorities towards the one end. But if life brought baggage, the man was equipped for a circumnavigation. He was on no Allied or Israeli list, hadn't been named by anyone in any public testimony to date, and yet spent most hours of every day looking over one of his shoulders in the firm expectation of being presented with a bill for several old accounts.

They had never discussed the detail on these accounts, but Florian, careful as always to know the risks of association, had made enquiries. Like everyone else with a certain kind of past, Manfred had needed help to become someone else. In the immediate aftermath of the fighting, universal chaos and the mass displacements had offered false hope that it would be easy to slip out of one skin and into another; but the ease with which hastily-chosen identities could be exposed led to their panicked, wholesale abandonment and the acquisition – often the purchase – of stronger ones.

Manfred had resided in Berlin since 1947 and had a green ID card (those issued in what was now the Federal Republic were grey), so he had acquired his identity here. It had been a small matter for Florian to give his bloodhound Linde the full details on that card and a fistful of American currency, and point him at the local false papers industry. Within two weeks he had returned with another name, one which would ring any number of bells, and this had been placed by Florian into a deep (if incorporeal) vault with other useful insurances. Manfred was safer, but somewhat better known, than he knew.

The food was excellent, as always. Manfred's conversation was enticed out of its shell with the help of a second and then third glass of wine, and soon a fresh crop of gossip about a number of the Project's famous architects was spreading leaves. Florian himself had only the single drink; his meeting at the Rathaus was with Senator Schwedler, who was relaxed enough about conviviality during work-hours but whose awed respect for his subordinate's efficiency couldn't be allowed to slip even slightly. They had coffees and were standing outside *Carpathia*'s front door by 1.45, each glancing around to ensure that no-one was paying unusual attention.

Manfred's manner had more of the hunted prey about it, but then it almost always did. Florian was more relaxed, and better practised at spotting a more-than-fleeting glance without encouraging it to become something more. They walked together down to Flensburgerstrasse and parted at the corner there. Manfred's office was at the site's eastern edge, abutting the Bellevue Park (into which Florian had often imagined him fleeing in panic to live the hidden, foraging life as best he could in such over-cultivated surroundings), while Florian's was in the main site complex at Hansaplatz. They shook hands, and, as always, Manfred looked as if he wanted to say more but couldn't quite get it out.

It was a sort of guilt, Florian supposed, tinged with hurt and self-justification. The heart knew perfectly well what had been done, while the head counter-argued its necessity, or inevitability, or pretended that the choices had sat in other hands. The whole amounted to a particularly abject strain of hypocrisy, and in other circumstances it might have spoiled this and every other lunch they shared. But for a student of human morality and the heroic struggle to overcome it - and Florian regarded himself as such – modern Germany provided too varied and vast a buffet to forego for the sake of a delicate stomach.

On the day his appointment as the SPD's Borough Housing Secretary was confirmed, Fischer decided to test Jonas Kleiber's theory. Leaving Renate at the helm of his commercial enterprise he went next door to speak to Frau Opitz, and then to the door beyond to have precisely the same conversation with Frau Riehm. The first told him that yes, Herr Pfentzler had been speaking of his own retirement and urged her to consider the same. Frau Riehm, however, had a different and quite fascinating story. Pfentzler had mentioned to her that his Frankfurt purchasers were looking to open a hairdresser's boutique in their new Berlin store. Of course, given that women were very loyal to their own hairdresser, it seems prudent that they should look to place the franchise with a local, Lichterfelde woman, and they had asked if Herr Pfentzler knew of anyone.

It seemed to Fischer that Pfentzler was doing more than merely putting in a word on behalf his purchaser. He didn't begrudge the man's enterprise, but it was clear that he had to be considered one of *them*, not *us*. Both ladies had made politely non-committal noises to his approaches; both had told Fischer that they had no intention of doing anything other than what they presently did, tempting offers notwithstanding. With Herr Grabner (who almost certainly would want to pass or sell on the *Süd-west Berliner Zeitung* as a going concern), it seemed that he had collected his first constituency as a local politician.

He gave several seconds' further consideration to how he might amplify a barely-felt sense of grievance without offering any cause for it, and then he went to see Kleiber.

The young journalist smiled when the question was put. 'Herr Pfentzler won't like it.'

Fischer shrugged. 'He should expect resistance. Will you run the story? As a rumour, say?'

'Otto, you're learning the craft! I'll use my old friend, *unnamed source*.'

'Say something about Lichterfelders not wanting their charming district to become another monument to modernity, like what's happening in Hansaviertel.'

'You want me to mention the *Interbau*? Why?'

'It's a good example of what the future will look like. Can you think of anything more likely to frighten folk hereabouts?'

For a moment Fischer imagined that he saw a familiar look in Kleiber's eye (that of a stoat spotting its next meal), but it faded.

'Yeah, but that's not what's going to happen, is it? As far as I can tell, these Frankfurt people just want to put new knickers on an old block, not knock it down. Look, Otto, why are you bothering with this? If just one of you refuses to sell up, they'll have to back away.'

'I want to make a little mark.'

'This political thing you're doing?' Kleiber shook his head. 'You're the last person I'd have put down for the job. You don't even *like* people.'

'I'm getting fonder. Of some of them.'

'No, you're not. This would give you a name hereabouts, but why …?' The young man's eyes widened slightly. 'The House elections? Seriously?'

'A man should put something back into the pot, if he's been lucky.'

'Which part of you has *ever* been lucky?'

Fischer, far too aware of what nonsense he was talking, nevertheless tried to sound convincing. 'I've had a few good years here. I make a fair living, and no-one stares too much at my face any more. Seriously, I'm comfortable in Lichterfelde, so why wouldn't I want to contribute?'

'But … a *politician*? If you want to make a difference, volunteer for the Veteran's Fund, or trap vermin!'

'They have a bad reputation.'

'Rats?'

'Politicians.'

'That's what I said.'

'Shouldn't we be trying to raise standards, then?'

Kleiber scratched his head. 'I swear, Otto, you're the strangest one. What does Renate think about it?'

'I haven't said anything yet.'

'She'll vote for you, of course. But how can you run a business *and* be a political?'

'Well, I'll probably lose. And even if I don't, it's the *Abgeordnetenhaus*, not the *Bundesrat*. Voting regulations for half a city isn't a full time job - I could work mornings here still and fight for our little corner of Berlin in the afternoons. Anyway, the elections are two years away.'

'Which makes this little campaign of yours look even more remorseless. Alright, I'll run a story.'

'And you'll mention Hansaviertel and the *Interbau*?'

'If you want me to, but on one condition.'

'What's that?'

'That if you become famous I'm ghost-writing your *Mein Kampf*.'

Renate had taken two repairs and sold a wristwatch in the half-hour Fischer had been absent, a level of industry that (very briefly) made him think once more of sun-drenched retirement. She seemed a little happier today, so he assumed that wedding preparations had formed themselves into a reasonably disciplined line. It was also likely that their recent lodger's departure had smoothed her nerves. The previous day, Senn had scoured the *Zeitung*'s situations vacant column and then hurried up to the Botanical Gardens, presented himself at the Works Office and demonstrated something of his long-dormant carpentry skills to the foreman. Given the parlous state of the seedling greenhouses and dozens of park benches he had been hired on the spot and asked to start immediately. He returned to the shop at seven that evening, tired but as happy as Fischer had seen him since before the battle in which one of them had lost his freedom and the other his face. Today, he was out hunting for rooms close to the Gardens, armed with a small deposit loaned by his former comrade.

Fischer had hoped that the satisfaction of finding work and planning a future might stifle that other preoccupation, but after Senn left the shop that morning a small, ugly premonition made him check the drawer in his workshop where he kept his pistol. It was there still, and the end of the barrel was touching the side of the drawer as it should have been; but the base of the grip was in free space instead of its designated position, nuzzling the corner.

It might have moved as he opened and closed the drawer, which he did several times each day. Yet an unthinking part of that manoeuvre was to nudge the thing back into place with his hand, a habit as ingrained as flicking off a light switch as he left a room. He didn't believe for a moment that he had failed to do it, either the last time he had opened the drawer or on any previous occasion.

He hadn't known the old Rudy Bandelin well; he didn't know how the intervening years had shaped or warped the man who'd become

Walter Senn; he couldn't begin to guess what would constitute trust and what would be blind gullibility. Senn had been putting his face and hands where they didn't belong, which in itself wasn't necessarily bad - if Fischer had placed himself entirely in the hands of a near-stranger, wouldn't he examine the near-terrain carefully? Unlike Senn, however, he wasn't presently looking to commit a capital crime. A well-maintained Walther PP was a sore temptation to someone needing the means to kill someone else.

If he hid the thing Senn would know that he knew, so he removed the clip, emptied it with his thumb, replaced it, scooped up the bullets and put them in his pocket. It was hardly a solution, just another hopeful improvisation to add to the rest. Vengeance, espionage, politicking – he had as much idea where one was going as the rest, and as little influence over the various processes. Had he woken from it all suddenly to find only a grey, unchanging parade of days marching into each other, the endless ranks of broken timepieces his only companions on the path to senility, he might well have lit candles and prayed his thanks.

The thought resurrected the matter of the Hermle, his intended wedding present to the young couple. He'd examined it the previous evening and decided that its ailments were beyond even his power to cure. The ceremony was in a week's time, and it was a measure of his present dolor that he could see only a single option - more expensive than he could afford but almost certainly better than a last-minute stab in the dark that would sit on a table or mantelpiece for all the years of a marriage and be hated cordially. He waited until Renate was with a customer and then dialled a number in Trier.

'Otto! Who's died?'

'Only me, Freddie. Are the piles still singing?'

'Louder than ever. Kristin won't have me into our bed until I can stay still for more than ten seconds, so I'm residing on the sofa at present.'

'Can you do me a favour?'

'If it doesn't require movement, of course.'

'Do you know of any nice hotels in Trier that I wouldn't need to sell my soul to afford?'

'You'll be staying with us, you dolt!'

'It isn't for me. A honeymoon suite, for my girl and her new husband - a week, if possible, but it's short notice.'

'Ah, that's a nice thought. There's a pretty place on the river - small but neat, and the owner owes me for not reporting him to the local Hoteliers' Association.'

'What did he do?'

'It involved wine and water, and it wasn't a miracle.'

'Will he have any rooms available?'

'In March? I'll get you the very best. Give me the dates.'

Five minutes later, Holleman called back to confirm the booking and a price far lower than Fischer could have expected. That, and the hearty kiss and hug from Renate when he told her, almost put some colour back into the day; but he couldn't quash the thought that he had eased a toothache while leaving the disembowelments to nag on.

8

Gregor was not so much discouraged by his failure to get someone interested in his story as by the utter indifference he faced. The young man from the *Berliner Morgenpost* had lowered his spirits the most, because he had done it without meaning to (unlike the man from the *Kurier*, who had laughed in his face and left without saying a further word, not even goodbye). In fact, he'd looked quite regretful as he dispensed the bad news.

'I'm sorry, Herr Schultz, but that sort of thing happened a lot at the time. I doubt that anyone's going to be surprised by your experience, other than that you managed to survive it. I assume you were just an onlooker?'

'I was a *witness*.'

'Well, the thing is, the Allies haven't prosecuted anyone for it. If they'd been Jews, or Gypsies, or some other group persecuted for being who they were, that would be a story, I suppose.' The young man looked doubtfully into Gregor's fireplace. 'Though most Germans would prefer to forget about all of that, too. But this was different – a *political* crime whose punishment almost half the nation still thinks was justified.'

'It was murder, and done coldly.'

'Yes it was. But a lot of murder was being done in Berlin at that time, not least by Allied aircraft and Red Army artillery. What you saw was a tiny, bad event, gone and forgotten before the bodies were as cold as the act itself. If I tried to get my editor to print something about it he'd think I'd lost my head.'

The young man stood and held out his hand. 'I'm sorry I can't help, but ...' He paused and frowned. 'Look, you might try the *Sozialistische Volkszeitung.*'

'Who?'

'The KDP's Party Newspaper. They're based in Frankfurt, but they have a Berlin correspondent. I can find his number for you, if you like. The thing is though, your story might lose credibility if they run it.'

'Why?'

'Because they're always trying to embarrass the Government – *our* Government, I mean. They run a dozen stories a week about former Nazis still being in powerful positions here, so revelations about something they did back then aren't going to shake leaves off the tree, even if they're believed.'

For the next two days Gregor thought about contacting the *Sozialistische Volkszeitung's* man; but he had no great love for the communists and didn't trust them to print precisely what he said. It *wouldn't* seem very credible, and folk might wonder if Gregor Schultz was secretly one of them, despite his solid record of voting CDU in city elections. But if not them, who?

I'll write a book about it. The thought pleased him for a minute or so, until it came to him that his lack of literary aptitude was the least of its flaws. If a journalist didn't think the story worth running, why would a publisher invest money in it? And was the memory of a few brutal minutes capable of being stretched beyond a paragraph or two?

Once the doctor told him that his heart could bear a little light gardening, he took the problem out to his allotment. He asked the cabbages their advice, and then the potatoes, and neither had any better (or more) ideas than he'd already considered and discarded. They also couldn't help him with the Brenda conundrum. He hadn't yet decided whether he should tell his wife everything and ask her advice or let her discover the truth when – if – he told the world. Would she hate him for holding back the story, or damn him for burdening her with it? She wasn't nor ever had been a Nazi – in fact, she had long believed that politics and fish-smoking sheds should be kept equally distant from the home. He couldn't guess, therefore, whether she would regard his business as a secret withheld or a matter left decently unspoken. Like other Germans, she was happiest not thinking or being reminded about the twelve years of National Socialism, and almost as much time had elapsed now since its extinction. Would she think him a dolt for even brooding upon it still?

He told himself that he had already given his story to four people (including his bed-neighbour Lothar), so hadn't he unburdened himself enough to let the thing go? If the rest of the world didn't want to hear the story, surely he was absolved by default? The logic of this appealed to him, and for almost a week thereafter he was able to think of more pressing matters (living at half-pace was more difficult than he had imagined, and quite exhausting), until an evening radio programme on German-Israel relations brought him right back to the matter of crime, punishment and who should say what, and when.

It also held out a possibility he hadn't yet considered. If someone on the radio had the courage or insolence to remind Berliners of their past (however obliquely), they might be interested in hearing his testimony. An interview, however brief, would flush away every gram of his guilt for having remained silent all this time - in fact, it might be better than a newspaper story, because people would hear the regret in his voice and judge him more kindly for it.

But how did a man get on to the radio, if he wasn't anyone and didn't know anyone? Writing a letter would be as good as forgetting the whole thing, and Gregor was certain that if he simply telephoned the station, anxiety would make him stand on his own tongue and talk nonsense. The only alternative was to go to the studios, demand – well, plead – to speak to someone in authority and put his case face to face.

Which radio station, though - RIAS or SFB? The latter was a recent creation, inheriting the old NWDR premises in the British Zone. He didn't know much about them, other than that they were the creation of the City's Senate, while RIAS was run by the Americans. Who could he trust more to put his story, if (a huge *if*) they decided to run it?

Then he recalled that SFB, though only a year or so old, was already being criticized in some quarters for dwelling too much on Germany's Nazi past, rather than the half-Communist present. That gave him some hope that his story wouldn't be considered an affront, so he found the station's address on Heidelberger Platz, placed it in a coat pocket and waited for an opportunity to present itself.

It came quickly, though he hardly welcomed the cause. Brenda's sister Verena, who lived across the Line in Potsdam, fell seriously ill. Her two sons had died in the war and her husband soon after, and Brenda was her only living relative. Even so, on the day she received the news his wife hesitated to pack a bag, giving her husband long, worried glances. He reassured her that he would continue to follow his doctor's regime strictly – he hadn't had a cigarette for weeks, was eating his oatmeal and steamed vegetables religiously and actually enjoying the gentle exercises he'd been prescribed. Of course she should go to nurse poor Verena, and she wasn't to worry about him in the meantime.

Two hours after she climbed onto the Potsdam bus with her suitcase he was outside Heidelberger Platz 3, the offices of *Sender Freies Berlin*. He had no appointment, no name to ask for, no idea how he was going to start the conversation; but the fact that he *was* here put something in his veins, and he didn't think of not going on. Even so, he waited until two women stepped into the main entrance and then followed them, letting the proximity ease his nerves.

The office employed female receptionists, which calmed him further. He approached the oldest of them, a pleasant-looking, slightly matronly lady, and told her that he wanted to speak to someone on an important matter. Her smile might have been one of welcome or incredulity, but she pushed a pad towards him and asked him to state the subject briefly. He wrote a lot more than what might have been characterized as brief, but when he handed the pad back to her she gestured to a number of sofas behind him and told him to wait.

He sat down and tried to remain calm. His weak heart was beginning to accelerate, so he breathed deeply and slowly, forced his limbs to relax and imagined the line of kohlrabi he had planted in his allotment but had yet to show above ground. This eased him so effectively that he almost fell asleep twice, and after each wakening start he scanned the faces of the receptionists to see if anyone had noticed. The third time he must have gone all the way, because the hand on his shoulder nearly sent him into the air.

The matronly receptionist apologized, and eased his embarrassment with a gracious lie about how the new sofas (which didn't look at all new) were too soft. Herr Mathis was very busy at the moment, but in about half-an-hour he could spare five minutes to discuss the matter. It turned out to be forty minutes, but Gregor remained awake during that time by staying on his feet and circling the sofas like an Apache warrior trying to get a shot at John Wayne.

Herr Mathis was a middle-aged man dressed comfortably in a tie and *strickjacke*. He shook the visitor's hand formally, waved him to the only sofa that faced away from the reception desk and asked his business. Despite having thought about what he had to tell for some weeks now, Gregor hadn't rehearsed the order of words, so he forgot about introducing himself and told it as plainly as he knew how, without emotion or embellishment. It took almost all of his allotted five minutes, but having heard it all Herr Mathis didn't seem to be in a hurry to end their interview. He rubbed his chin and stared at the carpeted floor.

'That's ... interesting.'

'Will you do a story about it?'

Gregor tried not to seem hopeful, but the careful look that the other man gave him suggested that he was about to be let down gently.

'I doubt it.' Mathis sighed. 'It's a difficult subject, German against German. People don't want to be reminded, in case old grudges stir.'

'Many of the Jews were German, but you deal with that.'

'Well, that's different. Jews were targeted for *being* Jews, regardless of whatever else they'd done. It's officially a war crime, even if we do our best to forget it. *This* thing, though - I think I'd find it hard to get past the producer, unless there were other, peculiar circumstances.'

Gregor nodded, though he hadn't heard anything he could agree with. He felt as if he'd come to the end of a road he hadn't wanted to travel, and his feelings about that were mixed. He was disappointed, certainly, but a small, palpable sense of relief smoothed its edges. He'd done what he could, and he suspected that not many Germans would have done the same, or would have given up at the first discouragement. He had meant it as a confession, for something that wasn't his crime, and now he could put it from him.

He stood up. 'Thank you for seeing me.'

Herr Mathis shook his hand again. 'It was a pleasure. You're the second person I've had to refuse on this type of story, so ...'

He paused, frowning. 'You didn't tell me where the incident happened.'

Gregor gave the address to him, and his eyes widened slightly.

'Would you wait here, please?'

He returned within two minutes, not paying attention to potential obstacles as he flicked through a notebook.

'The gentleman didn't give the precise address. He said it was an old apartment building, on Holsteiner Ufer, the northernmost stretch.'

Surprised, Gregor nodded. 'That's it. It stood alone at that point, though more buildings survived just a few hundred metres to the east. What did this man say about it?'

'That he and his workmates took down and buried six bodies from the cellar there. All were just bones by then, but he said that one of them had a General's stripes on his pants.'

'I was there! That day!'

Mathis looked doubtful. 'That day also?'

'I went to watch them demolish the place! My wife told me that she'd seen them start on it, and that I'd probably be sad to see it go. I wasn't, of course, but then I've never told Brenda the story of what happened in there. She just knew it as my old workplace.'

'So you saw them take down the bodies? That was … December, three, four months ago?'

'No, I was shooed away by two men in suits who came to take charge of the business. But I knew very well what they'd find down there.'

'How? It happened, what, eleven years ago?'

'Because I was there when the squad bricked up the cellar door, thinking all the while that one of them was going to turn around and shoot me in the head. But all I got was a wink and a finger on the lips from one of them as they left.'

'It was during the last days. I doubt that they thought of you as any sort of threat.'

Gregor nodded once more. 'That's what I've thought since. I was just a coward.'

'For what? Not throwing yourself in front of them?'

'I sat in my little *portier*'s room while they did it. I could hear one man screaming, begging, and I put my hands over my ears to shut him out. Then my floor began to creak, and I almost threw up.'

'Why?'

'I was directly above the cellar. They hanged the poor bastards from the beam there, and they must have struggled.' Gregor wiped a tear from his eye, wondering how it could come back so strongly after all this time. 'They were pulled up, not dropped.'

'Christ.' Mathis rubbed his forehead. 'The other man who came, he was the foreman supervising the demolition. He told me that he'd been ordered to say nothing about what was found, but he was upset that he'd been forced to commit a sin, as he saw it.'

'A sin?'

'They buried the bodies on the site, without ceremony. Then he and his gang were given cash, to keep their tongues still.'

'Why would anyone do that? Surely a Christian burial was the least they could have arranged?'

Mathis shrugged. 'The site's going to be part of the *Interbau* – a big deal for Germans, and Berliners particularly. No-one wants ugly reminders of the past to soil the future before it's even built.'

'But wouldn't that make the story more attractive to you? The scandal, I mean?'

'At some other time, yes, but we're already getting flak for not pointing our finger across the Line as much as RIAS does. It's been decided that we should go after the Communists, for a while at least. We were given our broadcasting licence only two years ago, and there are plenty of people in Rathaus Schöneberg who think still that West Berlin doesn't need more than one radio station.'

It was a strong, comforting hint to Gregor that his quest was over, and that he had acquitted himself as well as he might. Why, then, he asked the next question he couldn't quite say, either then or later.

'I understand. Could you let me have the other gentleman's name and address, please?'

9

Herr Globnow studied the plane tree directly in front of him with all the care of a seasoned dendrologist.

'Local secretary for buildings and housing. That's … surprising.'

They sat on the same park bench as before, which Fischer found quite curious. Surely the CIA had sophisticated devices that could measure arse-fall on out-of-the-way seating, and set their surveillance accordingly? At least they *should* have, he decided, and began to consider the technological challenges. He wasn't, after all, too interested in whatever agenda Globnow had brought to the park.

Something was expected, though. He cleared his throat and lied. 'It was something they asked me to do. As a recent recruit I didn't think I could refuse. In any case, it gets me settled in the local Party, which is what you wanted.'

'Yes, it's a good start. I wasn't being critical – you just don't seem the sort to be excited about the urban environment.'

'I live in one. I shouldn't be indifferent to it.'

'No.' Globnow settled back on the bench. He didn't seem disturbed about surrendering the initiative. Fischer – had he thought about it at all – might have imagined that a handler would be more assertive, if only to remind his reluctant charges of their lack of options. He recalled that Major Zarubin had offered several dark hints about what his own agents might expect if they wandered from his narrow road, but that had been back in Stettin, at a time when the blood had hardly dried on the streets. Perhaps it was different now; perhaps people like Fischer were considered to be minor, freelancing civil servants, entitled to the occasional payment but no perquisites or job security, and definitely no notice of termination.

Globnow cleared his throat. 'Have you discovered anything meaty?'

'Meaty?'

'Notable corruption? Illicit cash for tenancies? Cocks sucked to jump a housing-queue?'

If he hadn't said it with a smile in his voice, Fischer might have thought he was serious. Perhaps he was and wasn't, like an angler with only half-expectations of landing something.

'I've only been in the position for three days, if it *is* a position. The fellow I'm replacing didn't exactly throw himself into it. The paperwork he passed to me amounts to a list of contacts in the City Works Department and some angry correspondence about the drains on Brahms-Strasse. If any cocks were sucked, it was effort wasted.'

'There must be some nagging issues you can point to.'

'I'm not sure. Lichterfelde survived the war quite well - there was very little damage here. Some of the northern parts of Steglitz weren't quite as lucky, but I don't know that area very well.'

'Get to know it, then. The city's population's been rising so there'll be housing shortages, even here. Put some complaints together and make noise about them. It won't be difficult, you'll raise your profile locally and ...' Globnow raise both hands as if weighing the matter '… you'll be helping people who need help. Think how well you'll sleep at night, fighting that good fight.'

The man really seemed to enjoy his work. That, too, was beginning to puzzle Fischer. It was a dangerous profession and the man had already lost much – not least, a wife and any hope of the sort of gentle descent towards the grave that other men plan for. He was too relaxed, too at ease, to be convincing in his role. Even Generals had their bad days, yet this man didn't give any impression of having to negotiate furrows on the way to the high spots. If it was merely fatalism, a peace made with whatever he could expect, Fischer envied it. Otherwise, he was watching a performance, but to what end he couldn't guess.

Globnow had said nothing more. The plane tree was getting his attention again, and Fischer felt a little like an actor who had come to a rehearsal without first memorizing his lines.

'Do you ...?'

The other man turned, his eyebrows raised slightly. 'What?'

'... want me to provide written reports? On my progress?'

'Why would I? We don't do career appraisals. Just let me know what's going on when we meet. If something urgent happens, call this number Here ...'

Globnow pulled a card from his pocket. It bore no name or address, just a typed telephone number.

'It's my direct line at the factory, so make sure the urgent thing happens during work hours only.'

'What sort of urgent thing?'

'I couldn't say. Perhaps someone will shake your hand and discern a faint hint of treasonable intent - we have to deal with the occasional denouncement. Or you may come across something wonderfully useful and wish to pass it on quickly. That, too, happens sometimes.'

Still smiling, Globnow stood up, and Fischer felt the same urge to punch his face that Zarubin used to incite. Perhaps it was a technique taught by KGB, to forestall feelings of affection between the mice and their cat.

'That's it? That's all you wanted to talk about?'

The smile broadened. 'Yes, there was no great matter. I didn't want you to feel you were being ignored.'

Globnow half-turned but paused, and when an eyebrow rose once more Fischer wasn't remotely convinced by the sudden thought it was meant to convey.

'That thing in your local newspaper - about the Frankfurt Store wanting to buy out the block on Curtius-Strasse? Was it your doing?'

'How did you know about that?'

'Lichterfelde's become my business. Your premises are on that block, so I didn't need to think too hard to make the connection. Are you trying to negotiate a price or discourage the attention?'

Fischer wouldn't have considered the former, though he could see its logic. He shook his head. 'I'm not interested in selling.'

'The comparison made with the *Interbau* project – it's preposterous, obviously. Was *that* your idea?'

'Lichterfelders are notoriously old-world. Throwing out a threat of modernity can't fail to raise the dust, even if it's a fantasy.'

Globnow nodded slowly. 'It's nonsense, and clever. I doubt that it'll earn you any kudos in the party, though. The SPD are solidly behind the project, even if it's meant to house bourgeois families.'

'Because it's Berlin's final bid to become the Federal Republic's capital?'

'Yes. And for that reason, of course, we'd love it to fail badly.' The other man pulled a face. 'Though I doubt your little initiative's going to cause any heart murmurs in the Senate.'

'It's not meant to. I just want to discourage the Frankfurt people.'

'Well, good luck with it.'

Fischer watched Globnow stroll off towards Unter den Eichen, and wondered if he'd been believed. It was hardly likely that the most reactionary Lichterfelder would worry that futurity was going to mutilate their neighbourhood with the redevelopment of a small site. At most, the *Zeitung* might get a couple of letters from the sort of folk who thought that things had been all-to-fuck since the Kaiser abdicated, and irate correspondence was the plasma in local journalism's blood – vital, pervasive and hardly noticed. To anyone else, linking what was happening in Lichterfelde to western Germany's most prestigious building project would seem a ludicrous overstatement, but he hardly cared about that. The less that Globnow thought of his judgement the better.

What if he'd told him the truth? Did KGB care if their foot soldiers waged private war out-of-hours, or might he have been commended for retaining something of his former killer's predilections? Was abetting a murder enough to get him sanctioned, or promoted, or merely squashed for risking unwanted visibility? His utter ignorance of the intelligencer's sordid world left him snatching at mist once more, aware only that whatever his hand managed to grasp would be slimy, and probably poisonous.

That morning, Kleiber had given him a list of names, lifted from the accounts of companies set up to supervise the *Interbau* project. Most were of little interest, their various expertises baldly apparent – architects and their assistants, consultant engineers, geologists and others whose view of the whole was bound precisely by the tasks before them. Only one man stood out at first glance, and that by reason of his title: Liaison to the Office of the Bürgermeister. The City had two Bürgermeisters, but Fischer had no doubt as to which one this referred – Rolf Schwedler, Senator for Building and Housing.

He went back to the name – Herr Geist, the *Herr* in lieu of an initial or given name, as though he were personal assistant (or chief hairdresser) to Marlene Dietrich. *Liaison* could mean no more than go-between, but he doubted it. Political careers were tied to this business and its success, so the gentleman was likely to be adept at dealing with squalls, inconveniences, sudden alarums and dropped eggs, a nimble sort who kept reputations at a remove from everything that didn't advance them. If any one man could know precisely who was what on the Hansaviertel site, it would be this one.

It was going to be a challenge. No doubt Herr Geist could smell shit before it departed the cow, yet Fischer had to get both his attention and cooperation without seeming as if he wanted either. As he walked back to the shop he played with several ideas connected with his new role as Buildings Secretary for the SPD's Steglitz/Lichterfelde Branch, but all of them fell into the gulf between the very most he could make of that exalted role and the very least that Herr Geist would assume of his own. If he went up to Hansaviertel in any official capacity he'd be given a souvenir pen and laughed off the site.

And then, as he read one of the accounts' preambles, setting out the purpose and intent of the company's fleeting existence, its noble and well-advertised aspirations leapt from the page and taunted him with his idiocy. He'd been trying to be clever, when really it was absurdly simple. The only thing that would get him the attention he needed was the unadorned truth.

10

Walter Senn was cutting out a small, rotten section of the Great Pavilion's lowest rain-gutter when he was given a second chance.

Lowest in this case meant eight metres above ground level, and though the Pavilion had permanent fixed-ladder access, the Work's Department's safety regulations stipulated that maintenance work at that height be carried out on raised scaffolding. Senn didn't care either way; neither his head nor legs had ever been bothered by altitude, but if the precautions comforted management then that was how it had to be. The other man on the job, Hans, was sixty years old and grateful for the support. From the moment he reached the platform he'd been on his hands and knees, spreading himself wider than a king crab, and was next to useless for anything other than passing tools when requested.

Hans had been prattling about Tennis Borussia Berlin for about ten minutes when Senn cut his hand with a hacksaw. He sucked on the wound and gestured to the toolbox, and Hans, who had just enough sense to realize that this was probably more important than football (if only for a few moments), clambered to his feet to get the roll of lint that all toolboxes belonging to the Works Department contained. Perhaps he'd been on all fours for too long, but some part of his body had been starved of its entitlement to blood, and as he straightened he staggered backwards.

Almost nine years earlier, one of Life's brutal whimsies had placed a burden of guilt upon the old Rudy Bandelin, though nothing about it had been his fault. On many occasions since he had examined the moment from different angles, trying to see what he might have done differently; but the truth was that he had merely been preoccupied by what his Soviet gang-masters had told him to do, and any sensible man wanting to eat at the end of that day would have done the same - which is why the real Walter Senn had been allowed to make his unthinking way into history unhindered, via a long drop and unyielding Stalingrad street.

It might have been that the reflexes of the man who stole his name thereafter had stood to attention ever since, waiting to make amends for their earlier failure; but the new Walter Senn couldn't ever recall having moved with such instinctive speed, his bloodied hand lunging and grasping Hans' jacket before the old man reached an angle at which inertia carried him – and anyone attached to him – into free space. The arms waved comically for a moment like pretend wings, and then he was safely back on his hands and knees, trying not to puke.

Senn's elation was as intense as Hans' relief, but the feeling was tested by his discovery that he had a new best friend – in fact, a follower. As soon as they were back on firm ground the story of the old man's deliverance, embellished at every retelling, circulated the Works Department. A good turn, a fortuitous swerve of happenstance, became a preternatural act of deliverance, a palpable proof of God's mercy and favour (though why Hans was eligible for either remained unsaid), the bloodied outline on the jacket its Turin Shroud-like commemoration. The first reaction to the news was a pat on the back for the new man, but within an hour he was wandering into conversations that became hushed whispers and almost-reverent looks, as if he'd just taken a short cut and walked across the Eichenteich rather than around it. Before the lunch half-hour had ended he'd been summoned to the supervisor's office, to be told that he was up for a special merit award.

He'd wanted to be comfortable in his new job, not prominent. Though common-sense reasserted itself over the course of the afternoon and awe subsided he remained the centre of attention, and by clocking-off time had received three invitations to help his co-workers drink their wages next pay-day. Hans himself continued to preach his gospel, swearing that he would never have his jacket cleaned, but rather carry the reminder that every day to come was one gifted by an ever-kind Providence.

Senn had found a room only half a kilometre from the Gardens, on Lepsius-Strasse, where the landlady provided a good breakfast and didn't care to know too much about her tenant. He went home that evening in an unsettled mood, torn between a sense that he had put a small thing partially right and fear of what it was doing to his resolve. Saving a man's life wasn't a small matter, however strenuously he had dismissed Hans' claims for a minor miracle. It had laid to rest the troubled memory of the wretch whose name he'd stolen, made the theft itself feel almost just and given the reluctant hero a strange, unfamiliar feeling of having put a virtuous mark upon a long-tainted manifest. Against that, he was plotting murder. No matter what its justification, it made him feel as if he were presently inhabiting two entirely distinct skins.

His mood didn't settle when he discovered that his new landlady had put flowers in his spartanly-furnished room. They were crocuses, a reminder of the early life that springs from hard-frozen earth. There had been crocuses at Okhvat, their shimmer of blues and white a premature lament for the many who would fall that day, but it wasn't their memory that disturbed him as much as this silent reproof - of beauty to his intention to do evil. And if he was thinking of it that way, his heart and soul might not be up to the task.

There was also a supper waiting for him - a hearty *eintopf* with two sausages. His landlady brought it to his room on a tray and told him she would have to charge him an extra mark, which couldn't nearly have covered its cost. It was the last, thoughtful twist in a day that had thrown him entirely out of his furrow. Having a single purpose, no matter how ugly, brought clarity. He hadn't thought beyond it because he wasn't sure there could be a *beyond*. Little accretions – of fellowship, charity and momentary well-being – blurred the view ahead. Worse, they cleared space for fates other than the one to which he'd resigned himself.

His choices had been pared down – first by the Führer, when he decided that mighty Poland was an unacceptable threat to the Reich, and subsequently by the Soviet holiday camp industry. It had been so long since he'd had more than one option that even the hint of alternatives could make him costive, and when they came with a measure of hope attached he was a rabbit between two crops, and likely to starve there. The possibility that there might be possibilities was sapping him.

When his landlady returned for the tray he was staring at the wall, following a hairline crack from one corner to another.

'Was it alright?'

He dragged his mind back from the tomorrow he couldn't make out. 'It was fine, thank you. Frau Halder …?'

'What is it, Herr Senn?'

'If you knew something about someone – something bad, that is; what would you do?'

She sighed. 'Was that *something* to do with the war?'

Surprised, he nodded.

'Let it be, I say. Things were done as they are in any war, and only the losers are held to account. Has there been any punishment for the Communists? The Americans? Of course not. We've suffered enough. After the First War they took Alsace and made Danzig a free city; after the last one they took everything else and hanged a lot of people too. It's time to forget - even the Allies think so.' She laughed. 'Why, Führer Dönitz himself comes out of prison next month! He's served his time. We've *all* served our time.'

Let it be. It sounded right when he repeated it in his head. The hurt belonged to another, dead age, raised only by the guilt of his helplessness to repair it. A million crimes – more - had been committed in those final weeks as the German world disintegrated. Each of them deserved redress, but collectively they blurred into untouchable tragedy, like the victims of the Chinese famine, or Spanish flu, or …

'I have a plum tart, if you'd like some?'

'Thank you. I've eaten enough.'

Since his return to Germany he had been smothered by a deal of kindness, from people who owed him nothing. Old Else the widow, his inquisitors in the Lubeck bar, the fearsome drunks in Moabit, the divinely-bodied young lady at the *Morgenpost* archive, Otto Fischer (who'd stood him a bed, food and money), the street-sweepers of Lichterfelde, his new workmates and this widowed lady - it was a weight of moral obligation, a heavy, generous shove towards something other than a life curtailed upon a point of (pointless) revenge.

What would his sister have said to him about it? They hadn't been close enough for him to know with certainty, though the circumstances of her last days - bringing comfort to others rather than fleeing the advancing Soviet armies - offered a hint he could hardly dismiss. And Anna Felder, her best friend – hadn't she urged him to put away thoughts of retribution? It added to the weight, and he had nothing to set against it except …

Himself. He had been suspended in amber for fourteen years, breathing but not living, concerned for nothing but eating enough to make up the calories lost during a work-shift. Coming back into the world was like birth - painful, confusing and much too loud to allow him to make more than a little sense of it. His only certainty was that he was attached still, umbilically, to one thing, and that was a matter left uncorrected. He wanted, badly, to hate the man who had raped and murdered Margret, but he could see him only in the mind's eye (and he could hardly see her at all). Yet it was because the Bandelins were gone now, because he was the last of a not-very-noble line still breathing, that it fell to him to prove that they had been more than nothing. He had neither read nor seen a Greek tragedy or play of Shakespeare, but had the same understanding of natural justice as any man. His only sibling – his last surviving relation – had been murdered, and that circle could be closed only by another death.

'Are you alright, Herr Senn?'

She must have thought him drunk, or addled. He looked up and smiled.

'Yes, very well, Frau Halder. Do you know if there's an ironware shop nearby?'

Though a native of Moabit, Gregor Schultz was not familiar with Rostocker *kiez*. In the days of the Republic and then the Reich, its communist sensibilities had attracted much trouble, and sensible citizens who weren't in any particular hurry usually made a detour either to the west or east in order not to fall unwittingly into a police van during one of the many raids on the area. Like the streets around Moabit Prison, it was said to hold bad luck in its cobbles the way that fields held a morning dew.

Today, though, he had marched – or rather shuffled - into the heart of the former political battlefield, and was standing outside Berlichingenstrasse 38, a small terraced house on a block that was surely overripe for demolition (its northern extremity was shored-up with a beaten lattice of timber spars). Nervously, he pulled a slip of paper from his pocket, re-checked the address for about the tenth time, clenched a fist and held it a few inches from the surface of its front door, ready equally to announce his presence or run away.

His internal struggle was resolved when the door opened and a pleasant-faced young woman, attached at the hip to a snotted infant, stepped out.

'Is it about the job?'

Gregor swallowed. 'I'm sorry?'

'The clearance work, at the Westhafen?'

'I'm afraid not.'

Her face dropped slightly. 'He's at the Labour Department. Do you want to wait?'

Clearly, Gregor didn't give an impression of wanting to collect rents. He smiled, nodded and followed her into a tiny sitting-room, its old-fashioned, dark décor made gloomier by the thick lace curtains over the window. She nodded him to its only armchair, a distressed item.

'He won't be long, unless they offer him something.' She smiled. 'Then you'll be disappointed and I'll be happy.'

'He has no work, then?'

She shrugged. 'They finished the demolition work in Hansaviertel and laid him off until something else comes up. It's what they do.'

Gregor didn't ask who *they* were. In Berlin's almost-permanently flat economy, most of the smaller building-trade companies employed men as and when needed. He made a sympathetic noise in his throat and then realised that he hadn't introduced himself.

'I'm sorry; my name's Schultz. Are you Frau Mattner?'

'Yes.' She shifted the child to the other hip and shook his hand formally. 'Can I ask what it's about, please?'

'Of course. I met your husband a few months ago. It was at the building being demolished on Holsteiner Ufer ...'

'The ghost house?'

An apt name - it had certainly haunted Gregor. He nodded. 'I went to watch it come down. I was *portier* there, before and during the war.'

Her eyes widened. 'Did you see what happened?'

'No, it was a secret business, and I wasn't so stupid as to be interested.'

He would have been a fool, a suicide, to have done anything other than hide from it, yet the words sounded craven, even eleven years late.

She shook her head. 'Franzi didn't sleep properly for days, afterwards. He said it was the sort of thing you saw in dreams, and he didn't want any more of ...'

The front door opened, and the man Gregor now knew as Franzi Mattner stepped in. He placed his cap on a hook behind the front door, turned, and the smile paused halfway across his face. When he spoke his voice shook slightly.

'I was thinking of it, just now, as I was coming home.'

His wife's eyes rolled. 'You're *always* thinking of it. Were there any jobs?'

'I think so, starting next week. Why are you here, mate?'

Franzi patted the infant's head and then held out his hand to Gregor, who'd risen from the armchair. He'd practiced several ways of saying what he needed to say, but not the one that came out.

'I want to get it out of my head. I want to tell what happened.'

'So do I, but no-one wants to listen.'

Frau Mattner nodded. 'It's best forgotten.'

Both Franzi and Gregor looked at her. She was right of course, but recognizing it didn't help any more than a diagnosis made a migraine go away. What had sat on Gregor's shoulder for so long couldn't be shifted by mere common sense, and whatever Franzi Mattner had witnessed the day after St Stephen's Day …

Gregor turned to the younger man. 'They chased me away before you went in. Was it bad down there?'

'Worse than anything I've seen. There wasn't any smell – they'd been dead and decomposed for too long for that; but the way they were hanging was … obscene.'

'How so?'

'Two of them had been wearing braces when they were hanged. They were dressed still. The others had belts on. When the flesh went, the trousers came down to their feet, like they'd been fucked and then killed.'

'Franzi!' Shocked, Frau Mattner cupped her baby's head and pulled it to her breast.

'Sorry, darling. You expect – you hope for – some dignity to death, but there wasn't any in that cellar. The way they were hanging, twisted still, it looked like they'd struggled. It wasn't clean.'

Gregor shook his head. 'I heard them die. It took time.'

'Who *were* they? One of them had a red stripe down his army trousers, so I assume he was a senior officer. But the rest …?'

'I don't know. I saw two of them being brought it, but they were civilians. It was a final cleaning of slates, probably - the Regime's last surviving enemies, the ones who'd thought they might just make it, being disappointed.'

Franzi shook his head. 'Me and Elle, we're too young to remember what it was like. My Father died in the fighting, and Mother wouldn't speak about any of it before she died. How could someone have been so spiteful, to keep on killing their own people when the Red Army was in shelling range?'

Gregor rubbed his forehead. 'We're a bureaucratic nation. If a piece of paper said they had to die, who would argue?'

'Snakes eating themselves. Christ!' Franzi sat on the arm of the sofa and gazed at something between himself and the threadbare carpet. 'You know that we buried them there, on site?'

'Yes, the radio man told me. It's despicable!'

'A single grave, too, for all six of them, in the garden. The boss who came to direct it, he watched until it was all done, then he gave each of us cash and told us to keep our mouths shut – and that if we didn't, he'd make sure we never got another job in Berlin, ever.'

'Who was he?'

'I don't know. Never saw him before or since. His sort of suit doesn't get out of the office much, I expect.'

Frau Mattner had put her free arm around her husband's shoulder, and was frowning down at his hair.

'Imagine making honest men do something like that! I told Franzi that it was nonsense, that this fellow couldn't stop him getting more work if he told the truth. That's why he went to the radio people with the story, but they didn't listen.'

Gregor nodded. 'I went, too. They told me he had, and gave me your address.'

Franzi looked up. 'So again, why are you here, mate?'

'I have an idea.'

'Television?'

'No, they're run by the same people as the radio – they wouldn't listen. I don't think we'll ever get the story out. We can only try to do the right thing and hope that it has an effect. If it doesn't, at least we made the effort.'

'What, then?'

'We write a letter – I mean, just the one, but we both sign it. I was there when the crime was committed, you were there when it was concealed, so between us we know as much about it as anyone.'

'Who do we send it to?'

'Whoever's in charge - of what's going on at Hansaviertel, I mean. It'll be a politician, so he can decide what to do with what we tell him.'

Frau Mattner pursed her lips. 'Whoever he is, he won't want any scandal around *that* business. It's going to be Berlin's big moment next year.'

'No, he won't. But then, he won't know if we're going to take it further, in which case he might wonder how bad it will look if folk find out that he was informed and did nothing about it.'

Franzi scratched his head. 'How could we take it *further*?'

'We couldn't. He doesn't know that, though. At the least, it might push him to get those poor devils dug up and given a decent funeral.'

The other man nodded slowly. 'That's only right. I doubt that anyone's ever going to pay for what was done to them.'

'No, it's history now.'

'Alright.' Franzi looked up at his wife, who nodded slightly. 'But you'll have to write it. My schooling wasn't much.'

Gregor reached into his pocket. 'I already have, most of it. Read what I've got, and we'll put in what you saw and did. We'll make it into a *remonstrance*.'

'What's that?'

'It's a protest, a reproach.'

'This politician, whoever he is – he didn't do the thing, did he?'

'No. But he stands in the shoes of those who did. We're citizens, telling him that it was wrong and shouldn't just be forgotten. If we all forget, we're ...'

'What?'

Gregor searched his memory. His own education had been decent enough (though he'd never made much of it), but time had let a lot of it slip away. Brenda used to tell him that he was a bag of words, and he'd never been sure whether she'd meant it as a compliment or something else, so perhaps he'd helped with the slippage, pushed it along …

Helped. Something like that. *Collaborated?* No, but not entirely no. Like being guilty, but in company …

'Culpable. If we forget, we're *culpable.*'

Florian re-read the letter. It was addressed to him personally, and that worried him a little. He liked to be known as a problem solver, but only for problems he could see coming and chose to solve, and only if he could do it to his advantage. This was unwelcome, not only for its nature but the fact that someone regarded it as his business.

It was respectfully stated, and phrased with a certain amount of delicacy, given the subject matter. It referred only to 'unfortunate events' occurring under a previous regime (Florian didn't imagine the latter was a reference to the Second Empire) that might impact, however unfairly, upon the reputation of the *Interbau* Project. That part seized his attention, obviously. An interview was requested, at which more details would be offered. It concluded with an expression of regret for having added to what must be a considerable burden of responsibility already.

Who was it pointing a finger towards? Florian knew of five, possibly six men involved in the project whose shoulders were slightly dipped from the effort of constantly looking over them. Manfred was of course the prime suspect, but the others? What if it was none of them? He had made an effort to know his colleagues, but a history - or part of it, at least - could be hidden. The *Interbau* was going to be the Federal Republic's first prestige project, an opportunity to show that the nation had moved on – what more vulnerable moment could there be for old, rotten floorboards, than when the World's heavy tread pressed them?

He'd used that metaphor before, most usefully upon Senator Schwedler when first asked what the risks might be. His considered opinion - that individual war records were going to be a potential problem for *any* public German endeavour until at least 1980 – hadn't been intended to reassure the man. It was best to be nervous; wise to assume that what could fall at the least convenient moment probably would; wisest of all to prepare for what couldn't be anticipated precisely. This had ignited the Senator's nerve-ends, as Florian had hoped that it would. He wanted to be trusted absolutely to do whatever was necessary to protect the project, and never to be asked the means by which this miracle would occur. He had put a rhetorical finger to his nose, and Schwedler had understood the gesture precisely.

So far, there had been few reasons to resort to *whatever necessary*. The little archaeological incident at the turn of the year had been reburied swiftly, and a single life, too full of terminal pain (with its defective but untrustworthy memory), had been given a merciful release. Neither had caused him to lose sleep, much less thrown a stick into the machinery. This, though, might require closer and more persistent attention.

Most likely, it was a prelude to extortion. Would someone dance around a matter if it wasn't necessary to be discreet? And discretion was probably necessary only to protect the source. No doubt the conversation would be equally oblique, and it would be left to Florian to put the hypothetical question about how the matter might go away. That wasn't in itself a problem – he had a sufficiently large budget to absorb reasonable expenditure - but it was a sad fact that those who managed to put a hand in someone else's pocket were often encouraged by their success to repeat the exercise. Another early death might forestall that threat, but only if it could be established that the *accident* would cauterize the wound entirely, and only fools didn't cover themselves. He reread the letter for the third time. It didn't hint at foolishness.

His secretary brought him a coffee, and the event only registered some minutes later. There was an obvious first move here, and it wasn't to call the telephone number given in the letter. He picked up the receiver, dialled and waited.

'Linde.'

'I have another enquiry.'

'What sort?'

'I'm not sure yet. I need information, obviously. After that, we can discuss the matter further.'

'The party?'

'Fischer, Otto Henry. That's Henry, not Heinrich, so we may assume at least one Huguenot ancestor. No address, but I have a Steglitz frank. He claims to be a member of the SPD, so look at the local Party.'

'Handwriting?

'The note is typed, so just a signature and the envelope. It's somewhat spidery. We may be looking at age or an injury.'

'Is this urgent?'

'I don't know, so let's say yes. I need a history. His financial condition would be very useful. Any prior criminal convictions of course.'

'Right. The fee ...'

'I'm doubling it, to enthuse you.'

'I'm always enthused.'

'I mean no offence. It's an appreciation, in advance.'

At the other end the receiver was replaced without a further word. Florian had known Linde for some years now (though they had never met), and trusted the man as much as any. He was former SA, whose paramilitary career had hardly survived that of Ernst Röhm. Picked up for armed robbery in late 1934, he served several years in Plötzensee and was then 'volunteered' for a punishment detail on the Eastern Front. The fact that he'd survived that experience was a testimonial in itself – that, and the lightness of touch he applied to every job he'd done for Florian. One couldn't speak of artistry in matters of intimidation and murder, but the lack of attention his work excited deserved more recognition than it was ever likely to get.

Florian had a busy day ahead of him. He was attending the Steering Committee as the Senator's eyes and ears, organizing a reception for the visiting Federal Minister (at which much air would be moved and nothing of note said) and greasing an Electricians' Union convener who made half-veiled threats of walkouts whenever things seemed to be going too well. Another man might have winced at the prospect of that crowded schedule, but being paid generously for playing people was as satisfying a transaction as he could conceive.

He should have put this latest matter from mind pending Linde's preliminary report, yet something continued to prod uncomfortably.

He didn't enjoy not holding the initiative, nor playing a waiting game when he didn't have full sight of the cards. It might all be nonsense – an old grudge, pushed by someone too stupid to have a sense of perspective. It might equally be grenade, tossed where it would do the most, and the most lasting, damage. If something more than an inconsequence was allowed to explode, the first head in the basket would be Florian's.

An SPD member. Why had he mentioned that? Florian himself had no political affiliations, so the purpose of it was directed elsewhere. Towards Senator Schwedler? Or to the entirety of the Party presence in the Senate, *Abgeordnetenhaus* and Mayoralty? Was he inferring that his loyalty could be assumed, or swinging a cudgel wildly? Was the implication that everyone was safe, or no-one?

Perhaps he should have risked the chance of collateral knowledge, and had Linde do the business immediately. Perhaps the lesson of a swift, inexplicable death would have deterred Herr Party Member Fischer's potential collaborators. Florian's hand lifted from his desk and hovered above the telephone – paused, like the head, between two options: to await further information or initiate a short, further conversation that would strangle a potential problem before it could find its feet and wail.

His heart almost leapt from his chest when the telephone rang. He swore quietly, then laughed at a sudden, mental image of an open-mouthed idiot who prided himself on his ability never to be surprised, and picked up the receiver.

'Florian? It's Rolf Schwedler.'

He relaxed. The Senator called almost every day, to be reassured that there was nothing he need be reassured about. He had an anecdote primed already, about how Walter Gropius and Otto Bartning had spent almost an hour earlier that week arguing with the site-designers, Jobst and Kreuer, about the placement of new buildings on Hansaplatz's southern flank, before consulting old minutes of meetings and discovering that they had agreed the matter almost three months earlier. Like most practical men (he was a trained engineer), Schwedler enjoyed stories that reinforced his prejudices about prima donnas.

'Good Morning, Senator! I was about to ...'

'Listen, Florian, I've received an awful letter. It claims that something ghastly happened on-site a few weeks ago ...'

Florian remained silent while Schwedler gave him the details (daubed with a collage of his worst fears) twice over. It was a measure of his lack of balance, that, when the Senator paused for breath, he asked for a copy of the letter when he knew perfectly well that not only would he receive the original but that it would come with a heartfelt plea to make it disappear forever, if not actually be un-written.

When their conversation ended, Florian gave the opposite wall of his office several minutes' scrutiny and fought a strong, insistent urge to call Linde once more and negotiate a bulk order. Was it a conspiracy – a gang of blackmailers, or just the one man using three signatures? Did Otto Henry Fischer, Gregor Schultz or – he searched his recent memory – Franz Mattner even exist, or was this something else, a...

Christ. The thought almost froze his blood, but he knew better than to squash it, or pretend it was nonsense, that it couldn't be the case. He picked up the telephone once more and dialled a number which, though well committed to memory, he would have preferred never to use.

'Hello, am I speaking to Wolfgang? It's Florian … yes, that one. Could we meet, please? It's *very* urgent. I can be with you in three hours, if that's not inconvenient?'

Afterwards, he told his secretary that he had go out, an unexpected meeting, and that he left it to her to clear his appointments and make his sincere apologies to everyone concerned. He had done the same only once before, when he'd had the chance of an afternoon of carnal pleasure with one of his married female friends and allowed his cock to rule his head. Predictably, once his passion had spent (several times, thanks to the lady's skills), he'd regretted his uncharacteristic weakness and its necessary lies. This time, he found no consolation in the fact that he was being entirely honest.

13

'Otto, why are you interested in the *Interbau* business?'

'I'm not, Jonas.'

'Hm.'

Kleiber said nothing more for a while. He stared without interest into the bowels of a 1930s-vintage HMV cabinet gramophone as Fischer lifted the player unit carefully from its mountings. It was a large item, delivered to the shop by two young men some weeks earlier and strategically forgotten since by the proprietor, who hated big, old jobs. He'd needed to ask Kleiber to help him move it from storeroom to repair room, and had expected that the price to pay would be an interrogation of some sort.

'It's an ugly great thing. Why didn't they dump it in the canal and buy a new one?'

'It probably has some sentimental value.'

'I've seen prettier commodes. In fact, I might easily have mistaken it for one.'

'Well, that would have complicated the repair considerably.'

'You had me mention the *Interbau* in that story I wrote. There must have been a reason for it.'

'Like I told you, I wanted to announce my arrival in the Borough's buildings affairs with a little splash.

'Yeah, but you could have had me mention ten things more relevant to Lichterfelde. I think this is about something else.'

Fischer looked up. 'Honestly, Jonas, if I had any sort of tale to tell, I'd give it to you gladly. I've never been to the site, I've never met or spoken with anyone who has, and I haven't heard anything bad about the project. Except that it's costing a fortune, but you told me that.'

'Is it a murder, then? That's your sort of thing, isn't it?'

'*My* sort of thing?'

'I mean, your speciality?'

'I hope to God not. I'm investigating nothing and nobody. Alright?'

Kleiber's frown deepened. His nose was twitching, but a scent eluded him. Nor could he read his friend's face – half of it was so mutilated that the good side always looked blank by default, and in any case the man was far too practised at hiding his thoughts. It was why none of the panoply of journalists' sleights of conversation had ever wormed anything out of him – in fact, their only effect had been to make Jonas feel that he was being gauche, even transparent, by deploying them. Fischer only ever revealed his emotions – and then momentarily - when a needle skipped on one of his records, or someone went on about how wonderful things were in the old days.

'Alright.'

'Anyway, you'll be married in a few days and then off on your honeymoon. Think about that, not ways to make more work in the meantime.'

'I do. Constantly.'

Fischer looked up again. 'You spent the best part of a year trying to persuade the poor girl that you were the catch of her lifetime. Since the moment she surrendered you've been moving backwards more quickly than the dog that snatched the sausage.'

'We're a fickle sex, we men.'

'One of us is, for sure.'

'I suppose I'll be more keen once we've sinned.'

'She's held out, has she?'

'Like the Knights of St John at … where was it?'

'Malta.'

'I thought that was the British?'

'Them, too. It's been a difficult island to take.'

'Not as difficult as taking Renate's …'

'Jonas! I'm walking her down the aisle, remember?'

'Sorry.'

'Think how wonderful your wedding night will be, plucking a first, ripe fruit.'

Kleiber shook his head gloomily. 'I'll probably be too nervous to perform. You know what a perfectionist she is. And *I'm* almost a virgin, too. She'll be my first German girl.'

'Really?'

'Yeah. English farm girls are all I've had experience of.' He brightened slightly. 'One of them told me I was the best fuck she'd ever had, better than any Englishman. Then she said I shouldn't take that as too much of a compliment. What?'

Fischer was grinning broadly. 'You've just made me feel better.'

'Better? About what?'

'About how the war turned out.'

The Press continued to hover (without further attempts to interrogate) until the RCA was fixed and the unit replaced, and then he helped to carry it back into the store room. Less than a minute after he departed his fiancée returned from an errand to the florist's, made a brief note in her wedding ledger (a loose-leaf volume whose girth was beginning to resemble that of the Wenceslas Bible) and then threw herself into the afternoon's dusting offensive. She hadn't spoken much in the past few days, and Fischer, sensing a growing pensiveness, had attributed it to the expense of a fraulein's transformation to frau. His own two weddings had been frugal affairs in more straitened times, when a feathered display would have been seen as bad taste, a reproof to what was the norm. These days, new money needed to be seen, and those who didn't have it didn't dare to have it known.

He said nothing about her mood of course, and at five she left early for a fitting. He finished a small repair on a wristwatch, closed the shop half an hour early and went up to the apartment, where a copy of his letter sat on the kitchen table. Reading it again, he tried to find ways that it could be misconstrued. Obviously, it could be taken as a blackmailer's opening move, in which case the reaction might indicate how closely the recipient was to the (unnamed) perpetrator of the (unstated) crimes it alleged. If all that came from it was a visit from the police, he could assume that Herr Geist was depressingly innocent of any knowledge of, or association with, the man who killed Senn's sister. Even if the request for an interview were to be granted, it might mean only that someone whose job-title was 'Liaison to the Office of the Bürgermeister' was doing that job by assessing a potential threat to the reputation of the *Interbau* Project before picking up the 'phone to report a half-faced extortionist to the authorities. Hell, even if he offered money to make the problem go away, could that really be read as culpability, or just an honest man's anxiety for his job?

Fischer was relying upon a thin, hopeful chain of logic - that a man in Herr Geist's position, whatever his ignorance or knowledge of past crimes, would want to know more of what the correspondent himself knew, and that somehow, in asking his questions, he would offer a glimpse of his own understanding.

It was risky, and Fischer's only ally was the Party membership he'd mentioned in the letter. It was what a good SPD man *would* do, knowing that the reputation of Berlin's Government was so tightly bound to that of the *Interbau*. Any shrapnel that flew from a revelation of historical offences would spray everyone from Willy Brandt down, and the similar embarrassment of the CDU Government in Bonn would hardly ease that pain. Being SPD was his unspoken alibi, for daring to stir the past's murk.

He could do nothing more until he heard from Geist, who even now might be having a heart attack, or checking how much spare cash he could squeeze from the Project without anyone noticing, or arranging a trap with the police for when his correspondent came to visit, or frantically trying to discover which of the many hundreds of men he dealt with was a war criminal. There was no way of knowing which it might be, no point in trying to guess how their interview would proceed. This was perfectly obvious, yet Fischer continued to try to work it until his head rang like a punched bell and hurt like the hand that punched it.

It hurt more because he was skirmishing in another man's war. Naturally, he was obliged to help Walter Senn, having not only stolen the man's identity but ensured – however unwittingly – that it could never be claimed back. More than that, though, the parallel lines upon which much of their histories had passed were hard to ignore. On the same day, if in very different ways, they had been removed from their old lives and cast into bespoke purgatories, and therefore Senn was almost certainly one of the last two living men (if a long-neglected brother-in-law survived still) who could recall Otto Fischer when his face hadn't caused nightmares. They both had – *had* had – a single sibling, a sister, and if Fischer's had met her end in the same manner as Margret Bandelin he was certain that he would want to put things as right as they might be put. They had a camaraderie of shit shared, of second chances come unexpectedly, and this wasn't a small thing. And yet …

He felt a little like Romania, in 1916, opening an offensive on one Front while the real threat hovered on a second. He was marching towards a minor affray, lending his hapless assistance to a solitary act of reprisal, when on his flank the hundred divisions of Globnow and the KGB were massed, ready to make a laundry stain if he put a foot wrong. There was no ideal time to collaborate in an assassination, but there could hardly be a worse one than this.

Find the man; get it over with. There was something in Macbeth about doing a bad but necessary thing quickly that sounded right, yet his gut churned when he considered how *that* turned out. It was probably going to be impossible to persuade Senn from his course, so the best he could hope for was a clean kill that didn't leave Otto

Fischer written all over it. But that was the problem – he was *hoping*. He had no real control over Senn, other than as a moderating voice that would be heeded or not, yet the consequences of a messy job would splash equally over them both.

Senn had considered the matter carefully, and decided to play to his strengths. He had been reasonably accurate with a pistol once, but so many years had passed that he couldn't be certain that his skills were unimpaired. He didn't want it to be too messy, or prolonged.

Given his *Wehrmacht* training, a seventy-five millimetre field-piece would be the ideal tool, but he wasn't sure that army-surplus depots stocked that kind of ordnance. In any case, putting together a trained crew, finding a clear shot in a crowded city and persuading the target to remain motionless would be problematic (as would the dozens of collateral casualties). Which left the soldier's trusted last resort, the in-close tool of every desperate brawl.

He found it in a shop on Schloss-Strasse, at the bottom of a large box of assorted military souvenirs that hadn't been banned by the Allies as Nazi memorabilia. It was in fine condition, cost him next to nothing and was sufficiently nondescript that the man he paid probably wouldn't recall the transaction the following day. He took it back to his lodgings tucked up his coat sleeve, taking care not to bend his arm and exsanguinate himself.

It was a Pack & Sohne dress bayonet, lacking a scabbard. At the moment it would require some force to do its job, but the Works

Department had an abundance of sharpening stones, and if he borrowed one for an evening it wouldn't be missed. His landlady might well discover it as she cleaned but assume that he, like millions of other ex-servicemen, had managed to bring home his old disemboweller as a keepsake from the days of inglory. No one would think of reporting it to the police.

A stabbing would require that he get as close to the victim as a murderer could, but that was only right. If he was going to do the thing it had to be intimate, not only that his sister's killer could look him in the eye as he did it, but also that the memory remain strong until the perpetrator stood before God and had to account for it. Killing in wartime was an occupation; in peace, a crime whatever the motive. If it didn't give him sleepless night afterwards he'd fear for his soul.

His landlady had left a bowl of beef stew under a tea-towel on his little window table. He ate it one-handed while the other played with his new acquisition. He felt cold about it still, too distant from a moment he only examined carefully when the light went out and he had too much time to think. It was like all advances into battle – one knew what was coming, but as long as the view to the front remained unhindered the mind could keep itself at a remove. He hadn't even begun to think about *afterwards*. Would he return here and go on as before, playing the staid, honest workman, or would he be caught in the crime and put back into a half-life in which other men determined his every action? He was sure that he could resign himself to either, but he should have been more curious about it than he presently was.

He felt detached, because nothing was real enough to form a perspective. A grey, dull sense of unbelonging made what was, or might be, *normality* a matter of guesswork for him. He responded to events and experiences with frustration, anger, sadness, and, sometimes, satisfaction or approval; yet only in the way that he might to a radio programme that offered no direct connection to what he was hearing. If he was experiencing *now* at such a distance, how could he even imagine a future?

In the camps he'd often wished that he had died at Okhvat – cleanly, of course, without knowing too about it. No-one would have mourned (except his sister, but she must have assumed him dead anyway), nor suffered for want of him. Looking back, he couldn't recall much about his life before the war that deserved to be carved into stone, or lamented for having been curtailed. He'd done nothing bad but nothing admirable either; made no mark that he might ever be cursed or praised for. He was, he supposed, the sort of man for whom war was best suited, whose loss represented the least tragedy and brought the least hurt – an ideal Unknown Warrior for the politicians to pretend to mourn once a year. It wouldn't be so bad, to sleep in that underserved immortality.

He picked up his empty bowl and stood. His landlady had a kitchen cupboard that was threatening to part company with the wall, and he'd promised to fix it – an easy, quick job that would make her grateful and him feel useful. If he could fill his spare time with that sort of thing he might not have time to think about what life was, and what it meant. If he survived, perhaps he'd advertise himself as a do-any-job man, evenings only, no problem too small, in Fischer's friend's newspaper. With the nine hours he put in at the Botanical Gardens he'd be too exhausted to think in bed, much less peer philosophically up his back passage.

The thought cheered him slightly because it was almost a plan, and people with plans had at least one foot on the ground. He went downstairs with his bowl and tool bag and had the cupboard fixed in ten minutes (notwithstanding his landlady's accompanying, unbroken commentary on her neighbour's alleged affair with a Bulgarian plumber). That earned him a slice of *donauwelle*, and though he had no sweet-tooth to speak of normally he ate it with great relish, and even used a finger to capture the last smears. Then, he was invited to watch her television for a while, and, not having previous experience of this miracle of technology, accepted gladly.

An hour later, as he lay in bed examining the ceiling, his thoughts were confused. It was time to brood about the usual things, but he couldn't dismiss from mind the spectacle of an entire orchestra – the NDR Radiophilharmomie – playing music for his personal entertainment. It had been light, forgettable stuff (his landlady told him the composer's name, which, being unfamiliar, he had forgotten already), but he had sat directly in front of dozens of well-dressed musicians, and at times the camera had carried him almost onto the conductor's podium. He couldn't recall being more delighted by any childhood Christmas - it had been a wholly novel, unexpected nightcap, and if the police hadn't arrived a few minutes later and taken him away he might have counted this as one of his better days.

Florian had been to Ruschestrasse 103 only once before. Many people could say the same but probably didn't - at least, not to anyone they didn't trust absolutely. Some could boast (if that was the right word) of having visited upon several occasions, and some of *those* were capable of eating solid food still. Very, very few of them had left immediately after their business was discharged, much less in a nice car, as Florian had previously. The Democratic Republic's Ministry for State Security issued a great number of invitations, but only the occasional one was phrased as a matter of choice for the recipient.

He gave his name at the main entrance and was saluted as smartly as if he'd been Ernst Wollweber himself. Inside, a rather lovely young lady in uniform met him before he could present himself at reception and distracted him all the way to the seventh floor with her cold, teasingly distant manner. He was met there, and on a doctrinally-sound red carpet, by Wolfgang Eder. Wolfgang was deputy head of Section IX of HVA - *Hauptverwaltung Aufklürung* - the Ministry's foreign intelligence department, which put him only two pay grades below Markus Wolfe, the *Stasi*'s spymaster. He was also vain and tremendously venal, a man who enjoyed every last shard of privilege that came with his job; which is why, several years earlier, Florian had made it his business to become the man's personal purveyor of western currency and luxury goods. He was the best sort of enemy – one who didn't allow profound ideological differences to spoil a conversation, a game of golf or an all-expenses-met evening at a brothel.

Today, Florian hadn't had time to organize anything less sordid than cash, which he carried in an envelope in his breast pocket. It was more than he'd disbursed on any off-the-books matter since becoming involved with the *Interbau* Project, and almost certainly enough to make their auditors squeak when the accounts were examined. What it could buy, however, was beyond any rational calculation of worth.

In a large but utilitarian office, Wolfgang waved Florian to a chair. As he sat, he removed the envelope and pushed it across the desk without making any attempt to tie a ribbon around the gesture. Equally baldly, the other man opened it, made a brief assessment of the contents and disappeared it into a drawer. With dance-like coordination, the door opened as the drawer closed, and a male *Stasi* officer entered with a tea-tray.

When he'd poured and gone, Florian sipped his tea (which was excellent, and almost certainly British), while Wolfgang watched him, an amiable half-smile on his rough, former stevedore's face. It seemed to be his only expression, one he doubtless deployed at his wife, his dogs, severely beaten guests of the Ministry and honoured visitors alike - a deliberate tool to give him time to think at his own pace.

'Who needs to disappear?' The thick Balt accent made a brutal question even more ominous. Florian put down his teacup and shook his head.

'It isn't that. I want to ask a question.'

'Just the one?'

'That depends on your first answer.'

'Ha! I like a conundrum. Go on.'

Now that he had come to it, Florian paused. Putting the question as directly as possible risked a nod and an amiable fare-thee-well, and he desperately needed information. On the other hand, skipping around the houses might bore Wolfgang, and when he was bored he became playful – which meant that whatever answer he gave might be honest, misleading or somewhere on a scale between. It was also a risky question, for both of them. Florian had no pull on this side of the Line other than that which his money bought, while Wolfgang might very reasonably baulk at answering something that could put him against a wall – or at least in a sentry box on the border - if discovered.

Make it a conversation, then. Florian cleared his throat. 'I've been wondering what level of interest Section IX has in the Hansaviertel project.'

'The *Interbau*? We wish it the greatest possible success, obviously.'

'No, really.'

'We've turned hundreds of your workmen, and ordered them to piss copiously into the cement mixers.'

'Wolfgang ...'

'And to use their fingers to inscribe 'Willy Brandt loves it up the arse' on all prominent drying surfaces.'

Obviously, Wolfgang had defaulted straight to *playful*, but that was better than *thanks for the cash, now fuck off*. It meant that he didn't feel threatened by the question, which in a way half-answered it.

'Let me ask then – are you investigating or following anyone who works on the Project. I'm not asking for names ...'

'Which I don't have. No, as far as I know, we haven't taken an interest *per se*.' Wolfgang leaned forward in his chair. 'That doesn't mean, of course, that someone who works on your thing isn't being used or watched by us for some other matter. Nor that there aren't one or more of *our* people who just happened to occupy positions there. We encourage our irregular employees to spread themselves around.'

'Understood.' Florian pursed his lips and thought about what he might or could ask next. As a conscious act of policy, the DDR was notoriously harder on German war criminality than the Federal Republic (mainly for the opportunities to embarrass that it afforded). To mention the present matter in too much detail might therefore create the very interest he wished to avoid. What was made of what he said next would depend upon how Wolfgang valued a professional coup over the occasional but very lucrative bribe he received from his *wessie* friend.

'Let me put a hypothetical situation. If someone employed by Section IX were to mention that he'd received information about a war record, would you regard that as sufficiently useful to … publicize it?'

Wolfgang rubbed his eyes with a fist. 'Oh, God, not the Nazis again? I wouldn't, personally. But the Section would regard itself as duty bound to pass what it had on to Section III, to see what propaganda value they could milk from it. You said *received* - you're implying that the person from whom this information came would be non-intelligence? What, a concerned citizen?'

'Possibly.'

'If they had information about someone in West Berlin or the Bundesrepublik they'd probably be *wessie* also. Why would they come to us?'

'They probably wouldn't. I'm trying to cover all possibilities.'

'What did this bastard do during the war to make you shit yourself?'

'I don't know yet. That's part of my problem.'

'Ah.' The amiable smile was back in place once more, but Florian didn't resent it. Wolfgang had lived on a razor's edge during the entire life of the Reich, a communist docker who'd risked his neck daily in the Kiel yards, working to rule as a rule, stirring the maximum industrial strife that wouldn't earn a visit to the guillotine, re-routing vital supplies to where they'd be least needed and altering consignment dates so that half the *Kreigsmarine*'s short-life sea-rations had spoiled before vessels cleared Brunsbüttel. Having survived all of that, he was entitled to bask a little in the discomforts of old Nazis.

Florian was attempting to phrase the most craven part of the conversation in his head when the other man unexpectedly earned his bribe. He sighed, slid a notepad in front of him and picked up a pen.

'Give me a name and I'll check whether any of our people are aware of it.'

'I have three - Gregor Schultz, Franz Mattner, Otto Henry Fischer.'

'A gang of righteous souls? How very inconvenient.'

'Only the first two are definitely connected. I'm not sure about the other one.'

'Well, I'll ask around. Don't hope for much.'

'I'm *hoping* for nothing at all.'

'Ah, yes.'

Their business was done, and Florian keenly wanted to be on the other side of the Line once more; but shoulder-rubbing was more an instinct than a skill, and he couldn't leave it at that.

'How are Hanna and the children?'

Wolfgang's wife, a Jewess who's dropped an 'h' from her name and put all her trust in her natural blonde hair, had been as lucky as her husband in remaining above ground. Florian hadn't met her, but the photograph was impressive. Unfortunately, their two boys took very much after their father, which was to say that neither would ever find his way on to a Greek urn.

'All well, thank you. She appreciated those flowers you sent last year.'

The lady's brush with cancer the previous summer had offered an opportunity for Florian to display his compassion side, and he'd leapt upon it. He treasured any inexpensive gesture that looked good however a diagnosis turned out.

'It was my pleasure, though not as much as to hear of her recovery.'

Wolfgang held his eye for a moment, and it was very possible that he was being entirely seen through. A man didn't rise to the seventh floor in this building on the strength of an open, trusting nature, but Florian didn't mind being caught out in his insincerities. It helped to keep both men clear-eyed about what they wanted from their association.

'That's very kind. I'll pass on your good wishes. Now, I have another meeting ...'

The same blonde lady escorted Florian back to the main entrance, where Wolfgang had considerately provided an unmarked Ministry car. It tore through Freidrichshain and Mitte and dropped him just south of the Charité, as if he were a virulent *wessie* virus being flushed at the safest point. From there he walked back to his Hansaviertel site office, seeing nothing around him as he tried to gauge how good or bad his visit across the Line had been. He was relieved by what Wolfgang had told him, and pleased that the man had offered to look further; what he couldn't decide was whether putting an arm around *Stasi*'s shoulder and pointing directly at his prize pig had been a shrewd gamble or a telling symptom of anxiety-fuelled derangement.

The day was only just into its stride when it put itself forward as Fischer's worst of the year so far, notwithstanding several other recent, strong competitors. To be fair, he hadn't expected much of it, having tasked himself that morning with the first of several unpleasant priorities. Though he'd been the local SPD Housing and Buildings Secretary for little more than a week, he had already accumulated a small pile of correspondence from local citizens (to add to a similar pile that the previous Secretary had thought best to leave unopened), and had determined to make a start on dealing with them.

His great work had hardly commenced when Renate's scream wafted up from the shop and flushed waiting-lists, robber-landlords, inconsiderate neighbours, parlous roofs, inadequate drainage and rising damp from mind. He was out of his chair, through the door and halfway downstairs before the thought occurred that his pistol and its ammunition now occupied different storeys. The best substitute to hand as he charged through the repair room was a clock pivot-locator steel; he snatched at it and pushed it through the bead curtains as threateningly as its tiny dimensions allowed.

She was alone in the shop, gripping the counter with both hands, sobbing heartily. He dropped the steel onto the carpet before she got a glimpse either of it or his murder-face, quashed the unworthy thought that this might turn out to be worse than a robbery and placed his hand gently upon her arm.

Asking what it was that had so upset her was breath wasted, so he waited quietly until her chest stopped heaving and then gave her his handkerchief. She took and filled it while he went to lock the front door.

'It's … Jonas.'

Of course it is. 'What has he done?'

'He hasn't …' She sobbed once more and buried her face in the moist handkerchief. This was by far the most emotion she had ever displayed to her employer, and he was hard-pressed to know how to react. If he hugged her with fatherly tenderness she might scream again; if he was brisk and matter-of-fact she might think him a brute; if he did what came most naturally and stood, haplessly immobile, she might pick up the locator steel and stab him with it. Reading Renate was like parsing a stone – it was possible, but one was more likely than not to miss something.

Eventually, her lower lip stopped trembling and she shook her head.

'I can't marry him.'

Every instinct urged Fischer's mouth to stand down, but his nominal role as her stand-in father demanded that he offer the line.

'Why not?'

'I don't love him. He's a good man, but I don't.'

Fischer was perfectly aware of Kleiber's manifold wanting parts, and in any case, trying to persuade her that she *should* love him was a mountain that no sensible person would attempt. He waited for further information.

'I …. love someone else.'

'Ah. Do I know the young man?'

'It isn't a young man.'

'Well, whatever his age …'

'I mean, it isn't a man.'

'Oh.'

Oh said it perfectly. He had been uncomfortable with wandering onto the unfamiliar ground of young love, but this was far out on the steppe, with nothing on the horizon to provide a bearing. His store of advice on heterosexual *weltschmerz* was pitifully lacking; what he could or should say to the matter of sapphic love in an unforgiving age wouldn't have crowded a pinhead.

She put her hand on his and squeezed hard. 'I didn't mean to lead him on. I thought I *could* love him, if I tried – God knows, it would be easier, if I did. But I love Lena, and ...'

'Not ... *Lena Gaebert*?'

Every workday, their lunch was brought from *Café Vier Jahreszeiten* by a sweet-faced, rather squat little girl, who always lingered a while to speak quietly and share a giggle with Renate. Fischer had assumed that they'd been schoolmates, or girlfriends in the entirely innocent sense – which probably said a great deal about his emotional antenna.

She nodded, and the movement deposited a tear onto the glass surface of the counter. 'For a long time we pretended we weren't ... but she stays at my house about three nights each week now. Jonas thinks it's funny – he teases us about it, that we're like a married couple. I've wanted to say something to him, but how can I? What would he do? What would he *tell* people?'

A suitor who had been hurt badly enough could do real damage. Almost certainly, Renate – and Lena, too – would need to move away from their *heimat* and never return. During the Republic it might have been possible for them to make a life together openly - but only in the city, and on matters of unconventional sexuality Lichterfelde wasn't, and never had been, Berlin. They would be lucky not to be spat upon in the street, if the word went out spitefully enough.

'He wouldn't, though. Jonas isn't the cruel sort.' It was a rash diagnosis, but unless Fischer had entirely misread the lad he was more likely to sink into a self-hating torpor than climb onto a roof to broadcast his humiliation.

She looked at him with half-filled eyes. 'I'm going to have to tell him the truth, aren't I?'

'Your wedding's in eight days. It would be twisting the knife to leave it any longer.'

'Yes, of course.' She straightened and reapplied the handkerchief briskly. 'I'll do it now.'

Fischer's stomach leapt slightly. He hadn't wanted to give her quite so much, or such sudden, moral strength. She was about to perform a form of surgery, and it required finesse if it wasn't to kill the patient.

'What will you say to him?'

'That ... he's a good man, a *very* good man, but that we couldn't be happy together. And he'll ask why, and that's when I'll tell him the truth, all of it.'

She put on her coat and checked what ravages had been done to her mascara, and Fischer held his tongue. In fact, he was holding his breath, as he had often done after seeing artillery flashes in a dark distance – an unthinking reflex, it had never managed to limit the incoming damage.

He found his voice as she reached the door, told her to take as long about it as necessary (as if her concerns for *Fischer's Time-pieces and Gramophones* might make her rush things), and put on his shop-jacket. The door had hardly met the jamb when it reopened and an old lady stepped in. She was met by a smile that needed to struggle greatly to seem welcoming.

'Good morning, Madam.'

She scowled up at him. 'The Council won't repair my toilet.'

Forty minutes later the door closed once more, and Fischer put down the pencil with which he had scribbled an epic tale of blockages not to be spoken of. He lifted the hand to his temple, trying to rub feeling back into it and loosen the knotted rope that had tightened around his head. He couldn't quite recall what promises he had made to the lady, but as the unpleasant detail was revisited (in ever more, and more horrifying, detail), his initially sincere desire to help had soured into an urgent need to get her off the premises. Under pressure, he feared he may have exaggerated his power to move officialdom into moving compacted fecal matter.

The rope had begun to slacken slightly when the telephone rang. He picked up the receiver and had half-recited the name of his business when the line went dead. He was relieved; a wrong number was the best that he could have hoped for in his present mood (other, perhaps, than a brief, recorded message from Karlshorst, telling him that his services to the cause of International Socialism were no longer required). His relief lasted the length of the carpet between two counters, and then the telephone rang once more.

This time he managed to give his business's full name and ask how he might be of service before the disengaged tone told him that he couldn't. He frowned at the bakelite lump in his hand as if it were conspiring to make this pig of a day worse, and then put it down beside its cradle.

At that moment, a customer, staggering through the door with a difficult repair, would have been as welcome as Christmas, but Fischer had to improvise distractions. He rearranged a few items in the display window, wiped the glass surface that Renate's tears had dimmed, rehearsed a few consoling phrases in his head for when she returned from her errand and gave a more little attention to the longer-term strategic decision as to which colour would replace the now-tired light grey with which he'd clad the walls four years earlier. None of this managed to lift his mood from its pelvic floor, so he decided to scrape the very latest of his pending unpleasant tasks from the slate. He replaced the telephone receiver and lifted it again, dialled the number for the pretty hotel on the banks of the river Moselle, gave the manager there the bad news and graciously accepted the loss of his deposit on a honeymoon-suite. This at least brought to mind the several torments he would now avoid – the father's wedding speech, the toasts, the probable loss of a valued assistant, his inevitable further conscription as a godfather and the likelihood of another poor little bastard being burdened with *Otto* – and he let their small mercies lift him a little. All things pass, he told himself, and when they do, who cares?

Assisted by this stoical observation the day was righting itself slowly, and Fischer was warming to the prospect of a coffee when Kleiber came in and sat in the chair that old ladies usually warmed while they waited for their mended clocks. He blew out his cheeks and made a study of the small prop-up advertisement for Hirsch watch-bands that sat at eye-level less than a metre from his nose. Given that his face at rest usually had a slightly morose cast, it was difficult to read the depth of his reaction to Renate's news, and Fischer didn't try too hard.

Eventually, the younger man released a long sigh.

'You'll have heard?'

'She told me just before she came to see you. Are you alright?'

Kleiber glanced up. 'What? Oh, yes, thank you. It was a bit of a shock.'

'Of course it was. Look, Jonas, take a little time to think about what she said ...'

'No, it's alright, Otto, really it is. If it had been another man, some successful handsome fellow, I'd probably have thrown myself onto the letterpress. But you can't argue against another woman – it isn't competition, or a statement about what's wrong with me, is it? It's just ...'

'Fate?'

'If Fate can make your balls ache, yeah.'

'You're taking it very well.'

Another sigh. 'I never really believed it, you know - that she found me good enough to marry? I worried that I might have pestered her into saying yes. When you look at husbands and wives, it's hard not think that a lot of women must have given in like that.'

'She thinks you're a good man, Jonas.'

'She told me that. I suppose she had to, given the beating she was handing to me.'

'You won't blame her too much …?'

Kleiber shrugged. 'She hasn't taken the easiest path, has she? Folk don't like that sort of thing, even if the pink triangle's gone out of fashion.'

Fischer was impressed by this unsuspected vein of phlegmatism in his young friend 'I'm making a coffee. We should talk. It's important not to do anything ...'

'What? Kill myself? Get Lena Gaebert drunk and try to seduce her? Stand on the *Zeitung*'s roof and shout out the news? I'm fine, Otto.

From now on, I'll keep my head down.' Kleiber stood and raised a hand. 'You're my witness: I hereby dedicate my remaining years to the noble profession of half-truths, distortions, gossip and slanderous inferences, and deny myself any pleasantly moist interludes.'

'You're twenty seven, Jonas. It's too early to sign off.'

'I'm perfectly resigned, believe me.'

With that, the spurned suitor picked up the Hirsch display card as it to test its tangibility, replaced it, nodded a farewell and departed the premises. Fischer was relieved that he'd done so before Renate returned (having, as he did, a horror of other people's awkward emotional moments), but the day pressed more heavily than ever. He told himself that the world's usage of innocents was no worse than that of its cynics, and as true as this was the pall refused to shift. He tried to raise the spirit of Seneca once more, and tell himself that nothing mattered one way or another in the long run; but that merely made everything else he had on his pending list seem equally pointless. His only respite that morning – though of course he couldn't know it - lay in his ignorance of something that was coming to light some two hundred kilometres south of Lichterfelde, where a man calling himself Linde was examining a black file of the Gehlen Organization, a body that would become the new Federal Intelligence Agency in less than a month's time.

He wasn't an employee of the Org but had several contacts there, men who mined the histories of others yet lived in fear of the damage that light would do to their own. They obliged him, not out of fear of what he might do or say, but because he was a comrade, a fellow traveller, a member of an unincorporated association devoted only to keeping a certain sort of past where it belonged. Like them he was methodical, a digger, a finder of lost or buried information; but whereas they took great pains to present an unimpeachable face to the world, he was comfortable with who he had once been, and if required to act upon the consequences of his discoveries needed only to know that the compensation would be adequate.

The file held only a single sheet of paper, headed by a name: *Otto Henry Fischer*. It summarized an extremely brief career with the Org, during which the gentleman (and an unnamed confederate) had out-thought and out-manoeuvred its two most senior officers and brought an active operation to a halt by subtly threatening to expose the degree to which former National Socialists – several of whom were actively being sought for so-called war crimes – had been offered gainful employment by General Gehlen. A proscription, underlined twice in red type, had been placed on file, permitting no further action against the subject.

Herr Linde returned the file to its nervous keeper (who had insisted that it not leave his presence), and, an hour later, sent a telegram from a Munich post-office. Its message was very brief, saying nothing that would be meaningful to anyone other than the addressee:

O.H.F. a definite problem. Linde.

Senn was tired and irritated, but he could hardly complain about his treatment. He had been offered a vein-clogging breakfast and several cups of almost drinkable coffee, and the *wachtsmeister* could hardly have been more respectful. He hadn't yet asked for an autograph or offered his daughter in marriage, but Senn didn't doubt that he'd tip up the price of a taxi home, if asked.

'I have to do this', he'd told Senn, grimacing like an arse-doctor pulling on a surgical glove. 'You were told to report to a police station within two weeks, and you didn't.'

'They never told me why, and I didn't ask. To be honest, I've had other stuff on my mind.'

The *wachtsmeister* pulled another face. 'Of course you have. It's shit, but there's a procedure. All men coming home from the East have to be interviewed. Those who raise a flag of some sort get sent to speak to the Suits; the rest just sign their statements and say goodbye.'

'Suits?'

'*Spooks*, as the Amis call them – General Gehlen's people. They worry that the Reds have turned you all into spies.'

Senn laughed at that. 'Yeah, that's why they kept me 'til now – because I was keen to come home and do their business for them.'

'I know – it's balls, isn't it? Sorry, mate.'

'No, it's your job. What can I tell you?'

The *wachtsmeister* referred to his sheet. 'Were you mistreated?' He looked up. 'Stupid question.'

'Put down that we ate and were beaten the same way as their politicals, and worked on similar details. That's true, actually. They mistreated *everyone*, without bias.'

'Politicals?'

'Ivans who didn't do the right sort of communism.'

'Oh. The *wachtsmeister* scribbled for a few moments. 'Number two: were you offered any inducements to become a communist?'

'Obviously, yes. German prisoners could volunteer for re-education. It came with a promise of double rations and no physical labour.'

'Did any of your comrades take this up?'

'Two of them. I can't recall their names, but they were removed smartly from among us before anyone could change their minds with a shank.'

'Right.' More scribbling, and then a longer pause. 'Why didn't *you* take up that offer?'

'For one thing, I don't think they'd have been persuaded by me. Also, I didn't care to be cacked by my own people. *And* ...'

'What?'

Senn had never spoken of it, and it took a few moments to find words that matched the feeling.

'We all knew we were fucked – that we'd never get home. But a man lets a kind lie sit on his shoulder, whispering that a possibility, however tiny, is worth holding on to and squeezing.' He looked up at the *wachtsmeister*. 'As it turned out, the lie was telling the truth.'

The other man shook his head. 'I was captured by the Canadians, at Caen. Me and the lads spent almost a year after the war in a British camp, making matches and broom handles. We moaned about it all the time – that it was against the Geneva Convention not to let us go home – but none of us went hungry, or got rifle-butted. You had it a bit worse.'

'Well, it's done now. And I've come home, to not-quite-a-hero's welcome.'

'It's fucking disgraceful, isn't it?' The *wachtsmeister* looked at his list once more and winced. 'I have to ask one more question, if that's alright?'

'Why not? We're having fun.'

'What … what do you think of democratic institutions, and the free-market economy?'

This time, Senn could hardly stop laughing. The *wachtsmeister* looked embarrassed, but eventually a smile worked its way to the surface.

'I suppose that if my answer's too earnest you'll assume I've been turned. So, I think it's all to fuck.'

'Ha! I can't write that.'

'You should – it's the truth. Whichever way we vote, the same sort of lying bastards get their knees beneath the table. However hard we work, some fat fucker gets fatter while the rest of us are always one piece of bad luck from the workhouse.'

'You think it's any better in Russia?'

'No. They put different labels on shit, but they still sell it as chocolate.'

'The … subject … expressed … considerable … reservations … about … political … and … economic … systems … generally.' The other man finished with a flourish, pushed the paper across to Senn and held out his pen. 'Just above where I've signed, please.'

Senn glanced briefly at what had been written, scrawled a signature, handed back the paper and then, surprised, clasped the hand that had been extended.

The policeman tossed his head over his shoulder, towards the door of the Interview Room. 'Next time, do what you're told.'

'Right.'

A minute later, Senn stepped out on to Augusta-Platz. It only just after dawn, and the pretty sound of birds returned from winter quarters was only slightly disturbed by traffic. He considered going back to his landlady's house to let her know of his release, but that would make him late for his shift (which was going to be enough of an ordeal already). He stopped at a coffee-hut on Neuchatellerstrasse instead, bought and drank two mugs of an industrial strength brew and went straight to the Gardens, where the head groundskeeper, a notoriously early arriver, acknowledged his presence with slightly raised eyebrows but said nothing.

He went into the workshop, to the bench he had been repairing the previous afternoon. It needed only the reattachment of its iron legs, but it took him a while to finish the job. He was distracted by thoughts of Walter Senn, and how safe he might be in that skin. The Authorities had managed to track him from Lübeck to Lichterfelde, and that surprised him unpleasantly. It meant that someone had been waiting for his identity card to register somewhere on the system, and they'd caught it quickly when it did. If they could do that, could they not also backtrack, to check which registration office had issued it? If they did, it wouldn't take them long to check memories also, and discover that no-one could recall his application.

But would they go to that much effort? His kindly *wachtsmeister* had done his best to raise no flags that the Suits might choose to notice, so it was more likely than not that the process had ended with his interview that morning. Unless someone from the real Walter Senn's past sprang out of the fog to point a finger, what other risk could there be?

He didn't know, was the short answer. A man's life was his own complex mess, whatever was done with it after his death. If someone had asked if Rudy Bandelin had any dark surprises waiting to ambush an unwary impersonator he couldn't have answered with any great conviction that they were safe or otherwise. No memory was complete; no history unmarked by stumbles or unwitting offences. He recalled half-conversations with Senn in which the man had expressed regret – but for what he either never knew fully or had forgotten since. What if he had done some mortal wrong that time couldn't ease?

The events of the previous night that unnerved him, he realized, but he couldn't entirely dismiss his anxiety. All the while he was planning revenge upon his sister's murderer, someone else might be looking for a chance to even scores with Walter Senn. He could never be sure that some sin wouldn't find him out, even if – particularly if – he knew nothing of it. Perhaps this was an inevitable transaction – a dead man's identity for peace of mind.

The bench, finally, got its legs back, and when one of the other groundsmen turned up they carried it outside together. The sun that had warmed the ground by now made a start on his mood also, dragging his head from police stations, men in suits and the hanging threat of historic grievances. His weariness helped, bringing an almost comfortable daze that blurred the morning and folded its hours pleasantly. He excused himself lunch (a full stomach would have coshed what remained of his consciousness) and volunteered for the menial task of path-sweeping, which kept him on his feet for most of the rest of the shift. Despite his body's heartfelt complaints he accepted an invitation to have a drink at a nearby bar 'on the way home' (which turned out to be a two-hour detour), and was almost comatose when he arrived at his lodgings. He managed to stay awake long enough to give his landlady an absolutely truthful account of the previous night's interrogation (her relief was obvious), but remembered nothing either of supper, the process by which he reached his bed, or, from there, a scaffolding high above Angarskaya Ulitsa, in the once-fair city of Stalingrad.

Walter Senn was laughing – but then, he almost always was. His abiding cheerfulness was a slap in the face to their Soviet guards, but only those who didn't know him took offence. When one of them told him to shut up he turned, gave Rudy Bandelin a slow, pantomime wink, and laid another brick on the uneven course he'd been half-working on for the past ninety minutes.

It was a cold day – Russia-cold - and the planking was icy. A single safety rail, mid-thigh height, was all that separated the platform from free air. Bandelin had great respect for that rail, and though he didn't glance at it often he could sense its presence every bit as much as a bat could a cave's wall. If Walter was similarly aware, he didn't show it. When he told a story, or cracked an appalling joke, he tended to use his body expressively to make his points, and twice already that morning he'd wandered so close to the rail that Bandelin's nerves had almost shredded.

He wondered why he felt quite *this* anxious, and then it came to him that he was only a wraith; that he had no power to effect the events of a day that had passed long ago. Soon, Walter would go backwards over that rail and fall thirty metres to the cobbles below (he'd do it silently, as if to make up at the last for all his gobbiness), and, as whenever a dreamer realises the dream, Bandelin had a sudden urge not to squander what little time remained. He coughed, interrupting an obscene and frankly unbelievable tale about a Danziger seamstress and what she did with her *muschi*.

'What is it that you regret, Walter?'

'Eh?'

'You told me that you had regrets - a few weeks ago, while we were playing cards.'

'I did? That you were fucking cheating, probably.'

'No, it wasn't that. You weren't specific, but I got the feeling that it was something about the war.'

'Yeah, not being born Swiss. Or Spanish. Or with a 'von' in my name.'

'Seriously ...'

But Walter couldn't be serious, not without surgery, and Bandelin felt his anxiety sharpen. It wouldn't be long now – perhaps a few moments – and then the man's history would be sealed by order of the angels, pending Judgement Day. A little hop backwards put him within a metre of the void; he crouched slightly, pursing his lips to assess the line of bricks he'd put in rough proximity to each other (technically, it was sabotage, but their guards were either too stupid or indifferent to notice), and then straightened.

'I don't think bricklaying's my thing.'

'I don't think *any* work's your thing.'

Walter grinned broadly. 'I didn't mind the *Danziger Werft* yard. If you were handy, you could thieve more in a day than they paid in a week. I almost got rich, that year.'

'There's a noose with your name on it, somewhere.'

The other man's face became almost serious. 'There might be. We forgive ourselves too easily. I ...' He pushed another brick on to wet mortar and tapped it down. For a moment, Bandelin thought he might say more, but one of the guards had heard enough chatter that he couldn't understand, and had put a finger to his lips. Both men knew better than to take this as a suggestion, and they set themselves to pretending to do the work they'd been assigned. The mortar was almost used up now, and Bandelin braced himself for another climb down and back up again with a fresh load. He turned to ask permission of the one guard who spoke a little German, but the man was staring, his mouth wide open, at where Walter wasn't anymore.

Poor idiot. Bandelin felt more badly about it now than he could recall at the time, and he wondered if it was both for the dead man and himself – a life gone, one assumed, and no profound memory shared other than this. He had never really known Walter Senn, and for all that he now *was* the man, he never would.

When he woke, he felt strangely empty. For most of his life he had been Rudolph Bandelin, and since soon after that tragic day in Stalingrad he had been Walter Senn. Looking back, he couldn't quite see either man any more, and it made him wonder if at some point during his long exile from the world he'd fallen into a dark space between the two.

Florian considered what he had, and what to do with it.

His first thought was that he could probably relax slightly with regard to Gregor Schultz and Franz Mattner. According to his information, neither Gehlen's people nor *Stasi* had prior history on either man. Their involvement with the incident on Holsteiner Ufer was explained in some detail in their letter to the Senator, and blackmailers tended not to give away too much about themselves. Also, if they had motives that didn't bear examination, they surely wouldn't have unburdened themselves to the most public face of the Project – at least, that's how Florian saw it. But of course, he couldn't be sure. If they were stupid it was very likely that they were capable of making stupid decisions, though the letter was fairly literate, respectful and hadn't hinted at any threat to move further on the matter. On his first and even tenth reading of it, he'd had an impression of decent men, unburdening itself to the proper authorities. He was almost convinced that he could leave it at pulling their noses, to remind them of where they shouldn't have pushed them.

A nose pulled, though, often goaded a reaction. It shouldn't, but it did. And *when* it did, a problem became harder to fix. The contents of the cellar on Holsteiner Ufer had been a nasty surprise, an unexpected gift from a different age, one that the *Interbau* Project was intended to sweep from memory. Then, he had acted swiftly - and, he'd thought, effectively; but Herr Mattner had cheated, pocketing his mouth-closing bonus then failing to honour the deal. That wasn't acceptable.

And then there was Herr Schultz. He had been an actual eye-witness to the historical event, innocent of the crime but daubed by it. Though Florian himself wasn't prone to second-hand guilt he understood that some people experienced it quite strongly, and felt they had to make some meaningless gesture to assuage it. Reason or self-interest seldom seemed to do their job in such cases, so while a pulled nose might sting briefly, he doubted that it would give the man any clear understanding of his situation.

And, finally, Otto Fischer. Both the Gehlen Org and *Stasi* had files with his name on them. Florian would know more about the former when he could speak at length with Linde, but Wolfgang's information was worrying. Between 1947 and 1950, Fischer had been a prisoner of KGB's predecessors MVD at Sachsenhausen, yet no charge, formal or otherwise, was stated anywhere. The Soviet system relished its deformed judicial processes, and a man who fell foul of them could expect to be hoisted high and publicly as an example. If Fischer had been buried without trace, there must have been a damnably good reason for it. According to Wolfgang's information, he'd been released within days of the Democratic Republic assuming control of all political prisoners on East German soil, picked up at Sachsenhausen's front gates by a senior *VolksPolizei* officer and disappeared over the Line without his feet touching the ground. If, for whatever reason, discretion had been necessary, it would have been easy to expunge the man without anyone other than his executioners ever knowing about it. Yet the system had ejected him instead, and as forcibly as a stomach would a rotten egg.

These days, he ran a pitifully modest clock-repairer's business in a starchy suburb of southern West Berlin, and Florian wasn't fooled for a second. A man who pulls himself out of a deep grave doesn't crawl into a new one - he runs, as fast and as far as his legs will carry him, to a place where he can't be found, much less touched. But Fischer was hovering, inviting a swatting, a few kilometres from where either *Stasi* or KGB could do the business without breaking into a sweat. What that meant wasn't clear, but the man was something other than he seemed.

According to his WASt medical record, he'd been *Fallschirmjäger* during the early part of the war, and a note appended to his discharge sheet indicated that he'd subsequently served with the War Reporters' Unit and then Luftwaffe Intelligence (East). The latter alone made MVD's forbearance inexplicable. During the war they had routinely executed captured German field intelligence staff, and one of them falling into their hands since the Surrender – wouldn't they just have assumed he'd become an Org man (like just about every other former Eastern Front intelligencer), drained him of what he knew and then ventilated the back of his head? It made no sense, unless …

Florian could think of only one reason for it – Fischer had been turned. It was why MVD hadn't killed him, why Stasi had released him and even chauffeured him to the Line, and why, even now, he lived and worked only a short bus-ride from men who could end him in a moment. They wouldn't, because he was one of them. He was *here* still, because he was one of them.

But that logic raised another question - why had Wolfgang offered even this much information? Surely he wouldn't point to one of his own people for no good reason? To have claimed that *Stasi* had nothing on Fischer would have been his easiest option - a bribe pocketed, a generous acquaintance told exactly what he wanted to hear, secrets kept where they belonged, and …

No. This was Wolfgang dropping as subtle a hint as he was capable of. The information he provided had drawn a line in early 1950, which was enough to say nothing other than that Herr Fischer was off limits. Florian had admitted why he was interested in the man, so either Wolfgang didn't care or he was actively attempting to embarrass the Project. If not the latter, why hadn't he reined in his man once he knew that he was doing?

Am I seeing too much in this? Florian retraced every stage of his thinking and couldn't spot a weakness. Unless the reason for Fischer's letter entirely escaped him, the man meant some sort of harm. He wasn't a well-meaning Party *schutz*, trying to head off damage; he wasn't an innocent messenger, bring bad news; this was a play of some sort, either for personal gain or at the behest of *Stasi*.

He had the telephone receiver to his ear before it could ring a second time. He listened while Linde gave him a concise summary of what he'd found during his trip to Bavaria and then hung up without even thanking the man. Being a courteous person he realised this immediately and regretted it, but the business was becoming too ugly to stand upon pleasantries. What he'd just heard seemed to confirm some of his assumptions and cloud others. Fischer was *something* bad, he could sense that - but what, exactly, was effectively hidden beneath several layers.

He had to meet the man, to learn more. That was fine – he'd asked for an interview, after all, to discuss the matter. It couldn't hurt to meet, provided that sensible precautions were taken beforehand. Whatever Wolfgang was hinting at with his half-revelations, this couldn't be allowed to get out of hand.

Florian picked up the receiver, dialled and waited.

'Linde.'

'I didn't thank you for your efforts.'

The other man laughed. 'You *always* thank me, and very generously.'

'You have what I have for Schultz and Mattner. As for Fischer, I need to understand what he knows, so I'll meet with him. When I've arranged a time and place I'll be in touch. Unless I decided otherwise, it would be better not to let things drag, afterwards.'

'I understand.'

'This is a *very* delicate matter, yes?'

'Of course. Nothing will appear to be what it is.'

Part Three

1

Jonas Kleiber had a good story in front of him, and couldn't raise the slightest enthusiasm for telling it. Camp Andrews had issued a press release the previous evening, no doubt at the same time as they informed the local police and the Senate, stating that one of their master specialists (a new rank in the US Army, introduced that year, the *speciality* in this case being left to the reader's imagination) had confessed to raping eight girls in the Lichterfelde and Steglitz area over the previous three months. Naturally, the man was to be charged and prosecuted under the US Military Code rather than handed to the German Courts, but insofar as a depraved criminal was off the streets, this was unequivocally good news.

It couldn't be left at that, obviously. *Will he be punished as he deserves, or are German girls not regarded as real victims?* had all but written itself as the sub-heading, yet Kleiber couldn't focus upon what followed. His artistic vision was clouded by a recurring image of his darling Renate and Lena Gaebert clasped together, moistly naked (or nakedly moist, he couldn't decide which), writhing in mutual gratification. He found it at once unthinkable, heartbreaking and horribly arousing - a tableau that was going to live with him as long as he had a libido or hadn't a girlfriend, and no amount of ace reportage would dull or remove it.

He was still a little proud of the stoic face he'd presented to Otto Fischer, as wildly misleading as it had been. A tragically brave demeanour wasn't the worst way to bleach out the stain of cuckoldry – at least, not when folk stopped laughing about it (as they would, heartily, he feared), and the man-who-walks-alone-through-the-dark-streets persona was one that any journalist aspired to, if dishonestly. He just hoped he could keep it up in the face of almost-inevitable daily stumblings into his former fiancée.

I didn't want to get married. Surprisingly, that undoubted truth didn't help much. Love lost outweighed domesticity avoided, and by a fair margin - at least, it did for the moment (a long moment, he suspected). His cold apartment was going to feel colder from now on; his evenings an opportunity to pore pathetically over how and why he had never seen any of the signs. So she hadn't worn trouser, or smoked cheroots, or let her eyes linger on a passing shapely ankle – he should have sensed *something*.

He was staring at the almost-blank sheet in the typewriter in front of him, trying to parse human sexuality's little by-ways, when it finally occurred to him that he was alone – not just in the life's-journey sense, but physically. It was almost ten o-clock, and Herr Grabner was always – *always* – at his desk by eight am, flicking through the syndicated pieces that trickled in during the night hours. It was his way of avoiding breakfast and the calories that might deaden the effect of alcohol.

Kleiber picked up the telephone receiver but then paused. Yesterday had been Grabner's birthday, and the two drinks they had shared in the Schloss-Strasse bar had doubtless become eight or ten after the younger man made his excuses and went back to his cold, empty, Renate-less apartment. That quantity would have got his editor home in a warm haze, to where he could begin drinking seriously. It was entirely likely that he was lying nearly on his bed still, in as close to a state of auto-suspension as medical science could envisage. The receiver went back into its cradle, and the almost-blank sheet of paper received a little more half-attention.

Old Georg the compositor came up the stairs a few minutes later and knocked on the glass partition (he had been told many times to walk straight in, but preferred to respect the traditional delineations). He nodded and hawked his throat clear.

'You've a visitor, Jonas.'

For a moment Kleiber both feared and hoped it was Renate, but the gruffness of a cough from the floor below stamped upon both. It was a cough he'd heard before but couldn't quite place, which interested him a little and dragged his mind from its awful preoccupations. He stood and peered down into the Print-Room.

It was a moment before the name came back to join the face, and Kleiber suddenly, sincerely, wished for the presence of his proprietor. It was Berend Kahl, Branch Secretary of the local SPD Party, a man so over-aware of his stature that he had never so much as bestowed a patronising glance upon Kleiber during several previous visits to the offices of the *Süd-west Berliner Zeitung*. Kahl preferred to speak only to editors, if he had to speak to the Press at all.

'I've told him Herr Grabner's unavailable.'

'You didn't say why?'

Georg grinned. 'Not my place to.'

'Send him up.'

On the evidence of previous visits, Kahl had come either to urge that some non-story favourable to the SPD be bumped up disproportionately, or that an unfavourable one be buried deeper than it deserved, or that something to the disadvantage of the local CDU be blazoned across the *Zeitung*'s front page with an appropriate stock of exclamation marks. The last usually gave Herr Grabner particular grief. Lichterfelde was a conservative district, which, left to itself, would have sent a CDU man to the *Abgeordnetenhaus* every time. As the constituency included the more populous (and more *populi*) Steglitz, however, the latter's taste for almost-socialism usually prevailed. The *Zeitung* was read mostly by Lichterfelders, so pleasing Kahl meant displeasing many of the people whose pockets financed the editor's protracted suicide-by-bottle.

As the *Zeitung*'s five-percent shareholder, Kleiber had the right to make editorial decisions in the absence of Grabner, but he preferred not to (in case the ninety-five percent disagreed violently when he returned). Consequently, as the stairs to the Press Room creaked under Kahl's weight, his provisional *decision* was to promise the man whatever was necessary to get him off the premises while begging silent forgiveness from the Gods of Journalism. He stood up, opened the door for his guest and offered a little bow as the perspiring object entered.

'Good morning, Herr Kahl. How may the *Süd-west Berliner Zeitung* be of service?'

The great gentleman took off his hat and frowned. 'You are …?'

'Jonas Kleiber: head reporter, chief correspondent and occasional columnist.'

'It'll be your fault, then.'

'What will?'

'Your rag's attack on the *Interbau* project, two weeks ago. My attention was drawn to it only yesterday.'

The inference that the *Zeitung* wasn't worth reading was meant to wound, and it did. Kleiber drew himself up slightly. 'Attack? I – *we* – merely mentioned it in reference to a local property issue.'

'You said that folk didn't want it.'

'Want it *here*, Herr Kahl. We make no judgement on its value to Berlin.'

Kahl's face descended the red-scale a shade. 'It's inferred. You make it sound like a ...'

'An ugly, vainglorious waste of money? That certainly wasn't our intention.'

'Both President Brandt and *Oberbürgermeister* Suhr have endorsed the Project wholeheartedly, so any slur upon it reflects upon the Party itself! What were you thinking?'

Kleiber wasn't very practiced at conveying integrity, but he gave it his best. 'Herr Kahl, the business of a free Press isn't to grease the path of politicians, however exalted. We're the servants of the people.'

'Servants my arse! You're doing the CDU's dirty business for them! What the hell's the *Interbau* got to do with what's happening to a five-property commercial block on Curtius-Strasse, for God's sake?'

'It was a metaphor, for what's happening to Germany.'

'It's getting rebuilt is what's happening! Nostalgic for rubble, are you?'

Kleiber managed to find another centimetre, though only by letting both heels leave the ground.
'There are good and bad ways of progressing. Look at *Germania*.'

Kahl leaned back against the editor's desk and rubbed his forehead. When he spoke again his voice was lower, and palpably trembling. 'You're comparing a state-of-the-times residential development, designed by some of Europe's greatest architects, to Hitler's megalomaniacal plans for a new Rome?'

'Only the ...' Kleiber searched frantically for the word; '... *hubris* of it, when there's so many better things to spend the money on - like proper plumbing for all Berliners, or decent housing for workers, rather than the middle classes. I would have thought *you* of all people would have been for that.'

The last was a particularly telling thrust, and Kahl almost winced. As an SPD man he represented the workers or no-one (whatever his personal indifference to their several plights), and he was quite aware that the *Interbau* didn't fit neatly into any socialist rationale for the betterment of the masses. Fortunately, he and his colleagues had seen the problem coming and worked on it. He gave the younger man a pitying, slightly disappointed frown.

'*I* would have thought that *you'd* see the logic of the *Interbau*. Berlin's been treading water for years, economically, while the rest of western Germany booms. A flagship project attracts investment, makes a statement about our ambitions and confidence – and, if it makes Adenauer think twice about putting the Government in Bonn, it'll have a huge impact on what Federal money gets spent here. I don't care if Hansaviertel gets rebuilt for pharaohs and robber-barons; it's what comes after and because of it that matters.'

Kleiber didn't believe a word, but visions could hardly be refuted until they fell all to shit. It went against a journalist's grain but he couldn't help admiring Kahl - a good politician could sell a fork to a soup bowl, and the man was definitely one of them.

He gave him his most charming smile (the one that Otto Fischer saw through every time). 'Well, I doubt that anything we wrote is going to bring down the Project, eh?'

'That depends on how much further you intend to go with it.'

'Oh, not much.'

'How much is *much*?'

It was a good question. Fischer – who could find trouble like a field mouse did a hawk's beak - wouldn't have shown interest in something that wasn't worth a newspaperman's time. Kleiber could hardly reveal his source, however, or hint that he was waiting, hoping for something to surface that would topple reputations. Local politicians were invaluable sources of innuendo, slander and hurtful inference, and couldn't be alienated entirely. As always, a journalist had to balance the urge to fire the barn against the likelihood of rain afterwards.

'I doubt that there's anything more we can usefully say about the *Interbau*, Herr Kahl. Of course, I can't give any undertaking that would tie the hands of the Press.'

Kahl stared at him, sniffed, and picked up the hat he'd thrown down at least three times by now. 'I get on *very* well with Ferdinand

Grabner. We have a long relationship, built upon an understanding of how things are. I wouldn't like to see it spoil for want of a little mutual goodwill.'

'Herr Grabner often speaks of how much he values your acquaintance.'

'He does?'

'Certainly.' Kleiber waved a hand at his typewriter. 'I should mention that we're very much involved in covering the Camp Andrews story at the moment.'

'The rapes? I understand they've caught the man.'

'That's what they say. Of course, we'll never be able to judge whether it's the right man ...'

'Because American military justice isn't open to civilian scrutiny?'

'Not German civilians, that's for sure.'

Kahl nodded. This was far safer ground, however much a friend to the US Willy Brandt was or pretended to be. Most SPD members looked upon Americans as a necessary though polluting presence, their near-religious faith in capitalism an affront to the spirit of social democracy. Anything Kleiber could or might say on the matter of their military justice system would be quite acceptable to Berend Kahl.

'It's a shame that decent German girls can't walk the street safely in Lichterfelde.'

'It is, Herr Kahl, a very great shame. My former fiancée was saying as much only the other day. May I offer you a coffee?'

'No, I have a meeting in Schöneberg in less than an hour.' There was a short but meaning-laden pause. 'With the Strategy Committee.'

Kleiber forced his eyebrows to attention. 'Ah! I mustn't keep you, then.'

Old Georg was cleaning his plates downstairs, so Kahl had to make do without an honour guard to see him out. He descended the stairs slowly, pausing slightly at every creak, and at their foot raised his hat to an elderly lady who was waiting to go the other way. For a moment, Kleiber didn't recognize her, but as her face turned upward his heart almost stopped. It was Frau Benner, who cleaned for several respectable families in the district – and also for Ferdinand Grabner. She seemed distressed, and the thirty seconds it took her to reach the Press Room stretched for Kleiber like an over-familiar sermon.

She clutched the door, gathering breath, her other hand waving feebly as if to explain what the mouth couldn't. Eventually, it paused and opened, heralding a revelation.

'Oh, Jonas, it's Herr Grabner.'

Kleiber had been fearing this moment for some years now. It hardly needed an expert diagnosis to see what Grabner had been doing to himself since his young wife had fled their home with an even younger American soldier. Each evening he drank enough to topple three bartenders, and the fact that he could turn up at the office the following morning and work perfectly well spoke only to the distance his body had travelled on its downward path. On optimistic days, Kleiber hoped for some salutary episode that would scare the man into seeing the risks of liver failure or a heart attack, but the probable truth was that nothing would strike Grabner with enough force to incline him to pull the pistol out of his mouth, short of the bullet itself. Whatever Frau Benner was going to say, it wouldn't be any sort of revelation.

'What is it, Else?'

'He won't wake up. He's in his chair in front of the fire, but the grate's cold. And he isn't wearing any clothes, nothing at all!'

Fischer had known the old Hansaviertel district only vaguely, though he'd worked barely a kilometer to the east, in Wilhelmstrasse, during the war's final two years. It was a place that one passed through, rather than dawdled in - a colony of nice apartments and villas encompassed and bisected by a starfish-spread of fast roads, separated from the rest of central Berlin by the Tiergarten and a broad loop of the Spree. He'd heard that it was pleasant enough to live in, and not nearly interesting enough to seek out.

It looked very different, these days. Everything west and north of the Victory Column was a vast building site where elements of Berlin's 1957 International Bauhaus Exhibition – the *Interbau* – had begun to rise from their foundations. On Altonaerstrasse, a vast billboard carried an idealized representation of the finished product - a parkland seamlessly blending into the Tiergarten, from which broadly-spaced, low-level housing blocks, seemingly placed with no reference to each other, gave way gradually to American-style tower blocks, a clutch of sentinels overlooking the rail-lines and river beyond. It all looked marvellous, and doubtless the real thing would be a pale, ordinary shadow of the dream. He stood in from of the hoarding for quite a while, his eyes flitting between the image and the chaotic mess behind it, until he recalled that he wasn't alone – that someone was waiting for him to get on with the business. He resisted the urge to turn and hand-sign an apology, and pressed on instead towards Bachstrasse.

The directions he'd been given were precise, and he found the restaurant almost immediately. Clearly, it wasn't long for this world, occupying the ground – and only surviving – storey of a pre-war building just south of the Hansabrücke. It was probably a strong recommendation for the quality of its cuisine that the gentlemen planning this new world had left a little of the old to service their bellies until the last moment. The name over the door was *The Munich House*, yet despite the hint of staid Bavarian fare, Fischer was pleased that the front window was a large, canteen-like affair of the sort that had been considered of-the-moment (for about six months) towards the end of the Twenties. It made his task much easier, that the interior was going to be well-lit.

It was two minutes short of noon, but he could see that one table was occupied already by a single diner. He entered, gave his name to the major-domo (the man tried and failed to conceal his reaction to the face) and was led to his host, who leapt up as they approached.

Herr Geist was a handsome, well-groomed man, probably in his late-forties (though only the grey temples hinted at this). He beamed at the new arrival as if they were old acquaintances and held out his hand, shook Fischer's firmly but not competitively, waved him to a seat and started the festivities by pointing to his own, full glass of wine. As the major-domo retreated, his eyebrows formed a belated question mark.

'Forgive me - you're not an abstainer, Herr Fischer?'

'Not at all, thank you.'

They sat, and Geist spread himself slightly, one arm resting upon the back of the chair next to him. The smile remained where it was, with a slightly self-aware slant to it that invited Fischer to see the absurdity of two civilized, clubbable men being obliged to discuss something uncomfortable. It defused tensions and invited confidences, and the recipient had no doubt that he was meant to be flattered hugely by it.

Nothing was said until a second glass of wine and two menus were on the table. Fischer looked briefly at the day's offering and found nothing objectionable among the three choices per course.

'It all looks very nice.'

Geist hadn't glanced at his own menu. 'I know the kitchen very well. Would you trust me to order?'

'Of course.'

A finger brought the one-man-show back to the table. 'The *sauerne suppn* and then the veal, please, Ernst. For both of us.'

Ernst smiled and nodded as if the correct answer had been proffered (though neither dish was on the menu) and retreated. Geist turned to Fischer, his mouth making a little *moue* of apology.

'Shall we deal with the unpleasantness now?'

As if it were incidental to the business of filling our bellies. Thoroughly feeling his pulled strings by now, Fischer cleared his throat.

'I received an anonymous letter, just over a week ago. The correspondent noted that I was now the SPD's Buildings and Housing Secretary in Steglitz Borough, and might be the appropriate person to pass on certain information.'

'To whom?'

'Not specified, though the SPD reference suggests that Senator Schwedler, or even President Brandt, might be interested parties – in the sense of not wanting to know anything about it, ever,'

Geist smiled. 'That would probably be the precise sense, yes.'

'I contacted you because you appear to have a foot both in the Senator's office and the Hansaviertel Project, and could judge how much further this needs to go.'

'I'm glad you did. So, what is it that's alleged?'

'That someone in a senior position within the *Interbau* Project has a war record that would embarrass both Bonn and West Berlin, were it to become known.'

'I take it that the party isn't named?'

'No.'

'Or whether he's currently the subject of a charge officially laid in some tribunal?'

'Nor that.'

'Hm. It's not the most precise denouncement, is it?'

'It's discreet, certainly, which is why I assumed that it comes from a friend.'

'Discreet enough to be almost useless. Is there anything else?'

Fischer shifted in his seat. He needed to give the impression that he was an unwilling messenger (which wasn't difficult), but not to the point at which Geist stopped feeling the threat.

'There's a reference to an involvement in the killing of civilians. It isn't more specific, but to me that's as bad as it could possibly be, if it were to come out.'

'It's hard to say. If the accused was a member of an Einzatzkommando, it wouldn't be so much. If he commanded it – or, God forbid, had a hand in policy in the Occupied Territories - then that would be considerably *bad*.'

'As I say, it was put broadly. But ….'

'But what?'

'It depends on how shrewd our correspondent is. If this was about a mere foot-soldier, would anyone have taken the trouble to write about him? Also, it occurs to me that if the accused is now a senior figure in the Project, it's likely that his talents back then would have raised him further than a rifle-rack.'

'Mm.'

The soup arrived, and both men applied themselves to it. Fischer, worried that he'd lost the man, could hardly appreciate its excellence, but Geist ate as if it were the first food he'd taken that day. Occasionally his eyes wandered up from the bowl and fixed upon his guest for a few moments, but they hinted as much at what lay behind them as would a cat's.

Eventually, the silence became oppressive, at least to Fischer. He paused between mouthfuls. 'I can't recall ever trying this. I think the idea of milk soup didn't quite appeal.'

Geist laughed. 'I suppose it's like many things. Who would ever eat *blutwurst* a first time, if they considered what was in it?'

The ice cracked slightly, they discussed food and its loose relationship with army rations. Geist seemed to know a good deal about the latter, though his war service was implied without any detail coming close to the surface. To Fischer that was hardly surprising; most German men of a certain age had tried hard to excise six years of their lives from polite conversation, and he wasn't curious. He regarded it as his only blessing, that his own war service was written so starkly upon his face that very few people ever tried to go deeper.

The soup plates were removed, and the veal followed immediately. Geist tilted a hand apologetically over it.

'I'm afraid my schedule means that lunches are always hurried affairs. Please don't think that I allocate any more time to our architects when we dine. You'll have another glass, though?'

The refusal was halfway out when Fischer changed his mind and accepted. He couldn't yet read this man. He might be anxious about what he'd heard or supremely indifferent, and only more time spent in his company would offer a chance of knowing which. As they ate (something that Fischer could stretch out easily, as he detested veal), they spoke a little about the state of SPD politics and the prospects for the 1958 *Abgeordnetenhaus* elections, and though Geist spoke knowledgeably about both, Fischer had the sense that he cared equally whether the Party swept to absolute control of the House or plummeted into irrelevance. Whatever his job description, Herr Geist served only himself, apparently.

Lunch was almost over when the question was asked. Geist's face was open and the tone that of a man who'd just had a thought, but Fischer wasn't fooled by either.

'May I see the letter, Herr Fischer? I'd like a copy, if possible.'

'I destroyed it after reading it through. I have a shop assistant who's very good at finding things, and this wasn't something that needed to be found. My memory is quite acute, though.'

'Ah, that's a shame.' Geist managed not to look disappointed. 'Do you recall if there was a frank on the envelope?'

'No, it seems to have been hand-delivered. It was sitting behind the door one morning when I came downstairs to the shop. We don't get our post until around noon.'

'So, a local, perhaps?'

'Someone who lives in the Borough, certainly. Otherwise I doubt that he or she would have heard of my Party appointment.'

Geist nodded, moving his wine glass in small circles while pondering the smears on his plate. Fischer had given him enough to worry about and nothing he could address conveniently. If he was indifferent to the information there was no other stick that could be brought to bear; if he was concerned about it his only recourse was to find the accused and assess what damage his war record could do. Either way, all had been done that was possible to do.

Eventually, Geist looked up and smiled. 'And how are you finding local politics, Herr Fischer?'

'Call me Otto, please. Quite wretched, actually. I imagined I'd be spending less time in people's drains and more on redevelopment projects.'

The other man laughed, and for the first time it sounded entirely genuine. 'Then you must call me Florian. I imagine you're seen both as the foundation of these little grievances and their cure?'

'I'm the face of officialdom, for sure. Even if I'm not actually an elected official.'

'Ah, don't be too disheartened. People need someone to blame, otherwise the valve never gets released. I'm in precisely the same vise, though my tormentors are more - what, distinguished?'

Geist stood and dropped his napkin on the table. 'I have to rush away, but please finish your wine. The bill's taken care of, naturally. And thank you for handling this business delicately. I'll be in touch again soon.'

Fischer's wine glass was almost full, and there was nowhere he had to be urgently. As Geist departed he sat back and raised a hand towards the major-domo, who had just seated his second table of the day. He noticed and came over.

'This wine is wonderful. What is it, please?'

The man went back to his counter and not only brought the bottle for inexpert perusal but insisted that the gentleman finish the half-glass or so that it held still. For almost twenty minutes thereafter, Fischer sat quietly, letting another gentleman (apparently, one Monsieur Henri Emile of Chateau Guibeau, St Emilion) loosen the knot in his neck. For the first time in several weeks the clouds gathered on his horizon were partially occluded, and though he knew that it would last only as long as the wine in his glass he found himself not caring, a pleasantly unfamiliar feeling.

Outside on Bachstrasse, Florian Geist paused at the kerb's edge for a few moments and frowned. Very deliberately and slowly, he shook his head before turning to his left and walking briskly towards the lunar landscape that would one day be Hansaplatz. Standing almost immediately across the road from the restaurant, Walter Senn saw this clearly, though he was momentarily distracted by a man wishing to buy matches from the small tray he was holding. A third concern was the fellow who had arrived about ten minutes after he set up his little enterprise and had since made a show of reading his newspaper in a doorway to Senn's right-hand side. Fortunately, a man selling matches needs to scan terrain for potential customers, which had allowed him to keep a frequent eye on someone who was obviously more practiced at this than himself.

Geist's head-shake was noticed by this other observer, who folded his newspaper, tucked it under his arm, yawned and walked straight up to Senn, who had to keep both his face and nerves straight as he sold him a match-book. The fellow paid, pocketed it and walked off southwards at a strolling pace. Senn forced his feet to remain still until he disappeared around the corner of Cuxhavenerstrasse.

To the north, Geist was visible still, though he had crossed the road by now and was almost at the junction with Altonaerstrasse. Senn dropped his tray and sprinted, hoping not to be caught by a back-glance (at which he would have swerved across the road, trusting that the manoeuvre would both dispel suspicion and not put him under a truck). By the time he reached the junction Geist wasn't in sight, but the man reappeared magically as he emerged from the gloom of the railway overpass on the northwestern edge of the Hansaplatz site. A moment later he turned to his left, and entered the chaos.

Eight minutes later, Senn had tracked Geist to his site office, a large, low, prefabricated structure on a plot just off the southern spur of Claudius-Strasse. He made himself comfortable some two hundred metres away on a half-demolished low wall at the street's junction with Flensburgerstrasse, from where he could see anyone entering or exiting the building. The previous evening he had begged a week's leave from the Gardens to nurse his sick mother (sick indeed - she'd been in the ground since 1930), and as he departed his lodgings that morning he had paid his landlady for the following week and told her he might be away for a few days. Probably, he was being pessimistic; but the rucksack on his shoulder was stuffed with tins of cooked meats, and the two jackets he wore would keep the worst of a night's chill from seeping too deeply into his bones. There was much about his new life that struck him as the best he had yet known, but he had no intention of going back to it until this man led him to the one who had murdered his sister.

As Senn settled himself on the wall, Florian was in his office, pacing, waiting for his telephone to ring. When it did he snatched it from the cradle.

'Geist.'

'Linde. Why did you cancel it?'

'He told me nothing.'

'Perhaps that's what he knows.'

'Perhaps, but I need to be sure. He's playing games, and I don't like that.'

'What, then?'

'You've given me his past. Now, I want the present – who he speaks to, sees, associates with, and, though it's highly doubtful, fucks. The risk needs to be measured, and right now I can't see either end of it.'

'And when you know? What then?'

'Herr Fischer irritates me, but I feel bad that he's terribly mutilated. I hate to think of someone continuing to suffer unnecessarily.'

'I understand.'

3

'I'm afraid he's dead.'

The doctor, a young man, looked up with practiced regret. She nodded and said nothing, but the tears that had been fighting to breach the dam flooded out now. He stood, and placed a hand on her arm.

'Given his … condition, it was likely to happen.'

She sniffed. 'He was warned, but he wouldn't listen, poor man.'

The doctor looked down at the corpse. It was his second of the day already, and he hated this part of his job. Medical school wasn't yet so far in his past that he'd become inured to the grieving of those left behind (unlike his two senior partners, whose patient-manner was rather like that of veterinarians who removed bulls' reason for being bulls), and he struggled to leave it at the diagnosis. He bent down again, as if to demonstrate that the dead man was getting a proper, respectful degree of attention.

He checked the pulse once more, lividity, the eyes, and then lifted the head slightly to examine the neck. What he had missed before was immediately obvious now, and though it was another little tragedy to add to the rest he saw how it could be used to ease her mind slightly. He straightened and place his hand on her once more.

'He wouldn't have felt anything, I can promise you that.'

'How do you know?' There was an edge of exasperation to the voice, as if she was being patronized and knew it.

'His neck is broken. It must have happened as he fell. Look at the way his head was lying across the bricks.'

Brenda Schultz peered down. It was true – she could see now how Gregor's head had been resting at an unnatural angle to the body, as if he'd been asleep on two deep pillows. His face was entirely peaceful, more so than she'd seen it since before his first heart attack, so it wasn't difficult to believe (and she very much wanted to) that his passing had been easy. Her husband of sixty-one years, he was gone but looked almost … *right* where he was. He lay among his vegetables, on the little plot he had often called his favourite piece of earth, its rigorous layout and startling productivity the achievement of a mind that had come late but eagerly to horticulture. That was so like Gregor – whatever he did he threw himself into it, reading everything he could find, experimenting, painstakingly recording his successes, half-failures and disasters, insisting on keeping his wife apprised of every detail of the journey and refusing to be put off even when she rolled her eyes or feigned deafness – for which, now, she longed to beg his forgiveness.

She looked around his neat little kingdom. It deserved another pair of enthusiastic hands, but that would mean selling their home, and she was determined that she would be carried out of it, cold, on the day she went to join her husband. They had no children to inherit what Gregor had built, no friends sufficiently interested (or robust) to put in the work to keep it going. In a few months it would be a half-wilderness, its produce rotting where it had grown. She felt the prospect almost as strongly as the loss of her husband.

The doctor had waved over the ambulance men, and mindful of the widow's presence they made a show of reverence as they wrapped Gregor and placed him on their trolley. She watched and then followed to the front of the house as they put him in their vehicle. Her sister would arrive soon from Potsdam, and her niece from Hamburg within the next two days, and then the house would be filled with wailing, and memories stirred by long-interred photographs scattered over every surface, and gifts of food from neighbours, and all the other protocols that accompanied a life's passing. For now, though, it was silent, and she had the time and space to wonder how she would be, alone.

If only she could have kept an eye on him, perhaps there would have been a sign, some slight betraying movement or expression on his face which would have allowed her a few moments to ... she couldn't think what, but a possibility, lost, felt like more than what it probably was. It wouldn't have been feasible, she told herself; the garden was laid out to the windowless side of the house, with high fences to the front and rear. It wasn't overlooked by anyone, so whatever sign he might have given would be seen only by the sparrows. Her kitchen window had been open all that morning, so she doubted that he had made any noise when it happened. A little earlier, she'd heard low voices in conversation, but they could have been from one of the gardens beyond the fence; or perhaps it had been a radio, keeping another of the street's *hausfraus* entertained as she cooked. It didn't matter, but she wished she'd had some better sense of the moment he went away.

Now, of course, he would never tell her what it was that had been bothering him during the past weeks. She had seen it in his eyes several times each day, the almost-decision to say something, weighed and then dropped before it could find air. You didn't live with a man for six decades without being able to read every twitch, line and frown, and while a heart attack might have given good cause to make him thoughtful she didn't think that it had been about that. She knew his anxious face, but this had been something subtly different – as if he were preparing to tell her something, or ask her opinion about a matter he'd rather not broach at all. If it had been a secret, it would remain so, now and always.

She dabbed her eyes occasionally as she set out the best china for when her sister arrived. Like the treasured porcelain in most Berlin homes, some of it was chipped - a badge of honour rather than shame, to distinguish it from the modern stuff. When the table was laid she decided to bake something. It could hardly be ready in time, but the task would fill the space between now and then, and she was already mindful of how much *space* lay before her that would need to be managed.

Om the northern edge of Moabit, barely a kilometre from where Brenda Schultz contemplated her kitchen wall, Fritz Mattner was running. Half his mind was on the traffic he was trying to dodge without breaking pace, the other trying frantically to conceive something that would convince his wife yet not be quite the truth. He needed her to agree, to be fully ready to do what he proposed, because any time it took to argue the thing was time in which someone might be closing upon his family. His plan was simple, and desperate – to run until there was no possibility of further pursuit.

The man hadn't looked like anything, for bad or good. His face was the kind that wouldn't be recalled an hour after being peered at carefully, inviting no interest or second glance. He was of medium height and build, neither young nor old, not ugly or handsome, and dressed in a manner that wouldn't be out of place in an office or factory but probably couldn't have got him into a concert hall. Fritz hadn't even noticed the man until he began to speak.

'Herr Mattner?'

Fritz was standing on a stretch of the Westhafen's Pool 1, checking brickwork that his men had laid the day before. He looked up, expecting another question about his references from a troublesome clerk in the dock office. When he saw someone else, he relaxed a little and nodded.

The other man glanced around once and stepped closer.

'You were paid well, to be quiet. But you wrote to the Senator. He's a good man. The one he asked to deal with it, not so much. So this is how it is ...'

By the time he crossed Beusselstrasse's s-bahn bridge, Fritz was winded, but he didn't dare slow down. He didn't trust the warning to be just that, as terrible as it was. He couldn't conceive that it might happen, but to allow even the possibility would be insane. As if a threat to his family wouldn't be enough, the grey, nondescript man had given the full detail, the forensic description of what it was like when human beings burned to death. As he listened, Fritz had been so terrified that the thought of beating this man to a bloody pulp, of bringing a brick down upon his head until it wasn't a head any more, hadn't even occurred to him. He'd stood, paralyzed, as the creature walked away, and it was only after he'd disappeared entirely that movement, and panic, became possible. He had paused only long enough to vomit, and then started to run.

His brother Auguste would take them in. He had a spare bedroom in his neat little house in Kiel, and a good job working on the reconstruction of the city's docks. It wouldn't be for long; Fritz could find work there too, and probably both better paid and more regular than what was available in Berlin. He'd always envied Auguste his wanderer's spirit without ever feeling that he could be the same. He was too fond of home, but home was now a fire-trap, a furnace, and no matter what his wife said they had to go, today, before darkness came.

He had enough money for the train tickets and a telegram to warn Auguste that they were coming. With what food they could carry, it would be enough to get to Kiel. After that, he could worry about things as they came, though he doubted that any challenge would seem quite as tall or as wide as it might previously. He was too young to have gone to war, but he knew when he had been dragged into one.

Kleiber wondered if there were any emotions on the shitty end of the spectrum that he hadn't experienced in the past few days. The quasi-bereavement of a fled fiancée had only just dulled to a sharp, stabbing pain in his heart when the Tiger tank of an actual one had crashed through, leaving him feeling much as the losing party looked in such circumstances. He had long practiced a cool cynicism without ever really becoming adept at it, and he felt his former editor's loss more deeply than he had a half-known father.

Ferdinand Grabner had given him a chance, at a time when his only evident talent had been the maintenance and repair of dry-stone walls (preferably executed in a tattered uniform, on bleak moorland, in a pitilessly damp half-gale). It wasn't one which should have recommended him to a newspaper proprietor, but Grabner had seen something in him that others had missed. The man had nurtured a tiny, sickly faculty, given it an easy gradient and forgiven its occasional wild swerves into what Kleiber had fondly imagined to be 'courageous' journalism. And now, at the last, he had given him everything else, too.

The will, read the previous day, was quite straightforward. Kleiber inherited the other ninety-five percent of the *Zeitung*, Grabner's substantial home and contents and a rather obese bank account – everything, other than a thousand-mark bequest to Frau Benner (a recognition of her long and discreet service as bottle-clearer, vomit-wiper and launderer of piss-sodden bedsheets). He had become a man of substantial means, just in time to have no-one with whom to enjoy them.

Pathetically, he hoped that Renate would now respect him a little more than previously, and at least mildly regret her choice of soulmate. Hell, if she did no more than tell him she was *happy for him* (surely, the most brutally kindness that any ex-paramour could offer), he would take it gratefully, and put it in his little box of crushed hopes.

There are other women in the world, and some of them are almost as pretty, Otto would tell him, rolling his eyes at the tidal surge of pathos that Kleiber couldn't seem to quell. It was true, obviously, but that didn't help much at the moment. Perhaps he should use some of his new wealth to travel to places where memories of Renate could fade, helped on their way by a few passionate trysts with the sort of women who looked out for well-set men and knew how to gain their attention. A reputation as a heartless philanderer wouldn't be the worst memento to bring back to Lichterfelde.

But he told himself that he had a newspaper to run now, and couldn't indulge his would-be dissolute self. To his surprise, his view of the *Zeitung* and what it should or could cover had already begun to shift, and not subtly. The allure of a big, shocking story remained, obviously, but now his feelings were tempered by its potential impact upon the paper's reputation and profits. He didn't want to damage shareholder return, particularly when it returned to him alone.

It wouldn't allow it be quite the *same* as before, though. Grabner had been a small town editor, in a city suburb that still thought of itself as not-quite-suburban. There had been no great exposés, no revelations that had rocked the syndication wires; only the steady, reassuring drip of local half-news, the stuff that made Lichterfelders think that the world wasn't changing quite as much as they had feared. It was by no means a dishonourable record, but it offered Kleiber little material for the rousing encomium he'd be expected to deliver at the funeral. He'd be obliged instead to focus upon Grabner's stubborn courage in keeping going through years of … well, discouragement. When Hitler came to power he had dropped anything that might be considered remotely controversial, but as other local newspapers had disappeared the *Zeitung* had carried on, offering to its increasingly perturbed readership the considerable balm of births, deaths, marriages, centenaries, church fetes, matchstick constructions and whatever was booked that week at the Titania Palast. Only the onset of war and disappearance of newsprint for all but the Party's favoured organs had halted the presses, and even then, Grabner had continued to decorate the front window of the *Zeitung*'s offices each day with typed sheets carrying local news and official information about what Lichterfelders could, must or mustn't do. It all added up to little more than survival, but that wasn't an inconsiderable feat in mid-century Germany.

With Ferdinand Grabner's legacy suitably enshrined the *Zeitung* would go on, but with the recipe adjusted slightly. In Kleiber's opinion, the old man might have done more with his greatest asset, which was the willingness of his readership to have its prejudices coddled. The nation (well two-thirds of it) had emerged into an age in which powerful men could be prodded without the prodder finding himself in an *arbeitserziehungslager* or ditch, but the former proprietor's caution had outlived National Socialism and opportunities had been missed. It was time, with appropriate degrees of gravitas and circumspection, to piss in a few puddings.

'Whose puddings?'

Kleiber almost left his editor's chair. The stairs to the newsroom, having been reconstructed, gave damnably little warning of visitors. Even so, he was tempted to check Fischer's feet for ballet shoes.

'Did I say it?'

'That and a lot more, though I heard only the last clearly. Where's the rest of your staff?'

'Old Georg? I gave him the day off. He's very upset about Grabner's death - the *Zeitung* was only a month old when he joined. What can the last man standing do for you?'

'For once, nothing. I came to see how you are.'

'Off balance. It's been a strange few days. How's Renate?'

'Less moody than of late.'

'Is she wearing men's clothes yet?'

'Hush.'

'Sorry. That was humour in adversity, not spite. Otto?'

'What?'

'Do you think Josef Pfentzler poisoned Herr Grabner's wine?'

'No, Jonas, I don't.'

Kleiber sighed. 'I suppose not. It must be a curse, then.'

'Curse?'

'You haven't heard about Frau Opitz?'

'The shoe lady? No.'

'She fell off her stock-ladder yesterday. Her hip's broken. If I were you I wouldn't mend anything that requires a sharp tool, or electricity.'

Fischer had noticed that her shop had closed early when he went to get his lunch the previous day (Renate had banned café deliveries now that Lena was officially the other woman), but thought nothing of it. One block, five businesses, two of which were now thrown sideways while a third was provisionally sold to a Frankfurt store chain – he could see the attraction in the conspiracy theory, but old Pfentzler hardly had the strength to pull up his own trousers vigorously, so a campaign of murder and mutilation seemed less than likely.

'Otto?'

'*Yes*, Jonas?'

'Why were you interested in the *Interbau*?'

'I've told you, I wasn't.'

'I don't believe you. I had Berend Kahl in here the other day, playing the flaming fiddle about that piece I put in the *Zeitung* - at *your* request.'

'Did you tell him …?'

'The Press doesn't betray its sources, not unless legal papers are served.'

'A pity. I was hoping you'd said it was my fault, so he'd get the local Party to kick me out.'

'Aren't you enjoying the politico's life?'

'I have about a hundred complaints on my desk, of which I've answered nine. Everyone seems to think I have influence, or a toilet-unblocker.'

'Housing was a brave choice, for sure. You should have gone for Delinquency, or Sports Facilities. Anyway, the *Interbau*?'

For a few moments, Fischer regarded the newsroom's glass ceiling, trying to make out the morning light through eight years' worth of pigeon commentary. 'It was … a favour, for a friend. You needn't know the detail. It's finished now.'

'Was the friend Herr Senn?'

'Yes. Is Kahl going to make more of it?'

'I don't think so. I gave him the impression the story was dead - which it is, because I don't know anything.'

'Good.' Fischer glanced around. 'You're going to keep the *Zeitung* going after this?'

'Of course. The only thing that's beyond me is the accounts, but I can pay someone to do them.'

'You've always complained about how mundane local journalism can be.'

'Well, I might try to add some hot pepper – look for a *scoop* or two.'

'Scoop?'

'It's what Americans say for *schauffel* - when it's a noun, that is. The verb is what they do to ice-cream.'

'Eh?'

'Never mind – English is a foul language.'

'Will you hire anyone else?'

'Probably, but not a beginner like I was. I'll find someone who's been in local news for years - the sort who wears house shoes in the office, and actually enjoys interviewing old ladies about how much better it was, Back Then.'

'You've been thinking things through, Jonas.'

'I've had nothing else on my mind.'

'You sure you're alright?'

'I'm not going to do what Grabner did, if that's what you mean.'

'I didn't, but it's good to hear.'

Fischer went as quietly as he'd arrived, and Kleiber, warmed by his obvious concern, felt things a little more lightly than before. In fact, he had told a small lie to his friend - he hadn't considered hiring anyone until now, but knew of several old hands employed by the competition in southern Berlin, any one of whom might jump ship at the prospect of better pension terms. It was a strange, novel feeling, to be wearing a boss's skin, and debating whether to move into Grabner's house and sell his family home (or vice versa), and to have a substantial financial cushion with which to fight off the wolves, and …

Suddenly, he realised that he wasn't missing Renate, and hadn't for at least ten minutes now. *That* was as pleasant a thought as the rest combined, and shined his morning considerably. He still fretted a little about whether he'd misjudged the depths of Herr Kahl's feelings regarding the *Zeitung*'s *Interbau* story, but Otto didn't seem to care one way or the other, and in any case it had been *his* prompting that had got the damn thing printed in the first place. Still, even fretting had a place in his new world. A proprietor (he said it to himself, several times, enjoying the sound of it) had to consider the impact that any story made upon his local community – and advertisers.

Kleiber needn't have worried (though of course he couldn't know it). Berend Kahl was by nature someone who covered his back carefully against any cold wind that threatened. Immediately following his visit to the *Zeitung* he had returned home and telephoned the office of Senator Schwedler, both to keep the Party apprised of a potentially embarrassing development and advertise his own diligence. The Senator's secretary had been quite brusque, giving the impression that this was a matter some kilometres beneath the great man's concern, but had offered Kahl the number of his official liaison with the *Interbau* project, one Herr Geist.

In contrast, Geist had been charming, and quite dispelled Kahl's growing anxiety about whether a man could be *too* diligent. He hadn't heard of the newspaper in question (though he took its name and address), but seemed hugely amused by the story itself. He assured Kahl that he'd done the right thing to report the matter, and also that Lichterfelders need have no fear that what was happening in Hansaviertel might subsequently be visited upon their charming, quaint district. In fact, he said, once the International Bauhaus Exhibition had been held, admired and officially declared a success, he had no intention of ever again being associated with anything involving architects - a very troublesome, self-esteeming species who never showed any appreciation for the quiet, necessary efforts a man made on their behalf.

Having feared that he was going to feel bad about it, Fischer did precisely that. He and Senn had not discussed the matter of what came next, so having pushed the bait in front of Herr Geist he had no idea whether it had been taken, whether Senn had managed to follow him to his workplace or whether Geist had subsequently found, contacted and warned whoever of his many associates had killed Margret Bandelin eleven years earlier. As strategies went, this one had much of the utility of a hand grenade tossed into darkness.

They hadn't even arranged to meet or speak subsequently. Senn might be gone forever, in which case Fischer could reasonably assume that his debt to the man had been discharged in full. He *wouldn't* assume it though, because *gone* might equally mean avenged, fled or dead in an alleyway. With his help, something had been set in motion, but its trajectory was as predictable as one of General Dornberger's early rockets.

He continued to brood about his part in a potential crime while sinking gradually into his correspondence, an epic tapestry of waiting lists, vermin, disputed leaseholds, dry rot, wet rot and drains allegedly laid by the first Germanic tribes to reach these parts. For all of his plaintiffs he was the final recourse, the last stop on a journey of deflection and disappointment, during which their instinctive deference had quite fallen away. Most demanded that he do something about this or that; a few threatened legal action, the withholding of taxes or outright violence if satisfaction wasn't forthcoming; one elderly lady in Steglitz was swearing by her husband's memory and the heavens he presently inhabited that she would immolate herself publicly if her leaking roof wasn't fixed soon (presumably having found somewhere less prone to inundations before making the attempt). A hundred angry voices cried out to Otto Fischer for the redress that others either couldn't or didn't care to provide.

This wasn't any kind of spy's life. He'd feared betrayal, or treachery, or the swift, deadly consequences of discovery by Gehlen's people; but for none of these parlous dangers had he envisaged serving a dung-shoveller's apprenticeship. He almost wished for some exceptional event – a collapsed spy-ring or major diplomatic upheaval – that would necessitate a frantic call-up of KGB's learner-cadres and catapult him (over the heads of his irate correspondents) directly into the front-line. Even then, he suspected that Globnow would require of him some ancillary service in the pursuit of dying badly, to reassure Moscow that they were getting full value for their roubles.

He'd almost reached the foundations of his pile of letters from Steglitz-Lichterfelde's disaffected masses when Renate called him into the shop to recommend a version of *Rigoletto* to a customer. It wasn't a difficult task (they carried only one version, Serafin's) but he made the moment last despite the obvious indifference of a lady who was buying it as a gift for her husband. His erudite survey was accompanied by a rather less musical treat, courtesy of Renate and the song of new love that she had been humming for the past three days. He wasn't sure that this was an improvement on her former dourness (or, as it now seemed, her misdirected sexuality), but it raised the retail atmosphere slightly.

The *Rigoletto* lady had just departed, her purchase in its newly-designed *Fischer's Music* bag (he'd wanting to include something about it on the sign outside also, but the shop frontage wasn't wide enough for further additions) when it came to him again, more forcibly this time.

Globnow.

What the hell was bothering him about the man, other than the fact of who and what he was? Fischer had no sense that they'd met previously, there was nothing unconvincing either in his story or manner, and it was hardly that ample warning of his coming hadn't been given – in fact, John the Baptist couldn't have done the job more effectively than had General Sergei Aleksandrovich Zarubin. Yet for all that, there was something wrong about more than his mission, and Fischer's peripheral vision, distracted by his war on two fronts, wasn't up to making it out.

'Are you alright ... Otto?'

He must have been frowning, or mumbling. Renate looked concerned, though her own frown lines had faded considerably since she'd given Jonas Kleiber the bad news.

'A slight headache, that's all.'

'You don't look after yourself.'

He *looked after himself* perfectly well, but it was the right and duty of every woman to point out a man's failure to cope with life. He smiled, hoping that it looked like half-agreement.

'Perhaps I need a little fresh air.'

She overdid her solicitude by helping him on with his jacket, and told him not to hurry back. Feeling considerably frailer by now, he allowed himself to be led to the door and pushed gently out onto Curtius-Strasse. There, the twin irritations of Senn's revenge and Globnow's plans for Otto Fischer got into step and followed him on his staggered course towards Unter den Eichen and the Gardens.

He had only just reached Drakestrasse when an elderly man raised his hat politely.

'Good morning, Herr Fischer.'

Fischer didn't know him, but he smiled and returned the greeting. Two minutes later, a policeman called a similar greeting from across the street, again using his name. They might have met previously, but Fischer couldn't recall the face; still, it was hardly unpleasant to be recognized, and he waved a reply.

At the corner of Margaretenstrasse he was intercepted by a lady who placed herself directly in his path. She nodded respectfully and opened her purse.

'It's Herr Fischer, isn't it?'

He admitted his guilt, and accepted an envelope. She tapped it with a finger, to place an emphasis on the contents.

'I was coming to your shop. This is about my arrears of rent. I've told my landlord he'll be paid in full in eight weeks when my son sends money from America, but he wants the entire payment by this Friday. What can I do?'

Fischer assured her that he needed to read the letter in full and consult his files before giving an answer, but that he'd look at it as soon as possible. She nodded, slightly disappointed not to have immediate satisfaction, and was turning away when the obvious question came to him.

'How did you know me?'

She looked surprised for a moment, and then flushed. 'I was told you had a terrible face.'

'By whom, may I ask?'

She frowned and thought about it. 'I can't recall, but a few people mentioned you.'

He continued on his expedition to the Gardens, trying to decide whether he was blessed or cursed by his new fame. It was exactly what Globnow wanted him to do, so that when some manufactured evidence destroyed the reputation of their Borough's current Deputy a finger could be pointed directly at the people's local champion, the man who fought rats, noisome drains and authority with unflinching zeal.

So, who's your new man at the Abgeordnetenhaus?

It's Otto Fischer. You must know him - the One with the Terrible Face?

He didn't mind a reputation so much as what it was built upon, and what KGB would want him to do with it once he was settled at Schöneberg Town Hall. If he became *too* respected by his putative constituents they might try to push him early (which probably meant his life or freedom would be over the sooner); if not *enough*, he might spend years at the rear of the chamber, neither effecting much (for better or worse) nor drawing closer to a release date. Of course, nicotine poisoning would have a fair chance of getting him first - he'd seen photographs of Deputies' proceedings clouded by a self-inflicted miasma, the occasional bald head shining through the gloom, and he didn't doubt that …

Stop it. He tried to put the future from mind, at least for a few minutes. There was no way to see what was coming. He couldn't avoid the rails that Globnow and his people would put him upon, couldn't conceive a strategy to lift himself miraculously out of the latrine his life was becoming. Anticipating things was just applying salt to the wound.

He returned a passing stranger's nod on the south side of Unter den Eichen and crossed the road. The Gardens had yet to put on their spring colours, but he needed space to clear his head, and a light drizzle was thinning the ranks of Lichterfelders who might otherwise have joined him. He entered the main south gate, took the first path to his left-hand side and strolled around the Eichenteich, having only ducks for company.

He had made two complete circuits of the lake when he decided that the solitary gentleman feeding its residents wasn't really putting his heart into the task. He hadn't been there when Fischer arrived, but was in position on the bridge over the narrow waistline of the Lake's slumping figure-eight shape when he crossed it for the first time. The bag from which he was dispensing his largesse was too small for the job (unless he had a favourite duck and was ignoring the rest), and could hardly have held enough to keep him there for more than a few moments; yet on his second lap Fischer found him in the same spot, pulling bread from it one piece at a time, eking out his supply like a marooned mariner.

It's his lunch. Amid the broil of his other concerns, the single thought came like a flippant interloper, but it stayed. Wasn't the man hungry? Had he tasted it and changed his mind? Why was it taking him so long to throw it into the Eichenteich? Why the bridge, when it was a dry walk down to the shore at almost any point on the lake's circumference, where he could have got closer to the ducks?

The answer to the last question was the most obvious, and unwelcome. The Eichenteich's odd shape ensured that there was no one point from which it all could be seen at the same time; but someone on the bridge could see every route by which a stroller might chose to leave the area. The path that crossed it dog-legged at either side subsequently, but the bridge's elevation enabled a clear view of the treeless gaps both ways. Looking directly across the lake's southern stretch from it, both paths that led from the shore back to the Gardens' southern gate were visible, and there were few trees on that side to hinder observation. A man who'd followed someone here, and who wanted to continue the pursuit, couldn't be better placed to do it. As for whom that prey might be, Fischer had passed no-one else so far on his perambulation of the lake.

As ugly as the logic was, it explained every other thing that was wrong about the man. It *had* been his lunch in the bag, and its conversion to duck food was an improvisation. Why? Was he KGB, keeping an eye on a doubtful asset? A Gehlen man, waiting for a discreet opportunity to preserve democracy the messy way? A would-be constituent, summoning the courage to speak about his outside toilet and the chances of getting one indoors?

The last was improbable, but it made Fischer pause. Even a small chance that this might not be related to his infant career in espionage made a degree of circumspection necessary. At the least, it removed the heavy-shove-into-the-lake option.

He kept walking, giving himself time to consider alternatives. Challenging the man or striking up a conversation would achieve nothing – except, possibly, to end the pursuit, and he wasn't sure he wanted to do that. He'd *made* his pursuer, after all; there was no guarantee that he'd make his successor (and doubtless there would be one, if this was about his association with KGB). Running would merely advertise the fact that he'd done so, and in any case it was almost certain that the man, whatever his motives, knew already where his quarry lived and worked. The only other option was to continue, apparently obliviously, and hope that this wasn't an execution.

He continued, circling the lake's northern stretch, and, via a woodland path, pointed himself at the Gardens' principal north-south drive. His follower would be able to see him for a few moments as he crossed the bridge road at its northern dog-leg; but if his attention was elsewhere there was a good chance that Fischer could be on the drive before he was spotted. Even on quiet days, it had enough human traffic to deter an assault - in any case, the man would need to recover the lost ground between them, and blown lungs weren't the best tool in an assassin's box.

It took an effort not to glance back as he walked to the main gate, crossed Unter den Eichen and Begionienplatz and turned into Tulpenstrasse. The street was dangerously over-provided with tree cover, but he kept his pace steady all the way to Enzianstrasse, where he turned left and crossed the rail lines. At the corner of Moltkestrasse and Gardeschützweg stood a general foods 'store', modelled on the American self-service system (the owner was a keen trans-Atlanticist). Fischer entered, turned immediately to his right and stood behind a shelf rack topped by several display signs for tinned goods. A few moments later, his pursuer stepped into view, glanced casually through the window without breaking step and continued past the front door.

From his hiding place, Fischer got a good, close look at the man's face before it was gone. There was nothing to it that was memorable, but there hardly needed to be - he would recognize it in a moment, because there wouldn't be a moment when he wasn't looking for it. As he paid a young lady for a loaf and butter at her shiny new till he realised that his earlier mood had lifted. All his problems remained and had been joined by a new one, but at least he was aware of the latest, and might even have the opportunity to duck before its effluvia arrived. It was a pitifully weak sort of initiative, but more than he'd enjoyed for several weeks now.

It was only after he made his secretary cry that Florian sensed he was letting things get to him.

She was good at her work in all ways except keeping his diary up to date. Every appointment was noted, but usually on a pad she kept beside her typewriter. If she was busy it often happened that a transfer didn't take place, and Florian had to remember to ask whether there was anything that should be, but wasn't, on his personal schedule. He didn't mind this, usually. In fact, he hardly knew why it had bothered him this morning – and so much so that he had allowed it to show, and then asked her if she was happy in her job.

When the tears came he apologized, told her to take an early lunch and then audited his mood. One of his greatest talents, or characteristics, was to project a sense of calmness and competence that soothed the less composed temperaments of his colleagues and superiors. When things went wrong his breathing and pulse tended to slow, prompted by the nervous explosions around him, and people took this to be an admirable quality rather than the reflexive twitch that it was. Today, however, he feared that the illusion would crumble in the face of another little crisis. He felt rather like a submariner, standing under the conning hatch, at the moment he realizes that someone has forgotten to close it properly.

Obviously, his vexation was the fault of Otto Henry Fucking Fischer. Not dealing with him immediately was beginning to look like a weak decision, whatever the man's relationship with *Stasi*. An accident, after all, could very well be just that – even an intelligencer couldn't gaze down at a smear on the u-bahn tracks and diagnose something darker than bad luck. If, subsequently, Fischer had turned out to be blameless, Florian could have regretted his promptness at leisure – and, in fact, had he proceeded without first apprising Wolfgang Eder of his interest, *Stasi* wouldn't have had any reason to think the man's death suspicious. In all, the intelligent, cautious approach had been atrociously bad judgment.

Whatever Fischer knew, it would go to Heaven or Hell with him. An accomplice – if he had one – would need to break cover to keep the thing going, and then Linde could deal with him, too. After that, Florian could return to the simple business of herding cats while juggling plates, take his fat salary with a pure conscience and ascend to further glories once the International Bauhaus Exhibition had been delivered safely. Bonn beckoned, he told himself, and even the name of that fair little city acted as an anaesthetic upon the wound. A little more minor surgery was required, and what remained after that would hardly constitute a memory.

Feeling a little better, he dialled the number. No-one picked up at the other end, however, which meant that Linde was following his instructions, gathering information that was no longer necessary to the decision. It didn't matter; a postponement of a few hours wouldn't change things, and it would give him time to speak to the last of his known war-anxiety sufferers on the Project and try to pry out a little of what the man had done back then. If any further unpleasantness were to happen, he wanted to know precisely what was at stake.

He's interviewed four of them in the past three days (not counting Manfred, whose crimes were largely known to him). Two had been with the Einzatzgruppen; one in Ukraine, the other in Latvia. He was quite relaxed about both men - neither had ranked higher than hauptmann, and their leaders had been dealt with comprehensively in '47 (the western Allies had been equally keen to prosecute war criminals and then to close the book upon them). The other two were potentially more problematic. After much prompting, Heinz Pohl (a draughtsman in one of their architects' offices) had admitted to a senior role in the Reich Ministry of Food, helping to formulate the 'hunger plan' under Minister Herbert Backe. Christ alone knew how many millions of Soviet civilians and prisoners-of-war had died badly because of it, but the Ivans would be very keen to open up that old business, should it become known (not least because Backe himself had managed to hang himself before the Courts could do it). The second, Martin Feigl (a financial analyst with the Project's lead

Bank) had passed a largely blameless war until his unit reached the Baugnez crossroads on 17 December 1944 and helped to shoot dozens of GIs who had imagined they'd surrendered already. From Florian's perspective that hardly looked like any sort of crime, but the Americans thought – and continued to think - quite differently about it. If Martin's little *faux pas* came to light, the *Interbau* might be over before it opened officially.

The last man on his naughty list, Franz Appenzeller, was artistic director of the office that publicized the Project both within Germany and abroad. Florian had met him on numerous occasions – a hearty, urbane fellow, always the first with a good anecdote if conversation faltered at one of their interdepartmental lunches. According to Linde's brief initial research at WASt, Appenzeller had served in France and North Africa before being captured at Salerno. On the face of it, he'd not had much opportunity to sin, but a dropped comment during one of those lunches – about the fighting during Operation Citadel - had put him on the list. Linde's second sweep had then determined that the man was a member of the SS veterans' association HIAG, and a third located him to 3rd SS Panzer Division *Totenkopf*. This meant three things: firstly, that Appenzeller had never served in the Italian Campaign; secondly, that at some point he had probably worked in a concentration camp (as had most of the personnel who constituted *Totenkopf*, despite the claim by HIAG that they only took in former Waffen, and not Allgemeine,

SS); and thirdly, that he'd had reason – and the connections - to falsify a more innocent record at WASt.

Naturally, Florian wouldn't have given a cold fart for his past, had circumstances been otherwise. The camp business might or might not be bad news (depending on his responsibilities there), but his current membership of HIAG rang a whole peal of bells. Florian's boss, Senator Schwedler, was as sensitive to unfortunate associations as he was to tooth decay, and the SPD had unfortunate history with those unreconstructed Nazis. Two leading Party members, Fritz Erier and Helmut Schmidt, maintained close contact with the HIAG hierarchy, and though they tried to moderate the organization's worst revisionist excesses the linkage was both unfortunate and much too well-known. The Jews were all over it, and the Americans liked listening to the Jews (if only to get up German noses). Appenzeller's past might offer them a perfectly-timed opportunity to point a finger at modern Germany's failure to address the outstanding embarrassments of its past.

Given his disordered mood, Florian decided to deal with the matter immediately. He telephoned Appenzeller's number. The gentleman was slightly surprised to hear from him, but yes, he'd be delighted to have lunch, particularly at the Hungarian place, about which he'd heard much but never visited.

Barley ninety minutes later, Florian was back at his desk, his stomach sated but nerve-endings dancing even more strenuously than earlier. He hadn't quite been told to fuck himself, but there were many ways to impart the message without using that precise form of words. Appenzeller hadn't seemed remotely perturbed by the revelation of an anonymous letter, and actually laughed when Florian suggested that he might be the target of it. He reiterated his previous lie about having been taken prisoner at Salerno, and offered no more than a smirk when Florian confronted him with his HIAG membership. He suggested that a man who worked directly for Senator Schwedler should make better use of his time than to chase *Yekkel* slurs, and, speaking for himself, would be more than happy to defend his honourable war service, if called to do so.

Florian couldn't decide whether to be relieved or furious. Appenzeller had told him nothing, and he hated knowing nothing. On the other hand, cheery indifference was an almost refreshing contrast to the pitiful aspect of once-ruthless men trembling for their careers and reputations. He could tell himself that he had one less problem laid at his door; equally, he could worry that at least one known landmine wasn't precisely located on his field-map.

Linde's call should have been welcome, but he preferred his troubles to form an orderly line, not leap at him free-style. He listened to the detail of the day's surveillance, finding nothing in it to move him from his earlier decision, until Linde mentioned his visit to Lichterfelde's Botanical Gardens and their pretty lake.

A cracked bell rang in his head. He pulled open a desk drawer, found the piece of paper he'd put there two days earlier and uncharacteristically interrupted Linde in mid-flow.

'Fischer's address – give it to me again, would you?'

'Um ... Curtius-Strasse 21. He lives in an apartment above his shop.'

Florian stared down at another address, three doors from there – that of the *Süd-west Berliner Zeitung*, the rag that had made the ridiculous reference to the *Interbau* Project – and his excellent lunch almost returned. A fool or an optimist would regard it as a coincidence, but he was neither. The shock gave way quickly to a sense of clarity, even relief, as several potential options fell away to leave his earlier decision as the only sensible course.

'Linde, listen. The problem we discussed has to be resolved, preferably today.'

'That might be difficult. The problem's now indoors, and may remain there.'

'You'll know when's best, but as soon and as cleanly as possible. Call me when it's done.'

Walter Senn told himself that he needed a camera, but that would have required money and the skills to use one - and a darkroom also, to develop photographs he couldn't allow anyone else to see, ever. It was a good idea, doomed by a weight of reality.

For five days now he had followed Geist. What the man did in his office, or in his apartment in the pretty block in Charlottenburg (literally within walking distance of the Hansaviertel site), he couldn't say; but he doubted that he'd risk dealing with the problem in either. What Senn was watching for was a meeting – or meetings - where Geist and the other man weren't likely to be seen by anyone who knew them; where a delicate business could be broached in an appropriately discreet manner.

It had been a hard detail. On the first two nights Senn had slept on the streets, and discovered that his fourteen years as a prisoner of war hadn't quite inured him to that level of hardship. On the third evening he found an Inner Mission in southern Moabit, where he got supper, a bed, breakfast, and, most importantly, no questions. It was enough to sustain him until he got what he wanted – until he got far more than he wanted.

After five days he had four suspects and no way to cull the herd. Geist had held five meetings in restaurants and cafes, and at most of these, Senn's casual walk past had given him a sense that nothing inconsequential was being discussed. The fifth man, the one he'd dismissed out of hand, had eyes that were more usually to been seen peering out of a fish-tank, and Anna Felder's description would surely have included them. It had been sufficiently vague, however, to apply to any of the other four men he'd seen in Geist's company, so at dawn that morning he'd gone back to her apartment in Wedding and asked her to come with him to Hansaviertel, to point a finger. She had refused, too firmly for him to hope for a change of heart. Worse, she had told him that she was no longer sure that the man she'd seen that day at her office had been Margret's killer. Yes, it had looked very much like him, but perhaps her head had told her what the heart wanted to hear – that there might be a possibility of justice for her friend. It wasn't as though she had tried to commit his face to memory that long-gone, frantic morning on Danzig quayside; it had been at most a distracted glance in the middle of carnage, the data retained only because of what had followed. It couldn't be trusted, she told him; it wasn't any sort of evidence with which to condemn a man.

For a little while he'd been too angry to speak. She had put him in this place, told him of his sister's murder, and now she was washing her hands of the consequences. If she had said nothing about it his new life wouldn't have been born with a deformation, a badness that was eating out its entrails. Naturally, he would have wondered about Margret, hoping that one day some kind freak of fate might reunite them; but if not she would have been at a sort of rest, if only one of ignorance on his part. *This* was torture, however unintended.

He didn't believe her new uncertainty. She had been too definite about the encounter, however unwilling she'd been to speak of it. This was an attempt to undo what was happening, a clock set back in the hope that time would follow. Could she really think that he'd fall in with it?

She was nervous, as if he might try to force her to help him; but how could he do that? He might drag her to Hansaviertel, grab her ears and hold her head in the direction of a man he suspected, but he couldn't make her tell the truth even if he had the will and heart to hurt her (which he didn't, though realising that brought him as close to slapping her as he ever thought possible).

He managed to make small talk, enough to disguise his mood, and then left. His head was throbbing, trying and failing to find a next step, an alternative, not-quite-so hopeful plan. He could of course kill all four men (if they were so biddable as to allow it), and hope that one of them was indeed the murderer of his sister, but he doubted that his soul was up for that sort of punishment. He might approach each in turn, accuse him of the crime and look for some betraying twitch. *That* wasn't a bad idea, if he chose well. There was no way he could do that, though, and if his first, and more so his second, approaches were misdirected, word would surely circulate and the guilty man would be off like a startled hare, never to be rediscovered. His only other recourse was somehow get hold of a list of *Interbau* people who had attended the Seimens meeting that day and identify the man from it. *Somehow* was the spike in that shoe, though. He had no contacts in either organization (except Anna, who wouldn't, and probably couldn't, help) and no idea how he might bluff his way into the confidence of someone who had access to the information - even if he had the means to identify that party in the first place. Every possibility was surrounded by the high wall of his helplessness.

A wise man knew himself, and that was as much wisdom as he could claim. His own mother wouldn't have called him a thinker, and he would have laughed at anyone else who did. For all his adult life, it had been his hands that had earned him a living. He was – had been - a good carpenter, a reasonably proficient handyman, and, in uniform, an effective commander of an artillery unit. For most of that, his head had been required to solve simple problems - trajectories had been his only complex challenge, and his *mittelschule* mathematics had met it comfortably. Finding, snaring and executing a murderer required a different sort of mind, one that that could move sideways and back upon itself. He wanted to do this thing, but he couldn't see how it might be done.

He found himself sitting on a bench in Westhafen U-bahn station, and had no idea which route his legs had taken from Anna's apartment. He stood up and went to consult the transit map on a wall nearby. To his surprise, his subconscious mind had chosen well; he could go directly from here to Rathaus Steglitz station, which was at most ten minutes' walk from his lodgings. Suddenly, the thought of a bed and good food appealed monstrously. He was stumped, pulled up short, and needed the comfort of what passed for home.

Ask Otto. Why would he think that? Fischer hadn't tried to dissuade him, but it was obvious that he considered it a bad, mad idea. He'd slowed Senn down, pointed out the problems, tied him to a plan rather than a lunge. Why would he be the man to speak now?

Because he had been right. He owed Senn nothing more than the use of an unwanted name, yet he'd gone to considerable trouble to preserve an idiot from a particularly willful form of suicide. This impasse wasn't Fischer's fault – he'd conceived the best plan that a forlorn hope deserved, and if Senn was walking rather than being carried out of it he could claim no credit for himself. If anyone could see a next step, it was the man who had thought it all a bad idea in the first place.

On the u-bahn train he noticed his own odour and decided to go his lodgings and change into his working clothes. He arrived as his landlady was finishing her breakfast; she seemed pleased that he was back, but waved a hand in front of her face, laughed, and insisted that he take a bath. It being an unfamiliar, uncomfortable indulgence still he got it over with quickly, scouring himself in lukewarm water, drying and dressing within five minutes. In a further two he was out on the street again, his stomach warmed by half a cup of coffee and the remains of the hot bread roll she had thrust into his hand as he accelerated towards the front door. He wanted to be at Fischer's place before his pretty, sour-faced assistant arrived and killed any chance of a discussion, so the twenty minutes' walk he shaved at a trot, and was sweating freely as he turned into Curtius-Strasse. A church bell sounded a single chime, marking the half-hour – seven-thirty – and his near-collision with a man who did a swift little dance to his left, smiled, and carried on down the street.

Startled, Senn almost stopped; but then he noticed that *Fischer's Time-pieces and Gramophones'* front door was open slightly. He feared that the girl had beaten him to it, but when he stepped in he saw only Fischer, leaning with both hands against one of his counters. He was staring down at the surface, frowning, as if one of the items beneath the glass had stepped out of rank.

Senn cleared his throat, but Fischer didn't look up. One of his hands slipped slightly on the smooth surface, and the opposite leg twitched, pushing out to rebalance him. It was what drunkards did, when the ground moved as they pissed against a wall.

'Otto?'

Fischer toppled sideways, catching his head against the corner of the counter on his way. Senn was kneeling beside him in a moment, cradling his neck, trying to make something of the noises that came from his mouth. The damaged hand waved feebly, snatching at something that the eyes couldn't pin, but when it made contact with Senn's arm they focused briefly. He gasped and managed a single word before the light faded from them.

'Needle.'

Lichterfelde being a district with an unusually large proportion of elderly inhabitants, the jarring sound of an ambulance siren was too familiar to seize the attention of locals. Jonas Kleiber, who had any young man's sense of his own immortality, noticed it only because it rose to an irritating crescendo and then stopped suddenly. Even so, the phenomenon couldn't tempt him from his editor's chair and the congratulations he was drafting to mark the sixtieth wedding anniversary of Herr and Frau Robert Becker, both retired schoolteachers, of nearby Freiwaldauer Weg.

Having no interest in the Beckers' achievement beyond its potential to interest his duller readers, Kleiber wasn't squandering his own talents on the non-story. He had extracted a form of words with which the late Herr Grabner had reported similar, a cut-and-paste that required a few moments' concentration only. That done, he was reaching across his desk for the day's syndicated news-feed when a shriek almost stopped his heart.

Renate was at the foot of the newsroom's stairs. She was crying, and for an intensely-hopeful moment Kleiber dared to hope that her romantic compass had swung once more through one hundred and eighty degrees. She looked too upset, too wildly out-of-sorts, for this to be a scene played out from a cheap romance, however, and he braced himself for more bad news.

'What's wrong?'

He was almost down the stairs before she could answer. Her hand reached out to grasp his arm, but she thought better of it and took a grip on her hair instead.

'It's Ott ... it's Herr Fischer.'

'What is?'

'He's dead, Jonas!'

'He isn't!'

Kleiber was dimly aware that this wasn't a memorable riposte, but his head wouldn't work properly. *How* seemed no more sensible than *why*, so he said nothing more until further data emerged.

'He was on the floor when I got to the shop. That man Senn was trying to rouse him, but he couldn't. They've taken him away!'

'Who?'

'The medics, of course!'

That it had been an ambulance rather than the meat-wagon was a good sign, but Renate's pessimism was infectious.

'Is Senn still there?'

'He went with them.'

'Which hospital?'

'Rothenburgstrasse, I think.'

Being editor-proprietor now, Kleiber couldn't just make an excuse and leave the office, not until Georg the compositor arrived. Nor could he do anything for Renate, other than pat her arm and make vaguely comforting noises.

'You'd better close up the shop.'

She wiped her eyes. 'I've locked the door.'

'Go and see Lena, then. She'll take you home.'

She nodded, gave his arm a little squeeze, and left. Her touch, and his magnanimity (hell, his nobility), put a little iron into his heart, but until he could get to Rothenburgstrasse he was useless for any further work. Dulled yet agitated, he tried to make sense of events. What had it been? Surely not one of the mundane ailments that struck down men in middle-age? Fischer was a walking slap to the Reaper's face, a try-your-damnedest dare that nothing and no-one had yet managed to meet. Nothing in today's newsfeed hinted at the Black Death making a come-back, so what, short of a tank shell, could have laid him out?

Christ, I hope it wasn't Pfentzler.

It was mad – the man was half a corpse, a pensioner-in-waiting, yet the other businessmen and women on the block were dropping like leaves in October, and all the while his dream of being bought out handsomely was creeping closer. It *was* mad, but Kleiber had read more unrealistic stories in his beloved, dog-eared library of pulp fiction – master criminals were inventive, after all, and more than slightly unhinged by temptation, or passion, or some disfiguring life experience. A poisoner wouldn't need to be strong, or intimidating, and how hard would it have been to grab Frau Opitz's ankle and pull sharply as she balanced halfway up her stock-ladder?

But she would have recalled the assault, surely? And Herr Grabner had never paused in his drinking habit for long enough to allow anything nasty to be slipped into glass or bottle. And Otto Fischer … well, if an old man could have put one over on *him*, then the world was truly inverted, and nothing more could ever be a surprise. Herr Pfentzler was guilty, but only of the crime of irritating persistence.

The *cause* wasn't the worst of it. If Otto Fischer was dead, he'd lost his last friend. Both Herr Grabner and Renate were gone, fled selfishly, and his mother had been cold in her grave for eight years now. The lads who had shared his bachelor-night were as close as any loud, copper-livered idiots could be (which was to say, not very), while his record with the opposite sex - the wonderfully generous young ladies of Lancashire aside - wouldn't have earned him two Hail Marys at confession. Just as his professional life was turning a corner, everything else was falling off a cliff.

For almost two hours he watched the clock, willing Georg to the office on wings. Twice, he called the Steglitz Krankenhaus to ask after one of their admissions that morning, but was told that only spouses, parents and children could be given information over the telephone (he couldn't bring himself to claim to be Otto's son or father). Finally, at eleven o'clock, the door opened downstairs. Relieved, Kleiber reached for his jacket and almost ran to the stairs, but stopped dead when he saw the wrong face below. Herr Senn was filling the space where Georg should have been. His face was grim, too grim, for him to be bringing good news.

'Is he …?'

'Dead? Almost.'

Almost was almost good news, such had been Kleiber's Renate-fuelled expectations.

'*How* almost?'

'The doctor's given him a few things and wrapped him in blankets, but he says it's going to be a few hours before he knows, one way or the other.'

'*Blankets*?'

'Yeah, enough to drop a horse. His body temperature was way down.'

'What is it? His heart?'

'That, and a lot of other things.'

Kleiber was no expert on human physiology, but *a lot* sounded like worse luck than even Otto Fischer should have expected. 'How could that happen?'

'Easily, if you're given a dose of something deadly. The doctor thinks it's some sort of barbiturate.'

'How did it not kill him? I mean, yet?'

'He was treated quickly, and because he felt the needle go in and told me about it. And it went in the wrong place.'

As confused as he was, Kleiber had a sudden moment of certainty. 'His lucky shoulder?'

'Why do you say that?'

'Every time Otto almost gets it, his shoulder gets it instead. It's very strange,'

'It *was* his shoulder, the injured one. There's a lot of bad tissue there, and the circulation's poor apparently. The doctor thinks that most of the poison stayed in a patch of skin that's ...'

'Necrotic?'

'Yeah, I think so. Long enough for them to be able to do something about it, anyway.'

Kleiber shook his head. 'Poor Otto. Does he have any idea who did it?'

'*I* do. A few moments before I found Fischer I ran into someone I've seen before.'

'Seen? Where?'

'I'm still thinking about it. Perhaps when Otto went up to Hansaviertel.'

The Interbau. Kleiber shuddered. He'd had a feeling since Fischer first mentioned the Project. Why in the name of Holy Christ had he kicked *that* nest? And what had he been doing *up* there? He looked at Senn, whose hard face gave away nothing.

'Are you going to look for him?'

'No. There's no chance he'll leave a trail. We – and by that I mean you and me – are chasing someone else.'

Kleiber's stomach lurched, but he told himself to locate his balls. Someone had tried to kill his only friend (it sounded pathetic every time he said it to himself, but it was the truth), so this was one chore he couldn't take a step back to avoid. He frowned, trying to look the part, and nodded.

'Who?'

'A man named Geist, Florian Geist. I need you to put on your journalist's hat and find out what you can about him.'

'What's he done?'

'He *may* have something to do with this. In the meantime, be cautious. If anyone comes asking, Otto's dead, yes?'

Kleiber pulled a face. 'I'd worked that out for myself already. I'll tell Renate.'

For the first time in his adult life, Florian felt the weight of a moral conundrum. The pain was anaesthetized slightly by the revelation that triggered it, which was so unexpected that he had almost gawped at the man who told him. Even so, it took a great effort to seem the correct sort of shocked.

'We'd hoped that you might have heard from him. He was due to present the official International Bauhaus brochure to the Senator and Mayor yesterday afternoon. He didn't show up, and his secretary couldn't tell us where he was. I went to his house this morning, but he wasn't there. I spoke to his wife - she's in a terrible state, says he didn't come home last night. I think there's something else, but she wouldn't say. I'm fairly certain she hasn't called the police yet, and it isn't our place to do so. The Senator asked me to tell you, and - well, if you have any suggestions …?'

Smug, relaxed, cocksure Franz Appenzeller. Geist wouldn't have bet a counterfeit dollar on him being the party, yet he must have been primed like a detonator to have moved this quickly, even with the help of his friends in HIAG. Everything had to have been ready - the necessary papers, the route, a line of credit with some shipping company, a Paraguayan bank-account and the balls to drop everything, including family, without hesitation.

His wife knew, of course. It was why she hadn't called the police. No doubt he'd left a note explaining things, told her she'd be supported – perhaps made a promise he might actually try to keep, one day. Latin American women were attractive, though, and a man forced into a new life often feels liberated from the ties of the old. The chances were that Frau Appenzeller was going to endure a long and lonely vigil.

I wonder who he was, and what he did. It didn't matter - he was gone, and could no longer hurt the Project. Someone might want to throw shit still, but how could it stick? *Yes, we heard about Herr Appenzeller's war record only recently and attempted to confront him with it, but he'd fled already. Of course, we should never have considered hiring him, had we known in advance. Senator Schwedler unreservedly condemns the trend towards overlooking past crimes of this nature, and believes that if the Nation is to move on it must first confront its part.*

Blah, blah, blah. Florian would have something ready for Schwedler by lunchtime; in fact, he wondered if it might be better to put out a carefully edited version of everything, rather than a mere denial-by-admission - an *it-has-come-to-our attention* mea non-culpa that both preempted the shit-thrower and laundered the confessor. The Senator was very good at playing the noble penitent, and played carefully it might even boost his man-of-the-moment profile.

But the conundrum remained, and its name was Otto Fischer. Appenzeller's flight meant that an unfortunate, untimely accident was no longer necessary. Linde had been given his instructions almost twenty-four hours earlier, and he was usually quick to act, once poked. Still, it *might* be the case that Florian had time to intervene, and save a life.

Why would he, though? Fischer had tried to poke a stick through the spokes. Worse, he had done it teasingly, offering nothing but the vaguest threat of some discovery, as if he wasn't aware of what he was wielding. *Faux* innocence irritated Florian intensely, particularly when it had the effect of taking a hammer to his nerves. His hand, which had twitched in anticipation of dialling a familiar telephone number, stayed where it was.

He had a statement drafted in less than twenty minutes, one that would remove both Schwedler and the Project from any prospect of contamination. It both admitted and denied nothing, and expressed regret so broadly that the reader would struggle to see what it was that was being regretted. He read it through three times, found nothing worth changing, and began to be very pleased with himself.

He recognized the feeling, of course – it was release, a sense of several loads lifting simultaneously from his back. The business with the house on Holsteiner Ufer had been entirely unforeseeable;

nevertheless, his failure to smother it immediately had felt like failure. Fischer's little ploy had threatened the Project more grievously (not least because its edges had been indistinct), but its defeat had been easier than he might have hoped just a few hours earlier. With both expunged, he could return to the less complicate business of keeping the architects in line, the unions content, the suppliers moving and his political masters from daily fainting fits over non-crises. That prospect felt like the first day of his annual holidays.

For the next hour he cleared outstanding matters from his in-tray, but a small part of his mind kept returning to his collection of pet war criminals. Their several reactions to his approaches over the past few days had been instructive. Predictably, poor Manfred Kunze had almost fainted when confronted with yet another probe into his record (he would never again turn a corner without first pushing a mirror around it), while Appenzeller had been a study in pretended nonchalance. Between those poles, the others had presented various shades from the pallet of Germans' curiously frozen view of their collective past. Florian had been met with fear, guilt, defiance and self-justification, bonded to an underlying anxiety regarding the chances of exposure – and something else, faint but unmistakeable. He had taken care to play down the threat (once someone panicked it was almost impossible to control things), but with the exception of Appenzeller all had given off something of the scent of the cleverest pig in the slaughterhouse, the one that didn't squeal or struggle but waited hopelessly, knowing that whatever was coming couldn't be avoided or wished away.

It had been amusing yet pitiful, and gave Florian cause once more to be grateful that his own record was a matter of little concern. He wasn't blameless, certainly - what man who went through war ever could be entirely without regrets, or not wish that some things had gone differently? Even today, Eisenhower was probably kicking himself that he hadn't pushed harder and further into Germany while the Soviets were still regrouping on the Vistula, and how could Churchill look back upon his own strategic decisions without wishing he'd left more of them to his generals? It was what all men did, whether guilty or not of what some regarded as crimes. The trick was to lose little sleep over any of it.

Florian thought of Manfred Kunze and the chances of him ever again sleeping soundly, and would have laughed had the telephone not interrupted the vision. He picked it up and said nothing.

'Linde.'

'Ah. Good morning. Have you news for me?'

'None at all. The matter is dealt with, fully.'

'Thank you. Goodbye.'

The tiniest tug of remorse shrivelled and died before it could mark Florian's mood. He was in tremendous spirits, the best for as long as he could recall. It had been a while since he'd organized a lunch for all the personal assistants, and the freshly-wiped slate of his concerns seemed an ideal reason to put out a new invitation. His guests wouldn't know what he was celebrating, of course, but among them were a few reliable wits, and he didn't doubt that the occasion would be enjoyed by all. The food would be fine, the wine excellent, the Project's gossip frothed by loose conversation, and afterwards they would all congratulate themselves that Germany's most prestigious enterprise continued majestically upon its proper course. If the price of all that was an infrequent stab of something resembling guilt, Florian was willing to step forward and take up the burden.

He had made twelve calls, secured twelve enthusiastic promises for his lunch and had just replaced the receiver when his secretary brought papers for him to sign. He felt bad still for having made her cry the previous day (though she seemed to have put it from mind), so he opened his desk drawer, removed a box of Swiss chocolates he'd intended to present to Frau Schwedler and humbly begged the girl's pardon. For a moment he feared she'd leap upon him, but it passed. Flushed, she returned to her own office, but gave him the benefit of an arse-sway as she retreated. He was flattered, but told himself to be more careful in future. Messing with one's employees never ended well; in any case, he much preferred his conquests to be spoken for already. There was something about the estate of marriage that induced a hunger one simply didn't find in the most adventurous *fraulein*.

There wasn't a moment that Fischer could pin as the one in which he became *aware* once more. Rather, he seemed to rise through layers of pleasant, warm dissolution that gradually re-focused to something resembling a waking dream. And then he felt that he may have vomited.

He was aware that he should be worried about how and where he was, but had neither the will nor strength to make the effort. Shapes passed in front of him occasionally and he tried to be interested, but they moved too quickly for his mind to fix upon. After a while he closed his eyes, though the light level remained steady. He might have slept for a while, or perhaps a great while, after that.

His name intruded several times, but he ignored it. He recalled at least three periods during which he was uncomfortably (and increasingly coldly) damp, and each time the shapes returned to make him dry once more. He wanted to thank them, but shapes being shapes he wasn't sure they'd understand if he managed it.

'… hear me?'

Yes. Go away. He tried to turn over, but his body was missing some of the parts necessary to get the manoeuvre going. That was curious, and he had just begun to consider what it meant when a sharp object interrupted things.

'Ow!'

Indignantly, Fischer turned from the doctor (who was replacing the probe in his coat pocket) to the stern nurse.

'Can he do that?'

'Of course. Please keep still.'

'You're awake, Herr Fischer!' The doctor said it as if it were news to one or both of them.

'I am now, yes.'

'Good, good. Consciousness is very important. Please try to remain with us.'

The warm, comforting haze having entirely dispersed, Fischer saw no reason not to comply. He tried to move his head to survey the terrain, but a hammer-blow dissuaded him.

The doctor seemed pleased. 'Oh, don't do that. You're going to be off-balance for several hours yet, I expect.'

Through the pain, Fischer caught a glimpse of his first sensible question.

'Will I be … alright?'

'Yes, we expect so. You've been very lucky, on the whole. Most of what was injected didn't enter your bloodstream, so we had a leap-start. And you've had the benefit of our new technology.'

'What's that?'

'Well, it isn't really *new*, but we've only just installed it. Our tank respirator.'

'Was I breathing badly?'

'Almost not at all. We think you were given some sort of barbiturate that attacked your respiratory system. You needed help during the first dangerous hours.'

Lucky would have been to have avoided poisoning altogether, but Fischer grudgingly entertained a sense of relief. His memory of events was blurred still; he recalled his shadow coming into the shop, seemingly anxious, asking if they might speak in confidence. It had been unexpected, something not from the spy's manual, and

Fischer had been sufficiently disarmed by it to half-turn and indicate the repair room. It had been opportunity enough, he supposed, for the other man to do the business, though not enough for him to aim right.

When he recovered sufficiently he'd doubtless be mortified, ready to kick his own arse for allowing it to happen. At the moment he felt consoled to be breathing still, and said goodbye to another portion of whatever incalculable store of luck he'd carried into the world. He very nearly had been another unremarkable heart-attack, a man whose weakened state was all too visibly written across his body. If Senn hadn't arrived before he lost consciousness, who would have thought to look for a needle mark in already-torn skin?

He gave the doctor a weak smile, to acknowledge his great good fortune. Without needing to turn his head, he became aware that his was just one of many beds in a general ward. That, too, seemed like a good sign.

'When can I go home?'

'Not for a day or two yet. Typically, barbiturates are flushed out of the bloodstream within hours, but their effect upon organ tissue lasts longer. We want to make sure your heart and pancreas are safe before we kick you out. In the meantime, can we get anything for you?'

Fischer's heart had always been a robust device (the occasional attrition of teenage romance notwithstanding), but a chemical assault wasn't to be ignored or dismissed, and he felt no urge to challenge the diagnosis.

'A newspaper? Ice cream?'

The nurse's eyes rolled up. 'I can rob the children's ward.'

Two hours later, Fischer had made a new friend, Karl, a steelworker from the Ruhr who'd been visiting relatives in Berlin when one of his kidneys went on holiday. He was a large, cheerful man of equally large and cheerful (and only moderately obscene) conversation, who knew more about the city's football teams than Fischer had ever wanted to know. From Karl he'd received a banana, a tip for the following day's races at the Hoppegarten, surreptitious sight of a pack of pornographic playing cards and valuable advice on what was and wasn't edible on the meals-trolley. In return he could offer little that was tangible, but Karl had insisted on knowing what the fuck had happened to his face and hand, so recollections of exploding aircraft and extensive burns surgery had filled the time pleasantly.

At midday Senn came to see the patient. Fischer's thanks to him were heartfelt, but badly received.

'No, it's my fault. I dragged you into finding Margret's killer ...' he glanced around and lowered his voice; '... and this happens. I should have left you alone.'

Fischer couldn't speak of his unwanted career as a KGB pawn, so was unable to offer an alternative theory. In any case, he suspected Senn was correct. The Soviets wouldn't assassinate their own for no reason, and it was highly unlikely that Gehlen's people would do the same without first attempting to turn him, or at least squeeze out whatever he knew. Unless he'd repaired a time-piece or gramophone particularly badly, the odds were that someone had been attempting to protect their own.

'Who knows that I'm not dead?'

'As far as I know, Jonas Kleiber and your shop girl. Her girlfriend too, probably.'

'You heard about that?'

'Kleiber told me, though I didn't ask.'

'I think he's trying to control his humiliation by broadcasting it.'

'What's your name, mate?'

Senn turned to Karl, who was making no effort not to eavesdrop on their conversation. 'Walter.'

'I'm Karl. Me and Otto's bin' talking about stuff all morning - horrible, gory stuff, eh?'

'That's right, Karl.'

Senn nodded warily at Fischer's neighbour. Not being ill himself he felt none of the instinctive camaraderie that one patient had for another.

'What do *you* do, Walter?'

'I work at the Botanical Gardens, repairing things.'

'Ah, lovely. I'm in steel.'

'A magnate?'

'Ha! So, who's trying to cack Otto?'

Senn looked helplessly to Fischer, who seemed undisturbed by the security breach. He turned his head carefully towards his bed-neighbour.

'We don't know, Karl. Someone seems to have mistaken me for someone else.'

Karl nodded wisely. 'It happens. My brother Heini got his teeth pushed in by a couple of scumsacks for not paying his betting debts, only they weren't his - he just looked like the fellow they belonged to.'

'Did he go to the police?'

Fischer earned a look that would have crushed Bismarck. 'The Snouts? Nah. Me and my uncles beat out their lights, stripped 'em and chucked 'em in the canal. They didn't bother any of us after that.' Karl leaned dangerously out of his bed and dropped his voice to a stage-whisper. 'You should find this bastard and do the same. Or worse.'

'I'll think about it.'

Fischer was still trying to give an impression of thinking about it when two ward orderlies approached and took the big man to have his potassium levels measured. Senn waited until they were halfway out of the ward, glared provisionally at an old man in the neighbouring bed on the other side (he was deeply asleep) and turned back. 'Are you going to tell anyone else?'

'Probably not.'

'He has a point, though. About doing something.'

Fischer stared up at the ward's strip lighting. 'I wouldn't know how to find the man.'

'Not him – he's just the weapon. I think I know who arranged it, though.'

'Who?'

'You had lunch with the man Geist. I wasn't the only one watching. Another fellow was outside, acting like he had nowhere to be. When Geist came out of the restaurant he shook his head for some reason. It might just have been a thought, but the other one saw it and went away.'

'A coincidence?'

'I thought so – at least, I didn't have a strong opinion, one way or the other. But this loiterer, I almost bumped into him again on Curtius-Strasse, a few metres from your shop. And then I found you inside, busily trying to die.'

'The head-shake was a no, or a *not-quite yet*.'

'It looks to have been, yeah.'

'So, Karl was right. We need to do something about it.'

Senn paused and rubbed his chin. 'I've done something already.'

'What?'

'I asked your friend Jonas to use his newspaperman's connections, to try to find out what he can about Geist.'

Fischer nodded slowly. 'He could have taken my approach as a friendly warning, but he didn't. So he was expecting it, or something like it. If he's trying to protect the *Interbau* he's a dangerous mother hen. If he's protecting the man then this is business as usual, and we may have a lot more than Geist to worry about.'

'More?'

'The rat-lines get wanted men out of Germany, but what about the ones who stay here? How is it they're not exposed? It can't be luck, or the depth of the holes they've found.'

'People want to forget.'

'They do, and that helps keep hidden men hid; but blind chance should have dug up more than we know of. How many veterans' organizations are there?'

'Probably as many as there were arms of the Reich.'

'A hydra, then. They exist for a purpose, and I doubt it's to arrange beer nights for old comrades.'

Senn considered this. 'You think Geist's one of them?'

'I don't know. He may just be very single-minded about dealing with nuisances, or he may be a cog in a grinding machine.'

'We may have fucked ourselves, you mean?'

Fischer leaned back on his pillows. 'We've advertised an interest, for sure.'

'I'm sorry, Otto.'

'It was my idea to use Geist to find your fellow.'

'And mine to involve you at all.'

'I owed you something.'

A bell rang over the ward door, and several visitors rose obediently from their chairs. Senn grabbed his cap. 'When will they let you come out?'

'Tomorrow or the day after, hopefully.'

'Will you go home, or …?'

'It's a very good question. If you would, ask Jonas if there's any chance of me staying at old Grabner's place for a few days. It's empty, so he shouldn't mind.'

'I'll do that.'

When Senn had gone, Fischer closed his eyes and let his pulse play arrhythmic games in both temples. It wasn't so much a headache as an assault group changing direction between his ears, but the doctor had told him to expect it, so he endured it until he had a choice of reopening his eyes or vomiting once more. He took the sensible option, and immediately wished that he hadn't. The pounding in his head had only half-drowned the nurse's protests, but he'd imagined that the altercation was none of his business. Globnow's face, looming only a metre from his own, put him right on that. Today, it bore none of its habitually good-humoured cast.

'Your condition was described to me as deceased.'

'It almost was. Who told you …?'

'There's a notice on your shop door that claims the premises are closed due to bereavement. I went to speak to your journalist friend. He repeated the claim. I chose not to believe it. He didn't require much persuading to be honest.'

'You know about Kleiber?'

The sour look curdled further. 'We're not amateurs, Fischer. Our recruits aren't strangers to us, even before we recruit them. Everything that General Zarubin ever knew about you, we know – and more besides.'

'You seem irritated that I'm not dead.'

'No, it's that you may be playing games with us. You wouldn't be the first to have 'died' as a means of terminating your service prematurely.'

'Oh.' Of his various half-options, death hadn't really occurred to Fischer. Perhaps he'd dismissed it at a sub-conscious level, given that his face was always going to be a problem in any resurrected life. He liked the idea, though; it had an elegant finality that even retirement in Portugal couldn't match.

'You can check with my doctor. I'm definitely not well.'

'I will, believe me. So, what is it?'

'I collapsed. It's my heart, apparently.'

It was as much as the doctor would admit to Globnow, who wasn't a relative and whose KGB credentials weren't going to get him very far in a Steglitz hospital; but Fischer sensed he'd bought himself very little time. What value the First Chief Directorate might put upon a man under sentence of death was unclear. They might decide to wash their hands of him - either indifferently (with a bullet to the back of his head) or in a tide of blood (that of Geist and his accomplices – and Fischer's also, for causing the inconvenience), and he wasn't sure which was least to be preferred. He had two large, pressing problems, and one had to be settled, quickly, before he could begin to deal with the other.

Globnow had continued to glower, but now he reached down into his briefcase, removed a small package and put it on the bed. Fischer stared at it.

'What's this?'

'Grapes.'

'Thank you. May I ask for something else, also?'

'What?'

Fischer explained briefly. Globnow's eyebrows rose slightly, but he nodded.

'Alright. Now, get well quickly, or else.'

'Is it true?'

Kleiber had been practising the look (the more diligently since it had failed on one of Otto's customers earlier that morning), and he deployed it now with a sigh.

'I'm afraid so, Herr Pfentzler.'

Pfentlzer stared down at the floor and shook his head slowly.

'It's so terrible. First Herr Grabner, and now Herr Fischer - what good is a man's striving in the world, if it's for nothing?'

Though he regarded himself as something of a philosopher, Kleiber always side-stepped questions about Life's meaning, rhetorical or otherwise. He made do instead with another sigh, which conveyed all that was necessary.

Pfentzler looked up. 'And Frau Optiz, her fall from the ladder! It's as though we're cursed.'

You are, mate. Though Kleiber had persuaded himself that the old man couldn't be physically responsible for the dire luck that had fallen upon the block's tenants, he was more than half-convinced that the Curse of Pfentzler walked abroad in the world (well, in Curtius-Strasse). He was his mother's son, and a childhood watching her in search of a sweep's hand to shake on New Year's Day, crossing the road to avoid walking between two old women and never passing an oak table within knocking on it hadn't left him unmarked.

Believing in a thing gave it legs, of course; but wholesale ill-fortune tested a man's faith in coincidence. Herr Pfentzler wanted his Bavarian retirement home, and *something* was lending a hand with the arrangements. Whatever that something was – demon, troll or drude – only Kleiber himself and Frau Riehm, the hair and nails lady at number 19, were in the way still. Even an iron rationalist's bowels could be moved by that thought.

Pfentzler was looking around the newsroom. The expression on his face was open and innocuous, and Kleiber was entirely unconvinced by it. When the question came it was an octave higher than genuine disinterest would have delivered.

'So, what will you do now, with your editor dead? Will you sell up?'

'I ... yes, probably. If I can get the right price.'

It was a despicably cowardly answer, but Kleiber comforted himself that he was being sensible. Of course he wanted to continue with the business, but what if the Frankfurt people offered enough money to make his eyes pop? Wouldn't a life in which he could afford to plan a future be preferable to slipping on a patch of spilled ink one day (and probably sooner rather than later), crashing through the newsroom window and head-first down into a print run? If he was still *thinking* about things, perhaps this plague of ill-luck might hang fire for the present.

Otto would say he was being ridiculous, but having added himself to the casualty list he wasn't qualified to comment. Too much good fortune had blessed Kleiber recently for him not to brood both upon its cause and possible transience. For the first time in his life he was set comfortably, launched on a fair and prosperous wind – he'd even stopped mourning Renate, given that there could be no viable future with a partner who'd be staring at the same shapely rumps as himself. This was *just* the moment at which Life would be dropping its trousers and aiming a load at someone who'd allowed himself to forget that a pushed swing always returns.

So he offered his undecided face, which, overlaying his sad and troubled faces, quite convinced the old man, who looked up and then down, gave the horizontal a final sweeping glance, added to the sigh count with a little one of his own, turned and carefully descended the stairs. Kleiber leaned on the chair's rear legs to watch his progress (and to reassure himself that some visible manifestation of ill-luck wasn't emanating from Pfentzler's body), and only relaxed when the front door closed.

He turned back to the notes he had been making. Lengthy telephone conversations to the major Press Agencies in the Federal Republic – DPA, EPD, KNA, Reuters and even Sports-Informations-Dienst – had given him dozens of media references to Florian Geist, not one of which predated 1952 (when the man had appeared out of the gloom, fully-formed, as Demag's press officer, commenting on the company's negotiations to build a steel plant in India). With no great expectations Kleiber had also called HIAG's Berlin office to enquire whether a man of that name had ever served with an SS formation, but had been invited – very politely, and only in essence – to fuck himself. Records for the Heer, Luftwaffe and Kreigsmarine were extremely fragmentary and unavailable to public access, and without any information on the man's war service he couldn't approach WASt to check whether Geist had ever been injured or captured – which at least would have dragged up a place and date of birth. Without those, municipal records (or those that existed still) were equally useless, which left …

Nothing. Kleiber had tested his powers of initiative until his head throbbed, but the fact was that Allied bombs and Soviet artillery had unpicked the skein of accumulated knowledge with which the modern nation retained a grip on its citizens. From being one of the most closely observed and regulated societies, Germany had passed into a fog of human happenstance – a place where folk had actually been required, en masse, to come forward to the Occupiers to prove that they were who they claimed to be. Anyone not wishing to do so had enjoyed every opportunity to try something different, with little fear of discovery. The past was too often a wiped slate, so even if Herr Geist were innocent of any intention to deceive, there was no starting place from which to rebuild his history.

Kleiber would have to go back to Senn and tell him, quite truthfully, that he had done his very best. All that might be said about Geist was that he had succeeded at every employment he had taken up in the past four years. His present position was by far the most visible, representing in effect the public face of Senator Schwedler and the political arm of the *Interbau* Project. Kleiber hadn't heard of him previously only because he hadn't taken an interest in the business (and still wouldn't have, had Otto Fischer not wrestled him into putting out that story), but now that he'd researched the man he found him about as interesting as any other apparatchik, which was to say not very. Still, he'd tried, and if a niggling sense of obligation remained, it was only because Otto's near-death might have 'something to do' with him (whatever something meant).

It was while he was considering his admission of failure (in a form of words that didn't sound like he'd half-tried and then given up) that a final, thin possibility occurred. It did so because the name

Demag had been doing a little two-step in his head since he'd first read it three hours earlier. As one of Germany's foremost engineering companies it was hardly unknown to him, but the persistence of the thing irritated him. A half-memory, of something quite recent, took up the dance, and soon Otto Fischer joined it, circling, teasing, until …

Willy Wessel – a fellow journalist, though operating on a higher plane than Kleiber as a young reporter with the *Morgenpost*. They'd been to school together, and the connection had brought an unexpected invitation to a Press Association dinner the previous year (Willy's girlfriend had refused to be bored for an entire evening). They'd got drunk together, of course; but Kleiber could still recall enough of the evening to bring to mind the silly moniker they'd invented and laughed about inordinately thereafter: *Wessel's Wetter Band*.

Willy's brother was a musician, a violinist, classically trained, who'd recently found a permanent position with an orchestra. That would have been impressive, and Willy would have been proud of him, had that ensemble not been the Wetter Works Band, Demag's official cultural sop to its employees, who were often serenaded by their in-house virtuosi as they ate their canteen lunch.

A couple of days later, Kleiber had told Fischer about it, expecting him to be amused. Instead, he had been obliged to endure a short, stern lecture on the rich tradition of German industry's financing of the working man's access to classical music. Otto could do sternly serious quite well, and the experience had been enough for the brunt of it to quite forget the thing, until now.

In 1952, Demag had hired Florian Geist to be their press officer. That was a responsible position, so they must have required references, but from whom? A legitimate question, if put obliquely - one that might be asked by someone preparing, say, a puff-piece on the Project's leading officers. Kleiber was very good at puff-pieces. For a long time, he had assumed that journalists did little else other than provide a pair of willing lips for influential people's arses.

He found the Wetter exchange, dialled and asked for Demag's main number. The telephonist who took the call put him through to their public relations department (clearly, they'd expanded that single press officer's role in the intervening years). He gave a lady his puff-piece story, and, quite truthfully, told her that he had no information about Herr Geist prior to 1952. He'd be *very* grateful, he said, if she could add to the sum of what he knew.

She told him to wait while she consulted her superior. He'd expected an instant refusal, so his effusive gratitude wasn't entirely pretended. It faded a little as the minutes passed, but when he heard a male voice he momentarily had hopes of hearing something definitive.

Later, he had to remind himself that optimism was a bad failing in any journalist.

The gentleman didn't offer his name. He spoke deliberately, formally, as if he were a legal representative reading out a prepared statement. Demag had no knowledge of any Florian Geist, apparently; nor would it respond to any further requests, either verbal or written, for information on this matter. Demag was proud of its record of recovery in recent years - particularly in view of the Allied decision to remove much machinery from its factories in the immediate post-war period – to become one of Germany's flagship industrial enterprises. He also reminded Kleiber that the Company's respected chief, Herr Reuter, had been awarded the Federal Cross of Merit only two years earlier, not least for his courageous refusal to obey the Nero order to destroy all resources in early 1945, and his subsequent arrest and imprisonment by the Gestapo. As for the Press, surely Demag had extended generous access and every token of hospitality over the years, and hardly deserved this sort of duplicitous approach?

Long after their one-sided 'conversation' had been terminated (and abruptly) by the other party, Kleiber continued to stare at his telephone. Why the hell had that happened? He couldn't have made his enquiry more innocuous nor put more grease into his voice, yet shaving a cat wouldn't have got him more badly clawed. What trip-wire had he stumbled through? Whatever Herr Geist's past, Demag could hardly be called to account for it, so why the absurd lie about his employment *before* any sort of accusation was made?

He couldn't begin to see the problem. It wasn't as though Demag had been involved in anything particularly *bad* during the war. As far as he could recall, they'd produced locomotives and a variety of vehicles (with engines) for the Wehrmacht. No-one could point a finger at a record like that – not unless Ford, Scammell and GAZ were equally to be condemned. He could understand if he'd called I.G. Farben, or Krupp, or Sulzer – enterprises like that tended to deny everything, ask what the question might be and then contact their lawyers. No major German company had been able to hide or disguise the nature of its contribution to the Führer's industrial strategies. If Demag had been Bad, he'd know something of it already.

And what did they do these days? Principally, make very good mobile cranes and hoists, most of which were exported. That contract to build a steel mill in India had gone ahead, as far as he knew, and they'd built other stuff in Egypt and Norway. The offended gentleman had been right – the company was something that any western German could feel pride in. And none of that answered his question.

Still, he could now go back to Senn with more of a reason why he hadn't been successful. If someone didn't want Geist's past to be illuminated, what could Jonas Kleiber do about it? He put a sheet of paper in his typewriter and managed almost to fill it with the copious details of his failure. It went in an envelope, which he sealed and addressed with Senn's name. It was ridiculously formal – he could have recited every detail and saved them both some time – but he wanted it to look as though he'd made the effort. It eased his sense of guilt for not having had the courage to go to the hospital and visit his friend.

Otto was coming out this evening, though, using the cover of darkness to get into Grabner's house unnoticed. Kleiber's guilt was eased further by the effort he'd made to clean it up (or rather, to pay Grabner's old housekeeper double her usual rate to do the same). The place was quite luxuriously appointed (its heavy, old-fashioned décor notwithstanding), a perfect sanitarium in which the patient could recover at his leisure.

He wouldn't, though. The information in this envelope was for a purpose, and purposes with Otto Fischer never left the slightest elbow-room for anything resembling leisure. For once, Kleiber had no intention of asking what came next. He didn't know if he could trust Senn, and while he trusted Otto absolutely he didn't trust Otto's luck. If this was something newsworthy he didn't doubt that he'd hear about it before anyone else; if it wasn't, then almost certainly nothing good would come of his getting the details. It had taken a lot of the wrong sort of experience (and the recent, unexpected acquisition of things not worth putting at risk), but Kleiber was finally learning the art of circumspection.

Down in the print room, Georg was busily cleaning his presses. The next issue of the *Zeitung* wouldn't be out for three days yet, the advertisers had been herded and most column centimetres were spoken for already. Herr Grabner would never have considered dropping his quill and finishing early, but Kleiber was not the old man. His Protestant work ethic was mildly Lutheran at best, and it was a fact that a man was less likely to die in harness if he took the damn thing off occasionally. Besides, it had occurred to him that there could be no better way to celebrate Otto's deliverance and homecoming than with a nice bottle of wine, beers and some cold meats, and like any nourishment it needed to be foraged. He stood, put on his standing-around-for-hours-doing-bugger-all jacket (a venerably threadbare but warm garment), picked up the radioactive envelope and thrust it into a pocket.

'Georg?'

Georg looked up from his plates. 'Herr Kleiber?'

Until a few days earlier, Georg had never called him anything but *Jonas*. Kleiber had ascended to the editor-proprietorship, though, and the old man would rather have found a vein and injected his own inks than forego the proper forms.

'I have an appointment, and probably won't be back. Would you mind locking up tonight?'

The squared shoulders and nod, the hint of deference, quite cut through Kleiber's man-of-the-people pretensions. He'd found already that enjoyed being a boss, even if he had only Georg to rule. It was a novel, reassuring estate, one that could comfort a man that he was at least three hops from an unmarked, unnoticed grave. Thinking about it once more, he wasn't sure that any offer by the Frankfurt people would be enough to tempt him. He had enough money now, a greater amount than he could ever have expected, and the prospect of more of *enough* couldn't make his pulse race. No amount of specie would buy the respect that a successful newspaperman could demand of right.

He was only halfway off the premises when he met Walter Senn coming the other way. Though the man always made him feel a little nervous he was glad of this opportunity to discharge his task a little early. He removed the envelope from his pocket.

'It's what I've found on Geist. There isn't much.'

Senn took it and nodded. He didn't seem particularly disappointed. 'I've taken Otto to your place.'

'Already? How is he?'

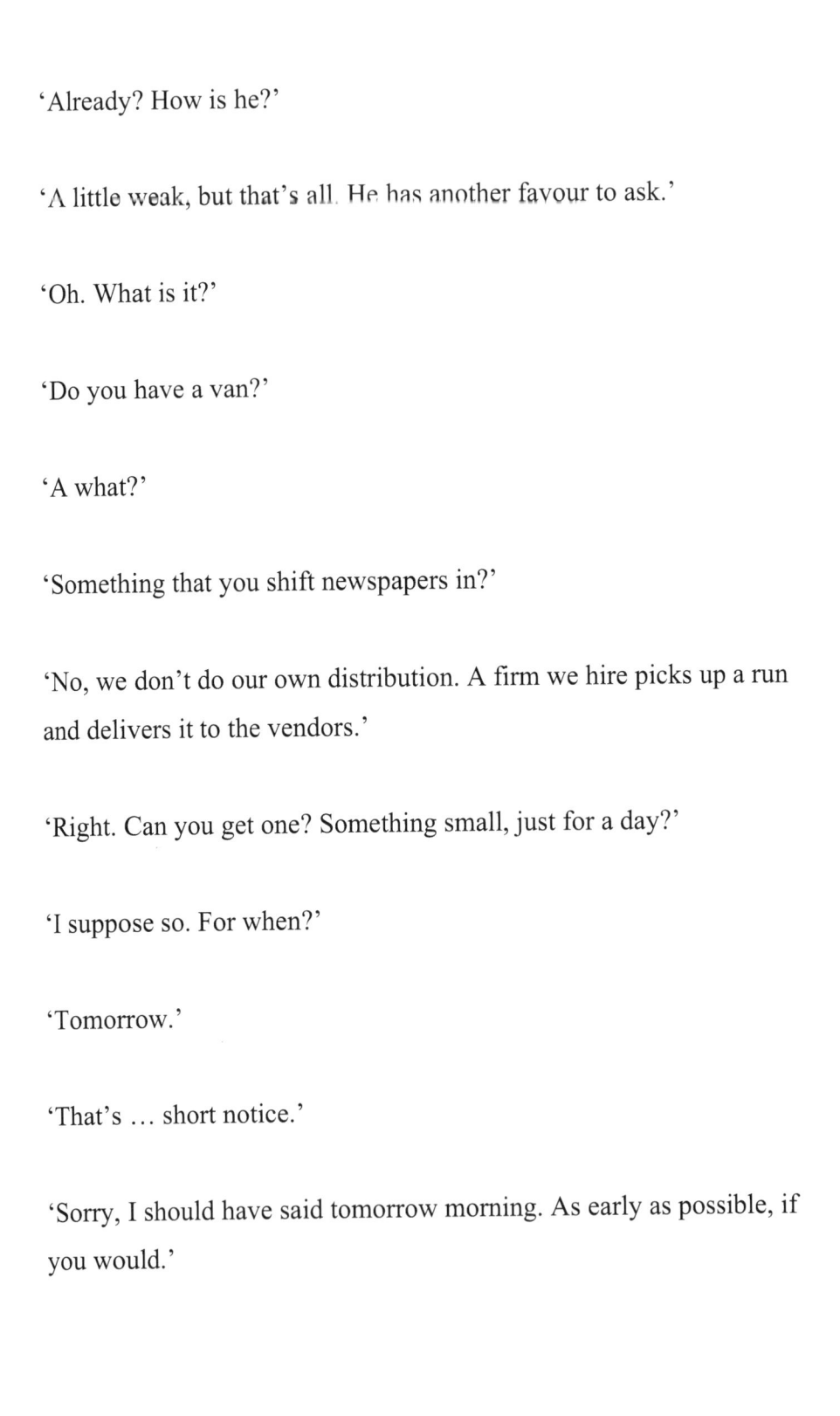

'A little weak, but that's all. He has another favour to ask.'

'Oh. What is it?'

'Do you have a van?'

'A what?'

'Something that you shift newspapers in?'

'No, we don't do our own distribution. A firm we hire picks up a run and delivers it to the vendors.'

'Right. Can you get one? Something small, just for a day?'

'I suppose so. For when?'

'Tomorrow.'

'That's … short notice.'

'Sorry, I should have said tomorrow morning. As early as possible, if you would.'

12

'Hansaplatz?'

Florian knew the answer to this already, but he made a show of consulting his notes. The Senator's face had been settling lugubriously for several minutes now (though he, too, knew most of the answers to the questions he was asking), so something was needed that didn't quite add to the effect.

'The square is scheduled to be completed only after the residential units, of course, so 1959 at the earliest. However, it's intended that all the major public artworks will be in place there by the end of the previous year.'

'Hmmph.'

'Our latest estimates are that at least thirty percent of all site work will be completed for the Exhibition's opening. The vision will be obvious, both to the expert and lay visitor.'

Visions were what most interested Schwedler. He'd known from the start that Hansaviertel's rebuilding couldn't possibly be finished before the International Bauhaus Exhibition commenced, but the creeping realities of a major project like this had gradually chipped away at his initial enthusiasm. A partially-built dream was still something considerable, but visions of futurity were beginning to be soured by equally convincing visions of important people marching through the site with copious amounts of mud on their expensive shoes. Berlin was known very well already for its exposed substratas; the Senator wasn't keen to attach his name and reputation to a new or enhanced one.

Florian could read all of this more plainly than if it were a large-print menu, and had the balm ready.

'The Berlin Pavilion material will be ready by spring 1957. I've seen the principal model already. It's almost complete, and quite wonderful - four times the size of the preliminary version, and precisely accurate. The visitors can look down on every detail of how Hansaviertel will look by 1960.'

'It's not *too* green?' The original model presented to Schwedler had been architecturally sound, but its 'natural' features – the broad landscaped and wooded areas between apartment blocks - too enthusiastically painted, like a child's colouring-book version of the world.

'The lacquers haven't yet been applied, but everyone knows what's required.'

'Hmmph.' This one sounded a little less disgruntled than the last. The *Interbau* was an exhibition of intention and progress, not an opening ceremony. Other nations would be exhibiting their half-completed or only-just-begun projects too, and it wasn't as though Hansaviertel would be a wasteland still. The Schwedenhaus and Vago blocks would not only be finished but fully furnished, giving attendees clear sight of how the middle-class family would live sixties-style, and several of the tower blocks, if not entirely fitted out, would be topped-off by then. The completed areas would be fully landscaped, and the more indolent visitors could choose to be conveyed around them by …

'The little train?'

'It's going to be ready by the end of the year. Volkswagen have promised it will fully tested on-site at least a month in advance. Its route will include the subway between Hansaplatz and Zoo Station, where there'll be artworks depicting the historic traffic jams that new Hansaviertel won't suffer from.'

'Good.'

The last had been Florian's idea, as had the train itself. Get visitors onto it and they could be shown exactly what he wanted them to see and hear what he wanted them to hear, and all at the right pace. It hadn't been hard to convince Schwedler; Volkswagen had offered to provide the train free of charge (why wouldn't they, given the worldwide publicity it offered?), and his politician's mind couldn't resist the idea of manipulating impressions mechanically. It had earned Florian a *well done*, which, though not bankable and definitely not something he treasured for its own sake, would add another layer to the shine on his curriculum vitae. For all his faults, the Senator didn't stint on due praise.

This meeting was all to do with nerves, naturally. The Hansaviertel schedule was proceeding exactly as it should, the obstinacy of its pedigree architects notwithstanding. It was just that, having been distracted by Otto Fischer and the two witnesses to the Holsteiner Ufer business, Florian had failed to keep Schwedler adequately supplied with daily reassurances. He made a mental note to bring a copy of the first-draft Project brochures to their next meeting. Its glossy presentation of the finished product was just the thing to keep the Senator's eye on the horizon, rather than the half-dug pit in all their foregrounds.

Gratifyingly, Schwedler was checking his watch, which meant that the worst of his latest panic-attack had passed. Florian had a final fillip ready to ease himself out of the office.

'I've arranged a lunch next Monday with the architects' principal assistants and the senior members of the construction committee. I called them myself, rather than have my secretary do it, because if any of them have issues they usually prefer to mention them in advance, so as not to have to admit to them in front of their peers. I haven't heard anything this time.'

The Senator almost beamed. 'Excellent! Let me know how it goes, will you?'

'Of course.'

Dismissed, Florian descended to the ground floor of the Rathaus and telephoned his office. His secretary had made no new appointments for him that afternoon, and, being only a kilometre from the apartment of the lewdest of his under-satisfied married ladies, he decided to make the most of the rest of his working day.

She sounded delighted to hear from him (the more so that he was calling from the very building where her husband worked), and within twenty minutes he was standing in a plushly-carpeted corridor outside her door. As always, he glanced around to ensure that he had no company and then adopted a stern, even threatening expression, unzipped his trouser-fly, pulled out his erect penis and knocked.

Almost two hours later, he hailed a taxi in the street outside her building. He was bruised but freshly showered and pleasantly relaxed, and while he had time still to return to the office and clear a few papers a sudden, irresponsible thought of going straight home instead and opening a bottle of something French recommended itself earnestly. He gave the driver instructions, sat back and devoted the journey to recalling every word of the obscene commentary with which Frau Jost had supervised her recent restraint, repeated violation and beating.

His apartment block stood back from the road, its front entrance accessed via a short, wooded drive. It was almost dark now, but as usual most of the windows on the first two floors were dark (many of the apartment owners were diplomatic types, often travelling or posted elsewhere). Irritatingly, the porch light that illuminated the entrance was either switched off or broken, and the *portier* hadn't cared to notice it. Florian paid his driver, climbed out and used the brief sweep of headlights across the front of the building to cross the gravel and gain the bottom step.

'Herr Geist?'

Florian turned, intending to give the *portier* a mild dressing down for his dereliction, but before the torch blinded him it gave a momentary glimpse of the pistol levelled precisely at his chest. In any case, it had occurred to him by now that the voice belonged to someone else, someone who had no right to be breathing, much less speaking. Astonished, he stepped back into what felt like a wall. Walls don't have arms, however, and certainly no access to what smelled very much like chloroform. Florian was reasonably strong for his age and build, but struggling didn't see to impress the arms, which held him carefully but tightly until he became quite still and disinterested.

'I haven't done this before.'

Senn said it matter-of-factly, but he was nervous, his hands continually moving, doing nothing useful.

Fischer closed the thick curtains, blocking the street-lights and plunging the late Herr Grabner's sitting-room into absolute darkness. He switched on a table lamp and turned to Senn.

'I have.'

'Abducted someone?'

'I thought you meant interrogation. No, I haven't done any kidnapping. Until now.'

'You've interrogated people?'

'I was a *kripo*, before the war.'

'I didn't know. It explains things.'

'Does it?'

'Why you don't have many friends, for one.'

It was a good return, but Fischer was in no mood to be amused. This was necessary - Geist had made it necessary, and still he dreaded what was coming. He rubbed his forehead, which was trying to turn inside out despite the impressive tonnage of medication with which he'd been issued to deal with pain.

'I'm might have to kill Jonas.'

'Why?'

'The van.'

'You mean 'Lichterfelde Van Hire' on the sides and back?'

'He couldn't have found something … plain?'

Senn shrugged. 'I doubt that anyone noticed. It was dark enough.'

'It was *unnecessary*.'

'We'll clean it out thoroughly.'

We'll need to. He may have pissed himself.'

He was slumped in a stand chair, though the hand-shackle attached both to his wrist and the leg of a heavy Second-Empire table kept him from toppling over. It was a scene from a cheap crime film, a b-reel pulp melodrama; but Senn needed to know which of Geist's colleagues had killed his sister, Fischer was somewhat curious about his near-translation to an untroubled state, and only the man in the chair could answer both questions.

Could, but what would be necessary to ensure *would*? Fischer had worked for several years in Stettin's Police Praesidium, but although Gestapo had worked on the same floor (and the screams of their suspects had percolated up from the cellars when the wind was in the wrong direction), he had never thought to enquire about their methods, much less study them. He doubted that he could use another man's face and body to extract what he wanted, not if it went beyond a couple of punches. Senn might feel differently, but there was a rare knack to ignoring human suffering while inflicting more of it.

He glanced at their guest. Neither of them had experience of administering a correct dosage (nor knew if standard-issue KGB drugs were more, less or similarly powerful than their western equivalents), and Geist had been unconscious for at least an hour, snoring occasionally to remind them of what they'd done. Kidnapping was a major offence, one whose tariff would excise most of whatever life Fischer had remaining. His three years in Sachsenhausen hadn't provided his fondest memories, and though a civil prison was no MVD Special Camp his spine was too old to endure twelve centimetres of mattress-padding for long. He wondered what Senn thought about it. The man's fourteen years' hard labour must have been as fresh as paint still, yet he'd not hesitated when Fischer had outlined his intentions. If it was trust, he'd greatly overestimated the thought that had gone into them.

The prisoner's eyes had opened, and he was squinting as if trying to focus them. Fischer put himself directly in their line of sight, and the shock he elicited was as good as a confession. Geist recovered quickly, though.

'Herr Fischer. You're looking remarkably well.'

'Thank you. It was the hospital rest, I think.'

Geist turned his head and gave Senn an up-and-down. 'An accomplice – how very professional. May I ask his name?'

'This is Walter. But he's more of an interested party.'

'Interested?'

'In a name.'

'Whose?'

Fischer shrugged. 'Your choice.'

'Well, I know plenty of names.'

'The one that belongs to a man you spoke to following our lunch, and regarding what we discussed. That narrows it to about five or six, I believe.'

Geist's eyes widened slightly. He turned to Senn again. 'You followed me. I didn't notice. I'm usually very good at noticing things. Alright, I'll give you some names, if it helps.'

'We only need the one.'

'Then tell me what he's done.'

'He's a war criminal.'

Geist laughed. 'They're *all* war criminals, in someone's eyes.'

'He murdered a girl, and probably raped her, too.'

'I assume you're joking? No court would even consider prosecuting a single murder so long after the event – the *alleged* event.'

'It won't go to court.'

'Ah. This is something personal, then?'

Senn cleared his throat. 'She was a young woman I knew.'

Geist pursed his lips. 'I don't doubt that any of the six could have done something like that. But I don't know which of them did.'

Fischer crouched down, to put him at eye-level with their prisoner. 'Then tell us what else they did.'

Geist glanced at both men. For the first time he seemed uneasy. 'No.'

'You were going to give us their names.'

'But not a blackmailers' charter. The ones who didn't do what you say can answer to God for their crimes, not you.'

'Why are you protecting them?'

'They're talented men. The Project needs them.'

'It's that important to you?'

Geist frowned. 'Far more so than anything they might have done during the war.'

Fischer looked at Senn, and tossed his head towards the door. As they reached it, the prisoner shifted in his chair and snorted.

'You know that I could just lift the table and free myself?'

Fischer half-pulled the pistol from his pocket. It was light, there being no bullets in the magazine - a detail he decided not to share with Geist. 'Please don't.'

In the hallway, Senn turned and scratched his cheek. 'Do we *force* him to tell us?'

'We could try, but how can we be sure he wouldn't be making up something? He must suspect one or two of them more than the others, so he'd try to deflect us from them. It's what I'd do.'

'Then we mention the killings on Palmnicken beach. Our man was part of that.'

Fischer shook his head. 'That would tell him exactly which of them he mustn't identify – *if* he knows that detail. If he doesn't, we'd be no closer.'

'Then what are we doing here, for God's sake?'

'Trying to get what we want while keeping this crime as small as possible. Whatever he tells us, we'll have to take it on trust. We can't continue to hold him while we go and grab the guilty party, confirm that he *is* the right man and then do whatever needs to be done. So, what Geist says *has* to be the truth. We need to make him want to tell us.'

'Appeal to his better nature, you mean?'

'I doubt he has one. We have to threaten the Project, rather than the man. If what we know – what Geist *thinks* we know – could hurt it badly, wouldn't he sooner lose the cancer cell than protect it?'

Senn shook his head. 'Hinting at something won't shift him.'

'It depends how it's done. Will you let me do the talking?'

'Yeah. I'd sooner slap him, anyway.'

They went back into the sitting room. Geist was peering at a lake-and-mountains painting of Hallstatt on the opposite wall (Herr Grabner's taste in artworks had been very conventional). Fischer pulled up a chair and sat down, blocking the art.

'You tried to have me killed.'

Geist's eyebrows rose slightly. 'I thought you might be a blackmailer. Or *Stasi*. In any case, you shouldn't bear grudges, Herr Fischer. They can shrivel a man.'

'It's a strange reaction, when a man brings you warning of a potential embarrassment.'

'You weren't being honest with me, as our present situation demonstrates.'

'I wonder why you went to such an extreme – I mean, as a first, rather than last, recourse. It suggests ...'

'Yes?'

'That I wasn't the first potential *embarrassment* your Project's faced.'

The ceiling received few moments' attention. 'The *Interbau*'s important to Germany. There are always people who don't want us succeed. It's my job to handle the sort of problems one can't see coming.'

'I doubt that Senator Schwedler would condone murder, even to see the *Interbau* succeed.'

Geist smiled. 'Of course he wouldn't. But who's going to tell him about it? Men who've kidnapped me? Really, threats aren't going to get you what you want.'

For a moment, Fischer was tempted to wave the pistol once more, but without either the intention or means of using it (other than as a club) he feared his red face would give him away. Geist was correct, of course; this whole thing was a bluff, and by their illegal actions the bluffers had made themselves incapable of more. They couldn't threaten any more than …

Wait. As he and Senn had driven north towards Wilmersdorf and Geist's apartment, he'd read Jonas Kleiber's notes on the man. He hadn't thought much about them since, because they'd contained so little that was interesting. But *little* wasn't necessarily useless.

'You're a puzzle, Herr Geist.'

The smile was mock-sympathetic, as though the man regretted being a nuisance. 'Am I?'

'You remind me of Venus.'

'Ha! My mother always thought me handsome, but that's a bit ...'

'I meant Botticelli's *Venus*, specifically. You stepped fully formed from somewhere, didn't you?'

'I don't understand.'

It was a cheap trick, but nearly always effective; Fischer pulled Kleiber's notes from his jacket's inside pocket and pretended to peruse them. As he'd expected, the smile faded slightly. No-one enjoyed being *known*, not when they didn't know what was known.

'In 1952 you took up a decent job with Demag.' Fischer looked up. 'Before that ... well, you weren't anywhere at all.'

'Your information is incomplete, then.'

'Yes, but only because it covers knowable things. Before 1952 you preferred not to be known, I think – like so many other Germans.'

'*Like* so many other Germans, it took a while to get my feet back on the road. I did many things, none of them likely ever to have found their way into the records. I'm actually very good at shifting rubble, for example.'

'Where did you serve? In the war?'

'Many places. I was an ordinary *schutz*, infantry. I went where I was sent.'

'A *schutz*? A well-educated man like yourself? What a terrible waste of talent.'

The smile was returning, and the shrug with it. 'Armies aren't meritocracies. I was called up in '39, with about two million others. I sat no written exam to find the best use for me.'

'I suppose not.' Fischer pretended to consult the notes once more. 'Still, you should have gone further. Any man who can step from rubble-clearance to the Press Office of a major company has some observable talent.'

'I was recommended to Demag. By a friend.'

'I doubt a recommendation would carry much weight – unless it was an informed one.'

'Well, he knew me.'

Fischer smiled. 'You were lucky, then. It's a good company, Demag, a proper phoenix – one of the few big ones to come out of the war in reasonable condition.'

'I suppose it's because most of their factories are in the British Zone – they weren't pillaged *too* drastically.'

'No, I meant reputation-wise. They made a lot of stuff for the war-machine, but nothing that might have embarrassed them in retrospect.' Fischer paused and stared up at the ceiling. 'Apart from the camp at Oberwengern, obviously. I recall that it was the largest industrial slave labour camp in the Ruhr, when it was built. What year was that?'

Geist had lost the smile entirely by now. 'It was long before my time.'

'Aah, 1943, I think. I was at the Air Ministry at the time. I recall wondering where they'd get the workers to fill it. I suppose the Todt Organization supplied many of them - and the camps in the East, of course. But as you say, it was before your time there – unless you got the job in '52 because of how helpful you'd been previously – in another life, so to speak?'

'I've done nothing to be ashamed of.'

'That's a curious denial. You could just have said no, or that I was talking out of my arse. I'm not, though, am I? You weren't ever a *schutz*, Herr Geist. Your hands are far too nice.'

'I served my country.'

'We all did. Walter did so blamelessly. Me, less so. You, I wonder about. I also wonder how pleased Senator Schwedler would be to hear of your military record.'

'You don't know anything.'

'No, but I could make up a great deal, some of which may stick. In any case, I think the Senator would play safe, don't you? *Or,* you could give us the man we want. Then, I'll find the key to those shackles, you can go home and everyone can forget things – you about being abducted, me about almost being killed.'

Despite his predicament, Geist was angry, his face flushed. He sat up in the chair. 'Then tell me what this man did! All I know is that he killed a girl – so what? If I don't know more I can't pull him out of the hat for you!'

Fischer looked sharply at Senn. He'd noticed it, too.

'Where are you from, Herr Geist?'

'What?'

'Home – where is it?'

'It isn't, anymore.'

'Where *was* it, then?'

'Why the hell do you care?'

'You said that our man killed a girl.'

'So? It's what *he* told me.'

'No, Walter said *fraulein*. It was me who said girl – *mädchen*. But you just threw it back at me as something else – *margell*. Hardly anyone uses the word anymore. Those who did – do – are displaced, aren't they? You're from Old Prussia, I think?'

Geist stared at Fischer as if he were demented. 'If it's *that* fascinating, yes, I am.'

'May I ask where?'

'I was born in Danzig, but the family was from Königsberg, originally.'

'Ah. You have no accent.'

'I made the effort not to. Sounding like a fucking *Samlander* was going to do me as much good as a horned helmet in the new Germany.'

'Hush. You'll offend Walter. He's from Danzig, too.'

Geist half-turned and stared sullenly at Senn. 'Is he? How remarkable. Perhaps we can share a drink and talk about the old, familiar streets.'

'Did you ever go back there?'

'How could I? The Poles aren't fond of the former residents.'

'I meant, towards the End?'

'Briefly, yes.'

'To find family, I suppose?'

Geist regarded Fischer closely for a few moments. 'My grandmother. The one to blame for my Old Prussian dialect.'

'Did you find her?'

'No. She'd left with friends, a few days ahead of the Reds. I heard much later that she died on the road to Cöslin.'

'I'm sorry to hear that.'

'It was hardly an unusual story. Most old folk didn't survive the treks.'

'So you got out of Danzig.'

'As quickly as I could.'

'Were you using the false name still?' Fischer turned to Senn. 'What was it?'

'Feyerabend.'

Geist's mouth dropped open. 'How the hell do you know that?'

'I didn't, until now. But knowing that, I know something else, too. *You* killed the girl.'

'Are you *mad*?'

Senn stepped forward. 'She was my sister.'

Bewildered, Geist's gaze went from one man to the other. 'I've killed no-one.'

'You were in the makeshift hospital, on the dockside. She helped you. You said you had family in the town, and wanted to find them. She went with you.'

'Y … yes.'

'Where did you go then?'

'To a street just off Vorzintischer Graben, where my grandmother lived. She was gone, as I said.'

'And after that?'

'To … the girl's rooms. She told me I could rest there for a while. I was a little dizzy still – from a small head-wound.'

'She was found on her bed, the next morning. She'd been raped, and then strangled.'

'No ...' Wide-eyed, Geist tried to rise, but the shackle kept him in a half-crouch. He raised his free hand as if to ward off Senn. 'She was very kind, and we ...'

'You *what*?'

'We had a drink or two. She had the best part of a bottle of something in a drawer - schnapps, I think – and we finished it while we talked about family, and getting out of the City before the Soviets took it. She told me she was leaving the next day with her friend. When I left her she was fine, I swear.'

'Did you *touch* her?'

Geist swallowed visibly. 'Yes. We were drunk, and we ... made love. She said she hadn't been with a man for almost a year, and I said it had been more than two for me. She was pretty ... but I never hurt her. I've *never* hurt a woman – I couldn't.'

Senn raised a fist and held it above Geist's head. When it didn't drop, Fischer closed the gap between them and took his wrist.

'A word, please, Walter. You, sit still.'

In the hallway, Senn grabbed his hair with both hands and pulled. His eyes had a mad cast to them, and for a moment Fischer mistook it for rage; but rage went one way, unhindered, and this was at least two heads of something, smashing into each other.

'You don't believe him?'

'Of course I don't. But ...'

'But?'

'It *might* be true. Christ!' Senn released his hair and looked up into the dark well of the staircase. 'She was found the next day – the *next* day. If Danzig was being ripped apart, full of retreating soldiers and fleeing civilians, who's to say it couldn't have been someone else?'

'A court might not convict him; anyone else probably would.'

'I know - I *want* him to have done it. I want to stab his eyes out, and know that Margret's been put to rest. I just don't want to spend the rest of my life wondering ...' Senn looked desperately at Fischer. 'You're cleverer than me; would *you* do it, after what he's said?'

'I don't now, truly. It's harder to kill a man, when he's not trying to kill you.'

'I was artillery, so it was never hard for me. You didn't see who you'd killed until later, and even then you could tell yourself that it was someone else. I'm not soft. Otto – in the old days I was in plenty of street fights, but I've never looked into a man's face and put him down forever. I'd need to hate him, and this one …'

'He's lying.'

'About Margret? Do you think …?'

'I don't know. About something *else* he said, definitely. Come on.'

They went back into the sitting room. Geist was bolt-upright still, his back against the table, waiting for the worst. He opened his mouth, but the plea, denial or threat remained in his throat.

Fischer took out his pistol and laid it on a small table, which, standing beside an armchair, Herr Grabner had been in the habit of decorating with a wine bottle. He sat down.

'You came to Danzig that day from Palmnicken, didn't you?'

Trying to parse the question, Geist took his time.

'From Gumbinnen. Ships were evacuating from there.'

'But you'd been at Palmnicken before that?'

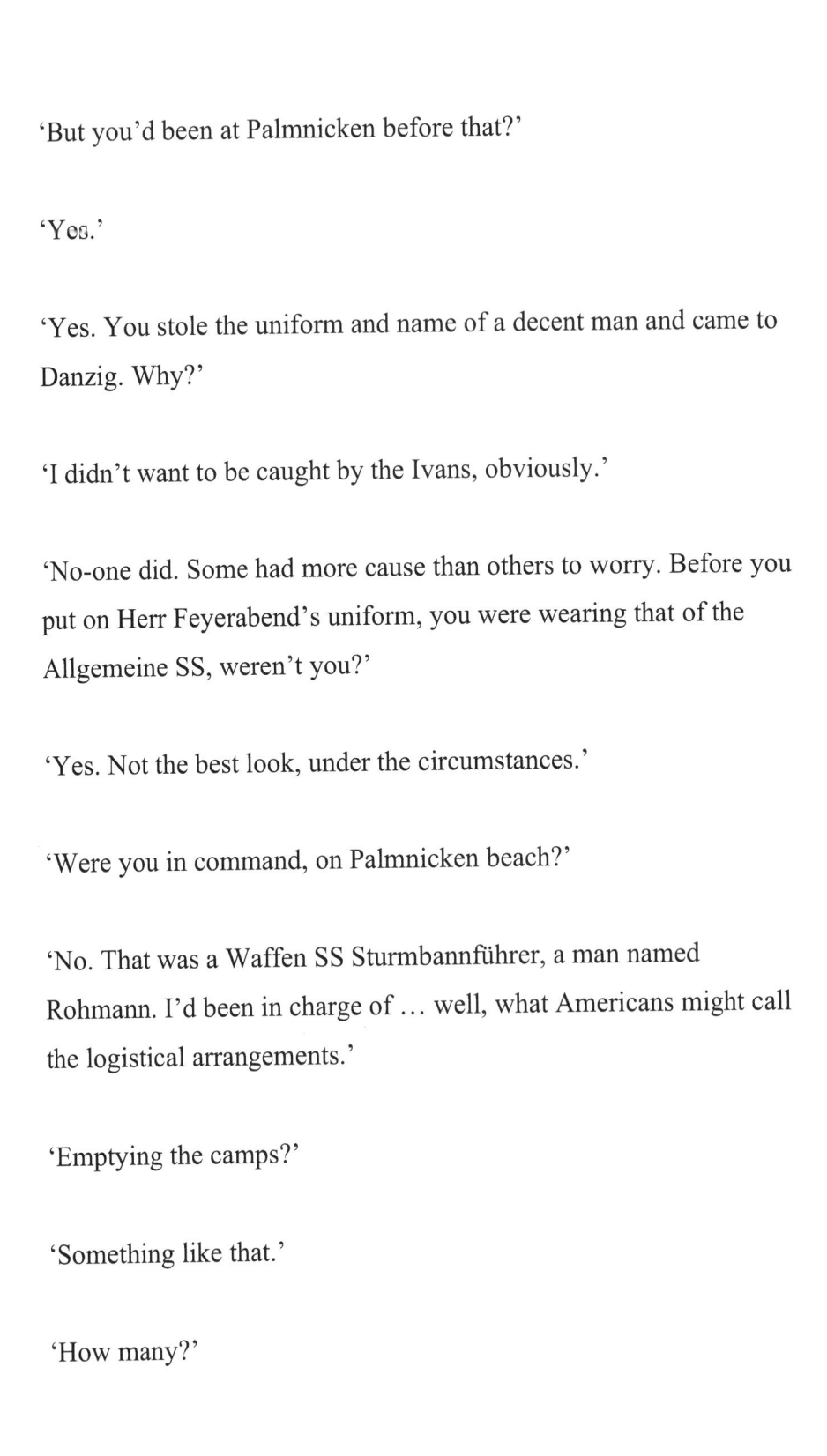

'Yes.'

'Yes. You stole the uniform and name of a decent man and came to Danzig. Why?'

'I didn't want to be caught by the Ivans, obviously.'

'No-one did. Some had more cause than others to worry. Before you put on Herr Feyerabend's uniform, you were wearing that of the Allgemeine SS, weren't you?'

'Yes. Not the best look, under the circumstances.'

'Were you in command, on Palmnicken beach?'

'No. That was a Waffen SS Sturmbannführer, a man named Rohmann. I'd been in charge of … well, what Americans might call the logistical arrangements.'

'Emptying the camps?'

'Something like that.'

'How many?'

'At the beginning of the march, perhaps thirteen thousands.'

'And by the time you reached the beach?'

'About three thousands.'

'And then you lined them up at the water's edge, and shot them all – three thousand women and girls. So, when you say that you could never hurt a woman, why is it that you expect to be believed?'

Geist stared at Fischer, dumbfounded. His mouth opened and closed like that of a half-stunned fish. He turned to Seen and back again, took a breath, frowning, as if the question were such as to confound a sensible answer.

'But … they were *Jews*!'

15

The park bench was in its usual place, but the coating of night-frost didn't encourage a lingering visit. Globnow was standing, hands in his coat pockets, hunched against the near-horizontal wind when Fischer arrived. He pulled his mouth out of a scarf long enough to ask the question.

'Why are we here, and at this ungodly hour?'

'To talk.'

'I'd guessed that. What about?'

'You.'

Globnow laughed. 'It wouldn't be a very interesting conversation.'

'To me it would. I've been thinking about you for weeks now.'

'Specifically?'

'That was the problem - it was nothing I could take a stab at. Just a broad, vague sense of *oddness*.'

'I'm flattered.'

'Last night it resolved itself. Someone told me that he'd feared I was *Stasi*. For a moment it amused me, though not how he'd imagined it might. But it stirred another thought. *Stasi*, he said, not *Stasi* or KGB. And then it struck me that he *wouldn't* think I was KGB.'

Globnow waited, saying nothing.

'If I were an American or Englishman, it might be different. *Stasi* know their place, even in Berlin, and leave foreign nationals to their Soviet friends. But KGB have no business, and probably no interest in, running a native German *in* Germany, not since *Stasi* expanded massively. I'd be a standard State Security asset, like the hundreds or thousands of other *wessies* they're said to have turned. This whole business, of getting me into the *Abgeordnetenhaus*, it's exactly what the gentlemen at Ruschestrasse regard as *their* primary sphere of responsibility, not Karlshorst's. And you, you're puzzling, too.

'Am I? How intriguing of me.'

'Why is a German a member of KGB still? You should have leapt the fence when the DDR took responsibility for its own internal security. None of this is usual, is it?'

Globnow examined his shoes but didn't reply. He might have been thinking of a response or merely letting the rope play out to a sufficient length, and Fischer had to remind himself that this was a conversation that might wander quickly from *interesting* to a suicidal statement of intent.

'So I wondered why it's happening this way.'

Globnow raised his head. 'What did you conclude?'

'Nothing. I can think of only one dislocating element that might explain why it can't be explained.'

'Which is?'

'General Zarubin, but he's no longer in Berlin.'

'He isn't.'

'Nor has any responsibility for Berlin operations?'

'None whatsoever.'

Globnow was, apparently, a low-ranking KGB operative, so he couldn't know that – unless he *knew* it. And if he knew it, he was closer to Zarubin than he'd indicated or hinted at. Fischer's sense of things not being *usual* intensified.

'Did you know that he came to Berlin last year, to speak to me?'

Globnow pursed his lips. 'He mentioned something about it. I don't know the details.'

'He told me then that KGB would have a use for me, that he couldn't interfere. It made sense at the time only because I assumed – and he more than inferred – that it was to do with my having served in the Gehlen Org. But this business about me joining the SPD, and standing for the *Abgeordnetenhaus* – it couldn't be further from that sort of work. I'd have no access to military or civilian intelligence, no way to put myself where decisions regarding national policy are made, and as an elected official I'd be shining a torch into my own face. If it were to infiltrate Berlin city politics I'd get the point, but I don't believe KGB have the slightest interest in the Senate or House, not since they passed that baton to *Stasi*. And that leaves only ...'

'Only?'

'My good friend Sergei Aleksandrovich. During our last conversation he hinted that he remained *of* KGB but stood apart from its mainstream Directorate operations. I don't know much about how the organization works, but *standing apart* requires a certain amount of pull, and not many people have it, I expect. One would need friends, and that would mean political friends.'

'He was tortured, when he returned to the Soviet Union. A man with friends would have avoided that.'

'He *survived* torture, which was surprising. It puts him in rare company, that of men like Marshal Rokossovsky, who's now ... what? The Polish Defence Minister?'

'So, he has some valuable connections.'

'I'm glad for him, truly. But if he somehow stands apart from KGB, what does that make you, and *this*?'

Globnow reached down and brushed water from his shoes, a pointless exercise. Fischer assumed that it was to allow him time to think of a serviceable lie, so what followed was all the more surprising.

'What I am is former KGB.'

'Former? I didn't know that was possible, for a foot-soldier. I'm sorry, I assumed ...'

'No, you're right. Do you recall what I told you about my wife, and how choices cease to be such?'

'Yes.'

'After she died I stopped trying – to be a good soldier, I mean. I grew to hate many of my comrades as much as I did my countrymen. It's a bad place to be, in no-man's-land with the enemy occupying both sets of trenches. Probably, I would have said something eventually that earned me a head-shot, but I found a friend before that could happen. His advice was always worth hearing.'

'General Zarubin?'

'Lieutenant Zarubin, back then. He urged me to transfer from NKVD into NKGB, where there weren't quite so many maniacs to avoid. He kept me with him – and others, I think – as he moved on and up. When he defected in '58 I was already out, so nothing came back upon me because of it.'

'How did you get out?'

Globnow smiled. 'He killed me off. Gehlen's people shot me, apparently, while I was doing stuff in the Black Forest.'

'Doing what?'

'He never told me. The paperwork was good, as you'd expect. In late '57 I had a new name and a couple of decent references, and joined the company I still work for.'

'Do you think the others got out?'

'Almost certainly. He was doing it for a reason other than mere friendship, and what I sensed of it – he never explained it exactly – suggests that he's been building some form of network of his own, of men and women who know how Soviet Intelligence works.'

'He's surely not going into business on his own behalf?'

'If he was, he'd be an idiot. Zarubin isn't that.'

'What, then?'

'It became a little clearer recently, when he instructed me to contact you. I asked why he'd want you – anyone – to get into West Berlin politics. He said it was because he didn't want gaps in the cloth. It suggests to me that he's been weaving.'

'Why, though?'

'I've thought a lot about that. And only one thing occurs.'

Fischer didn't ask the question. He was thinking about *apart* and its implications still. Zarubin had gone back to the Soviet Union with what he'd hoped was sufficient insurance. He'd lived, so it must have been. Events had gone his way – if Beria had lived and Khrushchev fallen, he might have expected them to start on his balls once the last fingernail had gone. But they hadn't. The uneasy settlement that the Politburo had fallen into had lasted three years now, and Zarubin had not only escaped execution but risen greatly during that time. Was it *all* a grateful Khrushchev's doing?

For the first time, he noticed something acrid in the sharp wind, as if the Gardens' staff had finally got around to burning the leaves that had fallen the previous autumn. He cleared his throat and coughed.

'Is there trouble coming?'

Globnow nodded. 'It may be. It's hard to believe that Berlin will continue indefinitely as it is, and almost inconceivable that the status quo in Moscow can last. The two cities share a fate, because what determines the future of one will shape the other's.'

'The Old Guard versus something else?'

'A few weeks ago, a rumour started. Did you hear it?'

'About Khrushchev denouncing Stalin?'

'The rest of the Politburo agreed to it only if he spoke in secret session. He did so, but then had about thirty thousand copies of the speech printed and distributed within the Red Army and Komsomol. Hence the rumour.'

'A bit of a slap in their faces.'

'It was calculated. It *must* have been. Malenkov, Molotov, Kaganovich – they're like deadweights on policy, terrified of any decision being made that's capable of rebounding. They look at the half of Europe they've coloured red and to them it's not only enough but a thing to be defended like the Atlantic Wall, or Maginot Line. They don't see it as an inevitable pause in an unfinished struggle. They think that the Americans are going home, eventually, and that only patience and caution are necessary to achieve it.'

'And Khrushchev doesn't?'

'He actually *likes* Americans, according to General Zarubin; but he isn't fool enough to wish them away. NATO is getting stronger, and the Warsaw Pact will only ever be as strong as the Soviet Union makes it. Time isn't on their side.'

'What does he want to happen?'

'Who knows? Zarubin thinks that a confrontation's coming. If Khrushchev wins, things won't be the same as before. What he does then is up to him, but it'll be *something*. The General isn't wasting time trying to predict the future, only preparing for it.'

'By placing spies in West Berlin?'

'By putting *friends* in West Berlin. If it were Karlshorst doing this they'd spoil everything by using their assets at the first seemingly opportune moment - it's what they do, unfortunately. Zarubin wants a constituency in place, intact and ready for when things change.'

'Why?'

'Were you here, during the blockade?'

'Briefly.'

'It was different, then. The western city was seen as a military outpost in the middle of Soviet territory, so removing it was a military goal. Now look at it. *West* Berlin is the largest city in either Germany. Every year it advances, becomes richer, more populous, more of a slap to Walter Ulbricht's face. Getting the Allies out is increasingly necessary, but it requires something different this time – a threat, but with cake attached, so to speak.'

Fischer considered this. 'A promise of non-interference?'

Globnow nodded. 'Free and so-called fair elections, no forcible re-union of the two halves. Moscow would agree happily to this of course, if they could achieve a withdrawal short of going to war. They'd even keep to the letter of the agreement. But the cultural and historical pressure to erase the Line and re-unify would be immense.'

'And influential people in West Berlin would be arguing the same.'

'People like us, Fischer – respectable, hard-working capitalists whose voices will be heard in the right places. It won't happen quickly, but that's good. Ulbricht will be kept on a short chain, *Stasi* likewise - nothing would be said or done to make the Americans want to reverse their decision. And within a generation the city will become the undivided capital of a country that's hardly viable at present.'

Fischer blew out his cheeks. 'It's a vision, for sure.'

'The General's done his utmost to make it Khrushchev's also. Of course, the First Secretary has to win the coming battle within the Politburo first.'

'If he loses?'

'Then all our futures become cloudy.' Globnow rubbed his shoulders. 'Now, I need breakfast. I'm glad we talked.'

He turned to leave, but Fischer touched his sleeve. 'There's something else.'

'Oh, God. I can't feel my feet ...'

'I'll be quick. If I mentioned the beach at Palmnicken, would you know what I meant?'

The plaintive expression on Globnow's face hardened. 'I would.'

'Forgive me for asking, but you're Jewish, I think?'

'I put that aside years ago.'

Fischer removed a piece of paper from his pocket and held it out. 'This is the name and address of a man who was there. He was second-in-command of the SS units who murdered the women.'

Globnow took off his gloves, opened the note, read it and looked up. 'Are you certain?'

'He admitted it, freely.'

'Why are you giving this to me?'

Fischer sighed and rubbed his eyes. He was missing a night's sleep and a lot more peace of mind, and the question was too pertinent to answer easily.

'Because it's too much, and too distant, for me to deal with. It isn't *personal*, and that's the only level at which I could justify taking action. The man deserves anything that comes to him, but I'm not comfortable in righteous armour, not with my own stains upon it. For a Jew, it *may* be personal. I'll leave it with you.'

'Why?'

'Because you have the means or connections to do something about it, if you choose to. Think of it as my thanks, for the acute arse-pain you've caused me.'

As he walked back to Curtius-Strasse, Fischer tried to concentrate on what he'd heard, but the lure of a warm bed kept elbowing it aside. He was ill still, and hadn't slept for almost thirty-six hours, and the prospect of letting Renate run the shop for the entire day recommended itself more than usual. He recalled that he had five repairs outstanding, none of which was urgent, and his small pile of unanswered correspondence on housing matters could wait until he summoned some enthusiasm to deal with it (which meant that some future civilization might find it undisturbed, like Tutankhamen's tomb). One of his large, pressing problems had gone away for want of the moral will to resolve it, the other had just stepped back a couple of paces and nothing else could possibly excite his attention sufficiently to keep him conscious for much longer.

The acrid scent in his nostrils hadn't cleared. He stopped and blew his nose, which encouraged someone to barge into him. Surprised, he turned, and a young woman put out a hand, excused herself and kept running. It was only an hour after dawn, and instinctively he looked back in the direction she must have come from, expecting to see a pursuer. Instead, he saw several – at least, they were equally in a hurry and moving in the same direction as her. Assuming it wasn't to do with a Soviet advance or plague of frogs he put it from mind and turned the corner into Curtius-Strasse.

Fire-vehicles lined the street on both sides, pouring water into a hole. At one side of it, a wall was still standing, and beneath it a printing-press hung precariously into space. To the right of the wall, *Pfentzler's Modes* was wholly intact, untroubled even to the extent of a cracked display window. To its left, nothing remained of four other properties, including *Fischer's Time-pieces and Gramophones*. It was complete, a total erasure, as if someone in the RAF or USAAF had consulted their aerial photography archive and returned to complete the sloppy half-job of several years earlier.

'Otto!!!'

Jonas Kleiber rushed across Curtius-Strasse, followed by Renate and her friend Lena (the girls wore matching dressing gowns, which must have wounded the young man cruelly). Renate threw her arms around Fischer's neck and sobbed incoherently, depositing a quantity of mucus onto his cheek.

'Christ, we thought you'd gone to heaven!'

'Not quite. I was at Grabner's place.'

Kleiber beamed. 'I saved your life, then!'

'Probably. What happened?'

'A gas pipe, they think. Earlier last night a drain beneath the street collapsed, and they blocked it off. It must have damaged the mains, though. Didn't you hear the explosion?'

'No.'

'You must be deaf. When I got here they'd dampened most of the fire. Frau Opitz's salon was only half-burned at that point, but her stock of nail polishes and removers ignited and started it off again. Look at it – all gone.'

'Is anyone …?'

'All safe and well. You're the only one of us who lives above the shop. A drain, would you believe it? Christ, you'll get the blame, being the local SPD's man on Drains, even if it was the RAF's fault. The *Zeitung* would defend you, but it can't now, can it? Renate, let the poor man breathe – Lena, pull her off, can't you? Old Pfentzler's in shock – they've taken him to hospital. He was over-insured, but thanks to Herr Grabner reinforcing the wall to soundproof the printers he's been left with everything. His Frankfurt buyers won't give a fart now, but that's his hard luck. The rest of us will be checking our policies and hoping to God that there isn't a collapsing shit-pipe exclusion somewhere. Just look at it - all gone, *all* of it!

What we'll do now is anyone's ... Otto? What is it? What the hell is there to laugh about?

'Otto?'

Author's Note

The 1957 International Bauhaus Competition (or *Interbau*) was considered a great success, both for the quality of architecture on show and its effect upon the reputation of the host city, West Berlin. The informal, widely-spaced layout of the residential buildings, interspersed with broad, landscaped areas that dispensed with the former, tightly-built urban pattern and seamlessly blended into the Tiergarten, provided a template that, for better or worse, was adopted by many town and city planners throughout Europe in the following decade.

For West Berlin, *Interbau* was an opportunity to present the city as more than a beleaguered outpost of capitalism and symbol resistance to Stalinism. It was a statement of confidence in a future other than as a Cold War pawn, and though it didn't (and couldn't) result in the relocation of the Federal Government from Bonn, the exhibition was an important marker in the process of integrating the city's economic and social life with that of West Germany.

The named architects involved in the Project are historical figures, though Florian Geist is fictional. The suggestion that several potential war criminals were also involved with *Interbau* is the author's alone, though their ready employment in so many other areas of western German economic life makes their complete absence unlikely.

The massacre of Jewish women on the beach at Palmnicken in January 1945 is a matter of historical record, as is the story of the virtuous *Volkssturm* commander Feyerabend, who shot himself rather participate in the killings.

Printed in Great Britain
by Amazon